The
LIGHT
of
HIDDEN
FLOWERS

BOOKS BY JENNIFER HANDFORD

Daughters for a Time

Acts of Contrition

The
LIGHT
of
HIDDEN
FLOWERS

Jennifer Handford

LAKE UNION
PUBLISHING

Published by Lake Union Publishing, Seattle

www.apub.com

Amazon, the Amazon logo, and Lake Union Publishing are trademarks of Amazon.com, Inc., or its affiliates.

ISBN-13: 9781503950870 (hardcover)
ISBN-10: 1503950875 (hardcover)
ISBN-13: 9781503947511 (paperback)
ISBN-10: 1503947513 (paperback)

Cover design by Elsie Lyons

Printed in the United States of America

For my grandmother, Anna Pauline Parker

PART ONE
FATHER AND DAUGHTER

CHAPTER ONE

I didn't usually mock my life. Really—my disposition was quite agreeable most of the time. In fact, people regarded me exactly that way: Missy Fletcher, a real sweetheart. The same way people described kindergarten teachers and puppies. And usually, I really did have an "attitude of gratitude," as my father had always taught me. *Count your blessings, daughter,* he was fond of saying. *We have it so good.* But today I felt a gremlin on my shoulder, egging me on.

A milestone birthday could have that effect.

Happy birthday, Missy Fletcher. Thirty-five years old and you've barely cast a shadow.

I locked the car and checked my reflection in the window. A disproportionately heavy head of hair for my little face, like a Tina Turner wig on a toddler. I reached into my pocket for a hair band and flattened the puffiness into a ponytail.

I began the block walk up King Street in Old Town Alexandria, Virginia, toward the financial firm I co-owned with my father. When I reached our building, I peered up the five steps to the copperplate at the left of the front door.

FLETCHER FINANCIAL, LLC
FRANK FLETCHER, PAUL SULLIVAN, MELISSA FLETCHER

Adjacent to our office was the community center, a redbrick building as old as the Continental Congress. It was the first working day of the month, which meant it was a Fletcher Financial seminar day in the center's main hall. I entered and saw that Dad was already there, moseying around the room and touching each long table as if bestowing on it a benediction. In a short hour from now, he would be up in front delivering a financial planning seminar, but mostly telling stories and entertaining his buddies and clients.

Let me tell you about the greatest guy in the world . . . my father would say. *Let me tell you about a gal who was the smartest in her field.* My father was this larger-than-life guy who started every sentence by complimenting someone else.

When Dad saw me, he brightened like his dimmer switch had been turned high. "There's my birthday girl! How's my beautiful girl with a beautiful mind?"

"Good, great!" I exaggerated a little. "You look handsome." Dad wore his perfectly tailored Armani suit, gleaming Rolex, and shiny Ferragamos. "I'm going to set up the buffet."

"Not so fast," he said, reaching for my hand. "Spend a few minutes with your old man. Tell me how you are. I mean really. It's your birthday, a milestone. Are you happy? Are you doing what you want to be doing?" He looked at me like an eager puppy awaiting a treat. "Seems like just yesterday, you were a little baby. I'd sit with you on the floor. I'd hold your little hands and you'd jump—"

"Up and down, up and down," I said, finishing Dad's sentence, one I'd heard so many times before.

Such was my father's daily conversation with me, his never-ending quest to tunnel into my soul. Why was I still single at the age of thirty-five? Why was I—his only child—working at his firm as a financial analyst, rather than pursuing another career? Why had I chosen to stay put, settling only a mile from him, in the same town I grew up in, rather than traveling the globe as I'd claimed I wanted to do when I was younger?

That Dad loved me was a given; that he thought I could live a larger life was a given, too.

"Dad, seriously," I said, exhaling noisily, like a child. "I'm great. Right where I want to be. Are you ready for the seminar?"

Dad peered around the room as if it were already packed with his treasured clients. "You know what my goal for today is? To talk to every person in this room." He smiled wide, pounded the table with his fist.

That was always Dad's goal. To talk to every person in the room. For everything to be "the best."

As for me, I could think of nothing worse. The exact opposite of my father, I preferred a quiet room, a cup of tea, and a good book. *Let's communicate by e-mail,* my quiet persona whispered. No need for public speaking. No reason for phone calls.

The clients and prospects filed in. Paul, our third partner, helped me set up the projector. Paul was a lovable Muppet with a heavy helmet of coarse salt-and-pepper hair, caterpillar eyebrows, and a smile that covered half his face. Paul was the best. He'd come to work for Dad before I had even left for college, and now he was kind of like a big brother to me. We laughed as we watched Dad work the room, greeting his old friends, meeting new ones: a touch and a thousand-watt smile. The attendees mixed and mingled, sipped coffee and nibbled on bagels.

"He never tires of this," Paul said.

"Never," I agreed. "Ever."

My father called the meeting to order and I kicked off the PowerPoint presentation, but I knew how this would go. Dad would look up at my first slide and would have every intention of sticking with the presentation, but . . .

"Good morning, friends," Dad began. "The other day I met with a new client. Let's call him Abe. Abe was a real worrier about the market. Watches it every day. CNBC is on his television set all day, he told me. He clicks on his online account a good twenty times a day."

I shook my head and smiled at Paul. We knew exactly where this was going.

"I told Abe, 'Abe, I want to know how far your house is from my office. When you leave, I want you to do me a favor. I want you to measure the distance, will you?'"

The audience hung on his every word.

"Abe said, sure. Of course he would do it. Then I handed Abe a ruler. 'What's this for?' he wanted to know. 'To measure the distance from my office to your house,' I told him. 'But Frank,' Abe said, 'I'm not going to use a ruler, I'm going to set my odometer—and measure it in miles.'"

Dad paused, looked around the room.

He went on. "'If you measure distance in miles, rather than with a ruler,' I told Abe, 'Then why are you checking on your investments twenty times a day? It's the same thing. Today's price isn't your price! Tomorrow's price isn't your price! When you wake up on your sixty-fifth birthday, check the price. That's your price!'"

The audience nodded, wives smiling at their husbands. Paul nudged me. This wasn't our first time to this show.

"Folks," Dad went on. "We don't pick the flowers to see if they're growing!"

More laughter. More approval.

From the corner of the room I watched as the crowd shook their heads and smiled and laughed because Dad and his thunderous personality had done it again. He spoke loudly, and often, and with conviction, and for these character traits, he was loved and admired.

Dad moved on. "Folks, you all travel, visit interesting places—vacations, to see the kids, to explore mysterious lands. So you tell me if I'm right. When you get on a plane, you want three things: to take off on time, to have a smooth flight, and to land safely."

Dad looked at me because his flying analogies hit a little too close to home, with his daughter who couldn't board a plane, even when nearly knocked cold.

Dad talked about hitting these goals, and when he was just about to make his point—to say that having a competent pilot was the same as having a competent financial planner—he paused, leaned against the podium, stared at the crowd. Time decelerated as we waited for Dad to continue. He cleared his throat, and through the speaker system, it sounded like growling. Dad looked at me again, issued a small cough, and wiped at his brow.

I couldn't fathom what he was waiting for.

Had he lost his place? I glanced at Paul, who knitted his eyebrows in worry.

Dad's eyes met with mine. *Help me.*

I attempted to send Dad a telepathic message, to prompt him back to his story, because for the first time ever, it seemed that he had drawn a blank. He could always find north, but today, Dad was in the dark, and couldn't seem to find the sun.

A few people turned from their seats and whispered to their neighbors.

My heart pounded in my chest, the same anxiety that preceded anytime I was forced to speak in front of a crowd. Saliva pooled in the back of my throat at the same time my lips adhered to my excessively dry teeth. My head itched with perspiration. When I looked again at Dad, his jaw was jutting back and forth, up and down, like he was trying to clear clogged ears.

My dad was trapped in a burning building and it was up to me to save him.

Run into it, Missy! my mind blared. *Save him!* I opened my mouth to speak, to rush headlong into the fiery heat, but nothing came out. The words I heard in my head were crushed by a flaming rafter. I couldn't help my own father.

Dad looked at me again. A look he shouldn't have had to give. A good daughter would have stood ready. A brave daughter would never have hesitated.

"So having a competent financial planner," Paul called, "is like having a pilot: takeoff, smooth flight, safe landing."

Dad's shoulders dropped an inch, and his jaw stopped shaking. It was as if he'd been under a spell now broken by the snap of the hypnotist's fingers. "That's it, my friend!" Dad said. He pulled out his embroidered hankie and wiped at his brow. "Forgive me, folks! Had a frog in my throat! Thanks for the assist, Paul," Dad said. "Paul Sullivan, folks, my brilliant partner!"

The grateful smile Dad sent Paul should have been for me. I should be the one with soot on my cheek, not Paul.

Again Dad's eyes flicked my way, and though he returned the smile I sent him, his eyes blazed feral, like a zebra cornered by a pack of lions. He pushed on. "That reminds me of another story . . ."

And like that, Dad was back on track.

CHAPTER TWO

After the seminar, I packed up the laptop and projector and then walked to the office. Inside, I inhaled my earliest memories: mahogany, worn leather and musty files, a hint of my father's Old Spice, and a touch of White Diamonds perfume courtesy of Jenny, his red-haired, red-fingernailed, red-lipsticked secretary.

At the sight of me, Jenny sang, "Happy birthday to you! Happy birthday to you!" She pulled a noisemaker from her desk drawer and tooted it ceremoniously while tossing into the air a handful of confetti.

"Thanks, Jenny," I said, "but I'm not celebrating, remember?"

Jenny honked the horn again, but this time at a decibel barely audible. "I know, honey," she whispered, sliding out of her chair, hugging me tightly and slipping into my hand a wrapped present with bow, anyway. Jewelry or makeup. Jenny always bought me jewelry or makeup, neither of which I had much talent for wearing. "Just in case you want to celebrate later."

Jenny was a Christmas tree of a woman, sparkling and gleaming, wrapped decorously in red and gold silk scarves and elevated on shiny hot-tamale pumps, with enough jewelry hanging from her ears and neck and wrists to melt down and arm a small country.

It wasn't until I was older that I figured out that Jenny had been angling all along for a different role than merely my father's dutiful assistant. What she was really hoping to be was his wife, and my mother. And though Dad never hired Jenny for the position she hoped for, the three of us imitated a family pretty well. When I was young, Jenny planned my birthday parties. When I was older, she treated me to shows at the theater, lunch at a fancy restaurant afterward. And she helped Dad shop for suits and ties, expensive wing tips, a gleaming Rolex. Dad and I reciprocated, blanketing Jenny with flowers on her birthday and Tiffany jewelry at Christmas.

"Thank you," I said, hugging her back. After all of these years, Jenny was still a wind chime, choked in necklaces and handcuffed in bracelets lining her arms.

"How was this morning?" she asked.

"The seminar went well, but . . ." I glanced down the hall to make sure Dad wasn't listening. "Dad was a little off."

"What do you mean, honey?"

I looked around again and then whispered, "He forgot what he was talking about."

"Oh, honey, he's seventy. What do you expect? We all have senior moments."

"Seventy isn't *that* old," I said.

"Honey, it's not young. I wouldn't worry about it. Focus on your birthday. You never know what the day'll bring!"

"That's for sure," I agreed, immediately thinking about my mother, who would have never predicted what the day brought her. She was just running an errand to the grocery store when an HVAC truck rammed into her car broadside, killing her instantly. I was four years old.

I breezed by Dad's office, the same office he'd occupied thirty years ago. To stand in it, to smell the mahogany of his massive desk, to hear the Frank Sinatra from his CD player (having finally traded in his turntable a few years back), felt no different than when I was five years old. On those Saturday mornings, Dad stacked and sorted, humming along to "Fly Me to the Moon," while I sat at Jenny's desk and pounded on her typewriter. Then I'd fish through her drawers, pulling out the stamps and ink pads and covering the back side of my paper with authoritative marks: FIRST CLASS. COPY. URGENT. There was no end to the fun with carbon paper and tracing paper and Post-it notes at my disposal.

Only now, I wasn't five, I was thirty-five years old—*exactly* thirty-five years old—and a partner in my father's business. A business that now grossed $5 million a year. I leaned into Dad's office. "Everything okay in here?" I asked, offering him a smile like a cube of sugar.

"There's my birthday girl." He looked fine, his usual, sunny self.

I put a finger to my lips and issued an exaggerated "Shh—remember, we're not talking about it this year?" Then I slipped into my own office next door.

I hung my sweater on the hook, clicked on my computer with its three flat-screen monitors fanned out on my desk like a tri-fold picture frame, then emptied my messenger bag while the screens came to life. Once the computer was powered up, I opened my to-do list via spreadsheet. Color-coordinated columns and rows based on prioritization—Urgent, Important, Later—glowed back at me.

In the break room, I filled my mug with coffee, added cream and sugar, and a shot of vanilla flavoring. Jenny had brought in a box of doughnuts. I chose a cruller. It was my birthday, after all. I was tall and thin with a hamster-on-a-wheel metabolism. In high school I ran twenty miles a week for the cross-country team and played tennis in the spring. Though now I was far from what someone would describe as athletic, I still maintained the happy ability to burn calories.

Paul walked in and headed toward the coffeepot. "I forgot to wish you happy birthday this morning."

"Forgetting would be good," I said.

"At least you're treating yourself to a doughnut," he joked. Everyone knew I had a sick addiction to doughnuts.

"Just the doughnut," I said. "I'm not celebrating this year."

"I *like* celebrating my birthday," Paul said.

Paul's simple truths had a way of grounding me. He never knew his father, was neglected by his mother, and grew up in foster care. He was owed more than a few birthday celebrations, I guessed. Paul was Dad's favorite kind of guy: a "bootstraps" kind of guy. A guy who made it because of hard work and tenacity. A guy with good character.

"Thanks for saving Dad this morning," I said. "That was weird, wasn't it?"

"He's gotten a little forgetful, that's all."

Gotten, I thought. As if Paul had noticed changes in Dad that I hadn't.

Back in my office, I glanced again at my screens. The technical charts, the moving averages, and the volatility indexes. I reviewed the portfolios I ran for our firm, noting my positions that had outpaced their peers yesterday and those that had not. My key designation was a CFA, a chartered financial analyst, which meant that I managed money. It meant that I could extract meaning from numbers, turn data into evidence, parlay evidence into decisions for our clients' assets.

I could write a stunning analysis, but dreaded picking up the phone. I could outline recommendations in tidy paragraphs and convincing bullet points, but couldn't sit face-to-face with a retiree and tell him why he could live on only $8,000 a month, not $10,000. Thus my father's and my working relationship: him, the strong topic sentence; me, the supporting data. Him, the hook that pulled the clients in with a great story, and me, the formatting of the margins.

My professional limitations extended to my personal life. I researched myself out of every big decision, charted my way out of meeting friends and going on dates, weighed the risk over my every opportunity, and if the possible outcome fell beyond two standard deviations, I ruled it out. I hadn't been on a date in over a year, and before that, my love life was sketchy at best.

If I were a company, I wouldn't buy my stock. Metaphorically speaking, I had failed to generate earnings, and could therefore go under at any time.

In Dad's office, I sunk into his leather chair and squeezed his sofa pillow to my chest, letting the velvety fringes tickle my chin. Had he had moments of forgetfulness lately? Now that I really examined him, I considered that maybe he wasn't his jovial self. When had a furrow etched itself between his brows?

"You feeling okay?" I asked.

"The old man's better than ever."

"How'd you sleep?"

"Like a dog. You?"

"The seminar went well," I said. I looked at Dad expectantly.

"Been better, but it was great to see the clients." He smiled.

But you lost your place, forgot what the heck you were talking about, I wanted to say. I *should* have said. My heart sped up and my mouth dried to cotton. I lost my courage, like always. All these years later, and I still just wanted him to be happy with me.

"It's your birthday," Dad said. "You don't have to be here today. I was hoping you'd take the day off—a spa day, a shopping spree with some girlfriends."

"What's on the schedule?" I asked, noting the irritation in my tone. Dad knew better. I didn't do spa days, I loathed shopping, and I certainly didn't have a gaggle of girlfriends to hang out with. If I had taken the day off, I would have stayed home and read a new book, drank a few glasses of Merlot, and rolled out homemade lemon-pepper fettuccini. Dad knew that. It bugged me that he pretended otherwise.

Dad issued a sigh of resignation. He looked down at his diary, a leather calendar that he still used, even though his computer was rigged with all the same information. "I love you, Missy, you know that," he said. "I just want you to be happy."

True enough. Dad did want only that.

Dad pulled a birthday present from his desk drawer. "Open it now, open it later. Whatever you want."

I smiled my best daughter smile and blew him a kiss. I needed him to know that I was happy, as happy as one could be, I imagined. How could one measure happiness, anyway? Truly, I was contented. I was satisfied. I wasn't a person who flew high on the fringes of life. I was the safety girl. The girl who stayed behind the line; I accepted the demarcation. I was happy, tucked securely in my groove. "I'll open it tonight, I promise."

I activated our firm's calendar on my tablet, and Dad launched into our day. "We've got a new couple at ten. The Andersons are coming in at eleven. We need to review his buy/sell agreement. The Kayes are coming in at noon to update their estate planning. After that, I'm hitting the golf course with Jimmy Jorgensen. What about you? Maybe you'll come along, hit a few balls, play some tennis? The club's a great place to meet eligible bachelors, right?" Dad flashed me an encouraging smile. "We could eat dinner on the veranda—the nice crab cake you like? A few Arnold Palmers to cool us down? A glass of champagne? Let me at least toast you for your birthday?"

"I'll stay at the office," I said. "I want to work on the portfolios for a while. I have a couple companies reporting earnings this week." In college, I majored in economics, and then pounded out an MBA. From there, I came to work for my father, learning the ropes and attaining

The Light of Hidden Flowers

licenses. By the time I was twenty-five, I had earned my Series 7 license for trading securities. The next year I became a certified financial planner. The Chartered Financial Analyst exam came next. I nailed each of these tests with nearly perfect scores.

"When are we going to celebrate your birthday, then?" Dad asked.

"We're not," I said. "Who are the new people coming in at ten?"

"A business owner and his wife," Dad said. "The wife just inherited money from her mother."

"They're big shots!" Jenny—who was always listening to every conversation—bellowed from the reception area. "Most of their money is at Goldman, but the Mr. wants someone local."

"Big shots, huh?" I said.

"No one's a big shot for real," Dad said. "People are people. They all put their pants on the same: one leg at a time."

Such was Dad. His entire life boiled down to putting on pants one leg at a time.

CHAPTER THREE

When the prospects came in at 10:00 a.m. sharp, I stood with Jenny to greet them. The man introduced himself as Mr. Charles Longworth III, sporting a crisply starched shirt and a million-dollar suit, and his wife, head to toe in tweed Chanel, Mrs. Elizabeth Longworth. When my father came out of his office to meet them, I smiled because my dad always struck me as Superman, his thick silver hair, his gleaming smile, his handshake that could crush cans.

At the sight of Dad, the prospect stood taller, puffed out his chest. "I'm Charles Longworth the Third."

Dad shook his hand. "Good to meet you. I know I'm going to end up calling you Charlie. One of my best friends growing up was a Charlie. Do you mind?"

"Well actually . . ."

Dad shrugged and smiled at him. "I'm apologizing ahead of time, *Charles*, in case I slip." My dad meant no disrespect—my father never disrespected anyone—he was just familiar, it was his way.

Dad held Mrs. Longworth's hand in his own, commented on her broach, and said it was as lovely as she was. "Charles, Elizabeth. This is my daughter, Missy."

"Melissa," I said, shaking their hands. "My father likes nicknames," I felt compelled to add.

"Feel free to call me Liz," Mrs. Longworth said. It appeared she was all for loosening up a bit.

"It's Missy's birthday today," Dad said. "We've got computers all around this office. But we don't need them. Not with Missy. A beautiful mind, this one has. Top of her class at the Wharton School, valedictorian in high school. Anyone who wonders how she ended up with a genius mind—well, they didn't know her mother. My Charlene. May she rest in peace."

I signaled toward the conference room. "Please, come in," I said. Meanwhile, Dad was still beaming, presumably thinking about me winning the math award my senior year or perhaps Mom completing her *NY Times* crossword puzzles.

We organized ourselves around the shiny cherry table. Mr. and Mrs. Longworth sat primly with their legs crossed and hands folded. I assumed my position, fingers perched above the keyboard of my laptop, reading glasses balanced atop my head. And Dad, he reclined in the chair at the head of the table, his legs crossed casually in the shape of the numeral four, smiling at us all. Jenny brought in a tray of coffee.

"Best coffee ever!" my father exclaimed, pointing at the tray. "Jenny's coffee."

Mrs. Longworth bobbled her head up and down. "Oh, yes, lovely—"

"Let me cut to the chase," Mr. Longworth said, opening his leather portfolio and turning the back of a Montblanc pen. "The bulk of my money is in New York at Goldman. I'm getting ready to retire and, thusly, there will be more money, from a buyout. My wife has recently come into some money, too, following the settling of her mother's estate."

Dad trained his eyes on Mrs. Longworth. "I'm sorry to hear of your mother's passing."

"Oh," Mrs. Longworth said, disarmed. "Well, thank you. I do miss her."

"I'm sure you do," Dad said. "It's never easy."

"In any event," Mr. Longworth piped back in. "I'm looking around for—"

"And what is your goal?" Dad asked, turning to Mr. Longworth.

"My goal?"

"All this money," Dad went on. "What's it for?"

Mr. Longworth twisted his face into a knot. "My goal is for the money to perform! Goldman has been a huge disappointment. When the market crashed in '08, my portfolio dropped 20 percent."

"Not bad," Dad said, shrugging his shoulders.

"Not bad?" Mr. Longworth sputtered. "Do I need to tell you how much 20 percent is on a multimillion-dollar portfolio?"

"The S&P crashed 40 percent," Dad said. "So yes, I'd say 20 percent isn't bad."

"And the more the market went down, the more Goldman wanted to buy," Mr. Longworth said.

"Liz," my father said. "Do you shop at Nordstrom?"

"I do," she said.

"Twice a year, they have a sale, correct?"

"A lovely sale," she agreed.

"If you went into Nordstrom during the half-yearly sale and picked out four or five outfits, would you tell the clerk to hold them for you until the sale was over?"

"Why would she do that?" Mr. Longworth bellowed, his fist coming down onto the table.

"I wouldn't," Mrs. Longworth said evenly, "because they were on sale. Just like stocks were on sale when the market was going down."

"Exactly!" my father boomed.

Meanwhile, Mr. Longworth harrumphed, not pleased at all by being one-upped by his wife.

To my "think first, act second" brain, the financial crash of 2008 was a predictable snowball of a disaster that gathered speed thanks to too much power put in the hands of reckless risk takers. For many years, "more leverage" paid off, making heroes of the rainmakers of these Wall Street firms. Caution gave way to the wind. Anyone who cried foul—who tried to alert their top management to the impending danger of selling these highly leveraged goods—was turned away. For our firm's portfolio, I began reducing equity exposure early, near the end of '06, while the market was still flying high. I had no idea how bad it was going to get, and we still got hammered plenty, but I knew the stocks were overvalued, so scaling back helped. Dad never once flinched. "We have reason to believe it's time to pull back." When the market fell off the cliff and we only dangled from it, I was relieved beyond measure, and so was Dad, as if the statute of limitations on him believing in me was about to run out.

Mr. Longworth went on. "Morgan Stanley has assured me that their portfolios—"

"Charlie," my dad said. "*Charles*, my apologies. You're a smart, successful guy and I hate to keep harping on this, but what's your goal? When all's said and done, what's the *value* of your money? Do you want to travel with your wife, spend time with your grandchildren, give back to the community? Let's forget returns for now. Let's talk about you and your wife. What do you enjoy?"

Mrs. Longworth's plaintive face brightened to a rosy pink. It looked to me like Dad was asking the question that she herself had wanted to ask, probably for years. She leaned closer to her husband, awaiting his response.

"Mr. Fletcher, I need to be clear," Mr. Longworth boomed. "You're not the only firm we're interviewing. We have a list of five firms; the four others are much larger than yours, but I agreed to meet with you because Jack Murphy recommended you so highly."

"I love that guy," Dad said, shaking his head. "You remember him, right, Missy? When you were little, we went boating with him and his daughter. Now there's a guy who's enjoying his retirement—a guy and his boat. Good times. Good guy, the Murph."

"As I was saying, this is just an interview," Mr. Longworth continued. "We plan to meet with each firm once, and then select two or three for a second round of proposals."

My father stood up, smiling widely. "Good for you. I wish you all the best." Dad extended his hand. "Liz, it was a pleasure meeting you. Take the time you need to grieve your mother. I know from experience that you can't rush the process. Remember the good times." Dad reached for her hand and cupped it between his. Mrs. Longworth shuddered as though she might cry.

"Thank you," she whispered.

Mr. Longworth, puzzled and confused, held up his piece of paper. "I'm not finished. I have a list of questions. We haven't even talked about your qualifications. I haven't seen your materials. Compared your returns."

My father, the towering, friendly Superman. "Charles, my buddy, I've been doing this for forty years. My clients are my friends. I would do anything, anytime, for any of them. The other day, a widow client of mine called me because she had a flat tire. I got on the horn and got her fixed up. This business isn't rocket science. It's about *caring*. It's about *trust*. You either trust me, or you don't. If you're a guy looking to compare returns, then we're not your firm. Sometimes the market will go up; sometimes it will go down. I can't predict the weather, but I can react to it.

"Missy here, sometimes *she* predicts the weather," Dad chuckled. "She's that good." Dad never missed an opportunity to throw me a compliment. My heart gonged with pleasure.

"What matters," Dad said, "is that my clients are living the lives they want to live. With all due respect, Charles, I don't do interviews. I wish you all the best."

Mrs. Longworth issued a little squeal, an indication she didn't want to let my father go. A hint, I thought, that she wanted my father to rub off on her husband.

"That's it?" Mr. Longworth said, his mouth setting into a thin line, gathering papers into his leather portfolio. "You're saying I should take your firm off my list? Remove it from consideration?"

"If you want to talk about goals, give me a call. Your goal is your life raft. The farther you get away from it, the more likely you are to drown. Until you know what your goals are, I can't help you."

"I'm confused," he said. "You're saying you don't *want* my business?"

"I'm saying that the fit might not be right."

With that, my father left the room and returned to his office, clicked on his Frank Sinatra, and hummed along while he shuffled papers.

I prepared to see them out. "It was nice meeting you," I said. "Let me give you our firm brochure."

Ruffled, bewildered, and dismayed, Mr. and Mrs. Longworth stood and straightened their designer suits. Jenny showed them to the door.

As I watched them walk away, I wondered whether Mr. and Mrs. Longworth had ever been refused service in their lives. I wondered what their conversation would be like as they drove down King Street, whether Mrs. Longworth would need to fluff Mr. Longworth's ego, whether my father had inflicted a bruise that would change colors for days.

I walked down the hallway and poked my head into Dad's office. "That was a lot of money you let walk out the door."

Dad leaned back, crossed his shiny wing tips across the corner of his desk. "I'm seventy years old. With every new person we take on, I need to ask myself: Would I be happy to hear they were coming in for a meeting? At this point in the game, it's like dating. I need to be sure before I jump into a relationship."

I slid into Dad's office and closed the door. "True, but you were a little *harsh* with them," I said. "You're not usually harsh with anyone." I took a tentative breath. "And at the seminar today. You kind of forgot what you were talking about, didn't you?"

My heart thumped. I never initiated confrontation.

"Honey, sit down," Dad said, rubbing at his eyes. "You know how long ago it was when I was in 'Nam? Fifty years."

I slipped my feet out of my flats and pulled them onto the sofa. When Dad got going on Vietnam, it wasn't an exercise in brevity.

Dad stared deep into his memory. "Missy, it seems like *yesterday*. I was just a kid, had barely heard of Southeast Asia. Then the next thing you know: jungle warfare, leeches, trench foot. Shooting at an enemy we couldn't see. Marching every day. We didn't know where we were going. We didn't know why. Pure insanity."

"I can't even imagine," I said. So young, and shipped off to war.

Dad shook his head. "Every day we were either bored out of our minds or scared out of our wits. At night, we'd peel off our gear: the flak jacket, the rucksack, the helmet, boots, and poncho. Some guys had their secret supply of cigarettes, their Bible, their favorite food. Me, I was all about my stash of jelly beans. My jelly beans and my joke book. My buddy Ralph and I would gather round with the group of guys, a two-man comedy show, we were.

"I'd open with 'A guy walks into a bar . . .' and then he'd follow with 'A priest, a rabbi, and a minister are out on a boat . . .' Back and forth, back and forth. Oh, Missy, the guys would howl, their heads jumping

The Light of Hidden Flowers

between me and Ralph like they were watching a tennis match. 'What do you get when you mix a German shepherd with a wiener dog . . . ?'"

"I'm not surprised," I said. "You've always had a way of holding court."

"Our buddy Timbo would always ask, 'How do you remember so many goddamned jokes?' Timbo was a laugher, a knee-slapper. He roared and roared and begged for more. What a guy, that Timbo. He was from Fairfax, I've told you about him, right, Miss?"

I nodded. "Yep, the one who played basketball for Thomas Jefferson."

Dad beamed. "You do remember! We figured out he and I actually played against each other in the state championships in high school. Crazy thing to think that our paths had crossed and then, there we were, in that godforsaken jungle."

I nodded eagerly as if this were new information, despite the fact that Dad had told me about Timbo before.

"'Tell the one about the pope,' Timbo would say. 'Okay, Timbo,' I'd say. 'For you. A guy's invited to the Vatican to visit with the pope . . .'" Dad shook his head. "Poor Timbo," he said.

"He died in battle, right?" I said for Dad, so he wouldn't have to say it himself.

Dad nodded.

"So sad," I said.

Dad and I sat in silence for a moment. "Going to play some golf today, Dad?" I asked, attempting to hatchet him out of the murky trail.

Dad remained introspective. He looked up with ghostly eyes. "I still know a lot of those jokes, Missy. Not the entire book, like I used to, but plenty of them. I still remember them like it was yesterday."

"Yep," I said. "You still got it, Dad."

Dad looked at me, and the burden in his face was both young and old.

23

"I forgot what the hell I was talking about today," he admitted. "Just a blunder. It won't happen again."

CHAPTER FOUR

At eleven and noon, Dad and I met with old clients, reviewed their plans, and made adjustments. Dad was the leader; I was the foot soldier, presenting data, explaining the why and what and where and how. Then there was chitchat and reminiscing. There were roars of laughter, and wiping of eyes, and mad appreciation for each other. Handshakes and hugs, and promises to get together soon. These were the relationships that my dad was in—fully loyal and totally committed.

Then Dad left for the golf course and I worked on my models. When my stomach grumbled, I headed out into the blinding spring sun, and down the brick-lined street to Ellie's. I reserved my eating pleasure for no one. I loved food, from a perfectly toasted English muffin with melted butter oozing from its golden nooks, to Ellie's homemade soup, to the fanciest five-star restaurant. In Ellie's little lunch shop, she made three soups daily. Today I was compelled to choose between (1) portabella mushroom, sausage, and kale; (2) broccoli cheddar; or (3) tomato-basil with pesto drizzle. I selected the tomato, and licked my lips as Ellie tore a nice hunk of bread from the crusty loaf. "A pecan bar, too," I said, pointing to her dessert case. It was my birthday, after all.

Back at my desk, I ate my tomato-basil while I charted beta. Today I was researching a stock I'd been following for a few months, ZelInc, a data storage company. I went through my twelve-step process. Though I had run these numbers countless times before, I now ran them again. I looked at revenue, because the health of a stock started with its ability to make money. Next I analyzed the earnings per share. If revenue was the measure of how much money a company was taking in, earnings per share was the gauge of how much was flowing down to the shareholders. Then I divided the average shareholder equity during the past twelve months by the net profit the company had made during that time. This gave me my return on equity and showed me how efficiently the company was producing a return for the owners. I went on to calculate the PEG ratio, the weighted alpha. I read up on what other analysts were saying about this stock, what the insiders were buying, as well as a handful of other metrics to help my decision-making process.

Before I knew it, hours had passed and it was already three o'clock. Jenny knocked on my door. "Guess who is on the phone?"

I shrugged.

"Mr. Fancy-Pants from this morning." She gave a smug smile.

"Mr. Longworth?"

"You got it."

"And?"

"He wants to talk to your father."

"Should I take it?" Dad had already been on the golf course for a couple of hours.

Jenny nodded and then left my office. I considered calling after her, asking her to take a message, but I had been a big enough coward today. The least I could do was take this call.

I inhaled a gallon of air, blew it out slowly. I smiled before answering, a trick Dad had taught me, a trick Dale Carnegie books and tapes had taught him years ago. "Mr. Longworth, hello, this is Melissa Fletcher. My father isn't here right now."

"We've decided to go with your firm." His tone was adamant. "We don't want to interview the others. We want your father. Your firm." Now his tone was pleading, almost frantic, like he was begging the store clerk at American Girl on Christmas Eve for the last Girl of the Year doll for his daughter.

"I'll talk to him," I said.

"Put in a good word for us, will you?"

"I will."

"And happy birthday," he added.

I called Dad on his cell phone, the flip-top variety that did nothing other than take and make calls. I told him about Longworth. "Missy, tell him I'll think about it. Tell him I'm not sure if it's a good fit. Tell him I'll consider it, and will get back to him by Monday."

"It's only Thursday, Dad. This guy sounds like he's going to blow a gasket."

"By Monday, Missy. Let me think about it."

I returned Mr. Longworth's call. "So now he's interviewing *me*?" he scoffed. "I'm now begging this guy to take my ten million dollars?"

"If he says yes," I said, "you won't be sorry."

Before I shut down my computer, I typed Mr. Longworth's name into the search engine: three pages of entries, all related to his business in wires. Then I typed in "Elizabeth Longworth," and I was surprised to see a fair amount of entries registered for her, too. Only hers were related to the work she did as a board member for the One by One Foundation, a nonprofit designed to aid in the development of Third World countries by building water and sanitation infrastructure. There were pictures of Mrs. Longworth—Chanel-tweed Mrs. Longworth—makeup-less in chinos and an unironed linen camp shirt, standing arm in arm with a village full of disadvantaged children. She had been instrumental in funding the local outreach organization that built the wells, and while the work itself was admirable and fascinating, I was mostly impressed by Mrs. Longworth herself. In person, she had struck me as passive and meek. Intelligent, yes, but not strong. Yet in these photos, fueled by her passion, she was courageous and fierce.

Before I decided to major in finance, I dabbled in the study of public policy. In my heart I was a Peace Corps girl with wanderlust and a dream of bettering conditions in the Third World. There were so many ways to organize a society, and yet the needs of the people were the same in every nation: food, clothing, shelter. To work, for life to have meaning.

The chance to improve another person's lot in life, through the development of farming, water, and infrastructure, exhilarated me. At William & Mary as an undergrad I declared a double major in finance and public policy. In the end, there was a fork in the road. To choose public policy and travel meant to leave Dad. To choose finance meant to stay by his side. For as much as my passions resided in tents and huts and yurts, I opted for Dad.

I chose Dad because I loved him more than anyone in the world. I chose Dad because I was already down one parent, and the thought of losing time with my one remaining was riskier than buying a tech stock at the height of the Internet bubble. And maybe I chose Dad because I wasn't brave enough to leave home. But if I had gone, I would have grown stronger and maybe, just maybe, I would have had the guts to step in to help my father this morning.

CHAPTER FIVE

At five o'clock on the dot, I packed my bags and headed toward the front office. From the looks of Jenny—her computer still glowing, her mug of coffee just refilled, her lipstick recently reapplied—it appeared she planned to wait for Dad, who was still on the golf course. "Tell Dad I said good night."

"Happy birthday, honey," she said again, blowing me a kiss.

It was the last week of May and though the month had started unseasonably cold, gushing rain and shooting ice daggers, Mother Nature was now handing out daily doses of sunshine like overstuffed goody bags. As I peered west over the faraway mountains at the Creamsicle sunset, I knew Dad was right, that it was a beautiful night to be at the country club, to be rallying on the tennis court, feeling the fresh air whiz by my neck. And while I did enjoy playing tennis, going to the country club was anathema to me. It was hard work. It required that I turn myself into someone else, demanded that I elevate my sociability many degrees beyond my comfort level, putting myself forward to a threesome in need of a fourth, most likely cheery BFFs from high school, then Chi Omega sorority sisters in college.

The tableau was all too familiar to me. I'd try, but I'd fail. For all of my efforts, I wouldn't look like them, talk like them, be like them. I knew the truth. The world loved extroverts: it valued the gregarious personality; it praised the person of action over the person of contemplation. To be me—an introvert, a sensitive sort of person who preferred the company of her own thoughts over the conversation of others—meant swimming outside the mainstream.

The few times I had made the effort—to play tennis, to be sociable—I'd met Dad on the veranda afterward and sipped an Arnold Palmer while he called over guys for me to meet. "Missy, this guy here—Tom Creighton—is a genius with the computers, just like you." The guy—Tom—would *Aw-shucks* and shake my hand and return the compliment to Dad, correcting him slightly, saying that he wasn't really a computer guy, more like a security systems analyst. "Either way," Dad would say. "He's a good guy. And Tom," Dad would go on, shaking his head, "Missy here has a beautiful mind. Never seen anything like it."

And I'd try, and Tom—or Bob, or Sam, or Max—would try, but our inane chitchat could never measure up to Dad's hopes for everything to be *the best*. For all of his efforts, the men would leave, undoubtedly feeling as though they had been sold a bill of goods: the spinster daughter who was single *after all of these years*. And I'd leave feeling just the same: like half-stale bread on the day-old rack. Dad's speechwriting was good—for me, for the guys—but something didn't line up. We were able to detect the spin.

I slid into my Subaru Outback wagon. When I purchased it a few years back, the salesman—an enthusiastic twentysomething—told me I *had* to have this car. *It's got all-wheel drive! It's got a hatchback that holds like a gazillion shopping bags! It's got a mammoth backseat with built-in tethers for your kids' car seats!*

That'll come in handy! I said, just to make him happy. The truth was that I had done hours of research and knew I wanted this car because of its fuel efficiency, reliability, and safety rating. I was a *Consumer Reports* type of gal, the kind that made life choices by comparing black and red dots.

Today the extra seats, all the space, and the roof rack mocked me.

Although I would have liked a special compartment to store my shame.

I clicked on the Rosetta Stone CD I listened to each night on my way home from work and repeated Italian after the narrator. *La donna beve.* The lady drinks. *La bambina mangia.* The baby eats. *L'uomo mangia zuppa.* The man eats soup. I had been listening to these CDs for years, and knew the vocabulary by heart.

"Take a trip!" Dad said all of the time. "Go see your beautiful Italy. Go see the Grand Canyon, for heaven's sake!"

"I will, Dad. Someday. I promise."

"What are you waiting for?" Dad asked. "For the old man to kick the bucket?"

"I'm not waiting for anything," I'd say.

"Just because it didn't work out once before, doesn't mean it won't work out if you try again."

Dad was referring to my last attempt to board a plane. Though I had read countless books on overcoming the fear of flying, visited the airport three times in preparation for my trip and taken my Xanax a half hour before takeoff, I still couldn't do it. I made it onto the airplane, but at the commencement of the flight attendants' safety demonstration, my heart wedged into my throat; had it not been for an extremely calm attendant who had once been an ER nurse, I would have hyperventilated and succumbed to a serious panic attack. She removed me from the aircraft and seated me in the waiting area. My luggage, already locked in the plane's belly, would go to Italy without me. I watched the plane soar into the sky and then sat for two hours, observing countless more take off.

That was four years ago.

At home, I dropped my bags on the kitchen chair, tuned my ears to the silence of my living-alone existence, grateful for the hum of the refrigerator.

I lived in a three-story brick town house in Old Town Alexandria. Only a few blocks from the water and a few blocks from downtown shopping, my location was desirable, by any measure. Dad lived only a mile or so away, in the same house he'd shared with Mom, so many years ago. Her framed photos still stood on the fireplace mantel, her macramé plant holders still dangled from hooks in the ceiling, her framed needlepoints still hung on the walls.

I didn't remember her. The memories I kept, the feelings I housed, weren't organic; they were from photos, an archive of images I contrived so that I could fake a recollection. A childhood forged from secondary sources. A dollhouse I filled with a hodgepodge of found items. That was the worst part. That I didn't get to keep a piece of her like Dad did. Dad remembered the real deal, when I had memorized the images. He was bona fide; I was just pretending.

In the kitchen, I chopped some onions, crushed some garlic, and sautéed them over a gas flame. Then I poured in a can of crushed tomatoes. The sweet aroma filled the air as the sauce simmered. I tossed in some basil and oregano, salt and pepper. In a separate pan, I boiled water and submerged fresh pasta. When it was heated, I covered it in sauce, and then grated fresh Parmesan on top. I poured myself a hearty glass of Merlot. I went to the family room and clicked on the television and DVR, chose a *Jeopardy!* episode from the lengthy list of them, and settled into my nightly dinner ritual, eating while watching brainiacs answer trivia. The only thing that changed was the food, whether it was pasta or soup or chicken or fish, all recipes I learned from *Molto Mario* while watching the Food Network. Soup, *zuppa*. Fish, *pesce*. Chicken, *pollo*. I sat there, stuffing my face with pasta, calling out answers. The Roman god of wine: "Who is Bacchus?" The country to the east of Sudan: "What is Ethiopia?" The founder of the Achaemenian empire: "Who is Cyrus the Great?"

A beautiful mind, indeed, I thought snidely, washing down my mouthful with a swig of wine. Look at where it got me. Alone on my thirty-fifth birthday, eating too much pasta in front of the television. A bottle of wine for one.

After dinner, I popped the button on my work pants and went to the freezer for the carton of pistachio gelato. I turned on the teakettle and sat on the granite countertop, shoveling the creamy treat into my mouth, as I waited for the kettle to blow.

With my cup of tea, I sat at my desk and turned on my computer.

"Let's see what everyone is up to," I said as I logged on to Facebook. Though far from the most social person on earth, I was a hell of a lurker. I relished checking not only on my high school and college friends but also distant cousins and great aunts and uncles I had never met. We were a small family to begin with—Dad, Mom, and their only child, me. But Dad was the youngest of five siblings, and both his parents died when I was just a baby. And Mom's upbringing was rocky. Her parents divorced when she was young—back in an age when divorce wasn't so common—and both remarried, starting new families. When Mom died, there wasn't much support for Dad and me. After a few perfunctory attempts by distant relatives, a few casseroles prepared and put in our freezer, the writing on the wall was clear: it was just the two of us. Dad bought me a shiny red Betty Crocker cookbook, and in a matter of years, I'd learned to prepare basic meals.

Still, I'd connected on Facebook with some of these distant cousins, great aunts and uncles, as well as with some old friends from high school and a few from college. Out there. Somewhere. I read their posts, the comments. I scrolled carefully over the photos of their children at soccer games and dance recitals. I grinned at silly pictures of family life, my friends and their husbands making goofy faces at their children. I watched as kids blew candles and gobbled frosting roses, babies attempted their first wobbly steps, toothless first graders dressed as Disney princesses. I delighted in watching them grow up, these children I had never met, a few that I had, once or twice. I witnessed anniversaries and trips abroad: the Louvre, the Coliseum, the Great Wall. I hopped aboard the Space Mountain roller coaster at Disneyland, stepped inside Hogwarts School at Universal Studios, rode the waves on the beaches of North Carolina. I imagined a life different than mine.

A few of these people—hardly close enough to call friends or family, really—had posted happy birthday greetings on my wall. Like a distant echo from one end of a tunnel: *Happy birthdayyyyyyyyyyyyyy, you person we barely know!*

But tucked within these faraway comments was a birthday wish from my high school boyfriend, Joe. My truest love. The man I had never forgotten.

Loving Joe had been like sliding on eyeglasses after a lifetime of poor vision. Joe was my revelation.

"Happy birthday, old friend. Good one? Hope so." Eight words. Our first bit of direct contact in fifteen years.

Though we had been Facebook friends for a few years, we had never messaged each other, had never posted on each other's walls.

I stared at the wish, an almost supernatural bridge from the past to the present, as if I could feel the tug of leaving one dimension for another. I captured the screen with his wish on it, printed it, and cut it out with scissors. I stared at it as if it were a prophecy.

As I brushed my teeth before bedtime, I remembered the gift from Dad. I went to my bag and pulled out the rectangular box. Inside was a necklace with a silver charm. In my palm, I examined it closely. It was a saint, but not one I recognized. On the back of it was engraved "St. Brigid, patron saint of safe travel." Also inside the box was an Expedia travel voucher with a note. "Take a month, take two! Travel, explore! Happy birthday, Daughter."

I sat down at my vanity, picked up the phone, and called Dad. "Thank you," I said.

"Will you do it?" he asked. "Take a big trip?"

"Someday," I said, staring at my reflection in the mirror, pressing on the blue veins pulsing against my ghostly complexion, the halo of hair that had sprung free from the ponytail.

"Okay, Daughter," he said. "Your choice, whatever you want."

"I like the necklace," I said. "St. Brigid, huh? When did you start believing in saints?"

"I've always believed in saints," Dad said. "Your mother was a saint, if there ever was one. She's smiling on you today, you know that, right?"

"I know."

"Boy did she love you."

"I wish I felt like I knew her," I said, like I always said.

"Know yourself, and you'll know her," Dad said, another one of his famous sayings. "You're a lot like her."

When I hung up, I sat on my bed with my gifts: Clinique skin care products from Jenny, my St. Brigid charm and travel voucher from Dad. And a wish from Joe Santelli. I picked up the piece of paper and pressed it to my chest as if it were a rabbit's foot.

CHAPTER SIX

Joe Santelli asked me to dance when we were both sophomores. It was the snowball dance, and I had gone with one of the neighborhood girls and he had arrived with his posse of guys. We slow danced to Bon Jovi's "Bed of Roses" and he nuzzled his mouth into the hair draped around my neck. "You smell so good," he said, and I remembered how pleased I was with myself for having done my research. I had read an article in *Seventeen*: "Drive your guy wild. Use coconut shampoo!"

"What happened to your date?" I asked, because I had heard that Joe had asked Sarah Myers to the dance.

"She asked me," Joe said, "but, I don't know . . . Lots of drama. Just as well. This worked out much better."

By the end of the night, we had danced ten times, exactly. I had kept track, assigning more meaning to each successive dance as though I were practicing ratios and proportionality in AP math.

When he walked me to the door of the gym, he leaned in and kissed me. I closed my eyes and let the shocks radiate off my marrow. When he pulled back, I would have given up food for a week just to taste his bottom lip for another second.

"Maybe we could get together on Monday?" he said. "Work on our science projects?"

"Science projects?" I responded, as the air left my tires. I no longer felt that ten dances meant true love. I felt more that I was being used. That being the smart girl in all the AP classes made me a hot commodity for a guy who didn't want to do his own work. That by Monday, Joe would ask me to "help" him with his science element project, that it would be me researching the radioactivity of promethium and hand-spooning him the information so that he would get a good grade.

"Sure," I said. "Of course." I smiled and then walked outside, where I knew Dad would be at the curb, waiting in his whale of a Cadillac, Frank Sinatra crooning on the cassette player.

"There's my beautiful girl with the beautiful mind. How was the dance?"

When I struggled to find words to tell Dad how the dance was, I finally said, "I think I'm being buttered up to do a science project for Joe. I thought maybe he liked me, but that would be dumb. Why would he like me?"

Dad laughed and squeezed my knee with his giant basketball hand. I tossed it back to him. "Oh, Missy," he said. "I'm not laughing at you. I'm just happy that if a boy is using you, it's for your smarts, not something else . . . If you know what I mean."

"Dad!" I shrieked.

"Missy," he said, now serious, his hand returning to my knee. "I'll tell you why a guy would like you. Because you're quick and funny, and smart and witty. And that mug of yours is pretty adorable, too."

That night, as I lay in bed, I replayed the splendor of the night. Slow dancing with Joe, the kiss at the end of the night, the offer that left me questioning his motives.

Monday after school, Joe and I met in the library. I approached him cautiously, businesslike, as though the other night hadn't happened. I wanted him to know that I wasn't clueless about his intentions, that I understood he wanted help with his homework, and that dancing with me was the price he felt he needed to pay.

"What's up?" I said casually, like I'd heard the cool kids say upon greeting one another.

"Hi, Missy," he said sweetly, not at all matching my aloof tone. "Friday night was fun."

"It was okay." My breathing was uneven.

Joe looked down at his notebook, as though I had hurt him.

"So you're researching promethium," I said.

"Yeah, and you picked neptunium, right?" When Joe opened his notebook and scanned his pages and pages of slanted, microscopic boy-handwriting, I choked back my tears, because what I had thought was wrong. Or so it appeared. He had already done quite a bit of research. Joe wasn't using me; he really just wanted to study together.

"Friday night *was* really fun," I said. When Joe looked into my eyes, I felt as though we belonged to each other. Try as I might to focus on the elements and their chemical reactivity, I was having a hard time extinguishing the chemical reaction that was heating my chest and pulling at my center of gravity. I just wanted to reach for him.

After high school, we went off to college. Joe chose a military college three hours from William & Mary, where I opted to go. Time and distance and circumstance pulled us apart gradually, the way a shoreline disappears at high tide, until we no longer had any contact. The years passed. One day Joe sent me a friend request on Facebook. He was married with three children. They lived in Jersey. He was a marine, now retired from the service, working as a security consultant. His wife, a brown-haired beauty who could have passed for his sister, looked adoringly at him, as the three children balanced on their laps. I accepted his friend request and now peeked into their lives, wondering what it would have been like, to be married, to be a mom. To have a different kind of life.

CHAPTER SEVEN
JOE

I found Kate crying again last night. I had just finished watching an hour-long show on FX—an edgy military drama soaked in gratuitous violence and debauchery. Not that I turned it off. I should have. The last thing I needed was more grotesque images to invade my brain while I tried to sleep. I had enough tape from Afghanistan to last me a lifetime. I should do myself a favor and watch *Happy Days* before bed from now on. I used to love *Happy Days*.

I had just clicked off the television and hobbled with my crutch to the back door to let our dog Scout outside to go "good boy." My leg ached tonight, as it often did with the rain. A below-knee amputee was shorthand for my condition. The IED that blew up my leg took my buddy Allen's life. As a lieutenant colonel, I didn't have to be on patrol with the guys, but I was. That was the part Lucy had the hardest time with: not that I had come home wrapped like a mummy, but that I was reckless.

I let Scout back in and had just checked the locks when I heard Kate crying. Weeping more than crying—the low, awful hum of my kid hurting. I crutched my way down the hall and poked my head into her bedroom. Kate was a real toughie, so hearing her cry hit me particularly hard.

I sat on the edge of her bed, smoothed the blanket on her back. "What's wrong, Kate?"

"Nothing." She stopped crying at the sight of me, wiped her eyes. "Just the usual."

"Tell me," I said. This first year of middle school had been an eye-opener. Girls we'd known since kindergarten had turned mean over the summer.

Kate backhanded her tears and turned to me. "Stupid stuff. I sat next to Anna. She got up and scooted down, so I scooted down, too. Then she yelled at me, 'Why are you following me? I'm trying to save a spot for my best friend!'"

"Oh, honey."

"Whatever," Kate said. "I was just scooting down."

Little brat, I thought, but of course didn't say. "Girls can be cruel at this age," I said. "I'm sorry that happened to you."

"I'm sorry that happened to you," she said, patting my reconstructed knee.

"Can you stay for a minute?" She moved toward the wall and I slid in next to her. We both stared at the ceiling with our arms crossed over our chests, saying nothing.

Just a year ago, Kate didn't care about all this girl drama. She was the happy-go-lucky kid who marched to the beat of her own drum, not worrying that her interests weren't mainstream, happier to read Anne Frank than to listen to Katy Perry on her iPod.

But then she started middle school, and rather than being satisfied with who she was, she found herself tormented by the attention drawn to her by differences she'd never even perceived before. Some days were fine, then others she realized—more like, she remembered—that she was not quite like the other girls. The girls who made friends so easily, ran in packs, paired up. And poor Kate just couldn't find her way in. She was made differently than the other girls were, and what she was made of didn't interest them.

I stifled the urge to give her advice. *This is what you need to do, Kate . . .* I couldn't help it—I was the dad, a guy, and my impulse, my job, was to fix things, even though I knew that that wasn't what this called for. *Just be there for her,* my wife—correction, soon-to-be-*ex*-wife—would say. *What about you, Lucy?* I'd want to scream. *Why weren't you there for her?* A thirteen-year-old daughter needed her mother.

"I can't do it anymore," Lucy had said less than a year ago. "I've been a wife and a mother. A *marine* wife," she clarified, "and Joe, I've had enough. *Enough.*" When she said the second *enough*, she cut her hand through the air for emphasis, like drawing a line in the sand.

Only days later, she accepted a job working as an event planner for an international law firm, setting up conferences and award trips all over the world.

"Kate's at risk, Lucy," I told her when she called the other day. "Middle school is a real battleground for her."

"Well, battlegrounds are your specialty," she said, throwing me under the bus. Lucy took every opportunity to indict me for deploying for my third tour, as if it were voluntary, as if it were my choice to return to Afghanistan. I didn't have a choice, but Lucy thought I should have tried harder to fight the system. As far as she was concerned, I chose the Marines over my family, and because of it, I lost my leg, lost time, lost years of our children's childhoods, and in the process, killed our marriage.

She never wanted me to forget that I made my own bed, and now it was time for me to lie in it.

I turned toward Kate. Asked her if anything else happened.

"Same as usual . . . girls laughing when I walked by."

"Why?" I said, like a stupid fool. Obviously she didn't know why. Kate just shook her head side to side.

Another wave of anger. Irrational thoughts poured over me, fantasies about defacing their lockers, spray-painting "Mean Girl" and "Bully" across them. Then I'd call their parents and warn them that their daughters are little brats and they might want to intervene before they grow into full-blown bitches.

Instead, I launched into nonsense.

"Girls who act like that . . . they live their life on the surface," I said. "Where everything changes from day to day: their friends, their moods. A lot of waves, a lot of stormy weather. You, though—you, Kate, you run deep. Still water runs deep." I was losing myself in this ridiculous analogy. It had sounded good in my head, but now it just sounded like I didn't have anything better to say. What good did it do to tell her that someday she was going to be an awesome adult, that someday these foolish girls would be struggling and she would be thriving, that someday she would realize that middle school girls were just an annoying hiccup in her otherwise extraordinary life as an award-winning novelist or classics professor or Nobel prize–winning scientist? Kate could be anything she wanted. She just had to make it through this first.

"I just wish . . ." she began, but was unable to finish. I could fill in the words for her. *I just wish I fit better. I just wish Mom wasn't in Costa Rica with her fancy lawyers . . . again. I just wish things were like they used to be.*

"Mom will be home next week," I said.

Kate just nodded stoically, though I could tell she was filled to the top. Next week might as well have been a year from now. Kate knew I'd walk through fire for her, but the one thing I couldn't do was be her mother.

"How are *you* doing, Dad?" she asked, burying her head into my chest.

"We're talking about you, not me," I said, kissing her head. "Let me check on your brother and sister, and then I'll come back." I left her room and tucked in Olivia and Jake, then grabbed my cell phone from my dresser, and turned off the bedroom light. With me in the chair next to her bed, Kate fell asleep in no time. When her breathing became rhythmic, I opened my phone and clicked on Facebook.

I wasn't a chronic poster, but I did occasionally post pictures of the kids. For my family. They liked to see what we were up to. All told, I only had about forty friends on FB, so it didn't take long to scroll my news feed. I got a kick out of seeing guys from my unit, now home with their families, in their new jobs, looking so clean and scrubbed, so unlike the camouflaged, dirt-caked warriors I'd spent so much time with. Bob Adams had been in my Marine Special Operations Battalion in Afghanistan, and was the most fearless guy I knew. He was on his second tour when he got hit by an IED. He lost his arm, but from the look of his posts, it wasn't stopping him much. Somehow he managed to play hockey with his son.

I liked to check in on my high school friends, too. Mike Marshall, a guy I played football with, had lost a ton of weight and was now an elite marathon runner. I never thought a linebacker his size could slim down so much. And Mr. LeFey, my civics teacher. He was a great guy. "Come see me after school," he'd say, and when I'd get to his room, he'd have college packages he'd sent away for. "Let's take a look," he'd say. It was because of him—him and a guy named Frank Fletcher—that I ended up at Virginia Military Institute and then in the Marines Corp. They were my mentors.

Frank Fletcher. I dated his daughter, Missy. She was my high school sweetheart. She was so sweet, so cute, and so damn smart. I'd never met anyone as smart as she was. I loved her and her dad. Missy never posts on Facebook, but she "likes" everything I post. That is so like her, to care for everyone else, but never one to get out in front.

Missy had been on my mind all day. It was her birthday—not that I needed an excuse for her to be on my mind. I sent her a happy birthday wish, just a generic "have a nice day." But if there were no rules, if there was no social etiquette I'd violate by doing anything more than wishing my high school girlfriend a happy birthday, if it didn't matter that I was a married—now separated—guy, if it was acceptable for me to lay it all on the line, I would have posted the memory of my eighteenth birthday.

We went to dinner at the Cheesecake Factory. Missy got me a collector's edition Mets baseball and a teddy bear wearing a T-shirt that said "Missy loves Joe forever." She told me she had it made at the T-shirt shop. After dinner, we walked through the mall. We took a strip of pictures in the photo booth kiosk. I still have that tattered strip in the middle of my yearbook.

That's what I would have liked to say: "Hey, Miss—remember my eighteenth birthday? That was a great night."

And then I'd ask her if she was single, and if she ever thought of me, and if she'd like to re-create my eighteenth birthday as much as I would.

CHAPTER EIGHT

The next week, the Longworths were back in our conference room. Mr. Longworth held a giant stack of documents, per our request. Our sheet labeled "List of Documents for a Financial Plan" sat neatly on top. That was our standard operating procedure. The first step was for new clients to collect their documents, the pile of paper that captured their financial life. Dad likened himself to a doctor: "If you're sick, you don't go to the doctor and give him half the information, and then go to another doctor and give him the other half. How could he treat you? I'm the same way: I can't make a diagnosis unless I have all of the information."

Dad wore a conciliatory expression today. As if he felt sorry for the stress he had caused by suggesting they might not be a good fit, Dad now worked extra hard to demonstrate his pleasure in seeing them again. He wanted his new clients to know that they were on the same side.

"I gathered everything you asked for," Mr. Longworth said cautiously, sliding the mountain of papers in our direction. "Tax returns, net worth statements, investment summaries, estate planning documents, retirement reports . . ."

"Thank you," I said, accepting the pile of papers. This stack alone would keep me busy for the next few days. I would pick through each document, input numbers and values into my software programs. I'd calculate and run scenarios. I'd assign projected returns, and then I'd spend a day or so reading through their legal documents, confirming that all bases were covered: revocable trusts, wills, medical directives, powers of attorney. I'd verify that their irrevocable trusts were funded properly, that gifts made to fund the insurance policies were "arm's length," that no impropriety could be detected by the IRS. Then I'd start in on my PowerPoint of recommendations.

And Mrs. Longworth brought her own stack of work, also gathered at our request: photo albums and a yellow pad with the title "Goals" etched in pencil at the top center. She opened the album. "These are our granddaughters—Loralie is six, and plays soccer. Emma is ten and is a real theater bug. I'd really like to be closer to them. They're in North Carolina. We have a condo there." Mrs. Longfellow turned the page and showed us a picture of their lovely waterfront home. From their veranda they could watch the pelicans slice through the horizon, and the sun plunge into the infinite sea.

"And I serve on the board of the One by One," she said, "a 403(b) foundation that works to improve the lives of marginalized children in Third World countries. I focus on issues of sanitation and infrastructure."

"That's fascinating," I said. "I have to admit that I looked you up and read all about the work you had done in India. I think that's admirable and so brave. How did you get involved?"

Mrs. Longworth pointed to her brown-faced granddaughter, Emma. "Emma was adopted from there," she said. "She lost most of her family due to poor sanitation."

"That's terrible," I said. "But it's wonderful that you're so involved in helping others."

Mrs. Longworth beamed. "Those are my goals: the granddaughters, North Carolina, charity." She sat stick-straight in her chair, folded her hands atop her stack of papers, and looked across at her husband. "Tell them, Charles. Tell them your goals."

Mr. Longworth hesitated—fidgeted in his chair, turned his Montblanc open and closed—clearly uncomfortable with our style of money management. His desires were private, and vocalizing them was like inviting us into his bedroom.

"Think of it from a business standpoint," Dad said. "If we were sitting here five years from now, what would you like to look back on in order to say, 'That's been a good five years.'"

Slowly, Mr. Longworth warmed, and when Dad was responsive to his every disclosure, he began to soften. By the end of the meeting, Mr. Longworth had morphed into a retiree who liked to golf, who wanted to spend time with his two sons, to whom he hadn't always been the most demonstrative father. "I was a bit distant, if you know what I mean," he said, his voice catching. "They're good sons, though. They've turned out good. Despite me."

"I'm sure you did just fine," Dad said.

"I've worked hard," Mr. Longworth said. "Damn hard. I worked long hours, at the expense of my family. But I've also been a lucky son of a bitch. My business—wires, technology—it was the right place at the right time. I acknowledge that I had the goods that were needed. Another place, another time—things would've been different."

Charles wasn't nearly the pompous, self-serving guy he presented to us at our first meeting. He saw himself as fortunate, comprehended that he had a responsibility to give back, to pass along his good fortune. Dad had exposed the better person inside Mr. Longworth, and now that momentum was building. By the time Mr. and Mrs. Longworth were ready to leave our offices, they were holding hands and Mrs. Longworth was glowing. How many years, I wondered, had it been since he'd held her hand?

As we stood in the hallway saying our good-byes, Mrs. Longworth admired a piece of artwork hanging on our wall. "What a beautiful painting," she said, pointing to the coral sunset descending on the ocean. "Reminds me of North Carolina."

"Beautiful place, North Carolina," Dad said. "Have you spent much time there?"

My stomach knotted. The Longworths' eyes begged for explanation. There was no way Dad had just said that. We needed a "Rewind" button to bring us back ten seconds.

"You're thinking of Myrtle Beach, Dad," I said, clutching his bicep with considerable force. "This painting was from Myrtle Beach. The Longworths have a house in North Carolina, right?" I forced my face to remain calm as I squeezed Dad's arm even harder. He would find nail marks on his skin later.

"Of course!" Dad said. "Sorry! I was looking at the painting and thinking South Carolina. My buddy who lives in Myrtle Beach painted this. He's a watercolorist in his retirement."

The Longworths softened a bit, but I could still see Mr. Longworth no doubt wondering if he'd just turned over his $10 million to a guy who couldn't remember basic facts. When the Longworths left, I pulled Dad into his office, closed the door, and said, "Dad, are you okay? You forgot they had a house in North Carolina. That's kind of big."

CHAPTER NINE

In my Subaru Outback, Rosetta Stone played. *Una macchina rossa.* A red car. *Un batello rosso.* A red boat. Car was feminine, boat masculine. I hit "Eject" and squeezed the steering wheel because something was wrong with Dad and the repercussions of that were twentyfold. For his own sake, what would it mean if his aging was accelerating, if he became increasingly forgetful? For the sake of the business, what would it signify to Fletcher Financial? And as for me—wouldn't I get burned without the shade of Dad's shadow?

I had aced every test I had ever taken, but I had also failed to grow up, and of that fact, I was now suddenly keenly aware. I was smart, but I wasn't wise. I had clung to my role as my father's child. How had it not occurred to me—strategic-planning, spreadsheet-producing, goal-focused me—that our roles might someday change?

Maybe he was just tired, overworked. Maybe he was just preoccupied, not thinking clearly. Maybe he just needed some green tea and supplements to give his brain a boost.

"Dad, are you okay?" I had asked him in his office.

"Missy, I didn't for a second forget they had a place in North Carolina," Dad assured me. "I was just thinking about Myrtle Beach, I promise. A simple mistake."

There was nothing simple about this.

We had one client, Tom Mercer, who suffered from dementia. Another, Ed Bailey, had early-onset Alzheimer's. Still another, Alfred King, had recently suffered a stroke. Were any of these a diagnosis for Dad? My father, who had never once faltered?

When I was little and Dad and I headed to his office every Saturday morning, he'd say, "You know the routine, Missy," and set me up at Jenny's desk, spreading out my McDonald's breakfast like a royal flush. I'd eat my pancakes and sausage and drink my orange juice from the hole Dad poked through the tinfoil lid, while he puttered around in his office, sorting and stacking files, speaking into his Dictaphone. How he loved his clients, his friends, his work. How he loved me. My father, who could draw joy from an empty bag, who found a silver lining in the most tattered scrap of fabric, who could find an honest man among a band of thieves.

Dad's life had meaning because he was meaningful to the clients he treasured like family. If he continued to blunder—because he was tired, overworked, or just getting older, or, God forbid, because there was something else happening to him—what would it mean to him to see his clients lose faith? It would decimate him.

Once home, I toasted a few slices of leftover focaccia and poured some olive oil into a dish. I took a bite of buttery Fontina, letting the nutty cheese melt in my mouth. I dredged a piece of bread through the oil. I savored a mouthful of fruity Pinot Noir. After I repeated these steps a few times, I called it dinner, deciding to cook the piece of chicken tomorrow.

With my carton of pistachio gelato, I sat at my computer and logged on to Facebook. When I clicked on Joe's page, I saw that he had added a few new posts. Katherine, the oldest daughter, was reading for a poetry event at school. The middle daughter, Olivia, was in a play. The little guy, Jake—the spitting image of Joe—had lost another tooth, and had the proud, wide-mouthed grin to prove it.

From the night of the snowball dance of sophomore year, Joe and I went on to date for three years. Dad loved Joe. Dad and I—just the two of us—led a quiet life. With Joe around, there was more life. Joe's house was chaotic and noisy with four loud boys, two parents, and a grandmother, all living under one roof. Joe sought refuge with Dad and me because it was peaceful at our house, a place where he could study, read. A place where he could tell someone about his day and someone would actually listen, ask questions. And for the exactly opposite reason, we loved having Joe with us: to increase the decibels, to multiply our house population by 50 percent.

During our junior year of high school, Dad started talking to Joe and me about colleges.

"Tell me, Joseph," Dad would say. "Tell me about your brilliant future."

"Mr. LeFey sent away for college packets for me," he said. "I'm really considering a military college."

"I'll tell you what's strong about that choice," Dad said. "The network after you graduate. You graduate from West Point or VMI and you'll have connections in every field of industry for the rest of your life."

"The world is changing," Joe said solemnly. "Globally, economically. If I could somehow be part of that change, I think I would have a good job."

"That's right, my friend," Dad said. "Go to where the puck will be. Wayne Gretzky, the greatest hockey player who ever lived, wasn't the strongest, wasn't the fastest, wasn't the biggest. And because of that, he knew he couldn't get right into the scuffle—where the puck *was*. He had to go to where the puck was *going to be*."

Joe's dreams varied widely. One day he wanted to go to law school; the next day he wanted to join the Marines Corp. The day after, he was considering a career as an EMT, and the day after that he wondered whether he would like to do what Dad did, advising clients on money matters. Listening to Joe weigh his options had a visceral effect on me. Even though I knew it was inevitable, I didn't want him to go.

"You know, Joe," I would say. "I just read about the number of lawyers being graduated—there just aren't enough jobs for them all. Plus, do you really think that you'd be able to sit at a desk all day?"

Joe would calmly answer, "I'm sure the market's as tight for lawyers as it is for just about any other profession, but I'd find a job. And I could always exercise during my lunch break or play soccer after work."

And then, because my obsession with his future, and disinterest in mine, was so apparent, he'd ask his own questions. "How about you? Any path that you're being pulled down?"

"I don't know." I would hem and haw, nervous to say what I really wanted for fear that my dreams would mean being away from him for a year. "It's hard to say. I mean . . . I'd like to help people, somehow. Maybe work for a nonprofit organization."

"Didn't you tell me once that you wanted to join the Peace Corps?"

"Yeah, that's true," I admitted. "I've always thought that that would be amazing."

"You should do it," he said. "Why not?"

"Well, *you*, for one. Dad, for another. I don't want to leave either one of you."

"Four years from now, Missy. Who knows what we'll be doing? You can't say no to your dreams when we haven't even started college."

While I wasn't necessarily the maternal type, pulled toward setting up a household and being a wife and mother, it still hurt me that Joe spoke like this of our separation, of everyone's eventual separation.

Constancy was my safety: Dad and Joe, our life in Alexandria. The idea of scattering made me nervous.

Ultimately, Joe ended up at Virginia Military Institute. It offered a strong liberal arts education with a top-notch engineering program, all in a military academy setting. As Joe put it, "This way I'll get a real taste of the military life. I'll know for sure if I want to go that route."

I studied hard and earned perfect marks, and while I was thriving at William & Mary, what I looked forward to the most was coming home on long weekends to see Joe and Dad. It became evident to me that my happiness was rooted in them. The thought that joy and satisfaction could be achieved without them never occurred to me.

CHAPTER TEN
JOE

Tuesdays were my toughest days, but they were also my best days. No longer just the second day of the workweek, the nondescript twenty-four hours following Monday, Tuesdays had become like a tough work-out: some dread beforehand and suffering during, but usually a great feeling afterward. It was worth it.

The day usually started at work for a half day, trying to get a full day's work done in five hours. I medically retired from the Marines four years ago following my injury, and went to work for a global security and aerospace company—basically a government contractor in busi-ness with the Defense Department. The job title they gave me was intel analyst, which meant that I took everything I knew about Afghanistan and Pakistan to help develop intelligence collection networks to defeat violent extremist organizations. Sometimes I felt like I was playing the game of war, rather than helping our government actually plan mis-sions. Some guys from my old unit couldn't stand that their lives now meant sitting at a desk all day. I was fine with it. I would be happy to never see the real deal again. At my desk, *playing* war games, I could convince myself there was a point to it. Over there, after a while, day after day of getting IED'd, it all seemed hopeless. Like the only way out was to raze the entire city or to die trying. I hated feeling purposeless.

From there, I rushed to my volunteer work at the National Military Medical Center, a veterans' hospital just outside of Newark. I met with my group in the lounge, a group of six who had all lost either a leg or an arm while fighting in Afghanistan. This was a "post-rehab group," meaning they had already endured months of therapy at Walter Reed in Bethesda, learning how to sit, walk, and function on their own. I'd been in their exact spot. Now they had been sent home to New Jersey, where each of them once resided. It was recommended that these guys would meet in a group for at least a year.

Most wounded warriors were resilient and determined, but this group in particular had yet to find the Zen in being an amputee. None of them was ready to commemorate the day he was wounded, his "Alive Day," as a way of refocusing on the life ahead. These guys were in the pits, still struggling with what had happened to them, miles away from accepting that there was any good to being half-whole. They sneaked smokes outside, drank buckets of coffee, looked down at their laps and, for the most part, acted like teenagers who had been forced into therapy, only because their parents wanted them to.

Over fifteen hundred soldiers had lost a limb in Iraq or Afghanistan; over 20 percent had lost more than one. In the physical therapy rooms of Walter Reed, the attitude as a whole was encouraging, uplifting. These were our country's finest men and women, and what brought them to dedicate their lives to fighting for our freedom was the same vigor and determination that drove them to walk again, to do the work necessary, to push themselves. They fed off each other, cheering one another on, a band of brothers. Many guys worked for five hours a day. There were a few remarkable guys: double and triple amputees with interminably positive attitudes. Indefatigable when it came to therapy, these guys were able to say "at least I'm alive."

Compared to many, I was lucky and I knew it. I was an amputee, too, but just below the knee. A lot of these guys looked at me like I had it easy. And when I thought about some of them—a lost arm, two lost legs, eyelids singed off, faces burned—I couldn't argue. With my prosthetic, I could walk. I had arms and hands to work and feed myself. I wasn't confined to a wheelchair. A mosquito bite compared to many of these guys.

I poured myself a cup of black coffee. When I signed up to volunteer, I had no idea that I'd end up here, with this bunch. I was more thinking that I could help guys secure jobs in the private sector after coming home. After all, I had done pretty well, getting hooked up with my job at a Fortune 500 company. But I got assigned to this group, like I had the qualifications to administer therapy to guys who were this far down in the dumps.

The coffee was sludge and instantly stained the sides of the Styrofoam. I added a few creams and a few sugars. I didn't trust drinking it straight.

I sat down and asked the guys to come to order, then initiated some chitchat that fell flat. No one wanted to talk about the Yankees, or major league baseball at all, for that matter. I opened my notebook, and called on my first guy. Tony was an above-knee amputee who lost his leg while on patrol, and had had a tougher time than most, having to endure over thirty surgeries, while battling grueling headaches, almost daily.

"How's your week been, Tony?"

Tony grumbled then proceeded to report in short, angry sentences how the week was crap, how physical therapy was a joke, how he couldn't sleep, the Ambien no longer worked, how the food sucked, and how he woke up in the night and felt like his leg was there, but when he reached for it, it wasn't. "It's like a goddamned prank, every night." At that, his voice cracked and he had to wipe at his eyes. "It's not fair."

The wipe at his eyes was my signal to move on. None of them wanted to cry in front of the others. "Andy, what about you? How are you making out?"

Andy had a better attitude than most. He lost both his arms when clearing a schoolhouse that had been booby-trapped by the Taliban. When Andy moved a box of books, it detonated and blew off his arms. Thanks to his buddy, who'd tied some expert tourniquets and administered blood-clotting powder, Andy was dragged away from the scene and then evacuated to Germany, and then to Walter Reed. A miracle, really. The fact that his face was spared was even more of one. I had yet to point that out.

"I'm getting used to this thing," Andy said, lifting his prosthetic right arm. "Still, though . . . what I'd do for just one arm. I'd trade a leg, even. At least I'd be symmetrical then."

A few of the guys laughed awkwardly.

I prided myself on listening more than talking. These guys had been through enough without having to hear a bunch of sanctimonious babble, but there were some facts about amputees and moving on that these guys needed to know.

"All right," I said. "Let's get to it. The sooner you accept that your limb is gone, the sooner you will heal—not just your body, but your mind and spirit. Every day is a challenge, guys, but it's not a challenge you can't overcome."

The guys shot me dirty looks.

"Think of Michael," I said. "Think of Rob and Derek."

Michael Gordon was a soldier who'd visited us about a month ago, a triple amputee—both legs and an arm. He had a wife and a baby waiting for him, and his determination was ironclad. He looked at my group of sad sacks and told them to get on with their damn lives, to live for the guys who didn't make it. After that meeting, a couple of my guys—Rob and Derek—had complete turnarounds. Started working harder at their PT and OT, reached out to family members, found at least some shreds of the spirituality they had lost. Those guys had since been moved to another group—a step two group, further in their recovery.

I reined in my urge for further platitudes. Lecturing them on why they shouldn't feel shitty wasn't going to make them feel less shitty; I knew that. I just wanted them to know they weren't alone, to remind them to hold in their heads the examples of three men like themselves—guys they knew, who'd lost pretty much what they'd lost, but who'd found it in themselves to push on to the next step. I believed in each and every one of them, but couldn't come right out and say it. Instead, I sounded like a hard-ass, telling them to man up.

Lucy had accused me of this more than once or twice: of being too hardheaded to let anyone in, of being incapable of just feeling rather than fixing.

I never claimed to be blameless in our divorce. There was plenty to go around.

After two hours with the guys, I left the hospital and drove to the kids' schools. Kate was at St. Agnes, the middle school, and Jake and Olivia were just down the road at Holy Angels. On my way, I called Lucy.

"I'm on my way to pick up the kids," I told her. "Anything you want me to pass on?"

"I'll call them later," she said. "I have good coverage from here." *From here* being the middle of New Zealand, nearly eight thousand miles away.

I squeezed the steering wheel, gritted my teeth. "I heard from your lawyer today," I said. "She said we've satisfied the waiting period for the divorce and she's ready to proceed."

Lucy sighed. "Don't act surprised, Joe. Don't act like you didn't know that was the direction we were headed in."

"What about the kids? What about Katherine?"

"I'm ready for something new," she said flatly, as though we were shopping for a new dishwasher and she suddenly decided on stainless steel rather than black.

"I didn't know that was an option," I said. "When we got married, I didn't know we were allowed to just walk away because we wanted something new."

"Don't make me sound so one-dimensional, Joe," Lucy said, raising her voice. "You know it's not that simple. We've been through hell and back. I deserve a little peace."

I pulled up to Holy Angels. "I'm here," I said.

"I'm sorry," she said, but her tone was anything but apologetic, the tone Olivia was famous for using when forced to apologize when her heart wasn't in it.

"Yep," I said. "Bye."

Once all three kids were buckled up, we drove downtown to a brick medical building where Kate saw a counselor once a week. This year of middle school had been tough, but we were assured that much of that was normal. "Middle school is hard," the school counselor told us. But then Lucy found a notebook of poems Kate had written. *I'm disgusting in every way*, a number of them began. That's when we decided to seek outside help. Just in case there was more to be worried about than what was considered "normal."

"She feels out of control," the counselor had explained. "We just want to keep a handle on it. We don't want it to escalate."

I was to blame as much as anyone. First I was gone, deployed. Lucy told me how much Kate worried about me when I was away. "What if he's killed? What if I never see Dad again?"

And since I had returned, her mother had essentially left, swept off with her new career, traveling to glamorous destinations every few weeks. And middle school was the biggest uncertainty of all. Kate didn't stand a chance in that group of girls. She was smart and kind and loved her books and her journal. There had to be another girl like her. There had to be a way to make her feel not so alone.

At the end of Kate's session, the counselor called me in. I was always included in the last ten minutes, so as to ensure we were all on the same page.

The counselor smiled at Kate. "It's May—you've almost made it through your entire first year of middle school." She clapped little claps. "What do you think the takeaway from that is? Any lessons learned to better equip you for next year?"

Kate shifted in her seat, stared toward the window. "I'd say the takeaway is to always save a round for yourself. Just in case you're captured by cannibals or headhunters?"

"I beg your pardon?" the counselor asked.

"That's what the soldiers were told to do in World War II," Kate said. "That's kind of how I feel about middle school."

"Kate!" I said sternly. "Are you being funny, or is there truth to what you're saying?" Being smart was one thing. Being a smart aleck was another.

She flashed me a half smile. "Just being funny, Dad," she said. "Can we go?"

CHAPTER ELEVEN

There is a photo on my mantel of Dad and me. It has been there since I moved into my town house a decade ago. Before that, it occupied space on Dad's mantel. In the photo, we are standing in front of the Lincoln Memorial. I was maybe thirteen—rail thin, a mouth of giant teeth I hadn't yet grown into, enough unstrained hair to cover five heads. Dad was in his late forties, early fifties, I would guess, with his thick brown hair, beautiful teeth, and shoulders as square and broad as the Hulk's. In the photo, I'm leaned into him as though he were a pillar—unstoppable, immovable. As though he wouldn't budge, no matter how hard I pushed.

Today, as I swung through the doors of the community center for our Fletcher Financial seminar and found Dad milling about, it occurred to me that I had never stopped seeing him the way he looked in that photo: robust, indomitable. But now, as I examined him closely, the artificial lens through which I'd been viewing him came into focus. Dad was a seventy-year-old man with thinning hair, a scattering of sun spots on his weathered skin, and purple circles under his eyes as delineated as the rings of Saturn.

Dad had aged, and I hadn't seen it.

Dad called the seminar to order. "Folks, so good to see you here!" This time, he was flawless throughout. Not a single blunder. Afterward, he circulated through the room, socializing while I broke down the electronics. As I was wrapping the cords into neat circles, Dad's longtime clients and friends, the Andersons, found me by the projector. With them was a good-looking guy, maybe forty.

"Missy, darling, hello!" Mrs. Anderson said. The Andersons had both been born and raised in Richmond—the west end, with the country clubs and private schools. Mrs. Anderson spoke with a drawl and dressed in Talbots twinsets; her hair was highlighted and bobbed.

"Hi, Mr. and Mrs. Anderson," I said, looking up from my cords.

"Have you ever met our son, Lucas?"

Lucas was their pride and joy; I knew that. "I've heard all about Lucas," I said, "but no, we've never met."

"I guess we might have mentioned him before," Mrs. Anderson said, blushing.

"The brilliant tax attorney," I said to Lucas. "Your parents are very proud of you."

"Parents make the best fan club," he said, holding out his hand for me to shake. "Nice to meet you."

"You, too," I said. "I imagine you're keeping busy in this crazy economic/political environment."

Lucas nodded. "There is a lot going on, tax-wise."

"True enough," I said. "I'm a bit of a tax junkie myself."

"Nothing to be ashamed of," he said with a grin. We held gazes until I felt my cheeks flush. Somehow, his parents had disappeared from view.

Lucas was tall with an athletic build, blond floppy hair, and earnest blue eyes. I had the urge to trace my finger along the ropy edges of his biceps.

"Your dad is quite a presenter," he said.

"Yeah." I laughed. "Most people dread public speaking. He craves it."

"Not me."

"Me either," I agreed. "I'd rather get my teeth drilled without Novocain."

Lucas smiled and lifted the projector into its case, placing the cords carefully in the side compartment. "So public speaking isn't your thing," he said. "But what about discussing taxes?"

I looked at his handsome blue eyes. "Oh, I'm all over taxes."

"What about lunch? Do you eat lunch?"

"Excuse me?"

"Maybe you'd like to grab lunch sometime?" he asked tentatively, less confident than his first try. "Talk about taxes?"

I looked up, let the pieces settle.

Lucas stammered again. "I mean, some people don't break away for lunch. Work right through. That's me, usually."

"I love lunch," I said. "And taxes."

For the first time in months, I had just been asked out to lunch. And with a guy who shared at least two interests of mine: lunch and taxes. Lucas said he would call to set up a time. When he left, in my flustered state, I unpacked the projector that Lucas had already put away so neatly for me. I checked my e-mail, though I had just scrolled through it a minute ago. And I sipped at a cup of coffee that wasn't mine. I was elated. I had a maybe lunch date with tax attorney Lucas Anderson, and rather than feeling my usual contentedness—a zero on the number line—I suddenly felt hopeful, eager, and expectant. A good twenty-five points off the norm.

My dating history left much to be desired. The truest relationship I'd ever had was in high school and the few years afterward with Joe. He was as good a man as my father. We were just too young. He knew before I did that being each other's first "everything" meant that we couldn't be each other's last. I begged to differ. I fought him on this, like a toddler who didn't get her way. It wasn't that I didn't want to have other experiences, that I didn't want to explore the world. I just wanted to do it with Joe.

After Joe, while in college and graduate school, I gravitated toward the Mensa crowd, brainiacs like me. All-night study sessions, coauthoring journal articles with top professors, earning assistantships. Then there was Jason, my on-and-off boyfriend of three years, when I had just turned thirty. With Jason, I attempted to re-create the passion I had had with Joe so many years earlier. Jason was dark, brooding, and athletic, just like Joe. He flew his handsomeness like a cape. Sometimes I would stare at his perfectly symmetrical features and compare him to Joe, yet I knew Joe was a thousand times more beautiful because his good looks penetrated to every atom of his being, unlike Jason's, which were skin-deep.

Jason was one of many siblings from a large family full of traditions, Catholicism, and delicious family-style meals. There were no boundaries with Jason or his family. They touched; they hugged and kissed. They overstepped, and I loved their every trespass. I adored how his parents kissed me like they kissed their own daughters. I treasured time with his sisters, how they fooled with my hair and handed me down clothing from their closets. *Try this on,* his older sister Mary would say, tugging at my shirt without regard for my privacy. Being a girl who came from very little family, it was exactly what I craved.

I tried to want Jason as much as I wanted the rest of his family, but he was the weakest link. While he had all of the physical attributes that Joe had, and while his family was everything I would want in an extended in-law family, Jason was sometimes cruel, bordering on misogynistic. He was insecure, and to build himself up, he often criticized me, his sisters, and even his mother. One night we were playing Trivial Pursuit with his family. I happened to be on a streak; I answered most of the questions. On the drive home, he looked at me with a cruel sneer. "So, what's it like to be such a know-it-all?"

I was stunned. "I'm hardly a know-it-all," I said. "Just lucky tonight."

"Whatever," he said. "It's cool . . . to date a girl who's more concerned with Trivial Pursuit than stuff like how she looks."

I had never been self-conscious about my looks—I was average enough, cute enough—but Jason was beautiful, and his comment was intended to make me feel ugly. It did. So much that the only rejoinder I could muster was, "Uh-huh."

CHAPTER TWELVE

The following week, Lucas called. In preparation for his call, I had checked him out on LinkedIn: bachelor of science in accounting from University of Maryland in College Park, master of science in taxation from American University, member of the Virginia Society of CPAs, practiced solo for five years, then partnered with the nationwide firm of Powell, Dunfee, and Hayworth, Chartered.

He wasn't on Facebook, though I certainly didn't hold that against him, as clearly I wasn't much of a Facebook participant, just a girl spying on more interesting lives than mine. I searched his name and read numerous profile pieces on him. I logged on to the Virginia Board of Accountancy and saw that he was squeaky clean—never had a complaint filed against him.

"Are you free for lunch?" Lucas asked. "Not today, of course. Maybe next Tuesday."

"Let me pull up my calendar," I said coolly, pretending to scan my empty pages. "Looks good to me."

"Where shall we go?"

"You choose," I said. "I like everything."

"I don't get out much for lunch," he said. "What do you suggest?"

"How about the Fruit Stand?" I suggested. "That's always good. And don't be put off by the name—it's mostly a sandwich shop. I think it used to be a fruit stand, like a million years ago."

"I like fruit," he said.

As a garnish, I thought. But not for lunch. Certainly not for lunch. "Great! So you've never been?"

"Never been," he repeated. "Looking forward to it."

I found it hard to believe that Lucas had never been to this Alexandria mainstay, always packed with an eager lunch crowd.

"You'll love it," I told him, "but we'd better meet at eleven or one; the noon hour will be too busy."

So at eleven o'clock on the following Tuesday, I met Lucas at the Fruit Stand. He was waiting for me on the front porch, wearing kha-kis and a golf shirt, his blond shaggy hair pushed back to the side. I straightened my posture and pasted on a smile because he was seriously cute. When I got close enough, Lucas held out his hand. We shook, and when we drew close, he smelled of soap and toothpaste.

The restaurant was crowded, but we got lucky and were seated in a lovely corner table by the fireplace. When the waitress brought us a basket of their signature homemade dill-pickle kettle chips, I moaned out loud. "These are amazing," I said.

Lucas popped one into his mouth. "Yum! You're right," he said, and then resumed his discussion about the new tax law, the Patient Protection and Affordable Care Act.

"I'm eating all the chips," I said. "Don't you want any?"

Lucas laughed as though I were making a joke. "I love watching *you* eat," he said, and continued to ramble on about the portability feature in the new health-care legislation.

When the waitress came, I ordered the walnut, pear, and Gorgonzola salad and a bowl of the she-crab soup. Lucas ordered the Virginia ham and brie panino with caramelized onions and cranberries.

"Sounds yummy," I said.

Lucas smiled, nodded eagerly. "But can we leave off the onions and cranberries, and substitute a slice of swiss for the brie?" he asked the waitress.

The waitress looked at him curiously, but Lucas just smiled and thanked her.

"Are you a health nut?" I asked him when the waitress had left.

"I guess I keep it simple," he said. "But not necessarily a health nut. I find it hard to resist pie with vanilla ice cream."

When the food came, Lucas was still explaining the difference between the filing necessary for a domestic entity versus an international one, and I was still picking at the leftover shards of dill-pickle potato chips. In the time that he explained it, I worked my way through the most intoxicating bowl of soup ever. When I asked him if his sandwich was okay, he looked down at his barely touched ham and swiss, and said it was perfect.

"What else?" I asked, steering the conversation away from work. "Tell me about yourself."

"Well, I've been in the area my whole life."

"Same," I said.

"Went to University of Maryland, and then to American."

"Tell me something that's not on your résumé," I said, smiling.

Lucas's face flushed red. "That's a tough one!"

Quickly, I thought of a laundry list of things that weren't on my résumé: I was an Italian-language learning novice, gelato lover, *Jeopardy!* genius. I wouldn't dare tell Lucas any of these things. "You're right!" I admitted. "Believe it or not, I read that question in a magazine: questions to ask when on a date. Kind of stupid, now that I think about it."

"No!" he said. "It's a good question. I just feel bad I can't think of anything. Makes me feel like a dolt!"

"Sports?" I asked.

"Yes, that's it." Lucas nodded wildly. "I work out at the gym. I run, play a bit of basketball."

"I used to run in high school," I said. "Because my father made me . . . insisted that I play a sport. And I used to play tennis, but hardly ever now."

"We should go running sometime," he said. His tone was sweet, considerate. His baby blue eyes were worth looking at.

"I'd die," I said. "But it would be fun."

"I'd dangle dill pickle chips in front of you," he said.

"I'd make you eat some."

After lunch, Lucas walked me to my car. A breeze mussed his hair. I reached up and cleared the blond swath from his eyes. "This was fun," he said.

"This *was* fun," I agreed.

"The restaurant was great."

"I think I like food more than you," I said. "I think I *ate* more than you."

"You haven't seen me with pie and ice cream," he said.

I hadn't converted him to my food religion, but maybe that was okay. I'd make a project of it. The good news was that he seemed sold on me, and judging from my sweaty palms, I apparently was interested in him. Lucas Anderson was cute and smart, smelled of soap and toothpaste, liked fruit, pie and vanilla ice cream, taxes and laws, and apparently, me.

As I slid into my seat, Jenny called. "Everything okay?" I asked.

"It's your father. He's at the country club and apparently misplaced his car keys. Do you have a spare set?"

"No," I said. "But I'll go pick him up. Tell him I'll be there in ten minutes."

As I drove to the club, I listened to public radio. The newscaster interviewed an elderly gentleman who had suffered a brain tumor. Was that a possibility for Dad?

That night, I typed a search into my computer: brain tumors.

The most prominent symptom of a brain tumor was headaches. I tried to remember if Dad had had many headaches lately. Other symptoms included seizures, changes in vision, difficulty walking. And then, there it was: memory loss.

Tumors were most readily removed through surgery. In instances when the tumor was positioned in such a way as to preclude surgery, radiation or chemotherapy was used. The only problem was the damage to the healthy cells, of course. Such damage could lead to the loss of certain faculties.

My first thought was Dad losing his ability to speak. My father bound and gagged. A storyteller who had lost his words.

CHAPTER THIRTEEN

I sat on Dad's sofa while he scowled at the computer screen. I saw him differently these days—actually *saw* him, for the seventy-year-old man that he was. I was so used to focusing on measuring how he saw me that I'd rarely reevaluated my assessment of him.

"If you would just come out of your shell," Dad would say to the teenaged me. "Then the world could see what's inside that beautiful mind of yours." My father—who understood human nature so well, yet never fully got me—deployed his brand of pragmatic optimism against me as the only panacea he knew. "Pretend you're social, even if you're not," he'd say. And as horrible as it sounded to the outside observer, my father wasn't criticizing me. He loved who I was, but he also believed firmly in emulating the achievements of others. And to him, sociability equaled success.

As I studied him now, he hardly seemed like the same man.

Dad looked up. "Tell me about this Lucas fellow," he said. "You like the guy? Is he good enough for my daughter?"

Since our lunch at the Fruit Stand, Lucas and I had seen each other two other times.

"Lucas is a nice guy," I said.

"But does he do it for you?"

"Dad!"

"I'm not talking about . . . *that*. I'm just asking if he floats your boat. Does he raise your blood pressure, give you chills, make your heart race?"

"He's a nice guy," I said. "A really nice guy."

Dad lifted his eyebrows at me, clearly doubting that "nice guy" status was good enough.

"What else?" he asked. "Are you happy? Are you doing what you want to be doing?"

"I'm good, Dad," I said. "Really, I'm happy. I'm fine. What about you?"

"Your old man is better than ever," he said, granting me his trophy wink and a smile. "Are we ready for our day?"

At ten o'clock, the Sherwoods came in. Dad had known Bob Sherwood for fifty years; they went to the same high school, played varsity football, worked at Dairy Queen in the summer. Both were deployed to Vietnam, and both came home with stories to tell and an urgency to marry their high school sweethearts. Bob married Laney, and Dad married Mom. Today, Dad and Bob reminisced, while Jenny brought in coffee. I attempted chitchat with Mrs. Sherwood, a stunningly assembled woman who put me to shame with her jewelry and makeup and matching shoes and purse.

"Been on any trips?" she asked.

"No, just around here," I said, trying not to hold this against her. It wasn't like she knew about my desire to travel and the paralysis that prevented me from it.

Jenny poured coffee.

"Best coffee ever!" Dad beamed, Jenny blushed, and the Sherwoods lifted their cups.

"Are you seeing anyone, dear?" Mrs. Sherwood asked. Another common question for a longtime family friend to ask, but still—she was on a roll.

"I am," I said. "A very nice guy. A tax attorney."

She pulled her coral lipstick into a broad smile. "Do you still like working in your dad's office?"

Working in my dad's office? I wanted to scream: Do you mean working *with* my dad as a partner and the firm's principal financial analyst? The person who manages your $2.4 million? I'm not some summer intern, filing papers and answering the phones, thank you very much! I have more degrees and certifications than most in this business, I wanted to tell her. Though of course I didn't. She was just a nice old lady asking nice-old-lady questions. And why wouldn't she see me *that* way? As the mousy daughter of the charismatic Frank Fletcher. Why would she think more of me than met the eye? It was true, wasn't it? Fact: I did still work with my father, *after all of these years.* Fact: I was still single, *after all of these years.* Fact: I hadn't gone on any trips, *after all of these years.*

Finally, Dad and Bob returned from memory lane and I cued up the projector, blasted their current portfolio onto the screen and felt compelled to deliver my part of the presentation with more technical acuity than I would usually employ. I used my red laser pointer to highlight their returns, and then, for show-off purposes, launched into a detailed explanation of the difference between "time-weighted returns" and the "internal rate of return." I drew a complicated equation on the whiteboard with brackets and parentheses, to prove my point. When Dad jumped in with a simple, "So great, we're making money!" I knew I had impressed no one.

Dad took it from there. He talked about seeing the lawyer, his buddy Roger, to update the wills and trusts.

"If we put money in the trusts," Mrs. Sherwood said, "how will we get to it?"

Dad carefully explained how putting money into a revocable trust meant nothing in terms of control. "It's still your money, L—"

Dad looked at me. Then Bob looked at Dad. Then I looked at Mrs. Sherwood—Laney. And I finally got it: Dad couldn't remember her name. *Laney!* I wanted to shout at Dad.

"That's right, Dad," I said. "With a revocable trust, Laney—Mrs. Sherwood—still has full access to the money. She only needs permission from the trustee. But in this case, she is the trustee, so she only needs permission from herself."

"You see, Laney," Dad said, "it's still your money, Laney." Dad couldn't stop saying Laney, as if, now that he had it again, he was desperate to cement the name in his memory. "Nothing to worry about, Laney."

After the meeting, I poked my head into Dad's office. "You okay?"

"Of course I'm okay. Why wouldn't I be okay?"

"You forgot Mrs. Sherwood's name."

"Too much time on the golf course!" Dad said, flashing a false smile. "My brain is in a sand trap!"

"How often are you forgetting things, Dad?"

Dad turned his mouth downward and waved me away. "I'm fine!"

"Dad. Seriously. Have you forgotten other things?"

"I forget things all the time, just like *anybody* else," he said. "I go to the refrigerator and can't remember what for. My father was the same way. But he didn't exercise his brain. My mind is working all the time."

"Sure, Dad, but there might be something going on—"

"The Dow 30!" Dad roared, clapping his hands. "Let's go: 3M, Wal-Mart, Amex, Disney, P&G, Apple, Nike, Pfizer, Boeing, JPMorgan,

74

Goldman. What else? Don't tell me, Missy. Chevron, Exxon, Intel, IBM." He stalled, tapped his head. "Let me think."

"Dad, stop!" I said. "Can you please stop for a second and consider that perhaps something is going on with your brain? Can I make you a doctor's appointment?"

Dad settled down, gave up on his Dow listing. "I'm good, Daughter! I'm good," he whispered. Then he looked at me long and hard. "Did I ever tell you about my army buddy, Dick McMurray?"

Though I had heard many of Dad's army stories, I hadn't heard about Dick McMurray. I settled into the crook of the sofa.

"Dick was a scrappy guy and that's exactly the way I always thought of myself—maybe not the smartest, but scrappy as hell, resourceful, hardworking."

Dad often referred to himself as scrappy and resourceful, traits he found admirable because they involved hard work. Being smart, like me, he considered a bit of a freebie, like athleticism. I was born this way. Fortitude wasn't involved in intelligence.

Dad zoned in on me. "One day, the fighting had gone on so long, we didn't know which way was up. Dark, murky hellhole: you couldn't see a damn thing. We were taking rounds from every direction. Mackie got hit. It wasn't until a few hours later that we were able to really take a look at him and see how his body was sprayed with shrapnel. We couldn't see the piece that was lodged in his head. He survived, though.

"When I was shipped home in late '68, your mother and I drove to Philadelphia to see him. His wife, Marie, told us to be prepared, he wasn't the same guy, because of the brain injury. She walked him out and sat him down. Gave him a snickerdoodle and a cup of tea.

"He looked like an old man, withered, shrunken—just skin covering bony limbs. When he recognized me, he cried like a baby. He pointed at me like he wanted to say my name, but for the life of him, he couldn't get it out. 'Frank,' I said. 'It's Frank.'

"Missy, dear daughter," Dad said, "that's how I feel sometimes lately. Like there's a piece of shrapnel lodged in my brain, a barricade preventing me from reaching up and grabbing the information I need."

"Can I make you a doctor's appointment?" I asked.

"Not yet," Dad said. "Not yet."

CHAPTER FOURTEEN

The first weeks of summer fell upon us. In typical fashion, the office slowed to nearly a halt. Many of our clients were vacationing around the globe. Jenny pinned postcards on the bulletin board in our lunchroom. In exuberant script, they gushed their thanks on the blank space of the card. *Thank you for making this possible. Thank you for giving us our retirement. Thank you for caring for us so well.*

And Dad was on the golf course every day. And selfishly, I was glad. When he would leave, I'd think, *thank goodness*, because I couldn't watch my father humiliate himself in front of another client. I didn't want to see him as anything less than the man I held him up to be. Our schedules nearly crisscrossed. Dad would arrive to the office early, dictate a few pieces of correspondence, instruct Jenny to schedule some lunches and golf dates with some of his buddies. And me? I came in late and stayed late.

And Lucas Anderson became part of my vocabulary.

The phone rang just as I had swept the Great Men category in *Jeopardy!* "Who was Charlemagne? Who was Pope Alexander? Who was Pericles? Who was Hannibal?"

What's it like to be such a know-it-all? I heard my old boyfriend Jason ask. But of course it wasn't Jason, it was Lucas, who called every night at seven o'clock. And Lucas would never say such an awful, angry thing to me.

Lucas and I chatted, made dinner plans for Saturday night.

"But I'll need your car keys early that day," he said. "No questions. I have a surprise for you."

Saturday morning bright and early, Lucas came by for my car, looking very pleased with himself. Then promptly at six that night, he rang my doorbell and kissed me hello. "Would you like to see your car?" he asked.

We walked down the few steps to a positively gleaming version of my Subaru. Lucas opened my door. I slid into the driver's seat. The interior was almost comically immaculate, as if I had just driven it off the showroom floor.

"Wow."

"I didn't just clean it, I *detailed* it," Lucas said. He reached down past me, showed me how he had scrubbed my carpets and degreased the wheels and waxed the exterior. "*And* I had the oil changed, and filled the tank."

"It's so . . . clean," I said. "And it has—a new car smell?"

"That's because I cleaned your air ducts," he said. "It's a hobby of mine. I spend a good couple of hours washing my car every Saturday."

"Thank you," I said.

"I shine shoes, too," he said. "I could do yours."

I peered over to spy his shoes. They *were* shiny.

"I'd like to do a lot of things for you," he said, a bit shyly.

I smiled, took in his blue eyes.

"It's just my thing," he said, backpedaling a bit. "It's a little weird, right? But Saturday mornings are for the car and the shoes. I'm a bit of a creature of habit."

"I'm the same way," I said. "Not the cleaning part, but my patterns." I thought of my morning routine at work: the computers, the charting, the testing. The listing, the filtering, the inputting of data. And my after-work routine: the Rosetta Stone CDs, the homemade dinners, flipping through the mail one piece at a time. The pistachio gelato in front of *Jeopardy!*, peeking in on my Facebook friends, planning trips on Expedia that I'd never take.

"Two peas in a pod," Lucas said, grinning widely.

In the restaurant, we were seated by the window. The sun was just setting over the Potomac, the ball of fire resting at the water's edge. When the waiter came, I ordered a glass of Chardonnay.

"And for you, sir?"

"I'm fine with water," he said.

"Sparkling, tap?"

"Tap's fine."

"And to start?" the waiter asked, looking at me. "An appetizer, a cup of soup?"

"You have to try the clam chowder," I said to Lucas.

"You go ahead," he said, placing his hand over mine. "I'm fine with bread and water for now."

"I'm good," I said, the disappointment audible even to me.

"Don't be silly," Lucas said. "Order whatever you want." He looked up at the waiter. "A cup of clam chowder for the lady."

The waiter nodded, jotted it down. When Lucas turned back to his menu, I looked up at the waiter and mouthed, "A bowl"—a tiny cup would only leave me wanting more.

I let my heart process Lucas's hand covering mine. It was warm, and he was sweet and considerate, and he adored me. And he had spent hours detailing my car and getting the oil changed and filling it with gas. I wanted to be with him. I wanted to be with a guy as kind as he was. On the other hand, he had just eschewed clam chowder and Chardonnay in favor of bread and water. When the waiter returned with my soup, I pulled my hand from under Lucas's and dipped my spoon into the bowl. I closed my eyes and savored the potato melting in my mouth, the hint of dill awakening my taste buds. I took a long sip of wine. For a few seconds, time stopped and Lucas hardly seemed relevant. I just wanted to enjoy my food. At last I looked over at him. "Are you sure you don't want a bite?"

"You enjoy it," he said, smiling. "I'm not really much of a fish guy."

In my mind, I began drawing columns and categorizing who Lucas was, and who he was not. He was a tax guy, a car-cleaning expert, and shoe-shining wizard. He wasn't a foodie, he wasn't a drinker, and he didn't care for fish. How would the two of us ever travel together in Tuscany? But then again, what were the chances that I'd ever make it to Tuscany, anyway?

When the waiter came for our order, I asked for the sea bass fillet surrounded by char-scorched tomatoes, broccoli rabe, a bed of orzo. Lucas ordered a steak and baked potato. He ate half of it, all the while chattering on about work, creating foreign entities, inventorying assets, and documenting policies for fraud prevention. When I asked about his family, he told me that he was pretty plain vanilla: great parents, one sister, his childhood home a redbrick Colonial still standing in the west end of Richmond. When I asked about trips he'd taken, he informed me that he wasn't much of a traveler; that he preferred to stay in the States or, even better, close to home. Instead, he regaled me with the details of a fascinating *National Geographic* documentary he enjoyed on California's Napa region.

"I adore good wine," I said, thinking of my favorite variety of red: its bouquet, ruby hue, plummy sweetness.

"I wish I knew more," he said. "But I'm sure I couldn't tell the difference between a ten-dollar and hundred-dollar bottle of wine."

"What did you like about the show on Napa, then?"

"I'm a huge history buff—geography fascinates me," he said. "Interesting terrain out there."

Interesting terrain out there.

"You must be interested in touring Europe then, right? If you're a big history enthusiast?"

"I'm sure it would be fascinating," Lucas said. "But there's so much to see here in the States. I feel like I've barely scratched the surface."

"True," I said, thinking I was foolish for pushing the point, seeing that I was the girl who had to be escorted off the last plane she boarded. Still, in my mind, I took a step back. In front of my eyes was Lucas Anderson, a guy who valued a good plan, discipline, and routine. If I were to list the qualities I respected in a man, Lucas's stability, reliability, and sensibility would top my list. So why then was I persevcrating over the fact that he didn't want to eat, drink, or travel?

When the waiter brought the dessert menu, I chose a flourless chocolate torte with salted caramel pecans. Lucas shook his head no, said he was stuffed. When I pointed out that there was pie and ice cream, he brightened. "Vanilla?" he asked.

"I'm sure they have vanilla," I said.

That was it, then. If Lucas Anderson were a flavor, he would be vanilla. I filed away this bit of information. Not a pro nor con, just a data point for me to chart out later. After all, I had nothing against vanilla.

Lucas drove me home and then walked me to the door. I unlocked it and pushed through. In the entryway, he pressed me against the wall and kissed me. I closed my eyes and thought about the clam chowder, the crusty bread and salted Irish butter, and when I did, Lucas's mouth became delicious.

CHAPTER FIFTEEN

"Goddamn it!" Dad roared from his office.

On the other side of the wall we shared, it sounded like a gang of wild raccoons was ransacking the place. I stood up and stared at our common wall. "Goddamn it!" he bellowed again, followed by a thunderous crash. When I ran from my office to his, I found him standing in front of his executive leather chair, regarding the bare expanse of his mammoth mahogany desktop, which he had evidently just wiped clear of its entire contents. On the floor were his lamp and day planner and iPad. Papers were scattered everywhere.

"Goddamn it," he repeated, this time in a small voice, an apologetic one.

I closed the door behind me. "What's going on?" I whispered. I kneeled onto the rug and began gathering the mess.

"Leave it," Dad said.

"Dad, what happened?"

Dad slumped into the corner of his leather sofa, wiped his eyes with his giant hand.

"My brain!" he said. "The shrapnel in my brain!"

"What happened?"

"I couldn't remember the ticker symbol for Chevron. I've owned that stock for forty years."

"CVX," I said. "No big deal. So you forgot."

"It's not just that, damn it."

"Then what?"

"I looked it up; I saw that it was CVX," he said. "But when I went to write it down—after I had just seen it—I couldn't remember how to make a *C*, for God's sake."

"It's time to see the doctor, Dad."

"Donny Kaye had a stroke. He's told me before that some days he feels like he's losing his absolute mind."

"Mr. Kaye had a *mini*stroke," I said. "And, yes! That's what I've been trying to tell you. There's a possibility that you've had something like that. We need to get you checked out."

That night I researched transient ischemic attacks and learned they were named "ministrokes" because the symptoms were like those of a stroke, but didn't last long. A ministroke occurred when blood flow to part of the brain was blocked, often by a blood clot. The blood eventually broke free and flowed again. Most likely ministrokes were warnings of a real stroke. Sudden numbness, tingling, weakness, or paralysis in the face, arm, or leg were some of the symptoms, along with vision changes, trouble speaking, and confusion. Brain cells could be affected within seconds of the blockage.

Dad could have suffered a ministroke that day at our seminar, when he froze in the headlights, when his jaw jutted back and forth, when his eyes looked as terrified as a man witnessing an execution.

I added a ministroke to my list of worries, alongside the possibility of a brain tumor. I hadn't a clue whether either was the culprit, but what I did know for sure was this: Dad's blunders could not be attributed to simple senior forgetfulness.

Three days later, Dad saw Dr. Bell who, because of Dad's high blood pressure, high cholesterol and triglycerides, ordered blood tests, an echocardiogram to check the heart's shape and its blood flow, and an electrocardiogram to measure its rhythm.

After the appointment, I grilled Dad on the details. "Did he take a CT scan to look at your brain?"

"He was checking out my ticker today," Dad said.

"Dad! Did you ask him about the possibility of a brain tumor? Don't you want to know if you had a stroke?"

"Daughter," he said, "I'm good. For now, I'm good. Enough tests for one day."

"This is crazy, Dad," I cried. "Did you tell him about the forgetfulness?"

"I want to get on with my life," Dad said. "Golf, work. Enough of this nonsense."

CHAPTER SIXTEEN

I had never been so angry with my father in all my life. I cursed his stubbornness. The man needed to have his brain checked, not his heart! For all the years he had accused me of living in denial of a larger life, who had his head in the sand now? I pulled the cork out of a half-full bottle of Merlot and emptied it into a water glass.

As I gulped wine, I distracted myself with Facebook. One of my dad's brother's grandsons had graduated from high school, another was accepted to a prestigious writing program for the summer, and a few of the little grandchildren were away at camp, canoeing and hiking and sleeping in cabins.

And Joe. His children were growing, too. The little guy, Jake, celebrated a birthday. But Joe's posts had decreased significantly. In June and July he had posted only once, a photo of the kids at the Jersey shore. In August, there were no photos, just one post he had reshared, a charity event for Wounded Warriors. I imagined Joe had a number of buddies who were wounded. I felt for them, and for Joe. Had my old sweetheart ever seen frontline action? Had any of his buddies been injured or killed?

Our first year of college, Joe and I did an admirable job of keeping in touch. This was the late 1990s, and e-mail was just beginning to sweep the nation. We each had AOL accounts and I, in the computer lab at W&M, and Joe, in his computer lab at VMI, wrote each other messages back and forth on our dial-up connections. As I waited for the screeching and squawking of the modem to connect, I'd flutter my fingertips above the keyboard, anxious to tell him about my day, to hear about his. On a few weekends, we'd meet back home in Alexandria, and for a while, it was like we had never left. Joe camped out in the quiet of Dad's and my house, and on the days when we went to Joe's, I drank in the chatter and laughter and mayhem that were the Lincoln Logs of Joe's family home.

Over Thanksgiving break, Joe and I went away to Virginia Beach, stowing away in a quaint seaside bungalow named the Sand Dollar. The little cottage was wood-paneled with floral curtains framing the windows that welcomed the afternoon sun. We walked on the beach, collected seashells, and lounged in the Adirondack chairs as we stared out at the shore. That night, we barely spoke except through our eyes, which conveyed the imperceptible looks we had grown to decipher in each other. *I want you, I love you, I trust you completely.* In the golden glow of the early evening light, Joe undressed me, and I, him. I kissed the pulse on his neck, the peak of his lips, the ledge of his cheekbone. He pressed his hands on the small of my back, traced the ridges of my ribs, pulled me closer to him than I had ever been.

That night, we made love for the first time.

"I love you," Joe said. He was on his side, and I ran my fingertips over his gorgeous body, his muscular biceps, his sculpted chest.

"I love you, too," I said, reaching to touch his hip bone, letting my hand curl around it.

"Never not," he said, leaning into me, his body filled with heat, covering mine. "I'll never not love you."

"I'll never not love you."

"You're so beautiful," he said, and at that moment, with the golden light, with the refusal of the shore to stop roaring, with our flesh sharing space, I felt more beautiful than ever.

"You're gorgeous," I said, lifting my face, letting his mouth brush mine.

Such was our teenage love, an intensity that bordered on insanity, a myopia that didn't see beyond our four walls, an urgency that the sky was falling and the only bunker was in each other's arms. That weekend, did we eat? I barely remember leaving the room. There were chips and soda, Red Vines and Snickers bars. But it was wholly perfect in every way.

Years later, when I was in my late twenties, I drove back to that seaside motel. It took a few passes down the drag to find it, for I had remembered it as quaint, immaculate. I had remembered the glow of the golden sun, the powder of the white sand, the turquoise scales of the ocean waves. Yet when I drove down the strip, I only saw motels and cottages and more motels—all the same. When I found the one named Sand Dollar, it hardly matched my memory. I parked, entered the lobby. In my heart I could still smell the cinnamon candle that was burning atop the registry counter, could still taste the banana of the saltwater taffy from the bowl next to the brochures, could still feel the moisture in the sea air.

"Can I help you?" asked a teenager behind the counter, some Jerry Springer yell-a-thon blasting behind him on the TV.

It was just a cheap beach motel, no better or worse than the one right next door. "Just looking," I said, inhaling deeply, a desperate, last-ditch effort to find the candle that once burned there. Down the pathway to the room where we once stayed, I closed my eyes and listened for the ocean's kiss against the shore, but all I could hear was the incessant moan of traffic.

Joe was my first love, but he was also my best friend back then. Would it be so wrong to send him a message, to say hello? It wasn't as if I were pursuing him. After all, I was serious with Lucas. I curled my fingers above the keyboard, took a giant gulp of air, and typed.

> Hi, Joe! I see your postings from time to time. Your family looks amazing. How blessed you are! I hope I'm not bothering you. I'm sure you're busy. Just wanted to say hi. No need to respond. Thanks!

I took another breath, positioned the cursor on "Send," closed my eyes, and thought it through. It was just an innocuous "Just saying hi" message, no big deal. I weighed the upside potential: he could write me back. I considered the downside risk: he could ignore the message.

I tapped my finger on the mouse. I was involved with Lucas. It was a risk I could manage. I sent the message.

And then I felt as though I'd vomit. I thought I had considered all of the possibilities. But I now imagined Joe being notified that he had a message, and then him reading it with a confused look scrunching his face, his finger hitting "Delete" before "nothing me" caused problems in his wonderful present life. Or I could imagine him telling his stunning wife over a gourmet weekday dinner she had made—coq au vin, perhaps, with a glass of heavy Cabernet—how his high school sweetheart sent him a message. How it was kind of cute, kind of sad. He was sure she had never married. Her profile just listed her profession, still working with her father. Never left Virginia. His wife would slice and butter a piece of French bread she had made from scratch. *Don't be cruel,* she'd say. *Not everyone gets to find what we've found. Count your blessings,* she would say. Then they would share a look—the kind that beautiful, popular people shared—that said, *But still, it was kind of sad.* Then they would laugh. At me. That night they would have sex like they hadn't had since their wedding night—grateful, we-are-so-lucky-not-to-be-alone sex.

CHAPTER SEVENTEEN
JOE

Some days my knee ached more than others. I thought maybe it was the rain, but tonight it was as clear as could be outside. Though I had been lucky in keeping my knee, the surgeries to reconstruct it had been tricky and numerous. Lots of scar tissue, fried nerve endings, infection. The phantom pain was chronic. Even though the cut was made above the zone of injury, sometimes I wondered whether it should have gone a few inches higher.

I was on a run to the store. We needed milk for the morning. "Kate, you're in charge," I had said, trying to give her a job, a sense of worth, a boost to her ego. I just wanted to see some light in her eyes. I just wanted to see her sweet smile. She gave me the thumbs-up, promised she wouldn't let Olivia and Jake play with knives or fire. I was glad she still had her sense of humor.

I was sitting at a light, rubbing at my thigh, massaging the quadriceps, as I obsessed on my unhappy daughter, when a horn blared from behind me. My cell phone beeped in the same instant—an e-mail—and the jumble of noises shot me out of my skin. Anyone who's been in a war zone stays a little jumpy, at least for a while. And sometimes forever. Way oversensitive to loud noises. Sights and smells, too, for that matter.

The light had turned green. Once I'd cleared the intersection, I pulled over and shifted into park, flexed my leg and opened my e-mail.

A Facebook message from Missy Fletcher. No way. Fifteen years. A lifetime ago. No way. I logged on and read the message.

I read her note over and over. Missy Fletcher, after all of these years. I knew we were "friends" on Facebook, but here was the thing: Missy never posted a darn thing.

Missy Fletcher—the coolest person in our school nobody ever got to know.

Before I dated Missy, I was with a girl named Whitney. Whitney's goal in life—at least in high school—was to be *just right*. We'd meet outside the basketball stadium, but we couldn't walk in until exactly halftime; otherwise, what would people think? She'd want me to buy her fries, but would only eat them if Sheila and Laura were around, girls who thought it was cool to binge and purge. If Marlene and Darlene (cheerleaders and identical twins) were around, she'd scowl at the fries in disdain. "Look at all that fat!" Whitney wasn't dumb, I don't think, but in her mind, it wasn't cool to do homework or stand out in any way.

Missy didn't give a thought to any of that kind of nonsense. She loved school, was a total brain, and wouldn't even consider not doing her work to impress the Whitneys of the world. She chomped into food, and the sheer joy of eating was written all over her face. She read nearly a book a day, worked extra math problems for fun, and sometimes strolled through the Smithsonian on the weekend all by herself. I'd be away at baseball camp and then ask her what she had been up to. "There was a contemporary art exhibition at the Corcoran," she'd say. As if it were totally normal to spend a Saturday doing that.

Missy was the most confident girl I ever knew. I told her that once and she nearly fell over laughing. "Me?!" She told me that she hated everything about herself, knew she was wrong in a thousand ways, but was helpless to change. One time she admitted she couldn't believe that I liked her. I thought she was nuts, but later I saw that she really did have this crazily limited, restrictive view of herself and her potential.

We were getting ready to apply for colleges and Missy all of a sudden dug in her heels, saying that she wanted to stay in Alexandria, that she wanted us to keep dating. This was nuts, considering she had already aced the practice SAT and colleges were courting the hell out of her. She had a 4.0 GPA and had proven aptitude in math and science. The colleges were all over her, throwing scholarships at her like candy. Every now and then she talked to me about studying abroad or traveling through Europe. I even think she filled out the Peace Corps application, but never sent it in. Something stopped her. She worried with anxiety about everything. I think it affected her more than she knew. Growing up without a mom probably played into that apprehension, I would guess.

Of course, she had her father. Frank. God, that guy was one of a kind. He loved me in an entirely different way than my parents did. My parents were good but we were just getting by. Their goals were maintenance: keep the kids fed, the mortgage paid, and never miss Sunday Mass. But Frank . . . the guy would take me out to lunch—just the two of us, sometimes—and talk to me, ask my opinion about things: politics, sports, and the stock market. He made me feel like my thoughts mattered. He valued me. My dad was great in a lot of ways, but I never once had lunch with him alone.

Later that night, I logged on to Facebook and wrote Missy back:

Missy, has it really been fifteen years? I look
at your profile picture and you look exactly

the same to me. Then again, I still feel like the same guy I was in high school, but you'd never believe how far from the truth that is. I spent most of the past fifteen years in the Marines. I served three tours. Now I work for a government contractor. But all in all, I don't have a reason to complain, not a reason for not being happy. I'm healthy and employed, and have three great kids. Katherine is thirteen, almost fourteen. Olivia is eleven, and Jake just turned nine. How are you and Frank doing?

CHAPTER EIGHTEEN

The next day at Fletcher Financial, I entered my office, turned on my computer and the three screens, and headed to the kitchen to fill my mug with coffee. Once at my computer, I checked the markets, reviewed the portfolios' returns, and scanned the to-do list. I opened the calendar, pondered the clients and the prep work needed for the meetings, and most importantly, penciled in a half hour for lunch. Then I checked e-mails.

"You have a message from Joseph Santelli." I smiled, logging on to Facebook. I pulled up the message. It had come in late last night. I was wondering why I hadn't heard the message alert on my phone until I found my phone dead in my purse.

Okay, then. A message from Joe.

I couldn't stop smiling. I wanted to savor this moment. I sipped at my coffee. I needed a doughnut. I returned to the break room, found a leftover Krispy Kreme from yesterday's breakfast meeting. I zapped it in the microwave, then returned to my office. I sat at my computer, clicked on the screen, and read the message.

I'd loved Joe more than anyone other than my father. I was glad to hear he was happy, and his joy inspired mine. Lucas wasn't Joe, but Lucas was great, and he and I could build what Joe and his wife had made: a home, a family, a lifetime of memories.

I wrote Joe back. I told him about Fletcher Financial and how Dad was the same great guy and how everyone still loved him and how he still loved everyone. Then I told Joe about Dad's forgetfulness, and how I wanted him to have a brain scan, and how Dad was resisting. "I just hope he's okay," I told him. "Thanks for writing me back, Joe. It's amazing to hear from you."

The following weekend, Lucas came to dinner. I cooked him Italian. It took me most of the day, but I managed to master saltimbocca. And while I was keenly aware that Lucas would eat only a portion of this plateful of food, I did it anyway. I wanted my house to burst with the aromatic smells. I wanted him to understand my passion. All the while, I sipped from my glass of Barolo.

While I finished up the dinner preparations, Lucas sat at the counter, sipping water and watching me.

"In Italian," I said, "saltimbocca means 'to jump in the mouth.'" I cut a small piece of veal and prosciutto and jabbed it with a fork, then leaned over the counter toward Lucas. "Open up," I said.

He took the bite, chewed. "That's cool that you're learning Italian."

I was being a bully; I realized this. But I wanted to know: "So what do you think? Is the food so good it 'jumps in your mouth'?"

"It's the best saltimbocca I've ever had," Lucas said.

I grimaced at his offhanded compliment. It was delicious, if I might have said so myself. During dinner, Lucas ate, but he didn't devour. Tomorrow I would savor our leftovers in private, and enjoy it a thousand times more.

I gritted my teeth and fought every urge in my body not to hold this against him, because after all, he and I were the same—except for this one point. So he wasn't a foodie. So he didn't drool at the thought of salted caramel, or ravioli pillows stuffed with creamy goat cheese, or Merlot sliding down his throat.

He was so much like me—a safety guy happy to stay put, a risk-averse chap who believed that testing the waters or working outside of the box could only lead to problems. I poured and downed another glass of Barolo. If we were so much alike, why was it taking me a half bottle of wine to get through dinner?

When I was a teenager, I was obedient and good. I never once rebelled against my father. His guidance didn't send me in the opposite direction. When he warned me not to cozy up with the boys too early, I listened. When other girls were pushing themselves into the arms of unsuitable boys just to spite their parents, I took Dad's advice to heart. He knew what he was talking about. When Dad told me to listen to his cache of Dale Carnegie tapes, I did. When he suggested I learn tennis because "country club sports" were essential to business, I grabbed my racquet. When he advised me to buy near the water because real estate proximity would always matter, I put in an offer.

But now, at age thirty-five, it seemed I was at last experiencing rebellion. The steadier Lucas was, the more reckless I wanted to become. When he ordered water, I ordered wine—one glass typically would have been fine, but now I ordered two. When he spoke of the safety of staying within the contiguous fifty, I argued for the value of adventure, of experiencing different cultures, not just watching them on television. Even with our tax discussions, as he argued for toeing the line of prudence and staying way below the IRS's radar, I argued that some techniques were lucrative enough to take the chance. The words coming from my mouth weren't my own, but those of a mutinous teenager arguing for the sport of it.

Home alone, I rebelled in another fashion. I planned trips. I'd spend hours on Expedia charting flights and finding hotels. I would fill my virtual shopping cart with all of the requisite pieces to make for a fine excursion: the flight, the hotel, the cooking school. The guided tours, the visits to the churches. Boat rides down the rivers bisecting cities. With ten different windows open, I'd work until I was only a click away—one "Submit" button on each page—from booking a trip.

Then I'd click on Facebook and stare at Joe. I would trace my finger over the delicate lines that now fanned from his eyes. I would close my eyes and imagine what a great father he must be to his children, what a wonderful husband.

And then I would exhale, open my eyes, and—one at a time—close out of all the open pages. Who was I kidding?

Lucas washed dishes while I put the coffee on. Deliberately, I sliced a piece of tiramisu for him—larger than I knew he would want—and one for me.

When I handed it to him, he covered his belly and shook his head no. "I can't eat another bite."

"But it's *tiramisu*," I said. I detected my mean tone, like a bully goading a weaker kid. Still: How on earth could he turn down tiramisu?

"Save it," he said. He stood up, slid his arms through mine, kissed my neck. "I'm hungry for *you*."

I wiggled away. "I think we should eat dessert first." I never picked a fight with anyone, but I was itching to kick Lucas for not wanting the tiramisu. I excavated a massive forkful of cake and crammed it in my mouth. Lucas took the plate from my hand, set it on the table, and then led me to the bedroom.

"But, wait . . ." I stuttered through my stuffed mouth.

"I don't want to wait," he said, laying me on the bed. He slipped off my flats, unbuttoned and unzipped my pants, slid them down my legs. He lifted my shirt and planted hot kisses over my belly. I allowed the full weight of my head to sink into the soft, downy mattress. I closed my eyes and tried to focus, strained to conjure up an ounce of desire, but my mind had only two thoughts: the tiramisu melting in my mouth, and Joe. I pretended Lucas was Joe: his olive skin, the blade of his hip bone, our beachside cottage. If I focused deep enough, I could feel Joe's lips, the terrain of his arms.

"You have no idea how beautiful you are," Joe used to say. I wasn't beautiful, I knew that, but at that moment, with my milky-white skin pushed up against his, the color of a perfect latte, I felt luminous.

My brain, my trusty ally, providing me with my faultless memory, remembering perfection.

And Lucas—so sweet, so adoring, yet so predictable. When I opened my eyes and looked at him—all the exotic tastes of Joe and tiramisu turned to boiled ham.

Later, Lucas fell fast asleep. I slipped from his grip and tiptoed into the kitchen, reclaimed the obscenely large wedge of cake, poured a cup of coffee still hot in the pot, and sat at my computer. I logged on to Facebook and stared at Joe's photo. "I love you," I whispered, and then exhumed another shovel of cake. *You would have loved this cake, Joe. You would have eaten it until you were sick. And I would have delighted in your gluttony.*

He had messaged me back: "Missy, sorry to hear Frank's gotten forgetful. Hard to believe he could ever age. I'm sure you'll convince him to see a doctor. Please keep me posted. I'm thinking about the two of you."

Following Thanksgiving break of our first year of college, Joe and I remained close. He'd given me my Christmas present early, a gold necklace with a seashell charm. We stood at his car, shivering, huddling together against the November wind, yet not wanting to leave the moment. We hugged and kissed and hugged some more. We stared into each other's eyes, professed our love with Romeo-and-Juliet passion. I cried when Joe finally slid into the driver's seat. When we said good-bye, I was sure that we'd be together forever. But only a few weeks later, Joe e-mailed that he wouldn't be coming home for Christmas break; that the residential assistant for his dorm had to go home because of a family illness and had asked Joe if he would stay on campus and do his job. It was a good opportunity to make some money; also, an internship had opened up in the ROTC office and Joe had taken it.

Joe came home after Christmas—briefly, for just a day and a half. I saw him once before he was whisked away by his big family. He looked different to me. All he could talk about was the military, the Marines. *What about us?* I wanted to scream, but Joe's intensity had transferred from his parochial life in Alexandria to a larger world in need of his services. He was a man on a mission, a guy with a goal, a world to save from tyranny.

By spring, our communication had almost stopped, but when I e-mailed him before Easter break, asking if he'd be coming home, he said no. I asked if I could come to Lexington, to see him, but he said it was against the rules, and besides, he had been handpicked to do research with the commandant of cadets.

Summer came, and although I was home at the end of May, Joe didn't arrive until July, having decided to stay through June to finish up his research project. When we finally saw each other, he tried to act normally, as if we were still a couple, and I clung desperately to the hope that we were. But we were hardly ever alone, as if Joe had contrived our meetings around his family or my dad. As if he didn't want to be with just me. When I finally orchestrated my own moment, sending Dad out to the store, I stood in front of him.

"What happened to us?" I found the courage to say.

"You're my first real girlfriend—"

"And you're my first real boyfriend," I said.

"That's the problem," Joe said. "We can't be each other's first *and* last." He looked down, and that's when I knew he had been seeing other girls.

"Why not?" I asked.

"Missy," Joe started. "I love you. Please don't doubt that. But there's a big world out there. For you, for me. We need to see what's out there. Before we settle down."

"I don't," I said. "I'm perfectly happy to stay here in Alexandria. With you, with Dad."

"Are you sure?" he asked. "Because I think there is more to you than that."

"There's not," I said and huffed away because Joe had just unwittingly maligned me the same way my father always had: revealing that me, as is, didn't cut it.

In the fall, Joe returned to VMI and I resumed my studies at W&M. After a few disappointing attempts, we soon fell completely out of touch.

Two years passed. I occasionally saw Joe's mother. Her eyes welled with tears when she told me of Joe's new girlfriend.

Then 9/11 hit. Could any of us claim to be the same after that?

If Joe were ever on the fence about joining the military, he wasn't after the attack on our soil. From his mother I knew that he had finished his degree in three years and then went to the Basic School in Quantico to become a marine officer. I also knew that he had married his girlfriend and that they had a baby on the way. By 2003, Joe was fighting in Operation Iraqi Freedom.

CHAPTER NINETEEN

By the end of September, Lucas and I had settled into a routine as predictable as a forty-year-married couple's. And while, admittedly, such a depiction of our relationship sounds disparaging at best, there was much that I appreciated about our stable schedule. Lucas was always on time. In fact, early. Lucas always had a full tank of gas, an immaculately clean car, and a wallet full of cash. Lucas called every night at seven o'clock on the dot. Lucas didn't care what I ate or drank, wore or didn't wear. Lucas accepted me exactly as I was. Correction, Lucas *adored* me exactly as I was.

We saw each other every Saturday night. For a number of weeks, we took turns picking restaurants. I mined the list of the top one hundred restaurants in the *Washingtonian* magazine, hoping Lucas might find a cuisine that appealed to him: Vietnamese? Russian? And on the nights when it was Lucas's turn to choose, we ended up at a chain restaurant like TGI Friday's or Applebee's. Even there, Lucas showed no interest in food. Even there, I did, delighting in the scorched swiss cheese edges atop a bowl of French onion soup. It seemed my affinity for food crossed all borders, both cartographical and star-rated.

Eventually, though, it grew easier for me to cook him a simple meal: grilled chicken with rice pilaf, a steamed vegetable, and a loaf of bread. So long as Lucas wasn't forced to choose among a menu replete with foie gras and sweetbreads, he was happy. And I was relieved not to confront this part of my boyfriend. So long as I wasn't antagonized directly by his aversion to fine dining, it was easier to cope.

Tonight I cooked a variation of the same. Roasted chicken, but this time with orzo rather than rice. Lucas wanted to know the deal: Is this pasta, or is it rice?

I gulped my wine, dislodging the dry chicken and orzo roadblock in my throat, then I tried some shock and awe. "Wouldn't it be great to take a trip to Italy?" I lobbed it in the air and waited for it to fall.

Lucas set down his water. "There are pickpockets in Italy. And I heard the food is nothing like the Italian we're used to. And Rome, it's dirty, I hear."

"Perhaps," I said, "but do you think you'd ever consider it?"

"Going to Italy?"

I looked at him levelly. "Yeah, with me. Going to Italy with me." I persisted in bugging Lucas this way, and I wasn't sure why, other than the fact that I knew it was a safe game for me to play. I'd ask, he'd say no, and in my mind I'd be able to blame him for our staying put, rather than my fear of flying. It was twisted, and had me questioning who I was, but questioning who I was had been the name of the game lately.

"I would love to go on a trip with you!" Lucas said, and when he did, my stomach turned. *What if Lucas actually said yes?*

"It would be awesome," I said, reaching across for his hand.

"But we might want to test the waters first."

"Test the waters?"

"Something local. A weekend trip to Williamsburg, for example."

I withdrew my hand. Another swallow of wine. "Williamsburg, Virginia?"

"It's so interesting there. All the Colonial buildings and the trades-people and shopkeepers dressed in Colonial garb," Lucas went on.

"You know I went to school at William & Mary, right? In Williamsburg?"

"Perfect!" Lucas said. "You'd be a great tour guide."

"What about Italy?"

"I'm not saying *never*," Lucas said. "But we'd need to travel together first. Do a ton of research. I wouldn't want to just hop on a plane and take our chances. I wouldn't want to cause you any undo anxiety."

"Because of my fear of flying?" I asked.

"Yes, Melissa, of course," he said, taking my hands. "I care about you. I don't want you to be scared. Ever."

Hmm. Did Lucas Anderson ever stop thinking about my needs?

CHAPTER TWENTY

A month later, Dad and I met with the Longworths to review their portfolio. Dad was smoking hot, remembering every detail: (1) Mr. Longworth's father-son golf tournament in the Outer Banks, (2) Mrs. Longworth's board meeting for the One by One Foundation, (3) the granddaughter Loralie's soccer tournament.

After we said our good-byes, Dad pulled me into a hug.

"It's a beautiful day, Daughter," Dad said. "Let's take a quick walk. Get some fresh air."

"Go ahead," I said. "I want to check e-mails before the Hoffmans come in." Our next meeting was in just half an hour, clients who needed to stop by to drop off some material.

When Dad hadn't returned in twenty minutes, I began to worry. The Hoffmans came in fifteen minutes later, and I had to apologize for Dad because he wasn't back yet. I led them into the conference room, took some notes on the changes they wanted to make. A half hour later, Dad was still AWOL. "I'm so sorry," I said. "Dad must have run into someone."

The Hoffmans were oblivious; they just wanted to relay to someone—Dad, me, Jenny—the amendment they wanted to make to their trust. They were happy to leave it with me. "Just have him call us," they said.

As soon as the Hoffmans turned the corner, I grabbed my coat and hollered to Jenny that I was going to look for Dad. I walked down the cobblestoned sidewalks of King Street, peering into the coffee shops and diners. I crossed Callahan and went into the train station—maybe Dad was there at the candy shop. He'd been known to frequent it before. I made a loop, checking the benches, in the restaurants, the shops. Back on King Street, I walked up to Duke. I eyed the steps, around the corners, down by the water. The memorials, the gardens, the firehouse museum, the Freedom House. *Where are you, Dad?*

On Washington Street, I decided to head back. As I passed Christ Church, I paused, doubled back. *Maybe.* Though Dad wasn't particularly religious, he did have a fondness for this church, where both George Washington and Robert E. Lee had once worshipped. I entered the darkness, inhaled the incense-infused space, and found Dad in the back pew. When I approached him, his face was in his hands. He looked a hundred years old.

"Dad?" I asked, slipping into the cherry wood and red-fabric pew next to him.

When he slid his hands down and rubbed at his eyes, I could tell he had been crying. His eyes—his bright eyes that smiled as much as his mouth—were bloodshot and lined.

I reached for his hands. "Did you forget about the appointment? The Hoffmans came in."

Dad shook his head no, wiped at his eyes.

"You're pretty far from the office," I said.

Dad nodded.

"What happened?" I asked.

Dad exhaled, looked at me. "I couldn't remember your mother's name," he said. "Charlene—her beautiful name that I loved so much—Charlene."

Dad rubbed at his face. He was an old man I'd never seen before.

"I ran into Jimmy Jorgensen and he and I were talking, and I was telling the story of the rainstorm that hit us just days before you were born. I started to say her name, I started to say, 'Charlene was ready to go to the hospital right then, just in case.' But the words weren't there. Her name wasn't there, like someone had erased it from my brain. I couldn't remember your mother's name, Missy. I couldn't remember Charlene's name."

I leaned into him, pressed my face against the nubby wool of his jacket. "So you forgot."

Dad issued a sad smile. "But then"—he again wiped at his eyes—"I started to walk back. And even though I knew the streets, the landmarks, the restaurants and churches . . . I couldn't remember how they fit together."

Dad looked at me, helpless to explain any of this. I had nothing to say in return.

"Missy," Dad said. "I was lost. I was lost in my own town."

Dad went on. "It's like everything I've known my entire life has been thrown in the air and has landed in different places."

At that, Dad started to bawl onto my shoulder.

PART TWO
CROSSING OVER

CHAPTER TWENTY-ONE

On the first day of October, the day my mother was killed exactly thirty-one years before, Dad and I crossed the threshold of Neurological Associates, a group of doctors who specialized in memory impairment. Dad was tested and prodded, underwent a brain scan, a neuropsychological evaluation. He patiently endured a battery of diagnostics: the Clock Drawing Test, the Mini Mental Stage Examination, and the Functional Assessment Staging Test. Naming, visual retention, patterning, and recall quizzes. Ad nauseam, he recited his family's history and submitted to physical exams, plus more tests that scrutinized sensation controlled by the central nervous system. Again and again, he was observed by technicians whose job it was to detect weaknesses in his memory's integration, his reasoning processes, his language recall. His blood was drawn, his urine collected, his vitals charted.

Finally, we sat with Dr. Bergman. He opened Dad's chart, then closed it. He told us Dad had indeed suffered a ministroke . . . and that there was evidence of Alzheimer's.

"We should have had you checked out," I said.

Dr. Bergman handed Dad a packet. I reached for it and began reading.

"Tell me about the medication," I said, pointing to a superlong word in the literature. "What's our course of treatment?"

Dr. Bergman rattled on about acetylcholinesterase inhibitors, drugs that work by helping to increase the amount of acetylcholine in the brain, a chemical that is important for memory and learning. Then he talked of glutamate pathway modifiers, another chemical in the brain that is important for learning and memory. There were also vitamins E and C, and a baby aspirin, once a day.

"How long until I'm totally cuckoo?" Dad wanted to know.

"Dad!" I objected. "Dr. Bergman is going to set you up with medication. You're not going to go cuckoo."

But Dr. Bergman didn't shy away from the question, however flippantly Dad had chosen to phrase it. "It's hard to say," he said. "But because you've already suffered a ministroke, it might progress faster. And, of course, the ministroke is almost always a precursor of more to come. So that's a worry, too."

After I had dropped off Dad at home and was on my way to my house, my phone rang. It was Lucas.

"We've just come from the doctor," I said. "There's indication that he had a ministroke. And what's worse, there's evidence of Alzheimer's."

I began to cry, so I pulled over to the curb. In that moment, I needed Lucas for one thing and one thing only: I needed him to ask how I felt about it. I would start at the beginning, explain that my father was my anchor, and how he and I have been braving it alone all of these years. I would confess that without my father, I feared I was nothing. I'd narrate my childhood, describing how Dad greeted me every morning with smiles and optimism, never missed one of my school events, and cheered on my every accomplishment. I'd venture to measure the size and weight of Dad's pride for me, how it was too large to hold in even his giant hands.

But Lucas was a problem solver and a tax attorney and a sensible, reasonable guy who was able to extract emotion from his decision making. "From a business standpoint," he said, "I'm sure you know that now would be a good time to put his and your affairs in order."

"Put our affairs in order?" I repeated, attempting to tamp down the anger rising in my chest.

"You know, your paperwork. The financials."

I closed my eyes and squeezed my hands into fists. "I'll talk to you later, okay?" I said, and then hung up without waiting for a response.

He was just being practical, saying what made sense, building a bridge of pragmatism over my river of emotional churning, but talking about business at a time like this made me loathe him. His misunderstanding of my father's and my relationship was so profound it left me shaking.

For hours, I sat at my computer and researched Alzheimer's disease.

The human brain is a remarkable organ. Complex chemical and electrical processes take place that let us speak, move, see, remember, feel emotions, and make decisions. Inside a healthy brain, billions of cells called neurons communicate with one another, receiving messages through electrical charges. Messengers called neurotransmitters move across synapses or microscopic gaps between neurons. This cellular circuitry enables communication within the brain. Alzheimer's disease interrupts the neurons' ability to communicate with one another.

And then I researched the link between Alzheimer's and stroke victims.

Neuroscientists have known for years that the risk of Alzheimer's disease is doubled for stroke victims. During a stroke—no matter the size or severity—the oxygen to the brain is depleted and as time goes by, the toxic chemicals related to the development of Alzheimer's disease accumulates. Even strokes that are without symptoms and thus undetected can serve as the catalyst for Alzheimer's disease.

I went to my bookshelf and pulled down my high school senior yearbook. I flipped to the index in the back, found Joe—pages 66, 134, 257. I opened to his senior picture, a gorgeous shot of him in a blue blazer and burgundy tie, his earnest gaze I held so dear. Next to his name it listed his activities: football, baseball, student council, the Lettermans Club. Then I found my page, plain-Jane me in my white blouse and beige cardigan, my puffy hair restrained with a headband, my rosy cheeks casting a glowing sheen, sitting up straight with my hands folded on my lap. Cross country, tennis, yearbook, Key Club.

I sat in my town house, having never felt so deserted in my life, so utterly depressed, rootless and alone. Yet the memories were *something*. They held value that I clung to fervently—my hopeless lifeline—even though I was certain my recollections, my attendant feelings, weren't exactly correct. How I remembered high school now—with such longing. How I perceived Joe now—as if staring long enough at his senior photo might invoke some telepathy between us. I knew I was floating in some make-believe froth of pointless desire, trying to will my past to be big enough to compensate for my present.

Then I thought of Dad and his now suddenly, horribly tenuous relationship with his own memories, a thousand times grander than mine. His wonder years growing up in the 1950s, falling in love with Mom, shipping off to Vietnam, and befriending all the guys like himself. Then a lifetime of service in a career he valued, along with his clients, his philanthropy, Jenny, and me. How would Dad survive without those memories? What would he do without his sacred ground?

I logged on to Facebook and clicked on Joe. I needed to talk to someone, and he was the someone I wanted. First I looked through all of his posts, all of his photos: his wife, his children, their activities, their *life*. And then I opened up a message to him and began typing.

> Hi again. There's a reason for my dad's forgetfulness. He's sick. Alzheimer's. It's hard to believe. I suspected something was wrong, but hearing the diagnosis felt like a dagger to my heart. It never occurred to me that he would be anything other than the towering guy he's always been. I know how much you liked my father. I just wanted you to know.

CHAPTER TWENTY-TWO

JOE

Tough Tuesday again. I sat in the waiting area of Kate's counselor. On the doctor's door was a giant poster. "How are you feeling today?" it wanted to know, followed by a hundred different cartoon face illustrations. A circle face with a smile = happy. A circle face with a squiggly-lined mouth = anxious. A circle face with a raised eyebrow = skeptical. A circle face with red cheeks = embarrassed. A circle with hooded eyes = exhausted. A circle with an O-shaped mouth = surprised.

Olivia listened to music through her earbuds. Jake played on his iPad. And I stared into space because today had been a rough one. My guys at the hospital were in a foul mood. On a number of the marine blogs this morning, there'd been a report of a Humvee hitting a mine in Afghanistan. Three confirmed dead, others injured. It hit me hard, too. I should have just sat around with the guys and commiserated, joined in on their "Everything is crap" chorus. Instead, I pulled out goal worksheets and asked the guys to plot out where they wanted to be in a month, six months, a year. Carlos and Andy made an attempt, but

Tony and Jerry both scribbled on their pages and then crushed them into balls, tossing them into the trash. "What's the point?" Tony wanted to know, and I didn't have a ready answer for him.

And then I picked up the kids. The second I saw Kate's face—her mouth a tight line, her cheeks flushed red, her eyes as wide as shields—I knew it had been a bad day for her, too. I didn't need the chart of circle faces to tell me she had been shaken and was ready to blow.

She slid the van door open, hurled in her backpack with more force than was necessary.

"What happened?" I asked.

"Another day in paradise," Kate said. "Girls laughing at me, no seats at the lunch table, Kelly telling me I couldn't listen to what she was talking about."

"What about Ellie?" This girl was a friend of Kate's. "Where was she?"

"I've been exiled by Ellie," Kate said. "She's best friends with Claire now. Doesn't give me the time of day."

My knuckles whitened on the steering wheel. I steadied my breath and reminded myself that I was only hearing one side of the story. Kate shucked off her sweater, getting it tangled with the seat belt. When she did, I saw that her blouse was on inside out. It must have happened after gym, when she changed back into her clothes.

"Kate," I said. "Your blouse is on inside out. That's probably why those girls were giggling behind your back."

"What?!" She scratched at her shoulder and seized the shirt's exposed seam.

"See? So, no big deal. It's not like they were laughing at *you*, per se. They were just being immature."

"Like it would have killed one person to tell me?" A tear the size of a water balloon sprung from her eye.

Luckily, Olivia and Jake were in the third-row seat with their earbuds in, oblivious to Kate rapping her head against the window.

Meanwhile, my head began to throb under the stress of having to shoulder all of these wounds. Battle was entirely worse in a thousand different ways, but this—feeling my daughter's hurt—was eviscerating. Who knew that I'd be a vessel for her every ache? When she was in agony, I suffered. When she failed, I crumbled inside. When she had a bad day, I had a bad week. How many more years until this knot in my stomach untwisted?

Kate finished her session and the counselor called me in. "Can I talk to your father for a minute?" she asked Kate. Kate joined her brother and sister in the waiting room while I took my turn with the doctor, who reiterated to me that my daughter was suffering a crisis of confidence. She'd asked Kate to write a story, and what she wrote was entitled "The Girl Who Tried Too Hard to Be Liked." *I'm wrong in every way*, it began. I pressed my arm into my gut, which felt like a cauldron of fire. I asked what we could do.

"Continue to fill her up with the things in her life that have meaning to her," the counselor said.

When we stopped at Chipotle for dinner, Kate was in a better mood; she always was following counseling. Unburdening herself seemed to provide a lift. I wondered if my guys at the hospital felt better after meeting with me. The kids chattered on, and I stared out the window and thought about my daughter, so smart yet so unsure. I didn't get it. Kate had always been so quick on her feet, sharp-witted. Why was she letting these girls call all the shots? Why didn't she just put them in their place?

Jake pulled up a YouTube video on his iPad—cats and dogs dressed in clothes, wearing eyeglasses and hats—and the kids collapsed in hysterics. To see Kate laughing, her real smile, not stressed for a second, almost made me cry.

We were still eating when my phone chimed: an e-mail message from Missy Fletcher. The kids were happily goofing with each other, so I opened it.

Frank, poor Frank. Missy, poor Missy.

She wanted me to know.

Later that night, in my bedroom, I opened my laptop and clicked on to Facebook. I had to write Missy. I had to tell her that my heart was aching alongside hers for the man who cared so deeply for the two of us.

No argument, my day had been pretty rough. The Humvee explosion, the guys at group, Kate and her tears, and then hearing about my buddy Frank Fletcher and the dagger to Missy's heart. A circle face with an ugly scowl. Really, the day couldn't have been worse.

But tonight, seeing Kate relaxed, hearing her laugh—a real laugh—and then getting a message from Missy, just feeling that connection with her, however thin it might be, lifted me up. It was a stretch—a desperate stretch, but maybe we had hit rock bottom and were on our way up.

A circle face with wide-open, optimistic eyes.

CHAPTER TWENTY-THREE

Late that night, I read a message from Joe:

> I'm so sorry to hear about your dad. There
> are only a handful of guys like Frank Fletcher
> in this world. I've been lucky to know him.
> I'll never forget how good he made me feel,
> like everything I did was groundbreaking,
> golden. I've always wondered where he got
> his enthusiasm for life.

I laughed out loud and then wiped my eyes because Joe remembered Dad like I knew him, he recalled the joy he transferred onto every person he came in contact with. I read on:

> For some reason, I thought back to the time
> you and I got him a computer. He resisted
> it, said we couldn't teach an old dog new
> tricks. But we set it up for him and then got

online and showed him how to use a Google search box. "What are you interested in?" I asked him. When he said Vietnam, I typed in "Vietnam 1965" and tons of pages came up, and Frank nearly fell over. He thought I was magic. "How'd you do that?" he wanted to know. "You're a genius!" he said, slapping me on the back. That was Frank, the guy who believed enough in me to give me credit for Google's search engine.

I dabbed at my eyes—tears, happy and sad. I finished up reading:

It's really great to hear from you, Miss. It's been too long, and reading your message was like coming home. Please keep me posted on Frank. Maybe a cure's right around the corner, right? Tell him his old buddy Joe says hey.

A month later, I got a call from Dad's neighbor. He found Dad in his yard in the middle of the night. He walked him home and put him back to bed, he thought I should know.

The next day, while Dad was at the office, I hired a group of guys from a hospital supply store to safety-proof his house. Childproof latches were put on the cabinets that contained cleaners and drawers that held knives. Sensors were installed on the doors and window locks, so I'd receive a text every time Dad left the house. An automatic shutoff switch was connected to the stove. Area rugs were removed so that he wouldn't trip on them.

At the office, Dad spent a lot of time talking on the phone with his buddies. They knew about him, and they were here to help. I had Jenny schedule two client meetings per day, first thing in the morning—so far, he hadn't had a lapse in the morning. I took up the slack in my own way. Dad's goal each day was to reach out to our clients, to check in on them, reassure them that they were on the right path. I wasn't comfortable on the phone, but I could whip up a pretty decent piece of correspondence and colorful report. Each day I composed three of these, and had Jenny send them out. A few days later, Jenny called to follow up, to see if the clients had any questions. I talked them through the charts—over the phone, in person. I could tolerate these conversations where there was an objective. *Yes, that's the yield. That's the dividend. That's the alpha and the beta.* When the clients asked about Dad, I explained to them that he was easing off a bit, enjoying more time on the golf course. *He deserves it, they would say. Good old Frank. No one deserves a nice retirement more than he.*

The next month, I tried calling Dad, but he didn't pick up. I hit redial for almost half an hour. Finally, I called the neighbor, Mr. Powell, and asked him to go over and check on Dad.

"I'm worried," I said.

When Mr. Powell investigated, he found Dad on the bathroom floor, his head bleeding. In the five minutes it took me to get there, the EMTs were already on the scene.

"Dad, what happened?" He was being loaded onto the gurney, and it was clear that he was confused, his eyes darting in every direction, his hands reaching for the gash above his eye.

At the hospital, hours later, Dad regained lucidity. He fell asleep in the tub, he said. It disoriented him, and he rose too quickly. When he stepped out of the tub, he slipped, cracked his head on the porcelain sink.

"Dad," I cried. "You're scaring me to death. What are we going to do?"

"It's not a 'we,' Missy; it's a 'me.' I don't want you involved in taking care of me. I don't want to be a burden to you."

"Would you stop!?" I demanded. "I'm *happy* to take care of you. I *want* to take care of you."

"I know you do," Dad said. "But it's not what you should be doing. You should be living your life."

Even in Dad's time of need, my desire—my choice—to care for him was somehow a reflection on my weak character. That Missy Fletcher could certainly be a nurse to her father, yes. But could she cultivate her relationship, get married, live a life of her own? Sadly, Dad thought not.

Dad spent three days in the hospital. Seventeen stitches covered the side of his shaved head. I told him it was a good thing he was named Frank. "You look like Frankenstein."

In the early mornings I sat with him at the hospital. He was lucid and tender and 100 percent the Dad I loved beyond measure. I held his hand and sat with him at breakfast, and when I thought he was as receptive as he was going to get, I broached the subject.

"So," I said, staring him squarely in the eyes, drilling my best, no-nonsense look into him. "Are you moving in with me? Or am I moving in with you?"

Dad slid the food tray away. "Daughter, I'm fine. Doc's going to dial up the meds, give me an extra dose of brain juice."

"Dad," I said, moving the tray to the side table.

"And no more tubs for the old man," he said. "Just the shower, with the handicap bar you had installed for me. I can't get in too much trouble with that, right?"

"Dad."

"You already turned off my stove, Missy. All I've got is my micro-wave oven. I'm fine."

"I want to take care of you," I said.

"I don't want you to take care of me!" he said, pulling his hand away. "I'm a grown man."

"This has nothing to do with you being a man, Dad. You're the strongest man I know! But your brain is playing tricks on you. I don't want you to get hurt."

"I have a *life*, Missy," he said. "A lifestyle I'm used to. An independence I'm used to."

"I understand that, Dad," I countered. "But I don't—"

"—have anything better to do?" he finished.

I shook my head no, brought desperately low by this jab at my stunted life, my spinsterhood. "That's not what I was going to say. I was going to say that I don't want you to get hurt."

"Come here, Missy," Dad said, his voice as tender as newborn skin. I nestled myself into him as best I could on the narrow hospital bed. "I love you so much. I love that you want to take care of me. But a man's got his pride, my love."

I started to cry. "I know, Dad," I whispered.

"I'm going home to my house, and you're going home to yours. Case closed."

CHAPTER TWENTY-FOUR

That night, Lucas brought takeout salads from Wegmans. Before he arrived, I'd been sitting at my computer and keying notes into my Dad spreadsheet, looking for patterns and precedents that might've precipitated his incident, some hidden-image stereogram, Magic Eye art, that could explain the how and why of Dad's brain degeneration. Was there a reason why the neurons spoke to each other at some moments, but not others?

"He wants you to get on with your life," Lucas said. "Let me help you."

I pushed around my food. For once, I was the one without an appetite. "What do you mean?"

"Do you remember a while back, I asked to look at your tax return? I wanted to see how you itemized your deductions, remember?"

"Okay . . . yes?" I said, confused. *Why this, now?*

"I want to give you your return back," he said. He reached into his computer satchel and pulled out my return.

"I really don't feel like discussing taxes now, Lucas." I wiped at my eyes and drank from my wineglass. The Zinfandel was warm with notes of black cherry, and I wanted to slide down into it like a warm bath. I looked across at Lucas with his glass of tap water and unbuttered bread and pale iceberg lettuce salad. I pushed my salad aside, picked up a piece of bread, and soaked it in the blue cheese dressing before shoving it into my mouth.

"I'm not planning to discuss taxes," he said. "I have a gift for you. I have an idea for you." He set my return aside, then reached back into his satchel and pulled from it a manila envelope, which he handed to me. "Open it."

I pried my fingernail under the metal tab and opened the top flap. Inside was a tax return. A 1040 in the top-left corner. "A tax return?"

"Look at it," he said.

I read the first line: Lucas James Anderson. The second line: Melissa Ann Fletcher.

"What's this?"

"It's us. As a tax return. A *pretend* tax return. Jointly filed."

"What?"

"We're definitely better off. I compared our individual returns to this one, if we were to file jointly. It would be beneficial." Lucas nodded vigorously.

I looked at Lucas oddly. "That's great, but I don't get it."

"Let's file jointly!" he said. "Let's get married. I want to be 'married filing jointly' with you."

Though stunned, I had no choice but to laugh—a gigantic, from the bottom of my belly guffaw. I laughed and smiled because up until now I was certain I was the biggest nerd I'd ever met. In front of me was Lucas, a man—a boy going through life as a man—proposing to me by filling out a future tax return.

And then it occurred to me that maybe my father was wrong. Maybe his assessment of my prospects was mistaken. I could have a life. A life as a jointly filed married couple.

"We're great together," Lucas said. "We're in the same field, practically. We have the same goals. Why not?"

My head swam. I was in no position to think clearly—with the wine, with my father, with a tax-return proposal. But I did ponder this question: Was that why people got married? Because they were in the same field—because when he spoke of someone having a high-income level, I was able to say, "So it wouldn't make sense to convert to a Roth IRA"? Because when I mentioned someone's thriving small business, he was able to say, "Of course, she does need to pay both sides of FICA"? Was it enough that the essence of our "same goals" was to make no changes in our lives? And was that even true of me anymore? Was Lucas's likeness to me a mirror, showing me everything that I didn't care for in myself? Was I the safety, stay-put girl I claimed to be, or might witnessing Lucas living my same life be just what I needed to understand that I craved more than that?

"You're sweet, Lucas," I said, and kissed him. "And I love your gift." And I did. From a creative perspective, from a unique proposal standpoint, for originality, I gave his effort—whether intentional or not—a solid ten.

"But . . . ?"

"But I'm not sure about marriage."

"I wouldn't expect you to give me an answer without thinking it over. Without charting out the pros and cons."

"Can you give me some time?"

"Of course," he said. "Absolutely. Do a Benjamin Franklin exercise: pros on one side, cons on the other."

What would Dad think about that? Of course I knew. He'd tell me that love and marriage were impulse purchases. That you bought in because you'd die if you couldn't have the guy, the life you wanted. Dad would tell me that love meant risking it all, charging through doors with no certainty of what was on the other side, betting against 100-to-1 odds.

"Where would we honeymoon?" I asked, testing him. "Italy?"
"If that's what you wanted," he said. My heart fluttered. "Or we could drive to Yellowstone. Nothing wrong with staying in the States."

That night, after Lucas had gone home, I got in my car and drove the few blocks down to the waterfront. Outside, I stared into the inky darkness and thought of Lucas and Dad and Joe. As I stared over the Potomac, I reminded myself that Joe wasn't mine. And Lucas was offering to be. And Lucas was everything I needed: steady, stable, risk averse. Good-looking, more than solvent, conscientious. And he would clean my car, every Saturday. And shine my pumps, even. And he would adore me. And never ask me to change. Lucas was lovely, and I was being foolish for not embracing him.

CHAPTER TWENTY-FIVE

Each day I picked up Dad and drove him to work. One morning we met with the Parkers. Toward the end of the meeting, Dad messed up the pronouns, twice calling Mr. Parker "she" rather than "he." The clients grew visibly uncomfortable, and later, after I walked them out and apologized for Dad being "a little off," I returned to Dad's office and told him what he did. With each blunder, his shame grew like a cancer metastasizing. The man with an open-door policy was now in the habit of shutting himself behind closed doors.

A few weeks later, Dad and I met with the Bradshaws. Dad admired the heck out of "Boomer" for his military service—two tours in World War II, and a later-in-life tour in Vietnam. Boomer was a pilot, and I was sure Dad would ask about the F-100 Super Sabres he flew. But today, Dad didn't ask, and when Boomer made reference to the nightmare of the Middle East, Dad looked up from his yellow pad, grinned his off-white dentures at him, and asked, "Did you serve?" Boomer looked at me, and I offered him a sad smile. When I walked Boomer out, I told him the truth, because he was the type of guy who would take it to his grave.

Lucas grew impatient. He wanted to know if I would marry him. Each time I saw him, he pleaded his case.

"Don't you want your father there?" he asked, pushing at my most sensitive button.

"You know how quickly the country club fills up," he said on another night, exploiting my need for advanced planning.

"The sooner we get married, the sooner we can combine our living arrangement. Imagine the savings."

"Give me time," I would implore. "With my dad being sick, it's just such a hard thing to think about."

"But Missy," he would press, "there's no *point* to waiting."

Lucas's pushiness and Dad's illness and my own weariness bit at me like a million tiny ants.

Every day I logged on to Facebook. Just to escape, just to stare at other versions of normalcy, just to see what people not affected by Alzheimer's were engaged in. Today I began a message to Joe:

> Dale Carnegie wouldn't be pleased with his once-top student, now Alzheimer's patient. No longer the king of making friends and influencing people, Dad's now making one mistake after another, forgetting people's names, mixing up pronouns. I feel so bad for him, and I know how much he loves coming into the office, but it's just so hard to watch him embarrass himself, addled so by this

horrible disease. I just want to tell him to stay home or on the golf course. It hurts me to see him sounding foolish.

I paused, felt guilty for taking up so much of Joe's time, for sharing the intimate details of Dad's illness, for talking to Joe when I should be confiding in Lucas. But I kept on.

I hope everything is great with you and the family. I hope your wife (Lucy, right?) doesn't mind that I write every now and then. Is it okay that I do? I saw from one of your recent posts that your daughter won a math award. That's so awesome. Does she like games? I wonder if she's ever played CrazyMath on her iPad. I have it on my phone. It's pretty fun.

CHAPTER TWENTY-SIX

JOE

I was in my van, stopped at a light and scanning the radio for a good song, when Missy's Facebook message chimed. I read it before the light changed. I read it again at the next red light.

I hope your wife (Lucy, right?) doesn't mind that I write every now and then.

No, Missy, she doesn't mind. First, she'd have to know. And second, in order to know, she'd have to be here. Last I heard, she was leading a reward trip for the lawyers with the most billable hours through New Zealand. And third, if she was here and she did know, I'd tell her that you were once my great friend and your father meant the world to me. But again, Lucy monitoring my FB account and questioning your message is kind of like worrying whether the kids are sneaking out at night to play laser tag with space aliens. Kind of irrelevant.

And yes, Katherine won a math award. Thanks for noticing, I would say to Missy, because some adult affirmation could go a long way for my daughter who seemed to be in the fight of her life.

I pulled around the back side of my office building into my marked parking spot right in front of the door, my name spray-painted onto the concrete. "Big shot with his own parking spot," I joked, ignoring the giant handicapped symbol in the middle of it. Inside, I pushed the button for the freight elevator. Nobody used it and I preferred the empty box to the crowded, paneled-and-mirrored one. People in this building were nice, don't get me wrong, but with Kate, Lucy, and all that was going on, I could use a few seconds of quiet.

In my office, I reviewed and responded to at least fifty e-mails. I met with my superior and discussed the new "anticipated demands" logistical model that had been beta tested over the last six months. We reviewed the results and talked about the bugs that needed working out. If we could get the program up to acceptable margins for error, we could get it into the field.

At eleven o'clock, I left the building and walked two blocks to Caribou Coffee. I was scheduled to meet Gunnery Sergeant Nate Reynolds there, one of the guys from my group last year. Up until his last deployment, Nate was a Scout Sniper Platoon Commander in the 1st Marine Division. Nate wasn't like the other guys, full of remorse over losing a limb. He celebrated his Alive Day and was already a pro in his wheelchair, fitted for his fancy prosthetic, a copper-bottom running leg under construction in a lab in California. But Nate also suffered from a traumatic brain injury, the signature injury of the Afghanistan and Iraq wars, as common as coming home from summer camp with poison ivy.

He was already sipping coffee in a corner chair next to a giant stuffed black bear, designed presumably to match the outdoorsy theme. "You and your friend been waiting long?" I said, signaling to the animal. Nate laughed, patted the bear. I shook his hand, and then went to the counter for a cup of my own.

"You look great," I said, slapping his back, sitting down across from him.

"It's a good trick," he said wryly. "Looking normal."

I knew exactly what he meant; there wasn't one of us that felt "normal" inside. There wasn't one of us who didn't wake up in the middle of the night, terrified and soaked with sweat. There wasn't one of us who didn't jump at the sound of a car backfiring.

Nate fumbled with the top of his coffee cup. "I look at myself in the mirror and I appear totally fine, like a guy who would make rational decisions, have rational thoughts . . . like a guy someone would ask for help if they were lost or had a flat tire. But that's the farthest thing from the truth."

"You're handling this like a champ," I said.

"People see my legs—my *lack* of leg—and they think that it must be the worst thing in the world, but goddamn, not having a leg is nothing compared to the hell that's going on in my head. It's like a freaking pinball machine in there."

"Did something happen?" I asked, because this wasn't usual talk for a guy with Nate's great attitude.

He took a swig of coffee. "My seventh grader needed help with pre-algebra the other night."

"Seventh grade pre-algebra is tricky business," I said, "brain injury or not."

Nate granted me a smile. "The thing is, before this, I was all about math. That was my job. Making calculations, assessing the arc, *doing the math*. But now, I stare at my daughter's math like it's hieroglyphics."

"You're no longer a sniper," I said. "You no longer need to hit the mark."

"You know what my daughter said? She said, 'It's okay, Daddy. It's okay that you're slow now.'"

I couldn't help but wince. "She didn't mean it like that."

"She's right, though!" Nate pushed on his thighs. "I am slow. And you're right: I'm no longer a sniper. I can barely figure out seventh-grade math. I don't know what the hell I am, anymore." Nate rubbed at his weary eyes.

"Part of your recovery is believing that you're more than a sniper. That you had a past, and now you'll have a future." Sometimes I heard the psychobabble spewing from me, and I wondered where it came from.

"All I ever wanted was to serve my country, and to be a good dad."

"And you've done an outstanding job at both," I said, "and you still are. Your service is just at home now. Right now your job is to take care of your family—to be that good dad and good husband. When you're well enough, the Marines will need you back, too. Just not the same way."

"I can't imagine that."

The two of us sipped our coffee in silence for a long moment before I said, "You're from Chicago, right?"

"The suburbs—Elmhurst."

"Have you been home since all this?"

Nate shook his head no.

"Do your parents still live there?"

"Same house I grew up in," Nate said.

"You have a good relationship with them?"

He nodded. "They're decent people. They deserve better than this." He pointed where his leg used to be.

"Sounds like they'll want to see you," I said. "Sounds like they've probably been waiting for you."

That just got a shrug and a look across the room, but I kept at it.

"Visit home," I said. "I don't know why, but there's something about sitting in your old childhood room, reclaiming your stuff, touching things that were important when you were a kid. The garage, the backyard, the tree house. Whatever it is, touch it, it'll replant itself on your memory."

"Did you do this?"

"I did, and you know what else I've done? I've reconnected with a friend from high school, and buddy, I can't tell you what it feels like.

It brings me right back—to high school, to being seventeen years old. When I read her messages or look her up in the yearbook, I feel hopeful, optimistic, like I did back then . . . like I couldn't wait for the next day. Do you remember what that felt like? To have so much *expectation* . . . like you were going to conquer the world?"

"I remember," Nate said.

"I do, too. I was so spring-loaded back then, ready to jump into the fire. I couldn't wait for a thing."

"You think that's good . . . to feel that way again?"

"You've gotta believe that the split second that changed your life— the brief moment that took your leg and bruised your melon—can't be the defining moment of your life. It was just an instant, a flash. Just *one* second out of millions of seconds. It doesn't get to own you."

CHAPTER TWENTY-SEVEN

On a cold day in February, Dad opened a can of soup and poured it into a stainless steel pot and put it into the microwave. The sparks and explosion that ensued were enough to cause a fire. Dad regained lucidity just in time to leave his house, to watch the flames engulf the kitchen. Had he not taken the extra ten seconds to go to the mantel on his way out and retrieve a framed picture of Mom and me, Dad would have never gotten injured. But the delay put him in the wrong place at the wrong time, just as a curtain whisked by, burning his right arm. A neighbor called 911, but the house was condemned for now, and Dad was hurt. He had no choice but to move in with me.

For the next month I relished caring for my father with the tenderness and concern a child bestows upon a newborn bird that has fallen from its nest. He was my injured baby and, if need be, I would have fed him drip by drip from a medicine dropper. The satisfaction I gleaned from making him his favorite meals, brewing decaf coffee afterward, and watching *Jeopardy!* with him was massive. At bedtime, I cleaned the burn on his arm, changed the bandage, and doled out his medication. I smoothed the covers on his bed and fluffed his pillows. I set a glass of water by his bedside, asked if he needed anything else. In the morning, I was up cooking eggs and bacon before he rose. I squeezed him fresh orange juice and opened the newspaper to the sports section. Together we drove into the office, and for these few weeks, I was happier than I had been in years. Dad would be okay, as long as I could take care of him. He just couldn't do it on his own.

Even so, in slight gradations, his personality changed. Most days he was grateful and appreciative. But some nights, he turned mean. He held my defects against me. Put me in front of the mirror and pointed out how pathetic I was. "Look at you, Missy. Playing house with your old man. You should be taking care of a husband and children. But instead you're playing June Cleaver with me."

Even in his state, Dad called me out. *Playing house* was exactly what I was doing. As if I were a child wailing for "five more minutes," I didn't want my playdate to end. I savored being the one who took care of Dad, even though I knew in my heart that he hated every emasculating minute of it.

"It shouldn't be this way, Missy," Dad said. "You've made some big mistakes in this life."

"Don't forget about Lucas," I said. "He asked me to marry him, remember?"

"You'd better grab onto him," Dad said. "Or it might be too late for you."

I settled Dad onto the sofa with an afghan tucked around his waist. When the sting of his words subsided, my rational mind told me that it wasn't my father talking. My father—never, ever—would speak of dreams being "too late" to pursue. My father was the consummate optimist, the one who could find beauty, hope, opportunity in any war zone. My father would never speak to me that way.

Meanwhile, Lucas continued to press me for an answer.

"I've got to be here for my father," I told him.

"But let's not forget about us," he said. "I want us to be together. If you waste the next year taking care of your father, that's one less year for us."

Forgive him, I told myself. *Pretend he didn't really just say "waste."* Forgive him because his mind tossed him *waste* when he really meant to say *spend.* Forgive him, because I now knew that a brain wasn't always the good friend I considered mine to be; sometimes brains set us up, sometimes they brought their buddies to hold your arms back so that they could punch you in the gut. Yet the blood was thrumming in my ears and all I wanted was to slap Lucas across the face, because whether he meant it or not, he just used the word *waste* in reference to my father.

"He's my father. I'm not abandoning him."

"Of course not. But there are people who could do for him what you're doing for him."

"I don't want to hire out my responsibility."

"Hiring a nurse to help you isn't giving up your responsibility," he said. "Let me at least do the research, find a service, and send you the information."

I had never been more ardently steadfast in a position. I wanted to take care of my father myself. Even so, capitulation was stamped on my forehead as visibly as a birthmark.

CHAPTER TWENTY-EIGHT

My father's agitation accelerated alongside the disease. I now kept him at home. Lucas had found a reputable service, and I had hired a nurse— a no-nonsense Jamaican lady named Dolly—to stay with him in the day. I didn't care for Dolly, but Lucas was right: I needed to gain some distance from Dad; I needed some hours in the office away from him. He begged to come with me like a dog scratching at the door.

As if there were a switch in him, he'd alternate between the two jobs he had in life: soldier and financial adviser.

Some days he rambled on for hours about Vietnam. In the murky water of his delusions, he would occasionally step on a dry rock and see for miles with mind-boggling clarity. He would rattle on about missions, spill out the names of soldiers, recall the head-splitting racket the Hueys made as they swept in over the thrashing treetops, whisper about the VC shadows shifting through the jungles, popping up out of tunnels.

Other days he was in his office, struggling in a near panic to protect his clients' life savings. He prattled and pleaded that he had to sell

Johnson & Johnson before ex-dividend day, that if he didn't dump Monkey Ward, it was going to be too late.

"Montgomery Ward went under fifteen years ago," I tried to tell him. "We don't have a position in it."

"You don't know what the hell you're talking about," he persisted. His sense of time and space was muddled, shaken. When I reminded him of the date, he looked at me as though we were living in some science fiction saga.

And then there were moments when he knew exactly who I was. Sometimes that was all right—sometimes it was lovely, he'd stroke my hand and say sweet things. But other times regret clouded his face, as though he was riddled with shame. "I never should have written that letter," he'd say. "But now I can't find it."

"What letter, Dad?" I asked, helping him look through drawers and his old briefcase.

"Did I send it to you when you were in college?"

"You sent me a lot of letters, Dad. Which one are you talking about?"

Then Dad would cover his face and cry. "I didn't mean it. You're perfect just how you are."

I would sit by him and press myself to his barrel chest and tell him that it didn't matter, that I was here—home from college—and that he shouldn't worry about it. Meanwhile, I searched my mind for the letters Dad sent while I was at school. They weren't substantive, just the usual confetti of Dad's optimism: *Here's some pizza money for my beautiful daughter with the beautiful mind! Here's an article I cut out about top women CEOs. Here's a wall calendar with photos of your beautiful Italy.*

Dr. Bergman upped his medication to the maximum dose, and for a few weeks, my father was back, at least in the mornings. He told me he couldn't even remember the things he said, but that I shouldn't believe any of them, other than the fact that he loved me. He made me promise that I would never believe what "Crazy Frank" said. He made me swear that I knew the truth: that I was his pride and joy, that God gave him the greatest gift the day I was born.

"I do," I said. "I believe you, Dad. I love you so much." I said the words, I meant them, but despite my greatest efforts, I could no longer look at him with eyes that saw him as Superman. I had seen ugly and cruel, and even though I knew he was not responsible for a word of it, I could no longer regard him the same way. His thousand-watt smile, his gleaming dentures, no longer looked like a stamp of approval. They now appeared oversized and discolored, and sometimes I wished he wouldn't open his mouth.

When the day-nurse, Dolly, arrived, Dad would look pleadingly at me. "Do you have to go?" He didn't like her. He told me she was lazy, sat around and watched soap operas all day. When he asked for his lunch, she harrumphed and made a big production of it, like she was doing him a big favor. Most days I prepared him a meal so that all she had to do was take it from the refrigerator.

I didn't care for Dolly either. She did the bare minimum; anyone could see that. But she helped Dad dress himself, and bathe, and use the restroom. She had to have a decent level of compassion in her to even choose such a field of work. Finally, though, I called the agency and asked them to send a different nurse. Of course they could, they had said, but I needed to provide a reason. Was there a problem with Dolly? Did I have a complaint? The thought of confrontation made me recoil. The last thing I wanted was a face-to-face altercation with her, the insinuation of wrongdoing. "No, no," I had backpedaled. "Never mind, Dolly is fine."

I texted myself a note to think of a reason why a new nurse was needed. A justification that wouldn't reflect badly on Dolly, but one that would get us a new, hopefully better nurse. A win-win.

Dad reached for my hand. "Do you have to go?"

I didn't have to go; I *wanted* to go. "Fletcher Financial needs me," I told him. "I'll be back soon." And left him in the care of exasperated Dolly.

And then there was Charlene, my mother, who Dad remembered every day. And forgot every day. A memory turned nightmare, *every single day.*

"Where's your mother?" Dad asked.

"Come on, Dad," I said, "we went over this just yesterday."

"Charlene!" he'd bellow, his hand to his mouth, his eyes darting wildly down the hallways.

"Dad, let's sit," I said, dragging him to the sofa. Next to him, I took his hands. "Dad, Mom died. Charlene died."

"No, no," Dad said, rising. "Where are my keys? I'll go look for her."

"Dad, Charlene died a long time ago. She was in a car accident. A big truck hit her broadside, don't you remember?"

"Well that can't be," Dad said. "Didn't she take you to school this morning?"

"Dad, Dad." I held his face in my hands. "Dad, look at me. I'm thirty-five years old. Mom—Charlene—died when I was only four years old. It's been you and me for a long time now."

Finally, Dad would understand. A healthy neuron would throw the ball to one of the other few healthy neurons, and the information would snap into place. When it did, Dad's face would twist and he would double over and the pain of hearing the truth would be as damaging as the first time.

Easter, this year, passed with little occasion. If not for Jenny—devoted, doting, dedicated Jenny—we might not have noticed. She cooked a beautiful glazed ham and two different pies, and the four of us—Dad, Jenny, Lucas, and I—sat around the small kitchen table, engaged in the strangest conversations. Dad hollering for Charlene,

Lucas attempting chitchat ("I was on the IRS website today . . ."), Jenny fussing over dishes, and me, staring numbly at the quirky players of my so-called family.

When I turned my attention from Dad, there was Lucas. I wanted to want Lucas, because I was tired of being alone. Yet the fantasies of my life with Lucas did not lay evenly atop my reality with him. I longed for him when we were apart. The thought of his companionship—anyone's companionship—was uplifting. But when the time came and we were together, I was left feeling empty, as if the movie had a depressing ending or the dessert wasn't as good as the description on the menu. Lucas barely knew my father before he was ill. He never spent time with him one-on-one, never fell in love with his giant heart. What Lucas knew was Dad now, and in fairness to Lucas—to anyone knowing Dad now—there wasn't much to love. But still. I needed Lucas to do better. I needed him to somehow erase the disgust from his face when looking at my father. I needed him to pretend better.

My only refuge was Joe, on Facebook, through the digital ether. He provided me with exactly what I needed: a recollection of my father, just the way I remembered.

"He's gotten really bad," I wrote to Joe one night. "He's a different person and doesn't remember me. I can't stand seeing him this way."

Joe wrote back:

> It's not him. Frank Fletcher loves his only daughter like a tree loves its last leaf. You're his world, Missy. Don't you forget that. His brain is not his own, but his heart is still beating, and I know it's beating for you. Forgive him a thousand times and know that this

disease has poisoned him and what he's saying isn't the truth, it's a delusion.

Remember when he took us to the Charles Town horse races in West Virginia? His goal wasn't to teach us to bet, it was to prove the absurdity of it. He gave us money to bet a trifecta, and of course, we lost. It's okay to gamble on love, you two. That's what Frank told us later, remember that?

"I remember," I wrote back. "That was an amazing day. How are your kids? You and your wife must be the happiest people on earth," I said. "You deserve it all, Joe. I'm overjoyed you've had such a nice life so far."

Then Joe responded:

I can't complain. But nothing's perfect, you know that. My life is good, but not anywhere near the idyllic picture you've painted. I have my kids. I can't complain. How about you, Miss? Do you see anyone?

My fingers hovered over the keyboard. Why was I afraid to tell Joe that I was involved with Lucas? He and I hadn't seen each other in fifteen years.

"Actually, I'm seeing someone," I said. "A very nice guy. I'm lucky."

"I'm glad you've found love," Joe wrote back, and as I read his words, I began to sob because I wasn't sure if I had found love. I had found something: security, comfort, reliability. Refuge, contentment, consistency. Or some other trifecta of safety and sameness.

CHAPTER TWENTY-NINE

On the twenty-eighth day of May, my thirty-sixth birthday, Dad's mood was particularly dark. I fed him soup, but he spilled it, and when I tried to clean it up, he shooed me away. "Let it be!" he scowled. And when I handed him his medication, he smacked the colorful pills out of my hand, sending them sailing in every direction. I had to move the table to find the green one. Hours later, he nodded off on the sofa and I hoisted him to standing with his arm around my shoulder. "Let's go to sleep, Dad. Let's go to sleep."

As we moved toward the bedroom, an agitated alertness overtook him, as though he were receiving enemy fire. "We need to get out of here," he snapped.

"Dad, it's me, Missy, your daughter. You're in my house in Alexandria. Everything is okay. Your brain is a little screwy, remember?"

Dad's eyes jutted in every direction.

"We're going to the bathroom, Dad. You're going to use the toilet and then go to bed."

"I don't need the head," he said, looking around.

"You should try."

"We've got to get out of here!"

"The toilet, Dad. You should try."

"Now's not the time," he insisted.

"Fine," I said, steering him into his room and sitting him on the edge of his bed. "Dad, listen. If you have to go during the night, you have to get up and walk to the bathroom. See the night-light? Dad, the bathroom, the toilet, okay? Dad . . . Do you understand, Dad? Dad, are you listening? Can you make it to the toilet, Dad?"

I left him, as he curled into the fetal position, ducking shells from the war that never left him, fighting another battle in his damaged mind.

The next day, Paul and I were presenting a plan to a new client when Jenny barged in. "Excuse me," she said with a wobbly voice. "Missy?"

When I met her in the hallway, she pointed to the phone. "Pick it up, Missy," she gasped, pointing to the receiver with a shaky hand. "Pick up the phone!"

As I reached for the receiver, I kept my eyes glued on Jenny, who had now covered her face with her finely manicured hands. Her little body bobbed. Paul had excused himself from the meeting, as well, and now stood next to Jenny.

"This is the Alexandria Police Department," the man said.

"Where's my father?"

"Miss Fletcher, we think you need to come home. Can you drive, or should we send a car?"

"I'm on my way," I blurted, dropping the phone and grabbing for my purse. When I reached Jenny, I lunged into her arms.

"I'll drive you," Paul said.

"I don't know what's going on," I said to Jenny. "I'll call you when we get there."

Jenny nodded but didn't speak, her worry rendering her catatonic.

Ten minutes later we rolled into the driveway of my town house. An ambulance was parked on the curb and my front door was wide open. There was a gurney being guided through the door and my father was on it. I ran from the car, rushing toward Dad—kicking off my flats and running across the lawn. He had been on a similar gurney just months earlier, following his fall. Then he was thrashing, agitated. This time he was motionless.

"Dad," I hollered, collapsing onto his chest. "Dad!"

My bare feet on the cool spring grass beside the sidewalk struck me as an omen. This was the season where life emerged from frozen soil. Dad loved the spring: the country club, the golf course.

"I'm so sorry, ma'am," a paramedic said. "We did everything we could."

I ignored this imbecile who was talking nonsense. I just needed to wake him up. *Remember, Dad,* I wanted to yell, *how you told me about the seeds? How they need to shed their shells and nearly destruct before they begin to grow? It's spring, Dad!*

"Dad!" I shook at his shoulders. "Dad!"

The paramedic placed a hand on my shoulder and tried to turn me around.

I tore away from him. "Dad, you have to feel the grass, Dad. It feels like spring! You'd love it. Dad, wake up. We need to get you out on the golf course!"

"Ma'am," he said, touching me again.

"Don't touch me!" I screamed, brandishing my fist at him like a knife. He held my gaze and when I saw in his eyes what I already knew to be the truth, I crumbled into the chest of this man I didn't know.

"I'm so sorry," he said.

"My father is dead?" I asked incredulously, because this wasn't how it worked. Superman wasn't supposed to die.

"It's okay, ma'am," he said.

I pulled away from him. "What happened?"

"We're not sure at this point," the EMT said. "Could have been a heart attack. Could have been a stroke."

I reached my hands for my temples. "Will there be an autopsy?"

"Most likely," he said. "With your permission."

My father was dead. His beautiful mind, with its uncanny gift for chitchat and making everyone feel special, had turned on him. I spied the sluggish nurse, Dolly, in the back of the room, crying. Paul was talking to her. I charged toward her like a deranged bull. My fury must have frightened her. She backed into a corner, pulled her knees to her chest, and covered her face as though I were going to hit her.

"What happened?" I asked her.

"I was in the bathroom," she said.

"How long were you in the bathroom?" I asked, trying to calculate if it were even possible for a man to have a stroke or heart attack, or choke, or whatever, in the time that she had used the facilities.

"We're trying to piece that together," Paul said.

"I was taking my break," she said. "I was watching my stories. I didn't hear anything."

My cheeks burned with fire. "Did you help him?" I wailed. "Did you give him an aspirin, did you try CPR? What did you do?"

"I didn't see any of it," she cried. "I was in the bathroom. I didn't hear him."

"Are you telling me you found him dead? That you did nothing to save him?"

"I'm sorry, I didn't know anything was happening."

"We'll figure this out," Paul said. He steered me away from her.

I slid my thumb across my phone. Five texts from Lucas: Can I come over tonight? Did you pay the deposit on the reception hall? Did you find a minister? Did you think about bridesmaids? I punched edit and, one by one, deleted every single message.

And then, there it was, my text to myself: NEW NURSE FOR DAD. REASON TO REPLACE DOLLY.

Had I not been such a coward—afraid of confrontation, fearful of offending Dolly—another nurse may have reacted differently to this situation. A better nurse might have saved his life.

Left in my care, my father died.

I killed my father. My cowardice made me a murderer.

Frank Fletcher was dead.

CHAPTER THIRTY

Frank Fletcher was dead.

My body was no longer whole—my limbs had been pulled from their joints, my oxygen stolen from me, my sight turned black. I was crippled, impotent, helpless. Just a second ago the sky was blindingly bright, the sun almost too much to bear without forming a visor out of my hand, the wet grass luscious between my toes. And then, like that, thunderclouds. Pure gray.

My breath: nothing but crackling gasps of regret.

The last words I had said to my father were the night before, urging him to use the toilet. "Do you understand, Dad? Dad, are you listening? The toilet, Dad." Bitchy, pedantic, humiliating words pouring from my stupid mouth, like a superiority-complex mom scolding her disobedient toddler for picking his nose.

The hate I felt for myself was teeming; the sight of my ugly face in the mirror nauseated me.

Dad was delusional; Dad had Alzheimer's; Dad was confused much of the time. But Dad wasn't terminal. I had no idea we were *there*. I had no idea that I'd never have the chance to say good-bye to him properly.

I had no idea that my last words would be a degrading critique of his bathroom habits.

If I had known. Of course, if I had only known.

"Dad," I would have said. "All my life you've said I was the one with the beautiful mind, but Dad, you were the one with the beautiful heart. All my schooling—high school AP classes, college, business school—all the reading and studying I did, taught me nothing as valuable as what you instilled in me: to care about mankind, to be generous to others, to pay it forward. To love without conditions, to take a chance on true love, to give it your all, even though you might lose everything. You are my hero, Dad."

But instead of professing my love and gratitude to the man who'd raised me alone, I chided him like a child who had spilled his juice. I couldn't hate my putrid self more.

Take me, too, I cried into my pillow. *Take me, too,* because without Frank Fletcher I was nothing much, never had been. Was never created to be anything more than an extension of my father. I was his appendage. He was my life source, and now, cut off from its nourishment, I would die, too.

I thought of Jenny, of how she loved to snip and transplant pieces of plants and flowers. She'd nestle them into the earth, then shrug. "Sometimes they take; sometimes they don't." I was just a snippet of Dad. Put me in the earth if you like, but I wouldn't take. I didn't stand a chance.

Being Frank Fletcher's daughter made me something, gave me value, validated my existence, but without him, I was just a girl too frightened to leave Virginia, too nervous to fire her father's indolent nurse, too scared to stick her tongue out and catch a drop of rain on the tip of it. I was Frank Fletcher's daughter, and without him, I was nothing.

Yet when I was his caregiver, when he was diminished and confused, and I was in charge, I'd felt important. The reality of this made me sick. I looked into the mirror and saw my disgusting self—stupid, scared me, who'd puffed up like a balloon as my father had been deflated. Dad knew it all along. He knew I could only be something in relation to him. If Death were a stock picker, if it profited from quality companies, then it just made a hell of an acquisition. And poor Life, forced to take the other side of the trade, was stuck with me. A speculative bet, at very best.

Three days passed. Lucas called, Jenny called; they showed up at my doorstep. They pounded on my door. I plodded zombielike to the peephole. "I can't," I muttered, benumbed to time or space. "I need another day." Still, the barrage continued: Lucas texting, Jenny forwarding e-mail condolences, cards slipped under my door.

"Honey, I need you to give me two minutes of your attention," Jenny pleaded. "I'm planning the service. I need to go through the details with you."

"You know what Dad wanted," I said in my listless stupor. "Whatever you think."

On the fourth night of living in this sleepwalking haze, I slid out of bed and onto the floor. I crawled on my hands and knees to my computer. I logged on to Facebook. I cradled my swollen, battered face in my hands. I had to tell Joe. I had to tell him Dad was dead.

"Dear Joe: Dad died."

Two words that had never shared space on a page before.

And with that, without sending the message, I slogged back onto the floor and belly-crawled to the sofa, where I grabbed the afghan and pulled it over me—all of me, head and all—and bawled for the next several hours, and then I slept. Bloated with shame and fat with regrets, I prayed to no one in particular to give me just one more day with my father.

I awoke beaded with sweat. I fished pieces of wool fibers from my mouth. I untangled myself, roused myself from my smog, and returned to the computer. I continued with my message to Joe.

He had a stroke and died. It's my fault.
I should have taken care of him myself.
Instead, I hired a nurse and she was
negligent—maybe, she was negligent. I don't
know. I just know I could have done better. I
should have done better. And now I'm stuck
with myself, and I don't want to be with me.
I feel vile, and I don't know how I'm going to
crawl out of this hole.

I hit "Send" and then returned to bed.

A few hours later, I heard my phone issue an e-mail. I reached for it. It was a message from Joe.

Missy, I'm so sorry to hear about Frank. I
can't believe he's gone. How can this world
survive without Frank Fletcher's enthusiasm?
What a guy. I'll never forget the day he and
I were out on the range, hitting balls. He bet
me I couldn't hit 250 yards and I told him I
could. "Hundred bucks," he said. He had
seen me hit that far before, so his motives
were a little transparent. It happened to be
right before prom, and I had told him the
week earlier that I wanted to take you to
the Chart House, but that I'd have to work
some overtime first. I have a feeling that that
$100 would have ended up in my pocket, no
matter what. Good ol' Frank. I hit the ball, it
sailed past the 250, and Frank just beamed,
handing me the two fifties. "Forget it," I said,

patting him on the back. "I don't want to
take your money." "You're like a son to me,
Joe," he said. I can still hear those words.

I smiled and cried at the same time because Joe remembered
my father so well, he remembered him like I did, got him like I did.
He knew that Frank was always in his corner. The memory of pre-
Alzheimer's Dad gripped at my heart with the pain and panic of holding
my breath a second too long.

There was more.

Missy, I know I'm overstepping here, but
you're talking to a guy who has the blood of
many men on his hands. I feel responsible
for each of them, and I know that will never
go away. They were in my charge. It took
a while, but I now know that I can't blame
myself for every detail that precipitated each
event. Just like you could not have predicted
the events leading up to your father's death.
Grief is heavy enough. That's all I'm saying.
Take it from a guy who knows. You don't
need to carry around guilt on top of it.

Oh my God. In my mind, Joe was still eighteen years old, idealistic,
indomitable. In reality, he was a man who had been to war three times.
He had the blood of men on his hands. He was a guy "who knew." He
carried his own heavy grief. This was for real. My dear, sweet teenage
boyfriend who I held in such high regard wasn't just a fantasy, he was
flesh and blood, heavy-hearted, forever burdened, and weighted down.

Thunder roiled through my chest and then my lungs were begging for air as the sobs came again. Only this time they weren't for my father and the loss of him, or me and my negligence. I now cried for Joe and all that he carried.

CHAPTER THIRTY-ONE

JOE

Frank Fletcher was dead.

I opened a search engine and combed through the pages until I found his obituary.

> *Frank Fletcher passed away on May 29. Frank was born in Chicago, Illinois, in 1945, though he spent most of his life in Alexandria, Virginia. He graduated from West Potomac High School, earned a BS in finance from George Washington University, and served in the United States Army. He was married to his high school sweetheart and loving wife, Charlene Hayes.*
>
> *Frank had a distinguished career at his own firm, Fletcher Financial, for forty-five years. Frank was an active member and past president of the Association for Financial Professionals, and was selected as one of the Top Ten Businessmen of the Year by the Alexandria Times. He was*

also a member of the National Association of Insurance and
Financial Advisors, and was honored by FINRA for his excel-
lence in service.

He is survived by his daughter, Melissa, two brothers, and
other fond relatives and friends. In lieu of flowers, expressions
of sympathy can be made on Frank's behalf to the Wounded
Warriors, a charity he supported and believed in.

At the end it gave me the information I needed. Services would be
held at Arlington National Cemetery on Saturday at one o'clock, with
a reception following at Christ Church in Alexandria.

I would go for just the night, to pay my condolences, to attend
the funeral. I owed that to Missy and to Frank, a guy who treated me
like a son. I needed to see Missy, to tell her again how instrumental
her father was in my life. I would assure her she'd be okay, even if it
might not seem that way—she could believe me, I knew this was how
it worked. It was true: she would go on. She was strong enough to live
without her father.

I called my mom and told her I needed to go to DC this coming
weekend. Just for the night. Could she watch the kids? After Lucy and
I were married and had kids, Ma and Dad moved up north to be near
us. Her kitchen in New Jersey was a replica of our kitchen when I
was growing up: flowered wallpaper dotted with her collection of old-
fashioned kitchen implements. I'd been staring at the handheld mixer
and potato masher my entire life.

"Where's Lucy?" Ma wanted to know.

"Out of town on business," I said. "You know that, Ma."

Ma harrumphed, and I imagined her pacing in the kitchen, wiping
down an already clean counter. "In my day, a mother didn't up and leave
just because she was tired of it."

"I know, Ma, I know," I told her. "What about the kids, Ma? Could
you watch them?"

"Of course I can watch them," she said indignantly. "I'd never turn my back on my precious angels."

That night, I told the kids I had a funeral to attend this weekend. I'd be gone for about twenty-four hours.

"Unless you decide to stay longer," Kate said in the sulky thirteen-year-old voice I never thought I'd hear from her. This was my kid who used to love everything, my daughter who couldn't wait for tomorrow, the light of my life who would decorate our house with streamers and balloons and homemade posters for every occasion, even Arbor Day and Chinese New Year.

"Kate," I said, raising my eyebrows at her. "I'll be back on Sunday morning."

"Whose funeral is it, anyway?" she asked. "Which of your buddies stepped on an IED this time?"

"Enough, Kate," I snapped, because her moping about her own life was one thing, but talking flippantly about the guys who put their lives on the line for our freedom was another.

"Sorry," she said. She looked up through her mop of hair, then pulled it back and twisted it into a bun. Through the click of my eye's shutter, I saw her when she was five years old, all eyebrows and cherry lips, before her heart registered pain.

"This guy was a soldier," I said. "But not in this war. Vietnam, years ago. I went to school with his daughter. He was very nice to me back in high school. He helped me figure out what I wanted to be when I grew up."

"Do you mind if I say war sucks?" Kate looked up at me, smiled just a bit. "All of them."

We were all casualties of war, and she knew it.

CHAPTER THIRTY-TWO

On the seventh day of my life in a world without Dad, I rose and showered and met Jenny for lunch. At Ellie's, we ordered soup and salad.

"Lucas has been calling the office," Jenny said. "He said it's been hard to get through to you."

"I don't know what to say to him," I said. I dipped my spoon into the mulligatawny and watched the steam bellow upward.

"He's concerned."

"I know," I said, "but he's pushing me too hard." I returned the spoonful of soup to its container.

"He's just trying to help, don't you think?"

"I'm sure."

"I like him," Jenny said. "You two are so much alike."

My eyes stung. My cheeks burned.

"Oh, honey, what did I say?" Jenny reached for my hand, curled hers around my palm.

"We *are* a lot alike," I said, dabbing at my eyes. "But I don't know if that's such a good thing. Is it best to be the same?"

"Don't overthink it, honey," she said. "There's no math involved in this. You either like him or you don't. You either love him or you don't. I'm just saying the two of you are peas in a pod. He doesn't push you to be anything you're not . . . and that's good, because you're perfect just how you are."

I blew my nose into the scratchy napkin. "Being with Lucas is like looking at my reflection. For as paralyzed as I am to go outside of my comfort zone, seeing him nestled safely in his irritates me. I want to shout: Eat the oysters! Travel across the border! Invest in something other than munis!"

Jenny smiled. "For as long as I've known you, you've sought the calm amidst the chaos."

"True enough," I said, picking up my spoon again.

"Maybe it's time for you to revise your understanding of yourself."

I took a small sip of soup, just big enough to scorch my tongue. "Meaning?"

Jenny looked at me as if I already knew the answer. "Meaning . . . perhaps the problem lies in the fact that you're not really the 'safety girl' I always hear you say you are. Inside there is a real tiger. After all, you're Frank Fletcher's daughter."

CHAPTER THIRTY-THREE
JOE

On Saturday morning, Ma was at our house by six. By six thirty, bacon was already sizzling on the cast iron, and pancake batter was being whisked in a mixing bowl. A bag of mini-marshmallows slumped over her handbag, ready to float atop the kids' hot cocoa.

Instead of driving my work-issued van to the airport, I called for a cab. When the driver honked in front of the house, I wheeled out my small suitcase. At the sight of me in full dress uniform, the cabbie leapt up the steps to retrieve my bag. Nice guy. Like most people do, he mentioned his connection to the military, to the war. "My brother was in Fallujah," he told me.

An hour later, I had made it through the TSA checkpoint, where I'd explained preemptively that I would most assuredly set off their metal detectors—I patted my leg, explained the prosthetic, the titanium joints in my knee, and they moved me along. I found my gate and boarded on time, and when the plane landed at Reagan, I made my way to the cab line. When it was my turn, I slid into the back and directed the cabbie to Arlington National Cemetery.

Once there, I ducked into the welcome center and looked up on the wall at a computerized schedule of funerals for the day. More than twenty-five of them. Frank Fletcher, Section 66, Grave 7708. I pulled open a map and located the spot. In no time, I was working my way down the walkway, along the Women in Military Service Memorial, wending my way by President Taft and then heading north and then east.

I arrived just as the inimitable sounds of "Taps" issued from the bugle. I slipped in behind a stand of mourners and saw Missy seated in the front row. At the sight of her, my heart cannonballed. She was beautiful. She was exactly the same. I fought the urge to rush toward her, to hug her, to touch her shiny, coconut-scented hair. I wanted to hold her and look into her eyes and launch into a string of sentences that all began with "Remember when we . . .": Remember when we walked down by the lake? Remember when we read *Macbeth* together every night for a month straight? Remember when we rode the Ferris wheel at the carnival and ate fried dough until we were sick?

Good God, was that Jenny next to her? She was Frank's assistant way back when, too. She had her arm around Missy, consoling her. Jenny always loved Missy.

A guy holding a stack of programs slid in next to Missy. Tall, Nordic. He leaned toward Missy, whispered something to her, kissed the side of her head. Then he glanced around and looked at his watch. *What a jerk. Who the hell was this guy and why was he in such a hurry?*

The service proceeded. Each speaker gushed on about Frank's service, his generosity, his loyalty. There were CEOs and ministers and community leaders, all who knew Frank personally. There were army buddies and neighbors and a much older brother. I watched as Missy accepted comfort from her boyfriend. Occasionally she'd bury her face into his shoulder. Once he cradled her head. He was caring for her. She was accepting his care. Okay, maybe he wasn't a total jerk.

The service ended and guests rose from their seating. Missy stood, turned around, and wiped her eyes. She scanned the crowd. Instinctively, I ducked, shielded my face with my hand, punched on my cell phone that was turned off. All of a sudden, the idea of Missy seeing me made me nervous as hell.

My heart hammered as if I had just been cornered by a group of insurgents with machine guns. I shouldn't be here. I had no reason to be here. I felt entirely out of place, woozy and disoriented, like I had been air-dropped into a foreign land where I didn't speak the language or know the customs.

Missy and I were old friends from high school, Facebook buddies. She had a boyfriend and a life, and all of a sudden I couldn't see the point in my interrupting it . . . if even just to pay my condolences. Not long ago I was a guy with a story to tell: wife, kids, service. I was someone who could have offered Missy support. But who was I now? How could I even explain my situation to someone else when it was still a mystery to me? My wife, gone and traveling all of the time. Our marriage on the way out. My oldest daughter, depressed and struggling. Me, a guy who had spent his life "in the field," now a desk jockey with one leg and a chronically achy knee.

If I went to Missy, if I offered my condolences, what would be the upside? It was nice of me to come? It showed how much I cared for her and for Frank? But what was the downside? An ex-boyfriend showing up could possibly be an issue for Missy's current boyfriend. I'd hate to think of landing any unpleasantness in her lap. Talking to Missy could have the effect of taking our friendship to a new level. Perhaps we'd message more on Facebook. What good would that do, for her? For me? And what would it do to me to see her up close, to hold her . . . even just her hand? It would make me love her all over again, and since

I was a married/separated guy with more issues than most, how could that be a good thing?

I turned and headed in the direction of the visitors' center, but this time I exited in the opposite direction, the long way—via the Kennedys, by way of the Civil War Unknowns, ending up back at the parking lot. A row of at least five cabs sat at the curb.

I slipped into the first one. "To Clarendon," I told the driver. I gave him my cousin's address.

That night, in my cousin Frankie's basement, I drank more beer than normal and played video games that I would never buy for my kids—*Grand Theft Auto* and *Call of Duty*. When I could no longer see straight—from the beer, from the games, from the enormity of the day—I crashed on his sofa.

"We have a guest bedroom," Frankie said. "Janet made it up for you."

"If you don't mind, I'm fine right here."

"Suit yourself," he said, and tossed me a water bottle. "Looks like you're going to need this."

In the night I awoke disoriented and covered in sweat. My eyes darted wildly around the room. I gasped for breath, felt the hammering of my heart. I pulled off my sopping T-shirt and wiped my face, grabbed at my hair. It was the same dark and dusty dream: I had stumbled upon a Taliban—two shots to the chest, one to the head. When the dust cleared, I watched as his children—presumably—tumbled out through a doorway and stormed his fallen body. Two girls—one maybe ten years old, the other probably seven—and a toddler boy on the hip of the older one. Kate, Olivia, and Jake. I told myself it wasn't the same; that those kids weren't Kate and Olivia and Jake. That those kids had grown up in this war zone and had seen horror on a daily basis. But still, three kids crouched over their dead father. The awfulness in their eyes. I would play that tape for the rest of my life.

Waking up feeling pure terror was normal—thank you very much, Afghanistan—but the frequency of the nightmares' visits did nothing to dilute the sheer shock of them. They were always the same—an instant replay of horrific events I'd seen, over and over. As if my mind could never move beyond them. As if a few seconds on the front line reigned over every other memory, past or future. I knew better than to give in to the bad guys, but damn it, in my sleep, they always seemed to win.

I sat up and worked on my breathing, a technique I'd learned along the way to deal with the night terrors: Inhale, exhale. Inhale, exhale. Inhale, exhale. Touching something real helped, too. I looked around, found one of Frankie's son's teddy bears. I reached for it, held it against my chest. Squeezed it like I was a little kid. God, it felt good to burrow my chin into something soft.

I peered around the room—at the posters on the wall, the black and chrome of Frankie's media room—and pretended I was sixteen again, a teenager who hadn't yet been to war, hadn't yet been married. Who knew only two things: the taste of Missy Fletcher's lips, and that the future was going to be awesome.

CHAPTER THIRTY-FOUR

A week after Dad's service, I prepared to face the task I had been dreading. I gathered the stack of legal documents, printed off Dad's most current investment statements, looked up values for his defined benefit and defined contribution plans, pulled from the file cabinets his life insurance policies, and spread it all out on the conference room table.

It was time to do the work I had done for so many other clients. It was time to file the claims, contact Social Security, request a tax identification number for the estate. It was time to take inventory.

I dug into the papers. When there is a married couple, and the first one dies, not much happens by way of estate planning. Because of the unlimited marital deduction, the majority of the assets pass from one spouse to the next—easily, no tax due. Where there are qualified assets—IRAs, 401(k)s—there is a beneficiary designation, and they too, pass seamlessly to the surviving spouse, and he/she assumes the contracts as his/her own. But at the death of the second spouse—as was the case with my father—there is work to be done. Unless every single asset has been placed in trust, or transferred via a beneficiary designation, the estate needs to be probated. Probate: the legal process to verify a will.

Because of this, we always tried to get our clients to title as many assets as possible in their revocable trusts.

In my methodical way, I began to chart Dad's financial life, as I would with any other client. First on my yellow legal pad, and then transferred into my spreadsheet, I began to build Dad's net worth. None of this was a surprise to me; Dad and I talked openly about his finances, and of course, the bulk of his investable dollars was with our firm, and thus, under my management. Four hours later, as the sun began to set, and the conference room had grown shades darker, I had completed my task. Dad was a wealthy man.

Jenny leaned in. "Honey, take a break."

"I'm wrapping up for tonight," I assured her.

Tomorrow I would look through the legal documents, even though I was with Dad in his meetings with Roger when they were drawn up and knew, for the most part, what they instructed. A large portion of his assets would be given to a variety of charities, those causes that Dad held so dear. He left money to the "locals," as Dad called them: the county library, the Rotary Club, the hospital, the Boys and Girls Club. He left money to the veterans: the Wounded Warrior Project, the Fisher House, the Paralyzed Veterans of America. He left money to my alma maters and to his: George Washington University, William & Mary, the Wharton School.

And a large chunk would go to me, outright. Dad and I cautioned every client against giving money unreservedly to their children. "Put it in a trust," Dad would say. "Give it to them in thirds; that way they have multiple chances to learn some 'life lessons' before getting it right. Just in case." Even so, Dad never worried about me. "No one has her head screwed on tighter than you, Missy," he'd say. "My money is your money. Do what you want with it."

As I stacked up the volumes of paperwork, my hand paused on the life insurance policies. I knew the New York Life policy would be paid to Dad's irrevocable trust, to pay for the estate taxes. The Colonial Penn life policy was for me. The Principal policy was for the Milton Hershey School for underprivileged children he supported so fervently. The last one, the John Hancock, I couldn't remember. I flipped to the back of the policy, to the copy of the handwritten application, and saw that my father had named Paul Sullivan as its beneficiary. My mind was short on a ready answer as to why Dad had a policy with Paul as beneficiary, but my mind was also spent, and grieving, and ready to crawl into bed with a plate of leftover pasta and a carton of pistachio gelato. If I saw Paul on my way out, I'd ask him. Otherwise, I was too weary to ponder, and would look into it tomorrow.

As I packed my bags, I saw that Paul was still in, but busy listening in on a conference call. I waved good-bye.

At home, I found Lucas sitting on my front steps, reading the *WSJ*. When he saw me, he glanced up over the rim of the paper. "Hi there."

"Have you been sitting here long?"

Lucas folded the paper neatly in half. "I called Jenny a while ago. She said you were on your way home."

I found my key and let us in. "I'm starving," I said, opening the refrigerator and pulling out a Tupperware dish of casserole.

Lucas took the Tupperware from my hands. "Let me take you to dinner. Your favorite—Pier 6. Soup, bread, a nice fish dinner, a few glasses of wine. Dessert and coffee."

"You don't like any of that," I said. "I don't mind eating here."

He pushed the hair from my face, traced his finger along my cheek. "I want to take you out," he said. "I want to see you happy."

"What about you, Lucas?" I asked. "What would make you happy?"

"If you accepted my proposal," he said. "If you agreed to marry me."

I could marry Lucas. Why was I putting him off, anyway? If not for Lucas, I would be utterly alone. I didn't want to be alone anymore.

"I do," I said, reaching up and kissing his cheek. "I accept."

Lucas kissed me and I let him, closing my eyes and melting into the idea of being married. And then I grabbed my purse and allowed Lucas to take me to dinner.

Later, after Lucas drove me home, I brewed a cup of decaf and carried it to my desk. I logged on to Facebook and stared at Joe's photo. I needed to remember that he left me.

One night—after a wintery January day of my college sophomore year—Joe showed up at my school. We had been officially broken up for at least six months by then, so seeing him in the lobby of my dorm was an apparition no less painful than seeing my deceased mother. "What are you doing here?" I asked.

"I can't stand that you're mad at me."

"I'm sorry that breaking my heart has been so tough on you," I said snidely, though my insides were simmering.

Joe dug his hands into his pockets—his Levi's 501s that fit him so perfectly. "I guess I deserve that."

"You didn't sign a contract," I said, hearing the unusual cutting tone to my voice. "You promised that you'd love me forever—'Never not,' remember? But I suppose it wasn't in writing. Just talk."

"It wasn't just talk," he said. "I meant it."

"But . . ."

"But I don't see how it could work."

"Why are you here?" I asked wearily.

"I don't want you to be upset. I don't want you to be mad at me. I want us to be friends."

"Fair enough," I said tersely. "Let me let you off the hook." I held my hand out for Joe to shake. "Friends."

"Missy," Joe pleaded.

"We'll 'never not' be friends," I said. "I've got to go." Back in my dorm room, I stared out my window and watched as Joe walked away.

CHAPTER THIRTY-FIVE

The next morning, I repositioned myself at the conference room table. I'd downloaded, printed out, and completed death claims for the first three life insurance policies. When I got to the John Hancock, I started on page one. The owner wasn't my father; it was Paul. Thus, Paul was the owner and the beneficiary; my father's only role was as the insured. This was typically the structure for a buy/sell agreement, where one partner buys a policy on the other so that there is ready money at the time of death to buy out the surviving spouse. I leaned back on the two legs of the chair and tapped my pencil to my mouth. Then I reached for the stack of legal documents—will, revocable trust, irrevocable trust, power of attorney, medical directive—until I uncovered a sealed manila envelope with my name on it. My heart hammered as I opened it and pulled from it a single sheet of thick bond paper.

"Missy," the letter read. "Call Roger Price. He recently updated some of my papers. He'll explain to you the changes I made. I hope you understand. Your old man loves you more than words, and he just wants you to be happy."

"Jenny!" I attempted to yell, but it came out more like a strangled cry. "Jenny! Do you know anything about Dad changing his legal docs?" Jenny rushed to my doorway. "I don't, sweetheart. I'm sorry."

"Where's Paul?"

"He's meeting with a client off-site."

I picked up the phone and attempted to dial Roger, Dad's long-time attorney, but my hands were shaking and I misdialed three times. "Damn it!" I tried again. Roger answered. "It's Melissa Fletcher," I said. "I need to speak with you."

"How are you doing, Missy?" he asked. "You hanging in there?"

"I'm fine, Roger, thanks, but Dad left me a cryptic note here to call you. What's up?"

"Can I come over?"

Roger was only two streets over, so it didn't take him long before he was sitting across from me in the conference room. "How are you doing, Missy?" he asked again.

I crossed my arms. "With all due respect, Roger, can you please let me know what's going on?"

"Missy, calm down."

"No, Roger. You tell me what's going on." I pushed back from the table, began to pace.

Roger lifted his reading glasses onto his forehead and looked at me squarely. "As you know, your father set up the business so that he and you were sole owners, with him owning a 70 percent share and you owning a 30 percent share. At his death, his 70 percent share would transfer to you, making you full owner of Fletcher Financial."

"I'm aware of that structure."

"What you don't know is that your dad changed the language, just a bit. He has now left you 21 percent of his shares, thus giving you 51 percent. The remaining shares are now an 'option,' meaning you have the option to keep them or sell them to Paul Sullivan. Your dad was hoping you would choose to sell to Paul. That's what the buy/sell agreement and the John Hancock life insurance policy is for. For Paul to buy you out."

"Why would he do that? Did he think I needed Paul to co-own the firm with me?" I sifted through this new information, finding nothing but senseless clumps.

"Your father wanted you to have options."

The vein in my neck throbbed. "Dad led me to believe that the business would be mine, should anything happen to him."

"It still is, Missy. If that's what you want. And if it's not, you can let Paul buy out some of your shares."

"But I could have sold shares to Paul anyway. I didn't need him to spell that out to me."

"Missy, your father left you a letter. Read it. Think about it. Then call me."

With that, Roger pushed back from his chair. He held out the letter for me; I didn't take it.

"How did I not know about any of this?"

"Just read the letter, Missy. Call me later . . . or tomorrow . . . or the next day. There is no rush." He placed his hand on my shoulder, but I felt nothing but revulsion. I twisted from him.

Roger dropped the letter on the table, a crisp white envelope with Dad's all-caps handwriting: MISSY.

Once Roger left, I brought the letter into my office and locked the door. I pulled it from the envelope. I unfolded my father's words.

Dear Missy,

Watching you grow has been the biggest thrill of my life. If only your mother could have seen you. What can I say, Missy? You've never let me down. You've been a good girl. You never got into trouble. You earned the best grades. You've been obedient and kind and good-natured. I couldn't have asked for a better daughter.

What I do want, is for you to ask more of yourself. I want you to be brave, Missy. I want you to get out of town. Explore. At the time of this writing, you're thirty years old and you've turned into the best financial planner and investment manager out there. I hope you're happy that you've chosen this career. I'm thrilled to have you by my side. But Missy, if you want to do something else, I want you to know, you can.

As for Fletcher Financial, you call the shots. Missy, I want you to be happy. But I also want you to be scared, and nervous, and unsure. Get out of this life you're in, Miss. Get out of your comfort zone. Let Paul run the business. You—take your heaps of money and do something amazing. Help people. See things. I want you to be thrown off course. It's exhilarating, Missy. To "not know." You were never meant to live in my shadow, my dear. Be brave!

You cannot discover new oceans unless you have the courage to lose sight of the shore.

CHAPTER THIRTY-SIX

How dare he? How dare my father make changes to our firm's structure without consulting with me? How dare he scheme with Paul and Roger behind my back, like I was a little girl who needed protecting? How dare he claim to know more about me than I knew about myself?

And how dare he sucker punch me when I was down.

And how dare he say that I wasn't brave.

And how dare he use one of his tired old clichés on me!

How dare he!

I reached for a throw pillow on my sofa and screamed into it. My blood was so hot the outside of my skin was warm to the touch.

Leave, some rogue rebel in my mind blared. *Leave!* But it was ten o'clock in the morning, and Jenny and I had a day's worth of work to tackle, and a client was coming in at one o'clock, and I was Missy Fletcher, who had never once played hooky in her life, who had shown up at school and work every day, whether I had cramps or a fever or a migraine. I was Missy Fletcher, who wasn't wired to just leave work because she was so furious she could hurl her three computer monitors out the window.

I gulped for air, exhaled like I was stoking a fire, and considered that Jenny and Paul and Roger were all waiting for me to address the situation. Paul—my dear, sweet big-brother-like Paul—was nothing more than a little sneak. In the five years since Dad concocted this scheme, Paul and I had worked hundreds of hours together, joked, shared, and never once did he say a word about their nefarious little agreement.

How dare Dad say I wasn't brave?

How dare he think I would give up my entire life's work, just because he gave me permission to leave?

How dare he insinuate that I was leading a false life?

Stay, my mind now said. Stay in this office until everyone else went home. Stay until midnight and then return at five in the morning. Glare at Jenny and Paul and Roger, and spread your arms wide to protect your territory. *Mine.* This is my office and don't you dare encroach on my territory. *Stay,* my ears echoed. Draft a letter to the clients telling them that I was now in charge. That they needn't worry about Dad's absence because Melissa Fletcher was on board and, while I might not be able to spin the yarn like Dad did, I had a genius IQ and portfolio returns that outperformed my peers'. You may be my employee, I would say to Paul, but I'm in charge. You run everything by me, I'd say, and don't even think of swiping so much as a Post-it note from your desk, because everything here belongs to Fletcher Financial.

Leave, my watery eyes begged. Go home and cry properly, and mourn the loss of your father, and grieve over the fact that your deepest fears have been confirmed, that he didn't really believe in you. *Leave,* go home and start a notebook for your wedding. Do what you do best: comparison shop, chart, and analyze. Go home and Excel spreadsheet your way through your marriage. And hook your claws into Lucas, because who are you kidding—he is quite attractive compared to what is out there, considering the pool of still-single guys who would be interested in a thirty-six-year-old rather than a fun twenty-one-year-old. *You ain't gonna do better than him, Missy.* You two go off with your jointly filed tax return and pocket protectors filled with mechanical pencils and Lucas's white bread and ham sandwiches and you with your stupid pistachio gelato routine. Live your boring, predictable, perfectly sanitary and safe life. It's who you are, Missy.

For the next hour, I tapped the tips of my fingers on the wood of my desktop and stared out the window, considering how the hell I was going to get out of my airless office while saving face. I was Missy Fletcher, the safety girl prepared for every contingency, so of course I had a fire escape rope ladder in my closet. I could always use that.

In a thousand ways, this was worse than I'd first imagined. When Roger told me the terms, I thought it was lame of Dad to think I needed a partner to run the firm. Merely needing a partner now seemed like an innocuous little stipulation compared to the real reason for Dad's plan: his belief that I needed a shove, that without his suggestion I would stay until I was ninety years old. Maybe I would have. Who cared!

Another hour later, I emerged from my office with a stack of files.

"Here," I said, slapping them onto Jenny's desk. When she ducked as though I might hit her, I said, "Sorry."

"Oh, honey," she said.

I shook my head. "Not now." I rambled off ten minutes of instructions, and asked her if she had completed certain other tasks.

At one o'clock, two of our clients came in, and today, rather than sitting in meekly on the appointment, letting Dad or Paul take the lead, I led the meeting myself. I projected the clients' statement from my laptop onto the screen. I used my red laser pointer to explain the allocations, the changes made, the percentages held, the pie chart that showed the breakdown. It was fine until I found myself rambling endlessly about a certain municipal bond's yield and tax-free status, and I could see the clients' eyes glassing over. It was obvious I'd gone too far, told them too much, and it was boring and confusing to them. They looked at me as if to say, *We hire you to do this stuff for us.*

I shook off their glazed-over stares, closed my eyes for a split second and pretended that I was Frank Fletcher. "How does Camilla like UVA?" I asked of their oldest daughter. Just that easily, the clients perked up— the mother beamed, and the father pulled out his phone to show me a photo he snapped of his gorgeous daughter in her dorm room.

God gave us two ears and one mouth so that we can listen twice as much as we talk, I heard my father say.

So even though I had planned to review their portfolio's dividend scale and projected income, I stayed quiet and just assured them that they were still on track, that there was plenty of money for Camilla's college, for their retirement.

Later, when I saw Paul in the break room, he put his hand on my shoulder and said that we should talk.

"Don't touch me," I said, yanking away my shoulder. "Ever."

Paul's face crumbled and his caterpillar eyebrows joined together into one long awning. "Missy, it's not what you seem to think. I'm happy to do whatever you want to do. It was your father's plan."

I laughed mockingly at the baldness of his lie. "Yeah, right."

"It's true," he interjected. "Your father—"

"Don't talk about my father like you knew him." I had never been the impertinent kid who talked back to anyone. I should have tried it sooner. Being a cheeky, know-it-all brat felt just right.

Io vorrei del succo di frutta. Io vorrei un caffè. Io vorrei del pesce. I tried, but that night I had no patience for my Rosetta Stone CD. I hit "Eject" on my car deck, and when the disc slid out, I grabbed it and snapped it in half, cutting my finger in the process. I threw the two broken half-moons onto the floor. I held my cut finger to my mouth.

At home, even though I had a piece of salmon defrosted in the fridge, I went straight for the pistachio gelato. When Lucas called at seven o'clock on the dot, I told him what I had uncovered today: Dad's nefarious plan, Paul's conniving conspiracy, Roger's culpability to the crime.

"This is a no-brainer," Lucas said. "You simply maintain your controlling shares. Everything will stay exactly as it is."

Everything will stay exactly as it is.

"He should have talked to me about this," I rebutted.

"Why, Melissa?" Lucas said. "Your father set this up perfectly. He gave you the option to stay put, something you would have claimed you wanted if he'd ever asked you, or scale back, something you might not have said in front of him."

I swallowed a colossal spoonful of gelato. "But how did he know that I would consider 'scaling back'? What made him think that? Wasn't I committed enough?" My eyes filled without permission and then spilled over. I had never cried with Lucas, and didn't want to do it now.

Lucas said, "He was just being nice—"

"Yes," I interrupted. "But he could have just given me the shares. If I wanted to sell to Paul, I would have. He didn't need to write the pathetic-Missy missive."

"The point is," Lucas said, "you're choosing the business, so why does it matter? He was wrong in thinking that you might choose otherwise. You *are* the business, Melissa. It's who you are. What would you be without the business?" Lucas made this argument as if it were all so obvious. Melissa Fletcher had no identity other than as a financial genius.

"You're right." I nodded. "It's who I am. Why would he think differently?"

"Exactly."

"Do you want to come over?" I asked.

Lucas was at my door within half an hour. I let him stay the night because he was the guy who asked me to be no one other than myself. He liked who I was and didn't need to give me a menu of options: (1) stay who you are: boring, predictable, safe; (2) turn into someone else: better, interesting, traveled; (3) become someone even more superior than the improved version of you: bold, gregarious, social—in other words, Frank Fletcher.

When Lucas fell asleep, I turned from him and curled into a ball. I closed my eyes and imagined what it would be like to travel to Italy, to walk into a café, to order a cappuccino or a glass of wine. I envisioned the Tuscan countryside, groves of olives, stucco walls obscured by ivy. I squeezed my eyes shut and imagined the oil-drenched olives, the crusty loaves of bread, the pasta, and the seafood. And then I remembered the flight attendant escorting me off the last airplane I'd attempted to board.

At two in the morning, I slipped out of bed and went to the bathroom. I stared into the mirror, gawking at my reflection as if I had never seen myself before. *Who the hell are you, Melissa Fletcher?* I pulled my hair back into a ponytail, studied my makeup-less face, my plain-Jane features and childish peaches-and-cream complexion. I opened the drawer of the vanity and fluttered on three coats of black mascara. I lined my lips red and filled them in with a scarlet matte lipstick. I pulled black eyeliner across the rim of my lashes. *Who the hell are you, Melissa Fletcher?* Was it even possible to be someone different? I lifted my chin, puckered my lips, raised a flirty eyebrow. Maybe I could fool a few. Yet through the cake of heavy makeup, I could still see little me.

I crept into the kitchen for a sip of juice, then sat down at my computer and logged on to Facebook. I pulled up Joe's profile. His younger daughter, Olivia, was hamming it up for the camera. In the background, I could see the older daughter cozy in a recliner, reading *The Hobbit*. She looked like me, back in the day, spending my time with characters in books instead of friends at sleepovers.

I started a pretend message to Joe, one written by the girl with red lipstick and heavy eyeliner. A message written by a girl who had another man in her bedroom. "I've loved you for as long as I can remember. I loved everything about you. I still love you." One character at a time, I backspaced until my message was deleted. Then I washed my face and curled up on the sofa.

I stayed awake until dawn. At five in the morning, I called the office and waited for the message machine. When Jenny's sweet voice asked that I leave a message, I told her I would be out this week. I told her I needed some time to think things over. As an afterthought, I told her I was fine, no need to worry, and that I was sorry if I was harsh with her. When I hung up the receiver, I felt as light as a meringue. Then I returned to my bedroom.

At six o'clock, the alarm on Lucas's phone trilled. He rolled over and kissed me. "Time to wake up," he said. "Early bird gets the worm."

"I'm not going in today," I announced. "I'm staying home. I'm going to cook all day. Maybe take a nap. I might watch an Italian film later."

Lucas looked at me as though I'd just announced my enlistment in the circus. "Why?"

I buried my face in the pillow. "I need some time to think things through."

"Get up, Melissa!" he said with mock cheer. "Grab a shower, put on your power suit, pour a cup of coffee, and get to work. Nothing will make you feel better than adhering to your routine. Trust me."

I pulled my face out of the pillow and looked at him. "I know you're right," I said. "But really, I'm not going in today."

Lucas buttoned his shirt. "You need to defend what's yours, Melissa. Trust me, don't spend too much time wallowing."

Just leave, I wanted to say. *Please, just leave, and stop talking.* "It's not that simple," I said, growing irritated. "Everything is different."

Lucas reached under the bed for his loafer. "What's different?"

I just shook my head, because what was different wasn't the obvious—that Dad was dead, that he had left me a crappy *You could do better!* letter, that I had a choice in my future. What was different was the cauldron inside of me, brewing a potion of anger for my father that I had never once felt before, a fury that could singe metal. I had never rebelled as a teenager; I had never screamed the iconic, adolescent *I hate you, Dad!* I had never felt a teardrop of ill will toward the man who loved me so well. Until now. Now, at this moment, only weeks after his death, I was ready to scream horrible epithets at him. The I Hate Frank Fletcher Club was holding its inaugural meeting.

I slept until noon, and when I woke, my head was cloudy and uncertain; for a moment I felt like a child waking from a nap, and for an even briefer moment I remembered my mother lifting me from my bed and holding me against her chest. "There's my girl, there's my girl," she sang.

With the nostalgia still clinging to me like shrink-wrap, I went into the shower and let the hot water and soap pull me into consciousness. With a towel wrapped around my body and another one around my head, I returned to my bedroom and slipped back into my bed. I pulled the towels from me and tossed them onto the floor, then covered myself with the down comforter, and shut my eyes. I padlocked my heart and tried to figure out if what I was doing today was merely a charade or if I was for real. *Who the hell are you, Melissa Fletcher?* I asked, and this time I needed an answer, because what I was thinking about doing required me to be bona fide, not just a pretender.

CHAPTER THIRTY-SEVEN

I spent the next week in unusual places. While my warm bed beckoned me to stay, I was too enraged with my father to surrender to the cozy cave of it. The people in my life were few in number—Dad, Paul, Jenny—but I had always trusted each of them implicitly. Jenny I held blameless, but Dad and Paul had lied to me. And because I didn't know to look for the worst in them, I'd never realized they were stunting my growth with their fake kindnesses. I'd stayed young and naïve and, just like a child, never left home. But now that I had shimmied into this new, mistrustful skin, now that I understood that everyone—even the so-called good ones—could be sharks, it was easier to step out. So long as I had my mace and safety whistle and healthy dose of skepticism.

I drove to the country club—the patch of land and collection of people I loathed the most, for how utterly out of place they made me feel. But I went because it was the geography my father cherished more than any other, and I wanted to be there, not to feel him, not to be near him, but to stomp on his sacred ground. That was the girl I was now: a spiteful, impudent, angry teenager, ready to defile a consecrated place.

I put my name on the "orphan" sheet as someone looking for a tennis match, and then went to the gym and attempted to jog on the treadmill. But my plan to spite my father on his hallowed ground backfired because everywhere I turned, I saw his ghost. *Die already!* my mind blared. *Leave me alone!* I didn't need to see his chatter-teeth dentures in the mouth of another old man, or hear his booming laugh from a guy goofing around with a buddy, or see the wink-and-a-smile combo my father had perfected delivered by some dandy at the coffee bar. My father was everywhere.

Just as I was rounding my last lap, my phone vibrated. It was the pro shop, notifying me that another single had shown up in search of a partner. I shot a snide look to an older guy pumping dumbbells who had the uncanny ability to clear his throat with the same tenor as my father, then wiped down the treadmill, ducked into the bathroom to splash cold water on my face, and headed to the pro shop.

There stood a woman, a slick alpha girl decked out in all the best gear, a one-piece tennis dress clinging greedily to her perfect curves. As if she were stepping onto the courts at Wimbledon with Venus Williams. I hated her instantly.

"I'm Melissa," I said. She eyed me like the other girls always had, no doubt wondering why I was wearing a tennis skirt with bulging pockets from the days of Chris Evert and Martina Navratilova.

"Devon Marchón," she said in her confident, corporate, hint-of-Charleston drawl. She was looking in my direction, but not actually making eye contact. More like she was looking past me, scanning for some cute guy who might delight in watching hotshot Devon Marchón kick my sorry butt. "My tennis partner got called back to work. She's a *surgeon*. I didn't even know about the *orphan* list."

She was a VP of marketing at a big firm, she told me as we walked. She rambled on, blabbing about her accounts, her corner office, her new Mercedes. Not once did she ask what I did. I was dying to tell her a lie, like that I was the president of her competitor.

At the court, she took a slug from her gigantic Vitaminwater and unzipped her pro-series Wilson tennis racquet. I set down my Made in China water bottle I got for free from the grocery store. I pulled my racquet from my bag.

"I had a racquet like that when I was in high school," she sneered.

Me too, I wanted to say. *This one.* "I haven't played in a while," I admitted.

"I'll try to take it easy on you," she said, smiling like a mean girl who'd just played a prank.

On any other day, Devon sizing me up as a nerdy, pasty, out-of-fashion easy win would have proved to be an adequate indicator of the game to come. But what she didn't know, what she couldn't have known, was that my father had died recently and, as a parting gift, had lobbed a grenade in my lap, and while the bomb didn't go off, it sparked enough to light embers inside of me. Whether the small blaze would kindle into an inferno, I didn't know. The only thing I knew was that I was burning hot with anger, and although I might not be able to hit straight today, I could crush the ball in my bare hand.

What Devon Marchón didn't know was that I had thirty-six years of people pleasing under my belt. That up until recently I was as agreeable and smooth as plush velvet—but now that my father called me out as a mimic at best, I was as sharp as barbed wire.

And what Devon Marchón also didn't know was that I had spent ten summers at tennis camp when I was a kid and played varsity in high school.

Devon spun her racquet, and I called "W," so I served first and we rallied for a while. Then I hit a lob over her head, and Devon leapt to return it—a scissors flying open—to no avail. I served again, smoking it. I'd always had a pretty decent serve. But today I was thinking about my father, imagining his too-big dentured smile painted across the ball. I beat the hell out of it. I won the game.

When it was Devon's turn to serve, I was sure to pivot into my forehand and follow through on my upswing, creating a nice topspin. She talked to herself—"Okay, Dev, let's do this. Okay, Devon"—and nailed one over my head that I couldn't return. "That's the way," I heard her say. "Now we're warmed up." I quelled the urge to ask if I could hit to the doubles court on her side, since it sounded like there were two of her over there.

For me, tennis was a game of math, a matter of statistics, a contest of who made the fewest errors. In order to win, I didn't need to be phenomenal, I needed to be one percentage point better than she was. I needed to not make mistakes. More points were given up in the net than anywhere else. Risk takers hit toward the alley, aiming for the corner shot, but they missed much of the time. At all costs, I positioned myself to use my forehand and I hit up the middle so that the ball never got caught in the net.

Devon was a risk taker, but she was good. She nailed a few I couldn't return, and it was indeed a tough match. I was out of shape and exhausted and made the wrong assumption about her having a weak backhand. She didn't. But I hung in there, and had my serves to help me out. I eked out a win, surprising the hell out of her.

At the sideline, I bent at the waist and gulped from my toxic BPA water bottle. "Here," Devon said, offering me a bottle of Vitaminwater from her duffel bag. "Drink this."

Funny thing about finishing on top. People look at you differently, almost instantly.

"Thanks," I said. "I'm fine."

"Great game," she said. "Do you want to get lunch?"

"I've gotta scoot," I said. "Maybe next time."

"Definitely!" she hollered back. "Let's plan on it."

I refrained from telling her that that wouldn't happen. If she didn't like me before the match, she had no business liking me after the match. As two-faced as the rest of them.

At home, I logged on to my computer. If I did as Dad suggested, if I got the heck out of Virginia, if I traveled—where would I go? To Italy, of course. I pulled up the research I had done so many times before, the reputable cooking schools, the ones with five-star reviews, the best places to go. In my exhaustive style, I had examined thoroughly the options available. Tuscany was where I wanted to be, so when I came across the cooking school in Certaldo, I knew I had found my place. I'd stay in a nineteenth-century villa surrounded by grape and olive orchards. I'd learn from local cooks. We'd focus on meat, cheese, wine, and produce. When we weren't cooking, we'd hike, tour Siena and Florence, and devour the delicacies of the local trattorias. We'd visit nearby artisans, farms, and vineyards.

I picked a date—two months from now—and planned the trip, start to finish. And then I booked it. I consulted no one, including Jenny or Paul. Including Lucas.

Lucas had been calling every night. "What's going on?" he implored. "When can I see you?"

"Soon," I promised, because in this tangle, he wasn't what had me snagged.

The following Tuesday, he was waiting for me on my stoop.

"Have you been to work this week?" he asked.

"No," I answered, finding my keys.

Lucas stood. "When are you going back?"

No answer.

"Melissa," Lucas said, reaching for me.

"Lucas," I said. "Let's go inside and talk."

We sat next to each other on the sofa. I scooted over a bit, placing more distance between us.

"I'm not going back to work," I said. "At least for a while."

Lucas blinked, and then blinked again. He cleared his throat. "Why?"

"I need to go on a trip. Alone."

"A trip?" Now Lucas was the one to place distance between us, pushing back into the corner of the sofa. "Why?"

Because I had a suitcase full of rage and unless I dumped it thousands of miles from home, it would find its way back to me. I could already tell how attached to me it was becoming, how needy it was, desperate for me to carry it around all day.

"What about us? What about our wedding?"

"I promise to marry you as soon as I get back," I said, and I meant it. I would marry Lucas, I would schedule a mammogram, and I would clean out Dad's house. All of the things I had been putting off.

This surprised Lucas. He brightened. "We need to set a date."

I reached for my desk and grabbed the paper calendar. "Let's do it," I said.

The relief on Lucas's face was evident. "This'll be great. Now I'll be able to check it off my list! I'll be able to get back to work, knowing how many weeks/months we have; I'll know how much work to take in between now and then, and when I'll need to wrap up my projects so we can go on our honeymoon."

I lived for checking things off my lists, so who was I to say, but still, his efficiency made my ears ring.

And just like that, two type A planners/organizers/schedulers inked their wedding date on the calendar, setting aside other obligations, such as dentist and doctor appointments. We programmed alerts and reminders.

Lucas reached for me and pulled me in. "This is good," he said. "Nothing like having a plan."

"Yep," I said, kissing his cheek. "Perfect for us. Two peas in a pod." I smiled and kissed his cheek again. Resignation settled in like the flu.

With Lucas appeased, I went about my next bit of business. With the same exhaustive research methods I used to pick stocks, I selected a counselor whose niche was my greatest phobia: the fear of flying. Her name was Susan McGillis, which reminded me of Kelly McGillis in *Top Gun*, with Maverick and Goose, and the MiG. (*So you're the one,* Charlie said to Maverick.) I took the accident of her surname as a good sign. And she really was a top gun: in another life, she'd been a naval fighter pilot, had flown F/A-18 Super Hornet jets over Baghdad, logged twenty missions in Desert Storm.

We met at Starbucks. "I understand the workings of airplanes better than most," she explained, as we sipped lattes and picked at scones. "And I get the worry, the anxiety. For me, it wasn't the fear of flying. It was the anxiety of *where* I was flying. Fear's fear."

I told her about my last encounter on an airplane. The near panic attack that left me at the airport while my suitcases flew to Italy.

"You know," she said, "the body doesn't know the difference between excitement and fear. They register the same."

"I haven't had much experience with either," I confessed.

The next Monday morning, I entered Fletcher Financial. I had e-mailed Paul, Roger, and Jenny and scheduled a meeting. We assembled in the conference room. I sat in Dad's chair, at the head of the table. I started the conversation.

"If Dad were here, he'd start by quoting *Alice in Wonderland*, when Alice asked the Cheshire Cat 'Which road do I take?' and he responded 'That depends on where you want to go.'"

The three of them issued small, conciliatory laughs.

"I can't say that I'm exactly sure where I want to go," I admitted. "But there are some things I know for sure. I want Fletcher Financial to thrive for many years to come. I want our clients cared for as well as if Dad were here."

"Agreed," Paul said.

I went on. "But I also agree with what my father said in his letter to me . . ." All of a sudden I felt clammy and flushed.

"Honey, what's wrong?" Jenny asked, standing and coming to me, placing the back of her hand on my forehead.

"Nothing," I said. "I just figured something out, that's all." When my father was delusional, he'd rambled on about "the letter he wished he had never written." It was this letter, I now knew—his missive to me to be brave. He regretted writing it.

"Sorry," I said, finding my place. "My father was right, in that it is time for me to get out of Virginia for a while."

Jenny clapped her little hands, then waved her fists in the air like pompoms, cheering me on as a mom would do.

"I never studied abroad," I said. "I was never shipped off to war, like Dad. I need to have an experience of my own."

"How can we help?" Roger asked.

I looked at him squarely. "I'm going to need for you to draw up some paperwork, some interim paperwork." I explained that I wasn't yet ready to sell my shares to Paul, but that I wanted to put him in charge of the firm while I was gone, while I was considering my next step. "So whatever needs to be done—new POAs, a new succession planning agreement—I'd like for you to work it up before I leave."

Paul murmured something about things staying the same, how that's really all he ever wanted.

I went on. "And Roger, I'll also need for you to draft some new estate docs for me." I looked at Jenny. "If my plane goes down over the Atlantic, I need to make sure that my beneficiaries are correct."

Jenny purred little "nos" as if that would never happen.

"I would want half of my estate to go to Jenny," I said, regarding her tenderly, the woman whose support of me had never faltered. "And the other half to go to the Fletcher Financial charity fund." We had established a "Give Back" fund years ago, into which we funneled our own philanthropic dollars as well as the money of some of our clients who believed in our list of charities.

Roger said he would get right on it. Paul and I exchanged smiles. Dad had handpicked Paul many years ago from a competitive pool of graduates looking for their first financial planning job. Dad knew he was one of the good guys. I knew it, too. And Jenny beamed through watery eyes. She was as much my mother as I could ever ask for.

CHAPTER THIRTY-EIGHT

Two nights before I left for Italy, I sat down at my desk, logged on to Facebook, and scrolled through the usual: the aunts, the cousins, the old friends from college. I clicked on Joe's page. Lots of photos of his children, but none of him and his wife. I was in a "what the hell" type of mood. I had no time for regrets. I had every reason to be brave, especially if my plane plummeted into the ocean.

"I'm off to Italy!" I wrote. "It made me remember how your parents used to always talk about Naples, right? I'll eat a piece of pizza in their honor. Anyway . . . no need to respond. Just thought I'd say hi. I'm sure you and Lucy have spent time in Italy."

My fingers hovered over the keyboard. *Seal it in cement,* Missy. Say it.

I began to type. "BTW—I'm engaged. Someday soon I'll be amongst your kind: the married." My finger tapped on the backspace key as I considered erasing the entire line. But why? How would that be fair to Lucas, the man I promised to marry?

I hit "Send" and then walked zombielike to my bed, face-flopped onto my pillow, and sulked, because telling Joe that I was getting married meant that I could no longer indulge in the fantasy of him showing up at my door, telling me he'd never stopped loving me, and pulling me into the arms I remembered so well.

The next day, I drove to Arlington cemetery and parked in the back row. I hiked up the path, passing the visitors' center, veering left and then right. My entire field of vision was filled with whitewashed tombstones, grave markers to our fallen soldiers. There were so many. There were too many. It never failed to impress me—the number of dead, the ages of the dead—so many, so young.

I found Dad's marker. For such a giant guy, the grave marker was diminutive, a sorry meter of his personality and its contagious effect. "Frank Fletcher. Husband, Father, Veteran, Community Leader. Gone, but not forgotten." I took the last couple of steps slowly, with apprehension, a child contrite after acting out at her father. Now that I had made some key decisions, I regretted that I had wasted a minute of my life feeling ill will toward the man I loved the most.

I knelt by Dad's gravestone, placed my forehead on the cool granite, and cried. I told him how I was trying to be brave, how I'd temporarily turned the business over to Paul, how I'd booked a trip to Tuscany, how God-willing I was going to get on a plane, how I'd set a date with Lucas, how I'd sent a message to Joe, the guy I'd never stopped loving. My heart swelled, and it was almost as if Dad were smiling his straight pearls at me. "Daughter of mine," he would say, "you win some, you lose some. But boy oh boy, when you win."

CHAPTER THIRTY-NINE

The next day—three months following my father's death—I entered Reagan National Airport. Lucas had offered to drive me. So had Jenny, so had Paul. *No thank you,* I had said to each of them, and now, as years of self-doubt clawed at my ankles, I wondered why I hadn't accepted a helping hand. Here I stood with seemingly miles of walkways before me. I inched my way toward a wall of glass, pressed my hands flat against the cool window, and watched my breath fog into thin clouds. I stared, wide-eyed, at the airplanes taking off and landing.

At the most inconvenient times, I remembered my father with a keenness that nearly buckled my knees. *Dad, Dad, Dad,* I murmured, reaching for the charm of St. Brigid that hung around my neck. I closed my eyes and let the pain of missing him prick pins on my skin.

Healing was proving to be a sneaky, power-hungry control freak who could have made my life easier all at once, but instead doled out my therapy like a close-fisted welfare worker in charge of the food stamps. *Here's just enough to get you by,* she'd say, handing me my first voucher: Anger. And when I was finished with Anger, I sold it for a loss and bought high on Love—a poor strategy for a seasoned stock picker like me, except for the fact that I knew sometimes you had to sell your losers and buy high to join the winners. I would profit from having Dad and his love on my side.

There were five steps to boarding the plane, my counselor, Susan McGillis, had told me. Count them, cross them off, reward yourself for making it to the next step. "Tell me the steps," she'd said at my last session.

"My first step is to choose a destination and to buy an airline ticket." *Check.*

"My second step is to pack my suitcase," I said. *Check.* I reported to her how I'd taken more than two weeks to pack it expertly, to fold my travel clothes—researched and purchased at REI—into perfect little squares; how my waterproof, bug-proof UV blouses and sweatshirts were arranged by outfit; how all colors coordinated with each other, so as to promote a mix-and-mingle attitude. How my quick-drying, microbe-material shirts could easily be washed in a sink, if need be. I told her how I'd packed my toiletries, my first aid kit, my electricity converters, and Tide stain sticks.

"My third step is to get to the airport," I now told myself.

I thought of Lucas, my known quantity, a good man who had been patient with me.

"Two weeks," I told him, in my most comforting voice. "Two weeks and then I'll be back to work and back to you."

"Get it out of your system," Lucas said supportively, as though I were trying to detoxify the sugar from my blood.

I had texted Susan when I got inside the terminal. She had texted back her unwavering Check!

My fourth step was to check in and to process through security. There was a part of me that secretly hoped I'd measured my three-ounce liquids incorrectly, that my pocketknife had jumped from my suitcase to my shoulder bag, that a security tag sewn into my pants would alarm TSA so that I'd need to be searched, and in the process, miss my plane.

The Light of Hidden Flowers

But security was a breeze—I was x-rayed and cleared and at the gate, lickety-split.

My fifth step was to board the plane. At the thought of this my heart seized, like a forearm in a blood pressure cuff, constricted to the point of panic. In just a few moments, they would call for boarding.

The alarm on my phone buzzed, reminding me that it was time to take my prescription medication, a sedative so strong it made my old Xanax seem like a baby aspirin by comparison. Susan and I had done a trial run with this medication and within an hour of taking it, I was knocked out in a dopey daze. I worried that taking the pill too early would put me in peril, should the plane run into a delay, such as a weather setback or runway change. I had no choice, though. I wasn't capable of boarding the plane unmedicated, and I knew it. I took the gamble, and swallowed the pill.

Minutes later, the flight attendant activated her microphone and announced to the waiting passengers that boarding would begin. In a cottony daze, I walked with the herd toward the flight attendant and through the turnstile and into the long tunnel that led to the plane. While the airport had been as chilly as a walk-in refrigerator, the tunnel was jungle muggy. I closed my eyes and practiced the techniques that Susan had taught me: *Inhale through the nose 2-3-4, exhale through the mouth 5-6-7-8. Inhale 2-3-4, exhale 5-6-7-8.*

When the passageway came to an end and the airplane was in front of me, I halted and stared down through the crack to the tarmac. My last glimmer of solid ground. I recited the statistics I knew by heart: (1) flying was twenty-two times safer than traveling by car; (2) approximately twenty-one thousand people died on the road in the United States in a six-month period—approximately the same number of all commercial air-travel fatalities *worldwide* in forty years; (3) more than three million people flew *every day*; and (4) a Boeing aircraft took off or landed every two seconds somewhere in the world—all day, every day.

197

But I also knew that my fear of flying couldn't be overcome with data.

I lifted my right foot and bridged the chasm between the tunnel and the plane, leaned into my now planted foot, and entered the aircraft.

"Welcome aboard!" the flight attendant chimed.

In my milky stupor, I said, "Same to you!"

I found my seat, an aisle seat, as recommended by Susan—more air, she said. I texted her and she texted back, and then I pulled out my on-board checklist.

1. Buckle up.
2. Earbuds in, iPod activated, soothing music playing.
3. Fluffy pillow across the chest.
4. Water bottle by side.
5. Eye mask on.
6. Commence breathing exercises.

I was on my third breathing sequence when I heard the flight attendant announce our journey. "Welcome aboard Flight 823 en route to Florence's Firenze airport. The flight will be approximately eight hours."

In the dark, cloudy world under my eye mask and the medication, I flinched when I heard my cell phone trill, alerting me to the fact that (1) I had an e-mail, and (2) I had forgotten to power down my phone. I lifted my eye mask and blinked frenziedly to clear my vision. I slid my thumb across the screen and opened my in-box.

A Facebook message from Joe.

I stared at his name. J-O-E. In my opaque blur, I considered the entirety of his name: *J* plus two vowels? I blinked more, and tried to tap on Joe's name. The message: "Missy, how exciting that you're off to Italy. Send me some messages and post some photos. I would love to see where you are."

He would love to see where I are . . . am! A happy, goofy grin swept over my face.

"I've been to Italy a number of times. Beautiful country, but you never get beyond seeing the Carabinieri and their machine guns right in a Roman square."

Carabinieri . . . machine guns . . . carabinieri—carbonara. Guns, pasta, eggs, bacon.

"Safe travels!! And PS—What exciting news that you are engaged."

Oh yeah . . . Lucas. Gonna marry Lucas.

"I'm so happy for you. In case I haven't mentioned it, I'm about to leave 'Club Marriage.'"

What? My eyes spread wide, but the weight of the lids dragged them down, little monsters tugging on the shades.

"After fourteen years, my wife has left me."

What? With my right hand, I slapped my cheek, forced my lids to comply.

"She has taken a job that requires a ton of travel, so we haven't seen her much for the last year or so."

What? Joe alone, a single dad with three kids?

"The kids and I are coping, but of course it's difficult."

What? What do you eat for dinner? Let me cook for you and your three beautiful children. I'll make you a delicious cioppino with a giant crusty loaf of bread. And what about the kids, what do they like? Chicken fingers, grilled cheese, Mickey Mouse–shaped pancakes?

"There's plenty of blame to go around. Life has thrown me some curveballs, and she's gotten hurt because of it."

What? What sort of curveballs?

"She decided she had had enough of being a marine wife. She wanted to try it alone."

What? Why would anyone want to go through life without you? Let me get this straight: She left *you?*

"Sorry I hadn't mentioned it. Up until now, we were just separated."

All these months we had been talking, Joe had been separated.

"Our divorce will be finalized in a matter of weeks. I hope this news doesn't depress you. I just wanted to let you know."

Those were the last words I read before I succumbed to my self-medicated sleep.

CHAPTER FORTY

I awoke to gray darkness, daylight obscured, only the low glow of book lights and backlit Kindles. Quiet, except for the heavy, ceaseless thunder of the jet pushing through the air. In the galley, the flight attendants chatted soundlessly with each other, flipped through magazines. I breathed carefully and quietly, as though I were hiding from an intruder in the bedroom closet. For a few minutes I just stared into the leaden air and processed what I knew: I had successfully boarded a plane to Italy. I had taken my pill and drunk my water and listened to my music and slept. So far, so good. At this hour, we were halfway there. We had been in the air for a good four hours.

Joe! It came to me like an ice cube down my back. The last message I read was from Joe and, perhaps it was just my imagination, but I was pretty sure he said he was getting divorced. Joe, divorced. Me, engaged. My pulse quickened, bile rose in my throat.

Could that be right? I reached for my phone. It was powered down. Was I allowed to turn it on in airplane mode? I wasn't sure. My heart pushed on the accelerator; my stomach rushed to catch up.

I counted the beats of my pulse for ten seconds. My breathing was a little fast, but nothing too worrisome. I eyed my neighbor, but she was fast asleep, as was the man in the window seat.

As much as I wanted to hover in the sticky middle ground of nighttime and post-medication, as greatly as I wished to think about Joe and his jaw-dropping news, as desperately as I craved to fit all the pieces of my strange life together, I knew I had to do as Susan instructed me to do: take another pill. "Even if you're feeling calm, take the pill."

I took the pill, chugged some water. I thought of Joe, his divorce, our homecoming dance, my Jessica McClintock pink dress, the itchy wrist corsage, Joe in his tux. I pondered Lucas, his spreadsheets and joint tax return, his unsalted food, his exceptionally shiny dress shoes. I remembered Dad, his vibrant expressions, giant dentures, and slaps on the back. "A beautiful mind, you have, a beautiful mind." In no time, I was back in the murky black forest.

When I awoke for the second time, the plane had just touched down, I guessed, as the passengers were agitated to the point of near hysteria. I opened my water bottle and guzzled half of it. I listened as some passengers yelled at the flight attendants, shaking their arms in the air. All around me, passengers were punching wildly into their cell phones, making calls, texting.

I rubbed at my eyes. "Hi," I said to my neighbor, an intense girl of maybe twenty-five, pounding away on her BlackBerry. A beautiful girl with flawless skin, turquoise eyes, and a thick ponytail of golden hair. She wore dark skinny jeans and a filmy coral blouse. Michael Kors flats hung from her toes. "Are we here?"

"If by 'here,' you mean Catania."

My stomach churned. A wave of nausea rose in me. "What? We're not in Florence—the Firenze airport?"

"Our plane was having a fuel problem. The pilot wanted to land to have the mechanics check it out."

I looked around wildly, out the small window. "So we landed . . . where?"

"Catania airport. Sicily."

My mind floated to my globe, my atlas. "We're down south?"

"Just a waterway across from Libya."

"How do you know?"

"How do I know where we are?" she asked, though her eyes were smiling. "Or how do I know that we're a waterway across from Libya?"

I chugged at my water bottle. "Either," I said.

"I travel 250 days of the year. I've spent time in this region."

My chest began to ache like a piece of hard candy was lodged in my throat. "What's going to happen? Do we just stay put on the plane? Will we be back in the air in no time?"

She smiled again. While the anxiety was arranging his meaty fists around my neck, my neighbor was as calm as could be. "Most likely."

A while later, the flight attendant made some announcements.

"The plane is fine—technically—but the mechanics want to replace a part, a part that won't be in until late tonight. The bad news is that we won't be able to take off again until tomorrow." En masse, the passengers moaned. "The good news is that the airline is willing to compensate you for being patient. That's the key word," she said, pointing her finger at each of us as if we were unruly schoolchildren. "We need you to be patient and flexible and just consider this as a little detour in your grand adventure. We're putting you up for the night at Novotel hotel. We're giving you money for dinner. Tomorrow, you'll wake, have breakfast, and by the time you're fat and happy, we'll have texted each of you to instruct you as to the time of our takeoff. *Capisce?*"

Another chorus of moans, no one willing to lead the way in the patient and flexible department.

My hands trembled and my breathing sputtered like a car engine ready to stall—in, out, in, out. Deviating from the schedule was my kryptonite. On top of that, an unexpected layover meant boarding another plane. I was considering the possibility of bus travel when my neighbor said, "Want to get a drink?"

"Me?" I asked. She nodded. "Yeah, okay. That'd be great." *Exhale 5-6-7-8.*

Her name was Reina Shephard, and she was twenty-eight years old. She graduated with her MBA from Harvard Business School, which she referred to exclusively as HBS, and now worked for UNICEF. The title on her business card read VP INTERNATIONAL LIAISON PUBLIC RELATIONS. Reina ordered a bottle of Bianco della Valdinievole, a typical white wine from the region, she told me, and a plate of *antipasti del mare*, appetizers from the sea, including anchovies, octopus, and mussels. I snapped a photo with my phone and jotted down the name of the wine. While my phone was open, I read the message again from Joe. It said what I thought it said: Joe Santelli was going through a divorce.

Reina told me that she'd been to over thirty countries in the last three years. That she'd fallen ill with dysentery from eating lettuce in Turkey, from drinking tap water in France—"Of all places!" she exclaimed. "Only drink from bottles," she warned, "even in 'First World' countries." For this she made dubious air quotes.

After our drinks and appetizers, Reina led me down the Via Patania to a quaint bar named Café Ambrosio. More living room than tavern, it was rich with plush sofa chairs dotted with overstuffed pillows, walls lined with bookshelves, and high vaulted ceilings with exposed oak beams. On the end tables were foreign newspapers and books written in various languages. Golden votive candles flickered in glass containers.

On the bulletin board were announcements and posters, fanning out like leaves, advertising literary events and music concerts, theater in the street. This detour that had nearly thrown me into a panic had already proved to be the most interesting few hours in my life. The thought that I was in Italy—somewhere in Italy—and not Alexandria, Virginia, astonished me. From this moment in time, I was no longer hemmed in by my parochial life, my triangulated space of home—office—Dad's. From this moment on, I could add to my vernacular: *When I was in Sicily* . . .

Reina ordered us two glasses of chilled white wine. When I took a sip, I detected a note of sweetness. "What's this?"

"Almond wine," she said. "It's a regional specialty."

We settled into two soft chairs and stared over the candlelight at each other. "What exactly do you do in these countries?" I asked.

Reina danced her head shoulder to shoulder as if to say, *How to explain my job?* "The mission of UNICEF is to improve the lives of children, through nutrition and environmental matters, equality issues for girls, HIV/AIDs treatment and prevention, protecting them from abuse and exploitation."

"Why are you on your way to Tuscany, then? Italy's a First World country."

Reina issued an ironic laugh. "Italy is postcard gorgeous, the food is delectable, the people are vibrant, the culture and scenery awe-inspiring, but believe it or not, Italy has the highest percentage of children living below the poverty line of twenty-five European nations."

"You're kidding. I thought Italians loved children."

"Hundreds of thousands of children go hungry every day. One in two minors in Italy lives in poverty—that means they only eat a 'decent' meal once every two days."

I circled that statistic, trying to grasp it: children in a nation of food-loving people, going hungry. "Why is that? It's *Italy.* The food!"

Reina shrugged. "It's mostly a structural issue," she said flatly, pausing to take a hearty sip of her wine. "The social infrastructure, if you will, is poor. We could make the problem go away, if only it were a priority among the government officials."

I shook my head again. "I just can't believe it," I said. "Italy is Europe's third-largest economy." I had just read this in my guidebook.

"Yeah, but Italy only allocates about 1 percent of its GDP to services like public child care—which of course would help parents go to work and feed their kids."

"Where are these children? In the countryside or in the cities?"

"About a third of them are right here, in Sicily."

"Then why were you headed to Tuscany?"

"Symposium on hunger," she said wryly. "A bunch of experts sitting around stuffing themselves while they talk about starving children."

"I wish there was something we could do."

"Are you up for a walk?"

"Definitely," I said. "But can you hold on one sec? I just need to send a message. The Wi-Fi should work here, right?"

Reina nodded while I pulled up Joe's Facebook message. In my mind, I drafted a response: "Joe, wow, I don't know what to say . . ." And clearly, I *didn't* know what to say, not a clue. Joe's divorce shouldn't mean much to me, but of course it did because, if I was being honest with myself, I had to admit that his availability was what I had wanted my entire life. But still, I was in Italy, I was engaged to Lucas, I was experimenting for the first time in my life with being brave. This was hardly the moment to time-travel back to high school.

"Jet lag!" I said, "I can barely string together a sentence. I'll send it later," and followed Reina out the door.

Reina led me through the streets of Catania. "So Catania is Sicily's second-largest city," Reina said, assuming her role as tour guide. "Above it looms the beautiful Mount Etna. Because of the eruptions of Mount Etna, the old city was leveled and built anew with dramatic baroque architecture. The main square—Piazza Duomo—is the perfect example of this, as are structures like San Benedetto, Teatro Massimo Bellini, and Catania Cathedral."

I looked around, drank it all in—the beauty, the archways. "Gorgeous."

Reina gave a sad smile. "That's the good of Sicily. What you also have to know is that Sicilians have been stepped on throughout their entire history. It's a triangular piece of earth perpetually hanging on by a thread. Stronger nations have always used Sicily as a base for launching expansion efforts. Let's see, also the birthplace of the Mafia. Sicilians have their own language—a blend of Greek, Latin, Arabic, French— though most speak Italian as well. Visiting Sicily is like visiting a dozen countries at once—very multicultural. But also very 'Third World.'"

"My cooking tour of Tuscany is sounding awfully bourgeois right now."

"Hey, there's nothing wrong with seeking out beauty if you can. And God knows Tuscany is beautiful. Nothing wrong with playing it safe and enjoying yourself."

I'd only known Reina for a few hours and already she had me pegged as a "play it safe" girl.

Reina wended her way down the populated city streets. When she turned down a narrow street, seemingly off the beaten path, I asked her where we were going. "I'll show you what I do," she said.

Down the street, left into an alleyway, then right down another street, we reached an area of town with apartments, kids running around, mothers sitting on stoops, men huddled around a fire pit, smoking.

"What's this?" I asked Reina, though my eyes were trained on a little girl of maybe two years old who was chasing after bigger kids.

"This is what we refer to back home as 'public housing.' Not the most desirable place to live, but it's all these people have. About 50 percent of the population lives in structures resembling these."

There was a cluster of maybe ten buildings, six stories high. Gray, industrial-looking.

I followed Reina up the three steps and into the first building. She knocked on Apartment #1, but when no one answered, she turned the handle and opened the door, calling "Yoo-hoo. Ciao?" When she saw my worried look, she touched my shoulder. "It's an office, don't worry."

"Giovanni?" Reina called. A dark-haired Italian, maybe forty, came out of the back room. His shirt was open, but while he looked at us, he buttoned up. I wondered if he had been taking a siesta, like I had read about in my guidebook.

Reina held out her hand and said hello to him. They chatted briefly in Italian, then switched to English. "We talked on the phone," Reina said. "From UNICEF?"

Giovanni brightened as comprehension flooded his face. Of course he remembered.

I stood behind Reina, wondering how many languages she spoke.

Giovanni pointed eagerly to the back room, leading the way. Reina followed him, and I followed her. In the back room were shelves and shelves of UNICEF-stamped boxes.

"What is this?" I asked.

"Eighty boxes of seventy-two freeze-dried meals."

I did the math. "That's 5,760 meals."

"The other boxes hold provisions: medicine, blankets."

"How does it work?"

Giovanni's job was to supply a meal to each child under age ten, once per day.

"How has it been going?" Reina asked.

Giovanni pulled out his clipboard. It appeared that he had been keeping track. But upon further inspection, Reina found that an entire shelf of MREs was ready to expire. "These should have been distributed," she said, showing him the date. He nodded, and said he would double up on the rations so that they didn't expire. Frustrated, Reina impressed upon him the urgency of dispensing the meals according to the schedule.

When we left, we walked in silence.

"Are you okay?" I asked.

"Oh, yeah!" Reina said, smiling. "Sorry. Just a little discouraging, seeing meals on the shelf, rather than in the hands of the kids."

A while later, Reina led me in the direction of stonework and arches, traveling through unassuming side streets and then down a flight of stairs. "The best restaurants are always hidden away," she whispered.

As I descended the steps, I wondered what the people in my life would think of me now. Dad would be cheering me on: *Look at you, stepping into unfamiliar territory!* Followed by an inspirational quip: *Until you lose sight of the shore, you'll never discover new oceans!* And Lucas, what would he say? *Surely there is a restaurant in the center of town, one recommended by Zagat, one that submits to regulations for food safety.* And what about Joe? Joe would be about the food: *Let's try the gnocchi in Gorgonzola sauce. And the fava bean with fennel soup. And what about the pasta with eggplant?* We would eat until we couldn't breathe.

Reina and I entered a restaurant that from the outside looked like nothing, but from the inside resembled the chambers of a castle. Once we were seated and served a glass of wine, we resumed our conversation.

"Harvard MBA," I said. "That's pretty impressive."

She gave me one of her half smiles I had already grown accustomed to. "I loved it in Boston," Reina said. "But it was a bit of a stretch for me . . . in terms of 'pedigree.'"

"What do you mean?"

Jennifer Handford

"I was there on scholarship," she said, pointing at herself with both index fingers. "Reina from Chattanooga, Tennessee."

"You must have had some awesome credentials."

"Straight As . . . and a *ton* of service work. It's kind of my thing."

"Still, you made it to Harvard."

"Very intense," she said. "We were all vying for the same spots, the same grades. HBS is all about 'creating leaders'—confident leaders who often have to make decisions in the face of incomplete information."

"I wouldn't do too well there," I admitted. "I'm a 'gotta have all the facts' gal before making any decisions."

"The problem is," Reina said, "there's no such thing as knowing all the facts. The times when we think we have complete knowledge, we're just kidding ourselves."

I let her profundity settle. "True enough," I admitted, and thought about my stock research, my charts and graphs. Surely they were complete, weren't they? But of course they weren't. There were always variables that I could never know.

"Do you like working for UNICEF?"

She shook her head vigorously. "Love it! I really do. But if I had my druthers, I'd start a project and see it all the way through."

"It must be frustrating to know that you did your part—sent the care packages—but they're sitting in a storage room."

"Yeah, it is," she agreed. "But . . ."

"But?"

"It's bad here," Reina said. "It's sad. Of course, it's sad. Anytime kids are disenfranchised, it's tragic. But there are worse places." She rolled her eyes. "Trust me, there are worse."

I nodded. "Asia?"

"Yeah. China, Africa, eastern Europe—there's plenty of bad to go around. But the worst? India. The girls in India—it breaks my heart." Reina proceeded to describe the slums of New Delhi. The huts, filth,

210

the water shortage, the sanitation crisis, kids scrounging through garbage for food, little ones orphaned and abandoned, kidnapped and victimized.

"And the 'lucky' girls," she said, shaking her head. "The ones who actually have homes and parents. They're just marginalized. When a girl is born, it is assumed that she will be sent off to be married, so she's not really considered the concern of her parents—she's her husband's family's concern, you know?"

"What do the girls do all day, then?"

She nodded. "Exactly what you would imagine. Cook, clean, sew. Take care of the littler siblings."

"And they're not educated? Ever?"

"Of course some girls are, always have been. The ones from wealthy families, who are taught by the nuns, sure. But that's not India, by and large. That's a small class of girls."

"That's sad." What a pitiful understatement. The thought of a continent's worth of girls being denied something so utterly vital to my own life, to my very sense of self—made my stomach ache.

"Only recently has the idea of educating them begun to even be considered," Reina said. "But it's all up to the fathers. The men are in control, and determine what their daughters will do. The schools that have sprung up recently—from global charity efforts—are filled with girls who have their fathers' blessings, so there's at least that. Without the fathers on board, there's no hope."

By the time we were about to leave the restaurant, it had just started to fill up. "Dinner starts late here, right?" It was past nine.

"Definitely," Reina said, "and lasts until 'indefinitely.' There's a big culture of lingering with one's food and company in this part of the world. Rarely will you see someone walking with a to-go coffee cup or eating on the run. It's all about taking one's time."

"I could get used to that!" I said.

"Well then," Reina said. "Let's order dessert."

Upon the arrival of the *dialogo fra il cioccolato e il pistacchio*—a slice of dense chocolate cake topped with a rich layer of cream and a dome of pistachio flan—both Reina and I smiled like kids.

As we sipped espresso, Reina asked, "You're single?"

I thought of Lucas, my engagement. I thought of Joe, his divorce, his children. None of that should matter, but still. I had loved Joe for my lifetime, and now I had learned that he would soon be divorced. Did that have any bearing on me? Did I factor in at all?

"I didn't think that was a trick question," Reina said with a smile when my pause dragged on.

"I'm engaged," I said. "Engaged, and in love."

"That's great."

"Only not to the same guy!" I said, laughing clumsily, regretting immediately such a stupidly revealing comment. But Reina took it in stride and, though obviously intrigued, let it slide when it became obvious I wasn't up for explaining it all just then.

That night, I lay in my Italian hotel room, letting settle the notions that were so brand-new to me: (1) that I was in Sicily, Italy, when only a day ago I was in my life in Alexandria, Virginia; (2) that I had made a friend—a good friend—after all of these years of having no friends at all; (3) that I was technically engaged to a great guy; (4) that I was in contact with Joe Santelli, the love of my life; and (5) that I had learned just hours ago that he was in the process of becoming divorced.

I needed to respond to his Facebook message; I needed to say something to address his news. But how could I, when I didn't know the full story? What did it mean that he was finalizing his divorce? That his wife took a job traveling a lot? That life had thrown him some curveballs? I needed to know more, but how would I ask? I rose from bed and walked to the window, stared out at the indigo sky, and followed one star to the next: star, star, star, void, and then another star. The *void*: the interruption to the pattern. That was my incomplete information. As Reina had just said earlier, we never truly have all the information we need to make a decision, yet decisions need to be made, nonetheless. Was that the first step toward being brave—hopping from star to star without knowing for sure whether you'd fall into space?

So I would write him, but what would I say? What set of words would I string together that would convey my true sorrow for his loss, while at the same time dropping a hint that perhaps he and I might someday reunite? But what about Lucas? And how would any of that make sense to Joe, seeing as how I'd just told him I was engaged? This level of nuance was years beyond my experience. I barely belonged in Relationships 101—heck, I was auditing the class, not even enrolled— and all of this—engagements, divorce, crafty wording of Facebook messages—was the stuff of Relationships 301. Maybe even a graduate- level class. Right now, I could really use the Chi Omegas from the coun- try club, girls who had been honing their tease talents for two decades. If only I could call them: *Whitney, Brittany, Tiffany . . . DEVON! I could really use your help*. I wasn't made for this: juggling, batting, the set and the spike. How I felt about Joe's impending divorce lived in my heart— a pounding, thumping ache. Poor Joe. My mind hadn't a clue how to translate these feelings into words.

I would think about it tomorrow. I would wait until I was settled in Tuscany, and then I would sit down and write Joe. Maybe the perfect words of my perfect truth would magically fall from my fingertips.

The next morning Reina and I met for breakfast in the hotel lobby. We drank strong coffee and spread jam on brioche. We indulged in a twisted, sugared doughnut that was quite possibly the most delicious fried dough variety I'd ever eaten.

"So last night," I said. "When you asked if I was involved? Maybe you'll have some advice for me." I proceeded to give Reina the short version of the eighteen-year-old-me/Joe story and the thirty-five-year-old-me/Lucas plus Joe/divorced saga.

"I don't think it's a matter of 'picking the right guy,'" she said. "It's a matter of closing unfinished business. As far as I'm concerned, you and Joe are 'unfinished,' and until you figure out how that story ends, you're not going to ever get past him."

We were on our second cup of coffee when our cell phones beeped in unison. It was the airline, notifying us of our departure. Four hours from now. When Reina noticed the pallor of my face, she asked if I felt ill.

"I have an irrational fear of flying," I admitted. "The fact that I made it this far is kind of groundbreaking for me. The last time I tried to fly—three years ago—left me hyperventilating." I laughed a crazy laugh, failing miserably to make light of my phobia.

"That's too bad," Reina sympathized. "And now you've got to get on another plane."

"That's what the medicine is for," I said. "To knock myself out. Thus the reason we didn't meet until we landed."

"Oh yeah! You were totally zonked."

"Sorry about that," I said.

"Hey, I got a lot of good reading done," Reina said. "But this time, before you go nighty-night, let's be sure we exchange info—cell phone numbers and e-mail addresses." We spent a few minutes punching into each other's devices, and then went upstairs to pack. In the bus on the way to the airport, Reina asked how I was feeling, taking a doting, motherly concern in me, even though I was nearly a decade older than she.

For the sake of superstition, I texted my therapist Susan through every checkpoint.

```
1. Suitcase packed. Check!
2. Arrived at the airport. Check!
```

```
3. Through security. Check!
4. On board. Check!
```

Once I fastened my seat belt, I looked back three seats at Reina and waved good-bye. She smiled and blew me a kiss, and then I got busy with my routine. I popped my medication, inserted the earbuds, guzzled some water, applied the eye mask, hugged the soft pillow to my chest, and began to breathe. *Inhale 2-3-4, exhale 5-6-7-8. Inhale 2-3-4, exhale 5-6-7-8.* Though my ears were filled with the music of ocean waves and my visualization was a lighthouse amid golden sunshine, all I could think about were hungry children and disenfranchised girls.

The staying power of my medication outlasted the short flight, so when we landed, I was groggy and hazy and thankfully Reina was there to help me off the plane. I gulped from a bottle of Perrier, splashed water on my face, chewed a piece of bracing spearmint gum. Then Reina bought me an espresso and by the time I had downed it and we were at baggage claim, I was starting to feel a little less cloudy.

At the taxi stand, Reina and I said good-bye, hugged like we were old friends, and promised to be in touch. Then I was off, back on track, on my way to my Tuscan destination, my cooking school nestled in the countryside.

My father was a romantic who believed in kismet, who trusted there were no accidents, that every person we encountered was sent to us for a reason. I was too pragmatic to believe in such providence, but today, after having spent time with Reina Shephard, I couldn't deny that there was a guiding hand involved in our meeting. I wondered if it was Dad's.

CHAPTER FORTY-ONE

By the time I arrived at the cooking school, the effects of jet lag, medication, and lack of sleep were squeezing at my head and turning my stomach. I hardly remembered the cab ride, registration, the valet leading me through the garden to my villa. I crashed in my clothes and slept for ten hours straight. As I awoke in the morning, feeling entirely refreshed, I almost needed to convince myself of the reality of the last few days. The plane ride, the detour to Sicily, my new friendship with Reina. If not for the automatic smile pulling across my face and the motorboat beat of my heart, I wouldn't believe it to be true.

Tuscany was every bit as enchanting as I'd imagined: the low, rambling hills blanketed in olive groves, the architectural jewels of the Renaissance, the vineyards, the cypress trees, the untouched farmhouses. My heart ached to enter this unspoiled world from seemingly the dawn of time. I itched to see it all. Romantic Florence, famous Pisa, palatial Siena. To absorb the art, to indulge in the food, to immerse myself in the culture. To drench crusty bread in the local olive oil, to tour the Galleria dell'Accademia to gaze at the works of Michelangelo, to walk atop the cobblestones and touch medieval cathedrals, to rub up against frescoed walls as I shopped through the quaint towns. That first night didn't come to an end until way beyond midnight. During those hours, I had made friends with Guthrie from Switzerland, Benita from Spain, Maelle from France. There were other Americans, too: Jolie and Todd, Carol and Adam. And of course our beautiful guide, Domenica.

When I finally sat down with my laptop and secured a wireless connection, forty-eight hours had passed since Joe had reported his news that he and Lucy were to divorce. In my in-box were four e-mails from Lucas. Short, fact-seeking ones: Are you wearing your passport and money belt? Have any pickpockets approached you? Then the wedding questions: Have you thought about the caterer? Will you invite your cousins?

I logged on to Facebook and made a funny discovery. The friends I had made just hours ago had already sent me friend requests. I accepted them, and then scrolled through their photos. They had already posted pictures, some that included me. It appeared that Jolie from Boulder was a chronic poster. When she posted, she tagged me, so her photos ended up on my wall. I wondered what Joe would think of these group photos, including me, cupping a glass of Chianti, scrunched in face-to-face with my new friends. "She's more outgoing than I remember," I imagined Joe saying. "Look at how social she is. Not nearly the introvert I remember."

I positioned my fingers over the keyboard and gave it a try. "Joe, I am so sorry to hear that your marriage is breaking up. I'm sure it's not easy on you and the kids. I'm here, if there is anything I can do."

It was a lame message and I knew it. I deleted it, and tried again. "Joe, Hearing your news has made me very sad for you. Mostly because I know how much you value family. I'm sure you fought hard to keep your beautiful one together. If there is anything I can do, please let me know."

Too sterile, too clichéd. Delete. I swirled my glass of red and sipped and sipped and thought it through. *From your heart, Missy.*

I lay back against my pillow and imagined it were Joe's heart beating in my chest, felt his hurt, his despair. I tried again.

> Joe: I don't know what to say. I haven't seen
> you in fifteen years. I only knew you when
> you were young. But back then I thought
> of you as invincible. You were the guy who
> would scale mountains, who would save
> children from burning buildings, who would
> lay down his life for a larger cause. When
> we became friends on Facebook a few years
> ago, it came as no surprise to me that you
> chose a career as a marine and were mar-
> ried with three children. I never expected
> anything less from you. The thought of you
> being a dad is the best, because is there any-
> one out there who would be a better one?
> When I knew you, you were this guy who
> believed in everyone and wanted to help
> anyone in need. A big, strong softie. So hear-
> ing your news that something in your life has
> caught a snag makes me ache for you, your
> kids, your wife. I'm sure it's a steep fall. But
> I'm sure you'll handle it. And your family will
> be stronger for it. I wish there was a way I
> could help. I'm thinking about you. Missy.

This was my truth. At least there was that. I sent it, and then I stared at Joe's photo. And then I cried for him because I would rather he be married and happy than unmarried and unhappy.

And then I responded to Lucas, and while I tried to inject emotion into my messages, they came out as brief and impassive as his own: "Yes,

I'm fine. No, I haven't contracted a stomach bug. Yes, I'm using my Lysol wipes on the remotes and door handles. No, I don't plan to invite my distant cousins. I miss you." I hit "Send" and then did the same with Lucas as I had done with Joe: I stared at his photo and waited for something to come and when nothing did, I simply rationalized that my relationship with Lucas wasn't an emotional one, but a practical, adult connection. A dry rock in a world of rushing water.

As the days followed, I snapped photos and posted them. In place of words, I provided images: pergolas of grapes, trellises of Provence roses, walkways flanked in rosemary, beautifully crumbling architecture the color of poached salmon. I posted them to Facebook and indulged in my wandering.

Cooking school exceeded my every expectation. The immersion program meant that we lived, cooked, and ate as the Tuscans did. In the mornings we ventured to the farmers' markets, seeking out the local produce: zucchini, eggplants, pears. We purchased fresh fish from the fishermen, cheese from the cheesemongers. Back at the villa, we walked the aisles of the organic herb gardens, snipping and placing into baskets what we would need for the next meal. After lunch, we rested and then met again in the afternoon to walk through the medieval walled towns, to visit a baroque monastery, to marvel at the spires of great churches. We explored Florence and Lucca, lingered in cafés, ordered cappuccinos. I ate real pistachio gelato, every day.

At night, exhausted, I took stock. Here I was in Tuscany, cooking, making friends, posting on Facebook. I had flown on an airplane. I had survived and even enjoyed a detour to Sicily, a potentially dangerous city I'd loved exploring. I had visited the projects.

I had been brave. By my standards, certainly, I had been brave.

And yet, as I negotiated the cooking and tours that made up my day, I thought of three things, in nearly perfect rotation, a Ferris wheel of contemplation. First I thought of Lucas, and whether our sameness meant that we'd stay on track or if it foretold of us careening off the rails. Then I chewed on my feelings about Joe, whether it was normal to harbor love for him because he was my first, and therefore would always be special to me, or if my affection forecasted doom, a lifetime of pining over a guy I'd never have. Was I just indulging in a fantasy, a sad-girl's version of What Might Have Been? Joe and I hadn't seen each other in fifteen years. What gave me any indication that he would be interested in me, after all this time? And my third thought was of Reina, and what she had said about the kids, their needs. I had money. I was—or liked to think I was—a generous, big-hearted girl, overflowing with philanthropic spirit. If there was something I could do to help, would I? Could I?

As time went on, it was this third thought that came to dominate. I was a First World girl with no problems on any measurable scale. But Reina had presented me with Third World problems—real needs that could be met, voids that could be filled, gaps that could be lessened. Nag, nag, nag. The thoughts slipped in, even when I'd rather they hadn't. When I was opening my mouth for toasted crostini topped with caviar. When I was swirling a Barbaresco as red as liquefied ruby. When I was stretched out, ready for sleep, on pressed linens and pillowy down. To have so much—and now to find almost no joy in it. Now that I knew how little others had. My version of survivor's guilt: abundance guilt.

A week into it, as I was lying in my bed, I pulled out my phone and texted Reina.

```
Just a random thought: If you had your
druthers and were able to stick with a
project start to finish, what would it
be? A school for girls in India?
```

I hit "Send" and closed my eyes, trying to visualize an entire town of girls who were being denied the chance to read.

That would be an amazing thing, Reina wrote back. Why? Have you hooked up with a billionaire?

Smile. What if I had enough to get us started?

Reina: Are you for real?

Real? Imposter, mimic, pretender? I don't know who I am, but I'm trying to figure that out.

Reina: If you're serious, then we should meet in New Delhi. So you can see the conditions. So you can see what I'm talking about.

Me: Just like that? Just fly from Florence to New Delhi?

Reina: You'll need a visa from the Indian embassy. We should be able to get that within twenty-four hours.

On the night I was packing to leave Tuscany, I sent Joe another message. "I hope everything is okay for you and the kids. Thinking about you. Leaving Italy, on my way to India."

He responded before I had even finished reading other messages. "What, what, what?"

"If I could explain, I would. But it's kind of a wild hunch I'm following. Will keep you updated." I sent the message and wondered who the hell I was, sounding like Indiana Jones, chasing after the Holy Grail. What would Joe think of me now? *Quiet Missy Fletcher, on her way to India?*

What did I think of myself: The girl who could barely save herself was now dreaming of rescuing an entire school of them?

CHAPTER FORTY-TWO

Feeling strong and confident, entirely different from the Missy Fletcher of old, I boarded a plane en route to India with only a Xanax, rather than my stronger sedative. I scooted into the open seat near the window. Missy Fletcher—looking out an airplane window. *Check!* Missy Fletcher—awake and lucid. *Check!*

Once under way, I practiced my breathing, I listened to my music, I visualized the girls in India. I ate my dinner. I even watched a movie. I remained calm for a good six hours.

And then, with at least five hours more to go, the restlessness battling against the fatigue and my sheer incredulity concerning what I now considered a foolhardy decision, I began to panic. With my lungs constricting and my throat swelling, I reached for the Xanax, popped two, and guzzled some water. *What was I doing? Really, what did I think I was doing?* My heart hammered and my brain churned, processing the fact that I was on my way to a developing country where anything could happen. Lucas had been right all along. I had no business detouring to India.

Hours later, the flight attendant alerted us of our impending descent. Whether I had fallen asleep or was just numbly drunk, catatonic, and paralyzed from the Xanax, I couldn't tell. I just knew I was foggy and had managed to soak my shirt collar with drool. I drank more water, chewed on gum, and slapped my cheeks. When the flight attendant announced our safe arrival into New Delhi, Indira Gandhi International Airport, I unclicked my belt and readied my bags for departure. Luckily, lucidity wasn't required to carry me through my next steps. I simply followed the hordes of passengers to customs. Once I was cleared through customs, I followed the crowds to baggage claim, and after that, was spilled out into the hustle and bustle of the modern airport, where there were shops and restaurants. The juxtaposition of grand Indian sculptures and paintings, only feet away from a Starbucks.

Gradually I emerged from my haze. Outside in the suffocating heat I watched swarms of tourists hurry to Fiat taxis and motorized rickshaws. Others slid into gargantuan black sedans. Travelers were greeted by their loved ones. I funneled into the transportation line and waited my turn for a taxi. Reina had instructed me to take a taxi to the hotel. "It's right down the street from the airport," she'd assured me. When I was first in line, the taxi driver popped out of his seat and hoisted my suitcase into the trunk. He had a thick head of black pomaded hair and a bristly mustache. He wore short sleeves, slacks, and flip-flops. He signaled to the backseat, where I slid in comfortably.

"Hello," he said. "How are you, miss?" His English was impeccable.

He told me about himself. His name was Raj. He was born in Calcutta but moved to New Delhi a few years back, hoping for better job prospects. He couldn't complain, he said. A year ago he was a rickshaw driver. Working as a taxi driver was an even better job.

"Are you married with children?" I asked, congratulating myself for being so social.

When Raj told me he was, and that he had daughters, I asked if they went to school.

"No, no." He shook his head.

Only minutes later, Raj stopped in front of the Hotel Blu, where I had plans to meet Reina. At the desk, the clerk informed me that she had left me a message: that she was out but would be back by five o'clock. The elevator lifted me to the fourth floor, where I found my room, a small space with a bed, desk, and tiny kitchenette. Ceiling fans spun overhead. Behind the curtains was a balcony. I pulled the fabric to the side and opened the sliding glass door. Beyond me, seemingly to eternity, were people and housing and more people and more housing. How different was it to live in New Delhi, India, versus Old Town Alexandria, Virginia, I wondered? Was lonely *lonely* wherever one was? Could one be lonely in a crowded society such as this?

I eyed the bed, crawled under the sheets, and fell fast asleep.

Two hours later, a knock at my door sent me flying from my slumber. Reina! I ran to the door and swung it open. There she was—striking, beaming, firecracker of a twenty-eight-year-old Reina. We grinned goofily at each other and then hugged tightly.

"Nice hair," she said, pointing to the windstorm on my head.

"You're here," I said dopily.

"I brought wine," she said, holding up a bottle and two plastic cups. "To toast your first time in India."

"It's amazing," I said.

"First things first," Reina said, pouring wine into water glasses. "Tell me more about Joe. About Lucas."

First I went to the sink and splashed water on my face. Then I popped the top on a cola from the refrigerator and downed it. Then I settled in and left my native tongue and switched over to the foreign language of love. With stilted starts, I searched for the words to explain that I wanted to love Lucas because he was my mirror and together we would build a nice life. With Lucas, I wouldn't be alone. And then, the harder issue to further explain, that Joe was unforgotten, my unforgettable. The man who would always claim me because I had given myself to him and never asked for any part of me back.

We settled in and Reina proceeded to tell me what she had been up to. "I hooked up with a buddy of mine. He works for a charity called water.org whose mission is to provide safe drinking water and adequate sanitation facilities to Indian families."

"The conditions don't look so bad here," I said, sipping from the wine, noting snobbishly that it was a far cry from the jewels I had been drinking in Tuscany.

"You'll see," Reina said. "Basically, India's population is huge. The more people, the bigger strain on resources. Most of the water is contaminated because of agricultural runoff and sewage, of course. You'll notice that there are very few toilets in India. I know my colleagues at UNICEF who work here have told me that over 20 percent of communicable diseases in India are somehow related to the unsafe water."

"That is so far out of the realm of our lives in the US," I said. "Can you imagine, not having clean water and toilets?"

"Missy," she said bluntly. "About sixteen hundred people die *every day* from diarrhea."

"Sixteen hundred?"

"Yeah," Reina said. "As if eight jumbo jets carrying two hundred passengers apiece crashed, every day."

I tried to fully absorb this horror, then finally had to add it to the list of this world's atrocities so grievous they beggared comprehension.

"And," Reina said, feigning mock cheer, "welcome to the land of the highest population of vulnerable children!"

"Vulnerable?" I asked.

"Orphaned, trafficked, diseased with AIDS."

"How many?"

"Over thirty million."

"How can that be?" I got up, crossed the room, and looked out at the people.

"We're talking about a country of over one billion."

"Aren't children required to go to school?"

"There is a compulsory education law, but how do you get to the disenfranchised, to the children in the margins of society?"

"But . . ." I wanted to cry out. How could so many people—so many *children*—be living like this? And how could so many people turn a blind eye to it?

Reina offered a sad smile. "Right now, some children are able to attend parochial schools, but of course, that isn't available to the poorest of children, and certainly isn't enough for all in need. If we open a school, we'll need to make it available to the poorest of children and we'll need to teach English. The Indian people know that learning English is one of the surest paths for their children to get out of the slums."

"How much would it cost?" I asked. "Have you crunched the numbers?"

"The costs would be related only to the start-up of the school. Once established, we would need to solicit donors. There are some schools supported by charitable foundations, like the Robert Duvall Children's Fund. We would need to gain an alliance like that. We would need benefactors."

"All right. What about the start-up?"

Reina pulled her mouth tight, looked at me with worried eyes. "Five hundred thousand?" She drew back. I realized she hadn't a clue what I'd meant when I said I had money. There wasn't a way for Reina to know whether I had a hundred thousand dollars or a hundred million dollars.

"Okay," I said. "What would be our first steps?"

Reina paused, pursing her lips before speaking. "Missy, you're being very cryptic. Do you have $500,000?"

I could. I might. I do. Uncertain as to how much I should protect of my privacy, I decided on full disclosure: "I could manage that," I said.

The next day started early. Reina hired a driver and translator named Salim to navigate us through roads jammed with taxis, rickshaws, scooters, and bicycles as well as bony, gaunt sauntering cows and pedestrians with arms full, blazing purposefully toward their destinations. Once we left the city center, once we left the houses and apartment buildings, I saw what Reina was talking about. Out the car window, my first thought was that I was seeing a global-scale scattering of cardboard boxes covering the earth. But then I realized what I was viewing wasn't the largest recycling plant on earth, it was *housing*. What I took to be cardboard boxes were rows and rows upon rows and rows of this society's housing.

"The slums," Reina said. As Salim coiled around people and wild dogs, dodging crater-sized potholes, I witnessed throngs of people jammed into the sides of the roads. I stared, transfixed, at the huts, sheds, and shacks—literally one connected to the other—lining the streets. As the taxi turned, I was able to see that the backs of these dwellings were draped resourcefully in laundry, so as to utilize every inch of space. Some rows of housing bordered a ditch, or canal, perhaps—some kind of waterway, anyway, if it could even be called that. The litter floating on it was dense—plastic bags, sodden cardboard, food refuse. The pollution evidenced by the grimy foam slapping at its shores was so vile, I wondered if it was also the runoff from the human waste fields.

"How can they live like this?" I asked, not really expecting an answer. I wasn't asking so much about how they managed to physically endure these conditions—I saw that already in the people, in their ingenuity and resourcefulness. I more pondered how they endured, in their hearts, in their minds. I questioned their dignity. How did one hold one's head high while plowing through sewage each day?

Reina read my mind. "They see hope; they strive. On a scale difficult for us to imagine. There is a spectrum, I've found. If you're on the bottom rung, among filth and starvation and depravation, then the next rung up—the one that offers even just one more cistern of water, or another five cents to buy one more meal—looks pretty attractive."

Reina had a list of schools for us to visit. Overcrowded, under-resourced. Teachers—women—determined, but exhausted from the daily chore of it. Teaching was the job—the calling, perhaps—but these women were also tasked with caring for far too many children. Before arithmetic could be taught, a certain level of sanitation, or sustenance, or care, needed to be achieved for these children. The parochial schools were like palaces compared to the state schools. The wealthy children attended these schools. They were dressed, fed. They had shoes on their feet. They were from a different class, and they knew it.

For three days, Salim drove us from place to place. We toured more and more schools. Certain givens were already apparent about India: (1) There was not enough space. According to Reina, the population of India was four times that of the United States, concentrated in one-third of the geography. People were crammed into small areas, forced to cohabitate, to share the same pockets of air that carried the scent of sweet foods cooked on open fires mixed with the odor of sewage piled on the side of the roads. In dark and dank passageways, groups of men, women, and children huddled, with only streaks of sunlight squeezing in between tarp-blanketed sheet metal roofs. There was no escape from the smoldering, suffocating swaths of people, just rows upon rows of shanties bunched together in misery, utility, and economy.

(2) There was not enough water. Multiple families relied on a single tap that might have been sufficient if water flowed continuously through it, instead of just a few hours a day. Wherever we encountered a precious tap, we found mothers and children crowded around it, waiting to fill their cisterns.

(3) Diarrhea and malaria ran rampant, and there were not nearly enough toilets. If you had access to a communal toilet, you paid for the privilege. Walking along a ditch line, you found viscous streams of green water and garbage and sewage sliding down the channels.

Responding to e-mails at night, there was always at least one from Lucas, demanding to know what I thought I was doing with this detour to India. In his mind, looking to educate girls in India was no less risky than distributing feminist propaganda to the women of Afghanistan. "You're going to get hurt," Lucas insisted. "Come home."

Reina and I began looking at buildings on the outskirts of New Delhi. The children would need to be able to walk to the school, and their fathers would need to know where their daughters were, if they were to agree to anything. In every scattering of dilapidated buildings we visited, I quickly applied the valuation method I'd learned in business school to assess how much each hovel might cost: earnings plus assets minus liabilities equals?

After hours of disappointing results from this formula, Reina kicked at the gravel, then peered ahead, and squinted her eyes.

"What?"

"This is going to be hard." The dirt on her face smeared into the sunscreen, making a Nike swoosh at her cheek.

"Let's get a drink."

We settled into a bench in front of a local store, sipping Coke from warm bottles. Parakeets pranced on the tree branches. Our elbows rested on our knees as we peered into the busy streets. Reina handed me a piece of ginger hard candy. I sucked on it, and thought it through.

"We need a building," I began. "We need children. Teachers. Supplies."

"Funding," Reina said.

"Ultimately, we'll need funding," I said. "But to start, we need a building, kids, and teachers, right?"

"At its most basic level, yes."

My heart somersaulted into my stomach. "We need an orphanage."

"What?" Reina gasped, half laughed, moved away from me a good foot.

I felt my cheeks flush, the backs of my ears burn, my lips adhere to my dry teeth. This was why I didn't make suggestions. This was why it was easier for me to be the backroom technician while Dad was the up-front guy. This was why the bell curve was so fat in the middle and the ends were so skinny—vulnerable, exposed, in danger of being axed. If you were strong, you didn't mind putting your ideas out there on the exposed tails and seeing them hacked off. But if you lacked courage, as I did, then the slice was devastating. There was safety in numbers, security in the middle, shelter under the cap of the bell.

"Stupid idea . . . I was just thinking," I stammered. "That there are probably orphanages around here that are just getting by. I doubt they're educating the kids."

"So would 'non-orphans' be allowed to come to school, too?" Reina asked, now leaning in my direction.

I eyed Reina skeptically. Was she considering this? I wrapped my hands on the sides of the bench. "Sure," I said. "I mean . . . I guess."

Reina and I locked eyes, our crazy grins mirroring each other.

"We could apply for grants," she said. "For local money, international money."

I bit at the chapped shards of skin on my parched lips. I looked at Reina. "You think it's a good idea?"

Over the rim of her Coke, Reina smiled with the eager eyes of a child who was just given a twenty-dollar bill to spend in the candy store.

CHAPTER FORTY-THREE

That afternoon, Salim drove us to the city center where we found the local magistrate. He sat behind a wooden desk, an oscillating fan only inches from his face. He gave us a list of the registered orphanages for girls.

"Is there one that's more desperate than the others?" Reina asked.

The official shook his head. "They're all in need."

"But is there an orphanage whose need is greater than the others?"

"Rohtak," the magistrate said.

Sixty kilometers outside of New Delhi, we found Rohtak. Down a dirt path, we found a crippled, elderly building holding itself up with shoddy crutches. The sign out front read: "Home for the Orphaned and Malnourished Girls. Home for the Destitute."

Reina smiled and clapped her hands. If we were looking for an orphanage in need, we had certainly found one.

Five concrete steps brought us to the front door, a striking, sturdy mammoth of a door, wholly out of place standing sentry before this pathetic structure. Reina had told me that India was that way: in the slummiest cities, you would find relics from an imperial age, treasures from dynasties of times past, inlaid jewels in sandstone and marble, propped up within the general hovel. I reached out and ran my fingers over the ornate etching on the door. On what palace did this door once hang?

We pushed open the door, stretched our necks through the opening, peeked in. "Hello?" We entered, pulled the door closed behind us. The room we were in seemed to be a warehouse of sorts. Boxes stacked, shelving stuffed with cartons and bags. Old furniture pushed against the wall; chairs stacked three high. We pushed our way through and found another heavy door. When we pulled it open, we were engulfed by a tidal wave of sounds and smells: the cries of babies, the laughter and whines of older children, the sweet aroma of curry, the harsh stench of urine. As we wended our way through the cacophony and commotion, attracting a growing crowd of children as we went, I realized the giant etched door we'd entered through must have been the back door.

The children clamored around us, grabbed at our shirts. "Hello, lady!" they said, impressing us with their English. A field of black hair in braids and ponytails encircled us, vying for our attention.

Reina fished the ginger hard candy from her bag, passed it around, but there wasn't nearly enough. The ones who didn't procure a piece hardly flinched. Surely they had learned long ago that complaining got them nowhere.

An older woman in a worn paisley sari emerged from the kitchen. She introduced herself as the director. Her name was Mrs. Pundari. She explained to us in measured tones that there simply wasn't enough of anything. "We get by," she said. "Just barely."

"Who funds this orphanage?" I asked.

"For many years we were funded by a charity in the UK, but it got involved in some questionable activities, and then the donations went down to nothing."

Flanked with girls at her feet and on her sides, Reina made a promise. "If we are permitted, we will help your orphanage."

On our last night in India, Reina and I sat on the banks of the canal and looked across the fields at the orphanage that would someday become a school for girls. Already I could identify the smell of impending rain. A monsoon was imminent.

"We have a plan," I said. Reina would stay on another few days to work the bureaucratic channels, while I would return home to secure our financing—our financing that would come from my own pocket. Money I would freely turn over if it meant that forty girls' lives would be changed for the better in the first year alone.

"I didn't expect this," I said. "Obviously."

"And you thought you were going to lounge in the hills of Tuscany, sipping wine and plucking olives from their stems."

"My father," I began. "Was this . . . this larger-than-life guy. The type of guy everyone loved. He loved everyone back, but he loved me the most."

"That must have been nice."

"It was. He loved me, but he didn't really believe in me." I waved my hands across each other like an umpire calling a man out at first base. "That's not true. It was more that he could never get over his disappointment that I wasn't like him—bold, gregarious, social. He was the lion and I was the mouse."

"Yes," Reina chimed in. "But you know the fable of the lion and the mouse. The mouse was able to help the lion, right?"

"What I'm doing now, what we're trying to do . . . is bold. I think my father would be pleased."

"So long as you are."

"I am," I said, almost too quickly. "I know that we're putting ourselves out there. That there is a huge risk of failure. But it's exciting, very exciting . . . to feel bold."

After Reina and I said good night, I sat on my bed with my laptop. With my head pushed back against the cool pillow, I smiled at the turn in my life: the prospect of being a philanthropist by starting a school for girls in the slums of India was the coolest thing I had ever done.

I was fueled with the courage of an extrovert, someone who acted in the face of incomplete information, knowing that there was risk involved, rather than the introvert I was, who would think through my every step before moving. I logged on to Facebook and pulled up Joe's page. Rarely did he post photos anymore, but today he had. The younger daughter was in a banquet at school—Egyptian, maybe? She was dressed in a gold headdress, turquoise armbands, posing for the camera.

I drafted a message I thought I would never send.

Hi, Joe, I'm leaving India tomorrow and will be back in the States on Thursday. What an adventure! I hope all is well with you and the kids. This is just a crazy thought . . . I have a layover in Newark; is that far from you? I was thinking that it would be nice to catch up. In person. Any chance you could meet me at the airport for a quick cup of coffee?

I allowed the message to sit. I permitted myself to imagine, to fantasize that Joe would read it, would respond eagerly: *Yes, definitely!*

I authorized myself to believe that I would see Joe Santelli again, after all of these years.

When Reina rapped on the door a half hour later, I let her in and told her about my message to Joe.

"Send it," she said.

"I'm not."

She strode across the room toward my laptop. "Send it, or I will."

"I'll vomit," I joked. "How would you like that?"

"I'm not afraid of a little throw-up."

I took a deep breath, looked at her seriously. "It's not a good idea."

"It's an excellent idea."

I read the message again, then again. "He and I used to have this thing we said to each other. 'Never not.' Like I'd say 'Do you promise to love me?' and he'd say 'Never not.'"

"Send it," she said. "You're *never not* going to send it."

I laughed out loud. Reina was the best. "You used it all wrong."

"Send it." She smiled with her tiger eyes.

Finally, I hit "Send" and then folded at the waist because sending this message was the bravest thing I had done yet. Or the stupidest. Were the two synonymous?

By ten o'clock at night, I still hadn't heard from him. Morning came and no message. By the time the taxi arrived to take me to the airport at noon, my in-box was empty like silence.

Taking risks on the fringes of the bell curve had left me nauseated. I just wanted to crawl my way back to the fat, cozy middle.

CHAPTER FORTY-FOUR
JOE

I was still at the office when the phone rang, an 862 number I recognized as Kate's school, St. Agnes. "This is Joe Santelli," I said.

It was Ms. Oliverio, the middle school counselor. "Katherine's had a rough day."

My blood heated at once to a rumbling boil. "Why's that?"

"Some of the girls played a prank on her. I'm sure they never meant—"

"What did they do?" Big or small, I would round up each and every one of them.

"They slandered her on Twitter," Ms. Oliverio said.

"What did they say?" I would send an armed drone over the Twitter CEO's house.

"It was simply nonsense."

"What did it say?" I demanded. I pushed on my knee, which had begun to throb.

Ms. Oliverio hesitated. "These girls intimated that Katherine 'did things' with her math teacher and that's why she got straight As."

I squeezed the phone until my fist ached. Jealous, insecure, hateful, bratty girls. I swallowed a mouthful of air. The words slipped from my mouth. "Has it been taken down?"

"Yes," she said. "They took it down immediately."

"Did you expel these girls?"

"We're meeting with their parents this afternoon. We have to be careful not to damage the reputations of the girls who were just, say, 'bystanders.'"

I silently pounded my fist on the table. "What about Kate's reputation?"

"We understand how you feel—"

"Where's my daughter now?" I demanded.

"She's with the head of the middle school."

"I'm coming to get her." Three tours in all varieties of war zones, and I had yet to feel this helpless.

"Mr. Santelli, let me assure you. The girls will be dealt with."

"Have my daughter ready."

I was still red-hot by the time I pulled into the parking lot of St. Agnes Middle School. I strode into the office, took Kate by the arm, and led her outside. When we turned the corner, I embraced her. "I'm sorry, baby. I'm so sorry."

When Kate pulled away, she looked at me with veteran eyes, like the guys I served with who had been through too much, too quick. "It's not your fault, Dad."

"Anytime I can't protect you, it's my fault," I said. "At least that's how it feels."

"Good point, Dad."

"I'd do anything to take away your pain. I'd cut off my arm just so you didn't have to hurt."

"Haven't we seen enough amputations?" she deadpanned.

"Fair enough," I said. "What should we do? Go beat up the parents of these bratty girls?"

"We don't need to do anything," Kate said. "I just want to go home."

"Can I at least buy you a sundae?"

"Sure, Dad. That'd be great."

We settled into a vinyl booth at Friendly's and ordered a quadruple-scoop sundae with caramel, whipped cream, and extra cherries. We ate in silence. When I spoke, I said what she probably already knew. "Those girls are just jealous, you know. Jealous of your good grades."

"Believe me," she said. "No one is jealous of me."

Kate's eyes turned glossy.

I slid from my side of the booth and scooted in next to her, holding her close as she cried. What could I say to her, that plenty of people would someday like her, that I adored her, that she had everything going for her? None of those stupid words would help her now. What could I say that wasn't a tired cliché? Of course I knew I wasn't supposed to *say* anything; I was just supposed to listen. I pried her from my shoulder, which was now soaking wet with tears. I handed her a napkin and she blew her nose. "Ice cream's melting," I said in total dad form, not knowing what else to say.

Kate wiped her eyes and nose again, then dipped her spoon back into the sundae.

"It's actually pretty stupid what they wrote on Twitter," she said, now smiling just a bit. A good cry was what she needed.

"Why's that?"

"Because it's really not that hard to get an A in Mr. Simon's class. Just do the assignments and the chapter review before each test."

I took another mouthful, staring at my beautiful, brilliant daughter.

"Plus," she said, "it was kind of funny, because they used the homonym 'aloud' instead of 'allowed.'"

"What? What's a homonym?"

"Dad. Come on, you know. They posted: 'Why is sixth grader K.S. aloud to spend her lunch with Mr. Simon?' Then they said the gross part. But get it, they wrote 'a-l-o-u-d' instead of 'a-l-l-o-w-e-d,'" she said, spelling out the homonyms for me. "Dorks."

"Total dorks," I said. "Homonym dorks."

We ate until the four scoops were gone.

When Kate went to the bathroom, I checked my e-mail. The first one was from Lucy, informing me that our divorce was final. "Just FYI."

Wow. I knew it was coming, but still, *wow*. I felt numb and sad, like I just wanted to crawl into a corner and hide under a blanket. Take off my damn prosthetic and curl into a ball.

I was divorced. Another day, another reminder of how little I controlled in this world.

Shake it off, man! For Kate's sake, I needed to keep it together. I drank some ice water, gritted my teeth, and pushed on my legs. Read the rest of my e-mails. A string of them from my team. A million things to do, never enough time.

Then there was a Facebook message from Missy Fletcher.

Oh Missy, if Frank Fletcher were still around, he'd warn you against what Joe Santelli has become. Remember that idealist you used to know, Miss? The one who wanted to save the world, who believed in so much goodness? Well, now he's a broken-down war veteran with half a leg, a chronically achy knee, a wife who left him—correction, *divorced* him—a daughter who's in pain, and more baggage than a Boeing jet. *Oh Missy, I'd love to see you, but what the hell would you want with a guy like me?*

Instead of responding to her message, I did nothing. Put my phone back in my pocket and waited for Kate by the front door.

CHAPTER FORTY-FIVE

Eighteen hours later, the plane touched down in Newark. Somewhere in the tenth to twelfth hour, when I woke from my haze (the strong stuff, not the Xanax), a thought infiltrated my still-hopeful mind: maybe Joe would show up, surprise me. Maybe Joe was waiting for me right now. Just in case, I brushed my hair and teeth and washed my face and applied lip gloss. When the flight attendant announced our arrival, when she instructed passengers that they could retrieve their items, there was a rush of people as thick as the running of the bulls in Pamplona. After nearly twenty hours aboard a steel cylinder, we were all ready to depart. Still feeling like I was wrapped head to toe in mummy bandages, I made my way down through the exit ramp and began walking in the direction of the main terminal.

The adrenaline accompanying the thought that Joe might be waiting for me helped shake off the jet lag and the medication. If he was out there, he would be somewhere beyond the security gates. I strolled casually through the main airport, furtively glancing around, careful to be casual and not conspicuous, just in case Joe was watching me. Finally, I settled at a Peet's Coffee and ordered cappuccino and a bagel.

Reluctantly, hesitantly, I turned on my phone and allowed it to cycle through its start-up process. When it was finally ready, I opened my mailbox. Nothing. The humiliating reality sunk in: Joe wasn't coming. With nearly three hours to kill until my connecting flight back to DC, I set an alarm on my smartphone, curled up on an airport chair with my shame and regret, and fell asleep.

After my short flight to DC, Jenny was there to pick me up. In perfect mom fashion, she detected that my emotions were schizophrenic. Sensing that silence would push me over the edge, she kept me talking, asking a million questions about the trip, the flight, the people, the food, the cooking school. Mostly, she wanted to know how I ended up in India.

Thinking back to only twelve days earlier, I told Jenny about the flight to Tuscany detouring to Catania, meeting Reina, seeing the slums of Sicily. I rattled on about the kids, the poverty, Reina's biggest wish to help the girls in India. Then I flew Jenny to Tuscany and drove her up the olive-groved hillside and the stuccoed villa where I lived, cooked, and tooled around for a week. I regaled her with my descent into New Delhi, the filth, the shortage of resources, and overpopulation. And the orphanage. I introduced her to some of the girls who dreamed of someday going to school. Of growing up and becoming teachers themselves.

"That's wonderful, Missy," Jenny said, reaching over to clutch my hand. "Your father would be so proud."

At the sound of the word "father," I reached for the St. Brigid charm around my neck, only to find nothing. "That's weird," I said. "I could have sworn I was wearing the necklace Dad gave me."

"It'll turn up," Jenny said, patting my leg. "So you're going to start a school for girls. Wow!"

"We have a long way to go," I explained, still reaching around my neck. "The bureaucracy is a nightmare."

"You know who you should contact?" Jenny asked. "Mrs. Longworth. She's on the board of a charity that helps projects like yours, right?"

"You're right!" I said. "That's a great idea."

"Do you miss the office, the work?" she asked.

"Of course," I said, and meant it. "But I miss how it used to be, working with Dad. I don't really miss the office without him."

"All this wonderful news," Jenny said. "So why the tears behind your eyes?"

At this, I began to cry. "I'm just upset I can't find the necklace Dad gave me," I said.

"What else?"

"I'm so tired"—I sniffled—"and jet-lagged, and groggy from the medication."

"Anything else?"

"I did something stupid," I admitted, regaling Jenny with the details of my Facebook message to Joe.

"Did you consider the fact that he might have a lot going on right now? A lot that has nothing to do with you?"

"It was just coffee at the airport. Anyone could have made time for that."

"Perhaps," Jenny said. "But don't presume you know his whole story. Maybe he wanted to. Maybe he just couldn't right then."

"Maybe," I conceded.

"What about Lucas?"

"I don't know," I admitted. "I really don't know."

Back home in the familiarity of my town house, I was greeted by the unfamiliar sight of a dozen red roses in a white vase. Next to the flowers was a stack of magazines: *Town & Country Weddings*, *Premier Bride*, *Martha Stewart Weddings*, *Get Married*. A handwritten note from Lucas: "I missed you. Check out the website I tagged in the *Get Married* magazine. It's an online wedding planner! It has charts and graphs and budget calculators. You'll love it!"

At the sight of these gifts, a wave of guilt rolled through my stomach. I had been messaging Joe—as an old friend, but if I were to be honest with myself, with Lucas, I'd have to admit that I had wished for more. I needed to consider that my silence about this truth was equal to a lie. Joe didn't want me, and Lucas did. I needed to say good-bye to my high school boyfriend forever.

I turned on my computer and waited for it to come to life, then I pulled up my Investor360 screen and reviewed my positions. Dad left me a wealthy woman, and with my ability to turn money into more money, I would never have to worry. Over $5 million. I could easily take $500,000, even a million, to fund the school, to renovate the orphanage into something sustainable. Even so, I was the type of investor who didn't like to touch a dime she had already made. My plan was to spin my current assets into more assets. For my earnings to fund the expansion.

I had a hunch, which for me was never a blind gamble, but an educated guess based on piles of research and pages of analysis. My position in a start-up called Genertech had tripled since I bought it, and now there was talk of a giant defense company buying it for its software capabilities. I went through my twelve-step process. I looked at revenue, the earnings per share, the return on equity. I calculated the PEG ratio and the weighted alpha.

When I was finished, my confidence level was high. Barring any surprises, this stock would continue to rise. I thought of Reina and her contention that we never act in the face of full information; there was always a certain amount unknown. She was right. With the stock market, there would always be unknowns—insider trading, instability in outside countries, political scandal that wasn't there yesterday.

My doorbell rang just as I was finishing up my analysis. It was Lucas, dressed sharply in starched jeans and a button-down polo, his hair thatched in expert crisscrosses. He looked cute. Adorable, really.

"You're home," he said, reaching for me.

"I see you used the key I gave you," I said, pointing to the flowers and magazines. "Thank you."

"I'm just glad you're home, safe and sound," he said.

I pulled back to look at him. Lucas was my future, and I was grateful to have him at my side. In the hours since I had sent Joe the message and in the time he hadn't responded, a new clarity had crystallized. The idea of reconnecting with Joe was a silly schoolgirl's fantasy I'd drummed up because I longed to return to that special part of my life. Joe and I could no more go back in time than I could be eighteen again. Admittedly, Joe represented a singular time in my life that would always be tender and dear, flawless and irreplaceable. I could allow that. I wasn't asking myself to forget Joe altogether, or to erase the feelings that suffused me at the thought of him. I would cherish those retentions like a family tie. The same way I remembered my mother. I would not demand absolute accuracy of any of those memories. It was okay that they were skewed, enhanced like the cover models on the wedding magazines Lucas had purchased for me. Those memories were mine; I could do with them what I liked.

Lucas represented the here and now. Lucas stood for my future. The interplay between the past and the present and the future suddenly made profound sense to me in a way I—with my linear, chart-minded way of thinking—hadn't considered. It was okay for me to carry my past into my present. It was okay for my present to represent only a portion of my future.

When I told Lucas about my trip, my detour to India, I watched him agitate and stiffen, as if my narrative about the plight of India was somehow going to land in his lap. His expression—heavy-browed and disturbed—seemed to suggest I was a door-to-door missionary who would soon ask him to convert. Like the PTA neighbor who would ask him for a donation to her kids' art fair. Like a beggar who would ask him for a few bucks.

"That's quite an undertaking," he finally said. "Are you sure you're up for it? With all that's going on? With the wedding planning?"

I assured Lucas that I was a multitasker and could handle all that was on my plate. And then the exhaustion hit me again, and all I wanted was to be alone.

CHAPTER FORTY-SIX

JOE

I should have gone to see Missy, I should have gone to see Missy, I should have . . . Over and over, the monotonous drone of my regret. It had been four days since she messaged me: *I have a crazy thought . . . I have a layover in Newark . . .* I should have gone.

I pulled into the National Military Medical Center and took the elevator to the third floor. My group of guys was waiting for me in the lounge. Tony was drawing hard on his cigarette; Andy was chatting with Carlos.

"Hey, guys," I said, pulling the door closed behind me, tugging down the shade for privacy. "How's everyone doing?"

"How are *you* doing?" Tony asked.

"Good!" I said. "Good."

"Your mug says otherwise," Tony pressed. "I know a sad sack when I see one."

"Not every day is great," I said with a shrug. "I grant you that."

"Sorry to hear, dude." Tony seemed to perk up, as if my being down in the dumps somehow excused him from being the guy with all the problems. I didn't mind a bit. It was gratifying to see him care to this degree. Maybe if I let him help me, his own self-confidence would be boosted. Plus, it wouldn't hurt to get my problems out in the open, let the guys psychoanalyze me for a change.

"What's the trouble?" Carlos asked.

"Had some bad days," I said. "My divorce became final, and . . ."

"And?"

"And I've talked to you guys before about connecting with the past. How it could be helpful to touch the life that was yours before this military life. I had been talking with an old high school friend of mine, and I have to admit, getting in touch with that part of my life—me, when I was young and ready to conquer the world—made me feel like I could do it again."

"What happened, Chief?"

I leaned onto my thighs, my forearm resting on the hardness of my titanium knee, the connectors that held in place the prosthetic. I looked up at the guys. "She wanted to meet. She was passing through— a layover in Newark."

"Well, that's cool."

"Except I chickened out."

Andy squawked like a chicken, but without arms to flap, the effect was less than convincing.

"What'd you tell her?" Carlos asked.

"I didn't tell her anything," I admitted. "I didn't even respond."

"Oh, dude," Carlos said. "And here you've been feeding us all this crap about how we don't have to be perfect, we just have to show up each day."

"I know," I admitted, hanging my head.

"So you made a boneheaded move," Tony said. "So make it right. Fix it. So how are you going to fix it?"

"Yeah, Chief," Andy said. "How are you going to fix it?"

CHAPTER FORTY-SEVEN

I spent most of the day watching my position in Genertech. That night, a message appeared from Joe.

> Missy, how are you? I'm so sorry I never
> responded to your last message. I would
> have loved to see you at the airport.
> Remember the Joe Santelli you used to
> know? I'm not that guy anymore. Kind of
> struggling at the moment. Wasn't sure if
> you needed that in your life. The thought of
> spreading bad cheer—in any small
> measure—made me feel like it wasn't a good
> idea. Write me back, please.

I didn't. The humiliation was too painful. Joe had turned me down—maybe not tacitly, but it seemed implied—and it hurt like hell. If he'd wanted to see me, he would have, no matter what was going on in his life. No one was that selfless, were they?

Over the next week, the market traded sideways, but Genertech rose just slightly. I bought at $4.50, and now it was at $4.65—up, but barely moving. Each day, I scanned my reports, looked for signs that might help me divine if CEO Evan Monroe was selling just because he could—a smart move to diversify what one would assume to be a portfolio top-heavy with Genertech stock—or if he knew something, that the stock price would decrease. I charted the technicals, watched the averages, squinted to read between the lines. To the best of my ability, I speculated as to the unknown information.

Each night I e-mailed Reina. She liked to FaceTime, but I didn't feel the need to stare at each other. I thought better behind my screens, was braver, bolder, willing to disclose more of myself through my fingers tapping on the keyboard. I had assured Reina that I could commit $500,000, and she continued to be baffled by this, as if she questioned whether I really knew where the comma went on such a big number.

In a week, she would use more of her UNICEF vacation days and head back to India. There were permits to file, officials to persuade. Together, Reina and I had assembled a presentation that tried to give practical shape to our desire to start a school for girls. It detailed the number of children we would accommodate at any given time. We had decided on forty girls for our first year. We described how the existing space in the orphanage would be used, outlining which rooms would continue to act as "board" for the live-in girls, and which would become classrooms for both the live-in and "day" girls. We designated a room to act as the library for reading and homework time. We outlined our needs for the kitchen, the amounts of food that would be required to feed the girls.

Following this descriptive narrative in our package were the financial reports I'd prepared, all of them airtight, certain to pass muster with any CPA or IRS agent. These reports detailed the investment needed to cover the start-up requirements, including new equipment and operational expenses, such as qualified teachers, books, and supplies. We then projected the school's needs into the future, spoke of a nascent board of directors, and our eagerness and confidence in our ability to raise funds from loans and donations, our willingness to apply to NGOs.

Reina had a classmate from Harvard, an Indian-born genius who now worked arbitrage at Goldman. She proposed to him a deal: if he went with her to Rohtak to help us get started, we would credit him for his work and name him as the chairman of the board of our up-and-coming charity. Amrit was happy to help, liked the idea of the pro bono title for his credentials, and was due for a trip home, anyway. And even though our school-to-be was located on the outskirts of New Delhi, and his family was in an upper-class neighborhood in Mumbai, he was willing to go. Reina told me how Amrit had a major crush on her in school.

And my connection, Mrs. Longworth. She and I had talked. "When your proposal is ready," she said, "get it to me and I'll make sure it's put in front of the right person. No promises," she said, "but I can at least make sure it's not buried."

On the twenty-first day of owning a nonsensically large position in Genertech, I turned on my computer and was flooded with over fifty Google alerts, messages I'd signed up for every time Genertech was mentioned in the news. It was happening. Lockheed Martin had made a bid to buy the company. The futures were going wild. In premarket trading, Genertech was selling for $16.00. When the market opened, I put in my orders. When my orders filled within the first half hour, I knew there was still plenty of room to go with this stock. But I was a disciplined money manager, and I wasn't looking to ride it to the top, just to make the fortune I needed to get the school started. I got what I wanted out of this bid, and I was happy with this. As Sir John Templeton once said, "Bull markets are born on pessimism, grow on skepticism, mature on optimism, and die on euphoria." I always got out before the euphoria.

When I'd once told Dad this maxim, and how I never waited for euphoria, he had of course translated the aphorism to my love life:

"Lovey," he said. "You're one hell of a money manager, but every now and then—in life, in love—you need to ride it to the top. All the way to euphoria."

I allowed the days that followed to suck me into their vortex. Working fourteen hours straight, I did the work that needed to be done to get our school off the ground. Each day I drafted and edited and revised what would become our grant application, to obtain money to fund our project. After hours of grinding away on our submission for funds, I pulled up a new document, the template for a letter to be sent to certain philanthropic organizations that funded causes such as ours. Where the grant applications were written straight, these letters were written with heart—leaning on pure pathos to appeal to the emotions of the readers.

"These Indian girls are marginalized from the start, their worth and value stripped from them at birth. They are born and raised to work, to submit to their father's rule, then their husband's. These girls crave education as plants crave sunlight. Our objective is to change the lives of however many girls as we can. This is a global initiative springing from a local application. Together, we can alter the course of India—one girl at a time."

CHAPTER FORTY-EIGHT

Thirty days after I had returned home, I prepared to board another plane back to India. This time, Lucas drove me.

In the last month, Lucas and I had settled into a comfortable routine. Plans had been made for our wedding: a small ceremony at a nondenominational church. Lucas's parents, Jenny, Paul, and a few distant relatives would stand up for us. An intimate dinner at the country club would follow. Soon enough, we would be Mr. and Mrs. Lucas Anderson. A joint tax return would bear both of our names.

When I arrived in India this time, what I saw outside the airport terminal—the terrain, the people, the dwellings—struck me not as shockingly depressing, abhorrently sad or dismal. Instead I saw optimism, because Reina and I were going to change the world. The idea that forty girls might be saved to go on and save others was mind-altering. It lifted me as surely as my father's zest for seeing the good in everything. *Think globally, act locally.* I knew I was thinking in terms of clichés, bumper stickers, and my Dad's well-known quips, but the adrenaline rushing through me was unstoppable. We were going to do this, one child at a time. We were going to educate a handful of girls, and these girls would take their new knowledge home, spread it to their younger siblings, and uplift their parents. My father—with good reason—had accused me of spending my life on the safe middle ground, of never reaching heights where I might occasionally taste euphoria, but he could no longer say that Missy Fletcher was insulated in her comfort zone.

And in a short hour from now, I'd meet Reina and we'd travel to the orphanage again. I had never felt so exhilarated in my life.

I turned on my phone and waited to hear from Reina. She was due to arrive from London any minute. When an hour had passed, I began to look around for my shiny friend. I checked the board. The flight had landed. But Reina was nowhere to be found.

When two hours had passed, I started to panic. I checked my phone again. I called her again and again. I texted. I waited. When three hours had passed, I acknowledged the truth: I was alone in India without a translator, without the cool confidence of world-traveler Reina, without a hotel reservation or a driver or a plan.

Just me. Just doe-eyed, naïve, ready-to-be-scammed me.

With the sun setting, the sky growing dark, and the crowds of people morphing from friendly to suspicious in my worried eyes.

I had read about scams in India. Restaurants that laced their food with bacteria, forcing the patrons to enter dodgy health clinics with whom they were in cahoots. I read about food infused with marijuana so that patrons would leave groggy and uncertain, making them effortless targets to pickpockets and worse. Left to my own devices, I would be an easy victim.

Up until this moment, I hadn't realized how much of my bravery was wrapped up in my role as Reina's sidekick. Now, alone, what would happen to me?

My chest tightened, my lungs fought for air. The onset of a panic attack. I reached into my bag, snapped a Xanax in half, considered swallowing it before I couldn't breathe.

But I wasn't in the United States. I wasn't on an airplane. I was on a bench outside Arrivals at Indira Gandhi airport in New Delhi. And Reina was nowhere to be found. And people were watching me, I felt. I would be robbed, or attacked, or tricked, I was sure. And I needed a clear head, at the minimum. No Xanax. I dropped it to the bottom of my bag.

Just then, a text message from Reina. It had been sent a good six hours ago but only arrived now, seemingly trapped in the lost dimensions of wireless transmissions.

```
Missy, Got delayed in London on UNICEF
business. I'll be to Rohtak by tomorrow.
Hire a car to take you to the orphanage
without me. I'll meet you there! Can't
wait!
```

I didn't need to go to Rohtak. I could take a taxi to the Sheraton that I could see from this bench. I could check into the American-based hotel and stay in my room and order room service and watch movies and hold out for Reina.

I could wait to be saved. I could rely on others. I could depend on everyone but myself.

Or I could get in a car and go to Rohtak.

Was it really that simple? Could I really just hop in a car and direct it to take me to Rohtak, a good hour's drive away?

I studied my options. There were taxis. There were town cars for hire. There was a train. As I was considering my options, the transportation steward asked if I needed a vehicle. Yes, I said, and glanced at the black town car. Before I knew it, he was holding the door open for me.

Inside the car, I plastered on a mask of false confidence. "Hello!" I said to the driver. "I need to get to Rohtak, please."

"Rohtak, so far," he said. "Have you been?"

I laughed heartily. "Oh yes, of course, many times." To my scaredy-cat ears, I sounded like a cartoon.

I glanced at his meter, and though I hadn't a clue what all the numbers meant, I could tell that he hadn't reset any buttons. Reina had warned me to always make sure the meters were started fresh. My chest squeezed. I peeled my top lip from my front teeth. "Is that your meter?" I asked.

"Yes, ma'am, this is the meter," he said, and did nothing to zero it out. My heart seared with anger. He planned to scam me. *Kindly reset it,* I needed to say. I opened my mouth, but no sound came out.

We bumped across town in his slightly off-odored town car. Was it traces of alcohol, vomit? The driver watched me from the rearview mirror. He was oily, shifty, and he was heading out of town in a different direction than we had gone the first time I had come. I knew Rohtak was an hour away, but time passed and he was still weaving through the city, just skating the outskirts. Anxiety, panic, fury grew in me as I considered what he might be up to. Was he running up the cab fare, or was he planning a scam? We entered and exited three different roundabouts. My sense of direction was now jumbled. I reached into my backpack for my travel compass.

"Why's it taking so long to get out of the city?" I asked.

"Traffic," he said. "Many detours."

I could demand that he let me out, and try to find a different cab. But being let out in a part of the city I didn't know made about as much sense as a preppy schoolgirl demanding to be let off on a ghetto corner, clutching her Kate Spade handbag against her chest. I closed my eyes and swallowed an imaginary dose of courage.

Then he turned left, off the city street and onto what might be considered a highway, except that there were no delineated lanes, just a massive tangle of six impromptu tracks trying to feed into one. Horns blared, fists threw out the window, bumpers threatened to nudge the cars in front of them.

"What's going on here?" I asked.

"Construction," he said.

Fifteen minutes passed and we'd hardly moved, then a half hour, then an hour. The bottleneck was ludicrous. We inched forward, jockeyed for position, made very little progress. Finally, the swollen jam thinned, and the six lanes that funneled into one spread again, back into six. Panic, anger, anxiety. I held the Xanax between my thumb and forefinger. My breathing was shallow. An hour had passed, and we were still in the city limits of New Delhi. The taxi meter ran.

My heart seared with anger; I reached back into my Chronicles of Cowardice, my internal record of the times in my life when I had been taken, used, mistreated because I wasn't brave enough to stand up for myself. In the third grade, when kids cheated off my spelling test. In middle school, when Cheryl Foxworth made fun of my jeans. In college, when a frat boy pushed his inebriated body against mine, admonishing me for being such a prudish bitch. In grad school, when my professor held my grade hostage every semester until I ate dinner with him.

My heart threatened to combust for every time I kept quiet. The rage poured from my pores. I wondered if he could smell my fury. "Why are you headed south?" I asked. "It doesn't appear you're going the right way."

He looked at me through his rearview mirror. Our eyes locked in a game of chicken. I didn't blink.

"You want to be the driver?" he said.

And that's all it took. Something inside of me cracked, snapped. Thirty-six years of people pleasing, of being agreeable, of taking the backseat to the bigmouths, was enough. This creep had just dumped gasoline on a flame, because all of a sudden I was burning and I wasn't the least bit worried about him hurting me. The only thing I was worried about was having to live with the humiliation of being duped, of having to fall asleep tonight knowing that this scammer took me for a ride just to see me squirm and then charged me ten times the price. I couldn't bear telling Reina that I'd let some jerk drive me around and terrorize me and that I'd paid for it. I couldn't live with that. More gasoline. My fire roared.

"Listen, mister, I've been to Rohtak before, I know how much I paid, and I know which route I took. I need you to zero out your meter and drive in the right direction."

I shot lasers into the rearview mirror, and this time he blinked. And reset his meter. He puffed himself up a bit and spit out the window, but we both knew what had just happened.

He turned west.

Soon he left the city streets and started down the road I had remembered. My nerves were shot. Sweat trickled down my rib cage. With the fire still burning, I revisited the perpetrators of my past. I walked up to the third graders and told the kids to keep their eyes on their own test, then I strolled into Brookhaven Middle School and broke the news to Cheryl Foxworth: "Hey, Cheryl, I may not wear the right jeans, but in a few years you're going to find yourself pregnant your sophomore year, and wearing the right jeans then will hardly matter." And then I found Scotty the frat guy pushing up against some other unsuspecting girl, and did her a favor, by spraying his eyes with mace and kicking him in the nuts. And then I located my skeevy professor in his book-lined office and told him he was the worst offender, because he used his position of authority against the people who valued him the most.

The driver drove. I texted on my phone. Every five minutes. To Reina. Just so she knew, just so someone knew my whereabouts. Just in case.

```
7:50 p.m.—Driving to Rohtak in town car
#34867.
```

By the time we arrived at the Home for the Orphaned and Malnourished Girls, I wanted to cry. I was so happy to get out of this creep's car. Maybe he was harmless; maybe he wasn't. I was happy to never know.

I paid him and watched him drive away up the dirt road, then I turned toward the sagging building. The long day of travel and the questionable car ride had dampened my enthusiasm from that of an evangelist to that of a telemarketer. I could read the script, but my heart wasn't in it. I wished for Reina. I was angry with her. She should have known better than to leave me alone. But maybe she didn't know better. Maybe I had fooled her into thinking I was brave enough to get here on my own. That was an interesting thought.

I walked toward the orphanage and pushed through the ornate back door, the same entrance we had used the first time. As I drew closer to the kitchen and the dining room, chatter escalated, as if I were slowly turning the knob on a stereo—first a low mumble, and then a graduated chatter, until finally the combined voices of a gaggle of little girls sitting with their backs against the wall sharing a meal crescendoed into a roar. I watched as they used their hands as utensils to swipe the food in the compartments of their tin plates. When the children saw me, they rose like flowers and waved their hands and granted me a roomful of the most beautiful smiles. The girls—little ones of two or three up to the bigger ones of eight or nine—ran to me and circled me until all I saw was a rainbow of saris and a carpet of braided hair. I was instantly rejuvenated, happier than I had ever been in my entire life.

"Miss Missy!" they cried. "Miss Missy, Miss Lady, it's you!"

"Hi, girls!" I cried. Seeing these beauties was better than a shot of adrenaline, and having them in my arms brought back every ounce of enthusiasm I had had hours ago when I landed in this country, plus some. I was an evangelist and a coach and Frank Fletcher's daughter, all in one. This orphanage—come hell or high water—was going to become a school for girls.

The next afternoon, Reina arrived. Brimming with energy, beaming her magnetic smile, eyes as bright as the desert sun, decked out in jeans and a T-shirt and a scarf looped casually around her neck, her Ray-Ban Aviators resting on her head, a shiny ponytail bobbing to her step. We hugged as if we'd known each other our entire lives. In a way, I *had* known her: she was just like my father with her optimistic energy, and being with her was almost like being with him.

CHAPTER FORTY-NINE

I no longer required the strong medication to fly. The Xanax had done the trick, but coming off of it was no easier than recovering from the stronger medication. Now back in DC, I picked cotton balls from my throat, ears, and eyes, trying to shake off the killer flight. My fat cow's tongue barely fit inside my papery mouth. My ears rang the same annoying tone that played when the television people tested for an emergency. *If this were a real emergency . . .*

Exhausted and hazy, I deplaned and beelined to the ladies' restroom, where I splashed water on my bleary-eyed face, slapped my cheeks, and subdued my tornado hair into a ponytail. "You made it!" I said to my reflection, as though it still baffled me that the Boeing jumbo jet hadn't plummeted into the ocean. I stopped at the first Starbucks and ordered a shot of espresso and a water bottle. I tore open a packet of sugar and poured it into the strong coffee, downed it, and then twisted off the cap to the water bottle. I chugged half the bottle until my stomach felt sloshy with liquid.

I proceeded through customs and the baggage claim, and was on my way to ground transportation when my medicated haze began to clear, leaving me with just the buzzy disorientation of jet lag to deal with. Jenny was scheduled to pick me up at two o'clock. The plan was that she would cruise by the Arrivals curb, and I would just hop in.

I found an edge of a bench and plopped down my bags onto the sidewalk and then sat, glancing at each passing car, trying to locate her whale of a pearl-colored Cadillac. I was excited to see Jenny, to fold into her warm arms, to inhale her familiar scent. I was happy to be home. I fished around my purse for a pack of gum, found it, and chewed two bracing pieces of spearmint, still trying to clear the gauzy film from my mouth.

Jenny was late. She'd probably just run into traffic, but I was beginning to worry. I set my shoulder bag onto the ground and bent over to root through the pockets for my cell phone. As I searched the bag, a tide of legs and feet and suitcases and children in strollers slid along the upper periphery of my vision until my eyes were drawn to a shiny prosthetic leg halted before me. I noted how neatly it sprouted from a colorful Nike sneaker, how tanned and muscular its opposite leg was. *God bless our veterans,* I could hear Dad say. Such a patriotic, grateful man, a veteran himself who never forgot his buddies who hadn't made it home.

I tucked down more deeply into my bag and finally located my phone. I started a text: Everything okay—

"Missy?"

The familiarity of the low male voice that had spoken my name hit me hard, like tasting Kool-Aid after thirty years and remembering exactly what it felt like to be five years old. I froze, the dissonance of knowing and not knowing at the same time striking a sort of paralysis in me.

"Missy?" he said again.

I looked up. In front of me was a mirage. A hallucination, a figment of my deluded brain. In front of me was my history, stepping into my present. Perhaps I was still asleep on the airplane, in my jet-lagged Xanax haze, loopy and dopey and dreaming a bunch of nonsense.

"Missy," he said for a third time.

"Joe?" I squeaked.

"It's me," he said.

"Seriously, Joe? You're here."

"I'm here," he said now. A statement.

"Joe," I repeated and, without an ounce of forethought, I popped off the bench and into his arms. I hugged him more tightly than I'd ever hugged anyone in my life because seeing him erased fifteen years, and touching him brought me back to the last time I felt deep love for a man, and holding him meant that he was real and so was I.

He didn't pull away and neither did I, until finally he had the sense to ground this moment in reality, to acknowledge that fifteen years was forever ago, and certainly there was a lot of time to account for. He released me, but we withdrew only inches from each other, and though I knew I had no right, I took the liberty, anyway: I placed the flat of my hand against his cheek, and then traced his thick eyebrows across his brooding eyes and let my finger find the crevice of his top lip. As I blinked, I paused with my eyes closed because feeling him and smelling him brought me right back; at that moment I could taste his lips without even kissing them.

"You're here," I said, still struggling to register this illusion. "You're really here." All these years I questioned whether my memory was reliable, or whether the image of him I held on to was an artificially beautified version of him. But my memory was spot-on because Joe was before me and the peak of his lips and angle of his jaw and generosity in his eyes were there, just like I recalled.

"Jenny's not coming," he said. "In case you were worried about her. She and I coordinated."

"You talked to Jenny?" The thought of my two favorite people conspiring to surprise me nearly launched me into a bout of tears.

"I talked to Jenny," he said.

Now we separated a little farther, far enough that my hands—hands that were respecting no boundaries—found their way to the terrain of his muscular shoulders, sliding down his tanned biceps. My eyes scanned his body and when they found their target—Joe's legs: one there, one not—I lurched into his arms again.

"I lost my leg in my last tour," Joe said.

"I see that," I whispered into his neck. My mouth on his flesh felt entirely at home.

"I didn't know how to tell you."

"Is that why you're wearing shorts?" I laughed.

"I figured I'd get it right out there," he said. "Just in case."

I hugged him tighter. "Just in case what?"

"I didn't know if you would care . . . about it."

I pulled from him, looked into his gorgeous eyes. "Of course I care about it. For *you*. Not for me."

He smiled. "As I recall, I owe you a cup of coffee."

Joe was parked in the lot across the way from the Arrivals curb. He led the way and I followed behind him, wheeling my suitcase. When we reached his van, he opened the back and approached my suitcase, ready to heft it into the back.

"I got it!" I said, aware of how clumsy, how slightly elevated my nervous voice sounded. "I've been lugging this thing everywhere. I could put it in."

"No, I got it," he said, and lifted it easily into the back.

"Do you want me to drive?" I asked, the words springing from my stupid mouth before I could call them back. *He drove here, dummy,* I reminded myself. Surely he could drive.

"I'm all set," he said.

A half hour later, we settled into a dark booth of a diner. We ordered our meals: a Reuben for me, a turkey club for Joe, a giant pile of fries for us to split. Two homespun milk shakes. We stared at each other, and hacked through the silence with stilted starts and stops. To me, Joe looked exactly the same. His hair was perhaps thinner, his skin a tad rougher, some lines etched into the corners of his beautiful hazel eyes. Finally, we found our rhythm.

"I'm so sorry about Frank," he said.

"I still can't believe he's gone," I said. "A year ago he was fine. The deterioration was especially fast for him . . . because of the stroke."

"In a way—"

"It's good, I know," I said, finishing his sentence. "It was horrible seeing him as less than the man he was. It was like monsters had invaded his brain."

"It's hard to believe that he was human, after all," Joe said. "I kind of thought of him like a guardian angel."

"He had a special way."

I gazed at Joe. Really looked at him. In front of my eyes was my love from fifteen years ago, and to me he looked exactly the same.

"Your dad used to tell us," Joe said, imitating Dad: "'Kids, who you are and what you're made of isn't a dissertation. You should be able to sum up your beliefs in a sentence or two. If *you* are clear on who you are, then people will trust you.'"

"Yep." I remembered. Dad and his elevator speech.

"I was there," Joe said solemnly. "At the funeral."

"What?" Goosebumps rose on my arms. The thought that Joe was nearby, as we buried Dad, made me want to cry.

"I'm sorry I didn't stick around," Joe said. "I chickened out. Convinced myself it was a bad idea, and kind of crept away before you saw me."

I thought back to the funeral, how when Taps played, I had been thinking of Joe. Had he been only feet away from me at that moment?

"I love that you were there," I said. "And as much as I would have loved to have seen you then, I wouldn't trade the reunion we just had at the airport."

Joe swallowed hard. My tough high school boyfriend had always been sentimental.

"Tell me what happened to you, Joe," I said, and then, brushing aside any doubts about the inappropriateness of my actions, I covered his hands with mine.

We stared at each other for a moment before Joe began. "I had been on patrol in Afghanistan. A routine mission. We were getting ready to cross a canal when all of a sudden I was thrown into the air and tossed into the water. The guy behind me—my buddy Allen—had stepped on an IED. God knows how I missed it." He shook his head. "Allen didn't make it, but I didn't know that. Not until later."

I tightened my grip over his knuckles. Fought the urge to lean over and put my mouth on his hands.

"At the time, I wasn't even aware of what had happened to my leg. All I knew was that a bomb had been detonated and I was fighting for my life. Somehow I dragged myself out of the canal. Somehow I was medically evacuated. I remember being on the helicopter, looking up at the medics. I remember their eyes. They weren't shocked by what had happened to me, to Allen. They just looked weary—sad and weary, like they were sick and tired of this happening so often. Like they were drained from seeing whole men taken apart."

When Joe paused, I saw that the waitress had delivered our food. He looked down at his club sandwich and said, "Let's eat!"

"I'm so sorry you went through all of that," I said.

"I'm honestly not sorry for myself," Joe said. "That's why I didn't tell you earlier. I liked that you didn't know, that you only knew me for me. When people see me now, I'm not just Joe anymore. I'm Joe with the prosthetic leg. I don't feel sorry for myself, but I can't force other people to not feel sorry for me."

"I didn't mean to," I said, "but I know I already did what you must loathe: say that I could get my own suitcase, drive the car. That must be aggravating."

"People just want to help. I get that."

We paused, ate some fries that happened to be ridiculously delicious. We dipped into a communal mound of ketchup.

"Tell me about your children," I said.

His eyes lit up, and he set down his sandwich. "My youngest, Jake, is a belly-laughing giggle monster. He's my reminder of everything good and pure in the world. He's nine and that blows my mind, because it's true what everyone says, I could swear he was just born. Of course, the effect was heightened. He's grown up for me—all the kids have—like time-lapse photography. I was deployed for much of their childhoods. I've missed a lot of years."

"He looks just like you," I said, remembering photos from Facebook.

"Olivia is eleven going on eighteen," Joe said. "We call her 'The Mayor' because she is involved in everything and everyone's business."

"She sounds hilarious," I said. "She likes to act, too? I think I saw photos of her in a play."

Joe laughed. "Yeah, kind of. Olivia doesn't so much want to act as she wants to lip-synch."

"And then there's your oldest—Katherine, right?"

"Yes, Katherine—Kate," he said, his face changing from light-hearted to serious.

"What's she like?"

"She's one of those amazing kids who practically raised herself. She's hardworking, studious. Straight-A student. High honors every semester. We've never had to stand over her to do her homework. She's just a good, good kid."

"A real smarty-pants," I said. "Thirteen?"

"She's fourteen, now." Joe's voice caught, like he was choked up.

"Are you okay?" I asked.

A half smile. "She struggles," he said. "She's a bookworm, and kind of lacks the skills to fit into middle school, you know? A lot of the girls her age are fighting over boys and jockeying for position with friendships, and Kate's at a loss on how to play that game. She's going to be fine, though. She's going to be an awesome adult. Still, she's alone a lot of the time, and the girls hassle her. There's been some bullying. It's a painful time for her, for me."

I looked wistfully at the window. I knew exactly what that was like. "It is hard," I agreed. "Clearly, I was—am—the same way, and the kids weren't always nice and school wasn't always a breeze. Despite my efforts to fit in, I knew I didn't."

"You always seemed excessively cool to me," Joe said. "The most self-possessed person at Abraham Lincoln High. Like everyone else could play their silly games. You had bigger plans."

"That was later, in high school," I said. "When you and I met. It was easier by then. Getting good grades was important to more kids by then, and I knew college was right around the corner, and . . . well, I had you. That helped."

Joe grinned.

"But in middle school," I said, "it was grueling. I remember, once, I was in the science lab with a group of girls. We had just taken an exam and had about ten minutes to kill before our next class. One of them got the idea to play hide-and-seek, and the teacher said it was okay. We all hid except a girl named Sandy, who was 'it.' One by one she found everyone except me. I was just behind the door! But she and the other girls were talking, and Sandy was saying that she found everyone, and all the other girls agreed. I just stood there. A minute later, they gathered their bags and left. I slipped out from behind the door and left, too. None of them even noticed."

"That's a crappy story," Joe said. "I'm sorry."

"It shouldn't mean much, but here I am—all these years later, and I can still recall it like yesterday."

"That's why I worry so much about Kate."

"It's probably worse on you," I said. "Just like it was worse on my dad. As a dad, you're helpless to make things better."

"Dads are supposed to fix things."

"My dad used to think he was helpful when he said things like, 'You'll come out of your shell,' but it wasn't helpful. I cringed every time he said it because it just seemed so critical to me . . . like he was suggesting that there was a better version of me inside the one that was on the outside."

"He never felt that way," Joe said.

"He didn't. You're right. The thing is, he was partially right. When it came to the social scene in middle school, I was in some measure responsible for my unhappiness. I *did* need to come out of my shell—not to change who I was, but to participate."

Joe considered this, then sighed. "I just can't stand seeing her in pain. And of course I worry about her hurting herself. I don't think she would, but it's there, in the back of my mind."

"Just make sure she's involved in things she truly loves. Even if it's some solitary activity, like writing poetry, try to encourage her to join a club—poetry club, or a teen writing program at the library. Just so she has contact with someone. And obviously, make sure she knows that you're there for her—totally open, with no judgment."

Joe sucked on the milk-shake straw until he heard scraping sounds. "Guess I killed this guy," he said. We studied the table and saw that we had powered through both of our sandwiches, fries, and milk shakes. "I forgot you were such a good eater."

I picked at a burnt end of a french fry.

"What about you?" Joe asked. "Tell me about your life."

"There's not a lot to say."

"Are you kidding?" Joe said. "It sounds like you've been crazy successful in business. And now you're off gallivanting around the globe—Italy to India. What's that all about?"

"All that's new," I admitted. "All post–Frank Fletcher. And it's a bit of a departure from my actual history."

"Tell me about it."

"I don't know how to explain myself," I said, then faltered, tapping at the plate with my burnt french fry. "People want an *accounting* of what you've been doing, you know? If you're married. How many children you have. In what school district you live."

"That's just standard conversation," he said. "People don't know what else to ask."

"To the outside observer, it probably looks like I haven't done much."

"How can you say that?" Joe asked.

"Because I don't have the *things* that matter."

"The things?"

"You know . . . a husband, kids."

"But—"

"But I've been happy—content, at least. And there's a lot to say for that. It wouldn't be many people's choice, but I don't regret for a minute that I stayed near my father, that he and I built a business, that I cared for him while he was sick. All that was meaningful to me."

"Missy, you don't need to explain yourself to me. I'm not looking at you like you've wasted your life."

Behind Joe our waitress moved between other tables, topping off ketchup bottles.

"It just went so fast—five years, then ten, then fifteen."

"You're sounding like you're looking at your life like it's winding down, instead of in the middle of a continuum that started when you were born. Who's to say, Miss? Maybe you'll live to be a hundred. Maybe this point on your time line is just the beginning."

"Maybe," I said, and though *maybe* was just a two-syllable word, I took my time with it, because all of a sudden my heart was creeping into my throat and my hands were sweaty with anticipation. *Who's to say this isn't just the beginning?* Was Joe intimating that he and I might have a point, a series of points plotted further down my time line?

Our waitress brought the bill. Joe handed her three twenties and asked if we could hang around for a while.

"As long as you'd like, sweetheart," she answered, whisking herself away toward the cash register.

"What happened with you and your wife?" I asked quietly. "If you want to tell me. You certainly don't have to."

Joe's face twisted in consternation, just as it had years ago when he would work a tricky trig problem. "Lucy is a good woman, a good mother. But all of these years she's been a military wife—a marine wife, to boot—and there is a lot involved in that. Moving, getting settled, and then moving again. She'd make good friends, have a network of people she could count on, and then we'd have to do it all over again. It's hard. Military spouses give up a lot."

"What happened?"

"I was gone a lot. She was home dealing with the kids. Her mother was ill at the time. And when I came home from my second tour, she thought it was for good. She had been itching to go back to work."

"Did she?"

Joe fiddled with the box of Splenda and sugar packets. "She was getting ready to—but then I deployed again. The surge in Afghanistan forced many of us to deploy unexpectedly, far sooner than we ever thought. Lucy was furious, for so many reasons. I guess there was already a lot of tension between us."

"And then you came home with one leg," I said.

"That was pretty much the straw that broke the camel's back," he said. "Because as an officer, I should have been safer than some. Wrong place, wrong time. Lucy was angry, but she shoved it down and rolled up her sleeves and got me through the tough times. Learning to walk, function. Those weren't easy days, and I was a lousy patient—depressed, withdrawn. My lost leg was the least of my problems. I also had a broken arm, which complicated matters tremendously, and a ton of aches and pains. By the time the cast came off my arm, my bruises had healed, and I was accustomed to living with one leg; by the time I was ready to reconnect with 'the living,' Lucy already had one foot out the door."

"I'm so sorry."

"There was a lot of recuperating involved, a lot of rehab. Lucy felt obligated to stay, yet every fiber in her was screaming for her to leave. She got me through the tough times, and then one day—when she sensed that I was fine—she started going out on job interviews. She landed a great job as an event planner for an international law firm."

"What has that meant to the kids?"

"It means that she's gone a lot of the time. She goes on these trips with the lawyers—business trips and reward trips. She's kind of like the on-site concierge. Last year she was gone over two hundred days. So the kids are with me."

"Doesn't she miss them?" The words left my mouth without thought. Of course she missed her kids.

"She needed a break from it all. She needed to find out who she was, other than a marine wife."

I couldn't judge her. She and I were doing the same thing, trying to figure out who we were after years of being someone else.

"Our divorce is final," Joe added. "Officially."

"I'm sorry," was all I could think to say. Then, "It's getting late."

"Let's get you home," Joe said, sliding out of the booth and up onto his two mismatched legs.

"You look great, Joe," I said. "I can't tell you how good you look."

The ride home was quiet except for my navigation instructions—*turn left here, you're going to veer to the right here, at the second light turn again. That's me, straight ahead, the second town house on the left.*

Joe shifted into park and turned off the car, then turned to me. "This has been an amazing day."

"What now?" I asked.

"I have a room booked at the Hilton. I'll drive back to Jersey tomorrow."

I reached for his hands. "I want to see you again."

"I want to see you again, too," Joe said.

I looked at my town house, thought about the rooms inside, the lifeless existence I had been living in that space. My wretched imposter of a life. I thought back and wondered what I was doing at the exact moment when Joe was in the fight of his life, when his leg was blown to bits and he was evacuated alongside his fallen comrade. What was I doing then? Watching *Jeopardy!* and eating gelato?

I looked at him. I'd never wanted anyone or anything more in my life. "Can we?"

"You're in Virginia—"

"And you're in New Jersey."

"And last I heard, you were engaged to be married—"

"And you're very recently divorced."

"Yes, I am," Joe said.

"Still." I leaned over into his space, settled in there, and let my mouth curl around his pillow of a neck.

At the door, Joe hefted my suitcase through the threshold. "I just wanted to see you," he whispered. "I'm sorry if I overstepped . . ."

"You didn't!" I said. "I'm so happy to see you."

"But . . ."

"But it's complicated."

"We should probably settle the open items in each of our lives before we consider something else," Joe said.

I nodded. I thought of Lucas, what I needed to do.

He nodded, and we stared at each other. Wordlessly we gazed into each other's truths, the thousands of steps that had brought us to this point.

"Okay," he said.

He walked down the few steps and I watched him smoothly manipulate his legs into his van, held my breath until he drove away. *I love you, I love you, I love you,* I whispered, over and over. Words I hadn't yet given to Lucas.

I thought of Dad, recalling again his wisdom. "Lovey," he said. "You're one hell of a money manager, but every now and then—in life, in love—you need to ride it to the top. All the way to euphoria."

Joe was my euphoria.

CHAPTER FIFTY

The first morning light sprayed in through the cracks in the blinds. Still awake, my emotions were taking me on a ride. The certainty I'd felt about Joe last night had been tempered by fear and anxiety. That I loved Joe was a given, and probably always would be. Still: I had loved him from afar all these years, but what was the reality? The truth was that Joe was an amputee war veteran, a brand-new divorcé, and a single dad to three children. How could his life have space for me? And what could I possibly add to it that would be worthwhile? I was Missy Fletcher, unmarried yet engaged, childless, kind of jobless, a woman who had never had a serious relationship in her adult life. How could I possibly have significance in Joe's life? His children would despise me because I would be the person occupying their father, attempting to replace their mother. And who was I joking about Joe wanting me as badly as I wanted him? Sure, he said last night that he'd like to see me again. Sure, he drove down from Jersey to meet me. Sure, the two of us together found the perfect rhythm in our conversation, a seamless fit in our touch, a flawless understanding of each other's situations. But still—how would it work?

The confusion I felt regarding Joe was the polar opposite of the certainty I felt concerning Lucas. Dear Lucas—good-looking, sweet-and-kind, tax-attorney Lucas. My mirror. My male counterpart. My safety-police partner. My risk-averse, nothing-wrong-with-staying-in-Virginia, who-needs-to-eat-raw-fish, crossing-borders-can-only-lead-to-trouble boyfriend-fiancé. He was a great guy, a man I would be proud to introduce as my own. A guy any girl would be honored to call her husband. But he didn't bring me to euphoria, and for that matter, I didn't think I brought him to euphoria, either. And for that alone—Joe or no Joe—we had no business staying together.

At seven o'clock, I texted Lucas. I asked him if he could come over for coffee—though *coffee* was mere shorthand, as I knew that Lucas would show me his water bottle and tell me he was fine, thank you.

An hour later, Lucas knocked. "You're back," he said, reaching for me, pulling me into a tight hug. "How was it?"

I hugged him and inhaled his scent, because Lucas was a good man and I was about to hurt him, and I wanted to create a scrapbook in my mind of the affection I felt for him, just in case this got ugly.

I spent a few minutes detailing the trip, the progress Reina and I had made with the local governmental officials, the paperwork we'd filed, the women we'd spoken with who were interested in teaching. Then I got down to business. "Lucas, we need to talk."

"Uh-oh," he said. "You're not going back to India again, are you?"

I took Lucas's hand and led him to the sofa. "Let's sit down."

"This sounds ominous."

"I want to be totally honest with you," I began.

Lucas dropped my hands and scooted away from me, pushing his back into the corner of the sofa.

"Do you remember once I told you about my friend Joe from high school?"

"You dated, right?" Lucas said warily.

"We dated. And then we went off to separate colleges. He got married, had kids, etc. We're friends on Facebook, so I've kind of kept up with his life." I went on to tell Lucas how I'd sent Joe a message when Dad was sick; how it had been important to me that he knew, because Joe and Dad were close. "From there, we began a correspondence—just friends, of course."

Lucas began to fidget. I eyed his hands opening wide and then balling into fists, a vein in his temple bulging. I watched him swallow hard, as if the involuntary act had become a difficult exercise.

I reached out and put my hand on his knee. "As it turns out," I went on, "Joe's a veteran. He served three tours. He actually lost one leg in his last tour. When I landed last night, I thought Jenny was going to pick me up, but instead . . . Joe picked me up."

Lucas sprung from the sofa and began to pace. "Whoa—wait, what? At the airport? Does he *live* here? Did you ask him to come?"

"He lives in New Jersey. And no, I didn't ask him to come. But—"

"But what?"

"It was great seeing him. He knew my father so well. We shared a lot of memories."

"Melissa, what's this *about*?" Lucas gasped for understanding. "Is Joe just an old friend? You said he was married?"

"He is, was—well, he's recently divorced."

"What the hell does that have to do with you?"

"Nothing," I said. "I'm just explaining why he came to see me."

"Why *did* he come to see you?"

"Lucas," I said. "Calm down, okay?"

"Are you breaking up with me for this Joe guy?"

I looked across the room while my brain absorbed the absurdity of Lucas's words. It was an absolutely ridiculous thought that I would be breaking up with Lucas because I saw Joe *one time*!

"Not exactly," I said.

Lucas didn't believe me. "Then what?"

"You know the Sir John Templeton maxim: 'Bull markets are born on pessimism, grow on skepticism, mature on optimism, and die on euphoria'?"

"I've heard it," he said.

I stood and took a step in his direction, but he backed farther away. "You and I, Lucas—our relationship—it's maturing on optimism. We're a great couple: we share the same interests, we're worker bees, we believe in playing it safe. But Lucas, lately—in India—I've tasted euphoria. The girls at the orphanage? They were so happy to see me, and when I saw them, I couldn't remember ever feeling such pure joy. Feeling that way, like my heart would explode? It leaves you breathless. The excitement of not sleeping at night because you're so eager for the next day to come. The thrill of building something that might actually change the lives of children for the better. The exhilaration of knowing that knowledge plus money plus sheer will and determination could save lives. I don't think I'm the same girl anymore. I don't think I'm the play-it-safe, stay-in-Virginia, work-ten-hour-days girl anymore."

"And Joe?" Lucas asked, clearly annoyed. "Does he leave you breathless, too?"

My heart raced. "I have no idea what will happen with Joe. I've only seen him once in fifteen years and I have no clue if our lives belong together, and if he would even want it."

Lucas laughed, a little maniacally. "You want it, though."

"If not with him, with someone else."

"But not me." Lucas's face had flushed bright-red, the vein at his temple throbbed.

"Don't you want it, too?" I asked. "Don't you want to be left breathless?"

Lucas headed for the door, then turned to glare at me when he reached it. "I kind of like *breathing*, Melissa," he said, pulling it open. "I kind of thought us breathing together was a pretty good thing."

"Lucas, wait!"

"For what?" He stepped out and pulled the door closed behind him.

The silence that followed was deafening. What was Dad saying from his perch? *You did it again, Missy. You blew another relationship. Here you are again—alone, same as before. You let a good one get away.*

Or was he proud of my decision, to give up Lucas for the miniscule hope that Joe might someday want me? All of a sudden, the rationale for the arbitrage I'd just committed seemed insanely weak. I'd sold my position in a solid blue chip—an established, money-making, dividend-paying stalwart—and bet it all on the mere idea of a start-up, a concept that wasn't even a thing yet.

Yet I couldn't deny it. The relief in saying good-bye to Lucas was palpable. It was time to take some risk. *Who am I to think that I can have greatness?* the old me would have asked. *Who am I to think that I can't?* I now pondered.

It was time to go big or go home.

CHAPTER FIFTY-ONE

The high of daring greatly, of acting brave, was short-lived, clobbered only hours later by a much stronger force: self-doubt. The malaise of breaking up with Lucas over *nothing*, really—over the idea that I wanted more from my relationship with a man—left me in a flushed, light-headed daze. When Joe called only an hour after Lucas had left and asked to see me before leaving town, I told him that we'd better not. "You were right," I said. "We need to tie up loose ends before anything else."

Each day I called Lucas. "I'm *fine*," he seethed through clenched teeth. "You don't need to call me." The fact that I had hurt him caused me significant shame, leaving me feeling wobbly and uncertain. I wasn't used to upsetting people. With so few people in my life, my starting point was to "do no harm." That Lucas was wounded at my expense made my chest ache.

And each night Joe called. We talked openly about his kids, the divorce, and his work. I told him about the orphanage, our efforts to turn it into a school. Without my telling him much, Joe knew of my breakup with Lucas. *Are you okay?* he'd ask. *Are you at peace with your decision?*

Days passed, and more than anything, I craved Lucas's forgiveness. As if I couldn't go on until I got it. I decided to employ my own twist on Dad's version of Dale Carnegie: get Lucas to talk about the things he loved.

"Don't hang up!" I blurted when Lucas answered the phone. "I need some tax advice, and I know you're the guy."

"I'm busy, Melissa," he said wearily. I could hear him pounding on his keyboard.

"I've been looking for hours on the Internet," I fibbed. "And I can't seem to find the answer I need. The orphanage/school in India is going to be tied to our 501(c)(3) charitable organization here in the States, but I can't seem to figure out how to apply for that: a US-based nonprofit benefiting an overseas operation."

He stopped typing, and I could almost hear him straighten up in his seat, tap his perfectly sharp pencil tip against his desk mat. "That's pretty standard, actually," he said. "Any tax attorney could help you with that."

"But what about filing the articles of incorporation?" I asked, not wanting him to hang up.

"You have to wait until your tax-exempt status has been approved," he said.

"What else?"

"Missy," Lucas said. "I don't want to talk right now." His angry typing resumed.

"Just one more question!" I exclaimed. "How do we set it up so that we can accept private and public donations? Just write that in?" I knew my nonchalance would rattle him.

"I get what you're doing, Missy," Lucas said, "and it's not going to work. I don't want to talk to you. You can't *fool* me into answering tax questions. You fooled me once already. I trusted you. I know you want forgiveness. I know you want us to be friends. I know you want me to say it's okay that you broke my heart. It's not. Please leave me alone."

He didn't wait for a response before he ended the call.

The weight of being an adult grew heavier by the day. Only a year ago the burden I'd borne was featherlight. A child's share. My default had always been to let everyone else take the lead. I didn't argue against it. It fit my personality, to walk in the shadow. I didn't crave the freedom to forge my own path. The old me would have never been in this position, because the old me would have never broken up with Lucas. The old me would have never asked for more.

The new me wasn't just asking for more, but demanding it, no matter how uncomfortable it made the old me, who still hung around, usually wringing her hands. The new me didn't care. She was making up for lost time, strapping on the yoke of responsibility and shouldering all of it, all at once: the future of Fletcher Financial, Paul's and Jenny's jobs, our clients' financial plans and assets. The hopes of forty girls in India. My renewed love and affection for Joe Santelli—a man with children and an ex-wife and PTSD and a prosthetic leg.

And now I'd added to the load Lucas's hurt and the knowledge that I alone caused it.

The following week, Joe asked if I could take the train up for the weekend. His wife would be home and would have the kids. He thought it would be fun to take in some "Jersey" sights: the shore, his favorite restaurant. "There is a nice hotel near my house. I could make you reservations."

"Yes!" I said, without giving thought to the logistics. The fact that I couldn't breathe, for one. When I hung up, I called Jenny. Dots materialized in front of my eyes, my chest squeezed, and my throat constricted. "Are you free for lunch?"

Jenny and I met at Ellie's and though she had made two of my favorite soups—roasted red pepper, and vegetable and kale—I declined to order either. Instead, I ordered a cup of tea and a lemon bar, and even that sat untouched.

"I'm in foreign territory here," I said. "Going to Jersey for the weekend! Who do I think I am?"

Jenny led me through it. "Let's talk about your expectations. What do you think this weekend will be about? What do you think will happen?"

Her question was a good one because if I was being honest with myself, looking at this as a dispassionate outside observer, this weekend would need to be characterized as nothing more than a first date. And maybe not even a date—more like old friends getting together. And even though I wanted it to be more, I was terrified of it being more. "It's Joe," was all I could manage to say, as if those words alone were adequate to explain fifteen years of caring for this man who once loved me.

Two days later, I boarded Amtrak's Acela Express en route to Newark. In my shoulder bag I had the latest *Businessweek*, the *WSJ*, *Barron's*. I had the latest Kellerman novel. I had my iPod loaded with music and podcasts. At the snack bar, I added a bagel and cream cheese and a yogurt/fruit parfait to the Starbucks latte I'd purchased earlier. I had enough food, beverage, and entertainment to last me across country. Spread out on my folded-out table, in the comfort of my reclining train seat, the food and entertainment sat, because all I could do was stare out the window and wonder what this weekend would bring.

Three hours later, I exited the train and made my way up the escalator toward the lobby. In the sea of people, I found Joe immediately, dressed in a black chauffeur jacket and hat, and holding a sign: MELISSA FLETCHER.

We ate dinner at Joe's favorite restaurant, a seafood place right in Newark. When he insisted I try the lobster bisque, I nodded eagerly. When Joe asked if I liked sautéed calamari, I told him I loved it. When

Joe couldn't decide between the swordfish or the tuna, I told him I was having the same exact dilemma. We decided to split.

Because of our history, there was a familiarity that fooled us into thinking that time hadn't passed. Eventually we learned to offer a preamble to every story, the backstory of our narrative. Joe spoke of the birth of his children, what it was like when he was deployed, the guys he'd lost in war and the ones who came home, with whom he would always have contact.

And I chattered mostly about Dad, how we built the business and what it was like to help our clients solve their problems, but mostly I talked about my trips to Italy, then India, and what it was like to feel true elation for once.

Through the hotel lobby, past a pianist playing a shiny grand piano, amid the glow of golden table lights and the muffled sounds of conversation and low laughter, we walked toward the elevator. Joe pressed "Up," and when he released his hand, it brushed against mine. I reached for it, squeezed it tight.

In the hotel room, Joe and I sat on the edge of the bed, our knees bumping against each other. He reached for my face, kissed me deeply. After years of researching myself in and out of every decision, listing the pros and the cons via spreadsheet, weighing the risk against the reward, I was now reckless and careless and fully willing to walk down this dark alley without my mace or safety whistle. I didn't care whether it worked out or if I was clobbered in pain from the rejection afterward, I just wanted Joe.

I lay back on the bed, pulled him onto me. We kissed and kissed, and then I reached for his belt buckle. My only goal was to touch every inch of his body, to have him entirely. Any thought of holding to a schedule of appropriateness had evaporated.

He moved my hand, though. "Just let me kiss you tonight," he said, and we lay there, staring at each other—two mirages from the past.

"I want to be with you," I whispered.

"I want to be with you, too," he said, kissing me again. "But let's wait, at least until tomorrow."

"You're turning down a sure thing," I joked.

"It's taking every ounce of strength," he admitted.

I wanted to laugh and cry at the same time, because Joe was still as good a man as he was fifteen years ago and the fact that he put the brakes on made me want him all the more. I loved that he was being respectful, offering me boundaries, because he didn't need to. I was already his. He could have me as soon as he wanted. I would follow him anywhere.

Or perhaps he was self-conscious about his leg. And then I questioned my motives, whether my wanting him was true desire, or my way of proving to him that I loved him completely, leg or not.

An hour later, Joe and I resembled teenagers who had staggered from the backseat of a car after a marathon make-out session. Our mouths and faces were red and swollen, our hair tousled and tossed, our clothes wrinkled and askew.

"I should go," Joe said. When we stood at the door saying good night, I—Missy Fletcher, the brave girl on a weekend trip to see her high school sweetheart, the cartographer treading into new territory—decided to stake my flag. "I love you, Joe," I said. "I've always loved you."

"I've always loved you, too," Joe said, and it wasn't until later, after he left, that I turned that phrase over and over, until I had examined it from every side. That Joe "had always loved me" wasn't exactly the same as his saying that he loved me now.

In the morning, I showered and dressed, and then waited in the lobby for Joe to pick me up for coffee. When I saw him from across the room, my heart thumped. "Does he do it for you?" I remembered Dad asking about Lucas.

We drove for a few blocks until we were at Rise N Shine. "I'm here every morning," Joe said as we approached the door. "Wait'll you try their butterscotch scones."

His face turned glum when we saw a sign hanging from the door: CLOSED FOR A ONE-DAY RENOVATION.

"Closed?" Joe said. "I can't believe it."

"I'll die without a butterscotch scone," I joked.

"There's another good shop, just down the road."

We drove a mile farther and parked in the lot of Earthly Paradise. We pushed through the glass doors. The aroma of dark-roast beans and sausage-biscuit sandwiches filled the air. We stood in line, then put in our order and lingered off to the side, commenting on the good smells, the artsy décor. Joe held my hand. I stared into his eyes and grinned crazily. The knowledge that I was here with Joe was a reality; I knew that. But still. This was *Joe*, the guy I had dreamed about for the past fifteen years.

Maybe Dad had been right all along, that I had been putting a ceiling on my happiness because I didn't think I deserved to have it all. Somehow I'd relegated myself to the back of the room, pushed against the wall, the girl with the glasses and the laptop who spoke only when spoken to, and who never offered an idea of her own. Why? And why did I think I didn't deserve Joe? There was no reason to think that this couldn't be the start of a brand-new future.

I thought of my old life on a spreadsheet: work, Rosetta Stone, *Jeopardy!*, Italian gelato, lurking on Facebook. Now my new life: jet-setting to Italy, setting up a school for girls in India, "gambling" with a portion of my investable assets, reuniting with Joe—the man I had loved for two decades.

A smile poured through my entire body. I was allowed to be this happy. The sky was not going to fall on top of me because my happy meter was smacking against the rails.

Suddenly, Joe dropped my hand and took an awkward step back. When I looked up at him, I followed his eyes to the front door. In the entryway was a woman and three children. I didn't need a translator. The warmth that had infiltrated me turned to nausea, as if the knowledge that I'd chugged sour milk had just hit my stomach.

Lucy, Katherine, Olivia, and Jake. Joe's family, only feet away.

I looked up at Joe, who—to his credit—was remarkably calm, but clearly uneasy. When the kids saw their father, a unified chorus of "Daddy!" sang from the mouths of the younger two. The older daughter appeared to eye her father and me somewhat skeptically, but joined her little brother and sister in encircling Joe in hugs. If I could have melted into the earth, I would have. I was cornered, and felt utterly exposed. If only I had a drop of my father's DNA to get me through this.

"Hi, Joe," Lucy said.

She was gorgeous. Of course she was. A thick mane of auburn waves, glowing and fresh-scrubbed skin, thick eyebrows, and mile-long lashes. The type of girl who hated me in high school because I was smart and she was pretty and we didn't mix well.

"Guys," Joe said to the kids. "Lucy. This is my friend Missy. She and I went to high school together, if you can believe that."

"You went to high school?" Jake said to his father.

"Back when the dinosaurs roamed," Joe said.

"High school in Alexandria?" Lucy clarified, speaking to me.

I nodded.

"And you live in New Jersey now?" she asked.

"No, I'm still in Alexandria."

"What brings you to our neck of the woods?"

Our neck of the woods. Like she and Joe alone owned New Jersey.

"Just visiting," I said lightly, smiling, but for all I knew I had the squiggly-lined mouth of nervous Charlie Brown. Lucy—ha! *Lucy*— would pull the football from me at any minute, landing me flat on my back.

"Visiting family, friends?" she asked.

"Geez, Mom," the older daughter, Katherine, said. "It's like you're interrogating her."

Lucy glared at Katherine.

"Me," Joe answered. "She's visiting me."

"Oh!" Lucy responded, slapping her own forehead. "My bad!"

"Joe," the barista called, signaling that our order was ready.

"Kids," Lucy said. "Can you say hello to Daddy's friend?"

A jangle of hellos escaped from them.

"Hi, guys!" I said. My falsetto was crazy, the voice of a strung-out druggie.

"We should go," Joe said. "Bye, kids! I miss you!"

"Where are you going?" Jake asked.

Joe halted, looked at me uneasily. "I thought I'd show Missy some of the sights."

"Take her to Emille's," the little guy said.

"Why would he take her there?" Olivia wanted to know.

"Because Mom loves that place and she's a girl, too."

"That'd be dumb," Olivia said. "Dad's not going to—"

Katherine took her little brother by the sleeve. "Jake, come with me." She steered him toward the pastry display, looking back at me with what I perceived to be a look of pity.

"But why?" Jake whined.

"Do you mind if I say you're a total dork?" Katherine said.

"Kids will say the darndest things!" Lucy piped in.

"We'll be going," Joe said.

We took our coffees from the counter and exited the shop. Joe drove us away, and neither of us said a word the entire trip back to the hotel. Inside the lobby, the same oxygen that left me euphoric only an hour before was now under pressure, and damaging my lungs. If I didn't get back into the atmosphere soon, I might die. Finally, I spoke. "That was a lot."

"I'm sorry," he said. "That was horrible and you must have felt ambushed."

"This might be more than I bargained for," I confessed.

"Don't say that," Joe said.

"I think I need some time alone," I said. I knew myself well enough to know that the clock was already counting down: 10-9-8-7 . . . and by the time it reached one, any confidence I had would have withered to nothing.

"I want to spend the day with you," Joe said, but if I was detecting his tone correctly, he was as freaked out as I was.

"Maybe later," I said. "I think I'd better go up now."

"Are you sure?"

"Yeah," I said. "Call me later?"

Joe nodded and I made a beeline for the elevator, stepping in and watching the doors close just in time. The tidal wave of childhood insecurity hit before I even reached the third floor.

Flopped onto my bed, the bed where Joe and I had just made out the night before, I cried silently as though all the bad news of my life were brand-new: We're sorry to tell you your mother was hit by a giant truck! You'll spend your entire childhood motherless. We're sorry to inform you of your father's Alzheimer's! Oh, by the way, he won't last long. The dementia will clobber him like a cartoon anvil. And then he'll have a stroke and the nurse you were too afraid to dismiss will let him die.

Oh, and Joe? We'll bring him back to you with such tenderness that you'll feel as though nothing in the world could keep you apart. Except for his wife and three children, the four human beings who will matter more to him than you ever could. Every time you see them, you'll know where you stand: against the wall, because there are only five seats at their table.

I had put on a good face, had acted brave traveling through Italy and then India, had made a good showing of being Frank Fletcher's

Jennifer Handford

daughter. But dating Joe, my high school sweetheart who had an ex-wife and children and one leg—who was I joking? I just wanted to be home in my town house, burrowed into the down comforter on my bed, my pint of pistachio gelato nearby. I wanted to recite my Italian phrases. I wanted to chart stocks. I wanted my father. I even wanted Lucas, because loving him was risk-free. I knew what he was—a tax-free municipal bond with a good yield. It would never make me rich, but it was steady and predictable and, under no circumstance, would it spike or plummet. There would be no conditions where I would feel like this.

Who the hell do you think you are, Missy Fletcher? You're no one's daughter or wife or mother or sister. You belong to no one, and no one belongs to you.

I lay quietly and stared numbly and watched movies and ate room service. At noon, Joe knocked on my door. We sat on the bed and held hands. "Promise me you won't make any decisions?"

I agreed, which was a lie, because I had already made up my mind: I had strayed too far off course. Charting new territory was one thing, but opening my heart so that it could feel like this was something entirely different. Living an adult life was still brand-new to me. Book-smart, I needed to work my way through some classes and tests before I was ready to be out in the field.

"I think I'll head home," I said. "There's a train leaving at 1:40."

"We barely spent any time together."

"I know," I said. "I'm sorry. It just made it so real. That you have a family: three kids, a wife. I can't possibly imagine how I would fit into that."

"That's because you don't know everything."

"What?"

Joe brushed my hand. "Straight-A-student Missy Fletcher doesn't know everything. Your IQ might put you at genius, but none of us knows what's planned for us. When it comes down to it, we need to trust in the grand plan."

290

"Do you?" I asked, though clearly he did, whether this plan was divine—driven by the God he had always believed so fiercely in—or just a knowledge he'd attained after seeing as much as he had.

"I have faith," he said.

"After everything you've been through," I said, "how could you have any faith left?"

"Faith is a choice, Miss. I choose it." He smiled. "It's not a coincidence that our paths have crossed again. There are no mistakes when it comes to me and you."

CHAPTER FIFTY-TWO

The weeks that followed fell into a predictable pattern, one I clung to. In the daytime I did the work of the orphanage—filing paperwork, soliciting NGOs for support. With the lawyer's help, we created our entity: Global Education Initiative, and were able to piggyback off our Fletcher Financial 501(c)(3) organization. Our firm had already proved a long history of giving to worthy organizations. From there, we created a new entity, funded not only with my personal money but also with some of the Fletcher Financial "Give Back" program's money.

And Joe. He and I talked every night. Our conversations were as familiar and warming to me as my childhood bedroom. He was exactly the same, and entirely different. He maintained a bubbling enthusiasm for life, organic gratitude toward mankind, a genuine desire to help others—that was the same as eighteen-year-old Joe. He was deeply thoughtful, contemplative, reflective—that was thirty-six-year-old Joe. There was nothing simple, dogmatic, easily definable about him. If I thought for a second that I would find in him a blind acquiescence to a creed or code, I would have been wrong. He hated the war he fought in, he believed passionately in each of his men, he valued all human life. Nothing was simple. Everything was difficult. Everything was gray. He was nuanced and pained and laden. He was mature. He carried his adulthood like a pro. He was a veteran, in every sense.

And with his children, he tried so hard, cared so much. He coached Jake's soccer team. He built sets for Olivia's school play. But Katherine he worried about the most. She continued to struggle with her self-esteem. A clique of popular alpha girls had decided they couldn't bear the fact that Katherine, with her straight As and passion for reading and writing, couldn't name a Justin Bieber song and chose to wear the wrong brand of skinny jeans. Joe didn't need to describe for me the hundred different ways they chose to punish her for these failings. I knew their work all too well. Joe shared his worries with me, and then, as if catching himself, would pull himself together with a tidy, "She'll be fine! Girls like her are the ones who do the best, later in life. Look at you," he always said, as if I were a shining example of the tortured girl in middle school eventually rising to the top.

I would agree, because I knew he needed me to agree, to affirm his belief that his daughter would be okay—eventually, but these stories of Katherine hit me in the gut. Later, after Joe and I had said good-bye, I'd lie in bed and think of her, because she and I were the same. Along with so many others. And not all of them were "fine." Not all of them made it out of middle school.

"When can I see you again?" he asked one night.

"Anytime you want," I answered without reservation because I ached for him, wanted my hands on him as badly as my heart wanted to pump blood. The resolve I'd felt in New Jersey, the certainty about not being part of his life, had faded almost immediately once I left. "But you have to come here." I couldn't stand the thought of running into his family again. I wanted him, but it had to be here.

A few weeks later, Joe called. "Guess what?"

As it turned out, Katherine had been chosen as a finalist in a Library of Congress writing contest. She would be honored in DC, at the Library of Congress itself. "We're coming to your territory," Joe said. "Are you up for meeting Kate again?"

I had thought about Katherine so often, I felt I already knew her. But who was I kidding? She was bound to hate me, because for her, I was no one worth knowing. Her parents had just divorced, and I was Dad's "new friend." She would have no choice but to hate me out of maternal deference, out of spite for her father, because she was simply a teenager, and she wasn't supposed to like the things and people her parents liked. But I still remembered that day at the coffee shop, how she stepped in when her mother was asking me so many questions, when she'd tried to defuse the situation by steering her little brother away, by stopping Olivia from saying more. At the time, I'd thought she looked at me with pity, but now, as I considered it, maybe it was empathy.

"I'll try."

The following weekend, Joe and Katherine arrived. We had decided that they would get settled—take the Metro to their hotel, rest a bit—and then meet me for dinner. When I'd asked what Katherine liked to eat and Joe said, "Believe it or not, she loves seafood," I knew just where to recommend.

When I pushed through the doors of Pier 6, Joe and Katherine were already at the bar. Joe was drinking a frosty ale, and Katherine appeared to be sipping from a soda. When Joe saw me, he signaled to his daughter, and they both smiled. Joe walked to me, leaned in and kissed me on the cheek, and then led me back to the bar.

"A formal introduction," Joe said. "Kate, this is Melissa."

"Congratulations on your writing contest," I said. "I read your essay. It was great!"

She seemed surprised. "Did my dad give it to you?"

"It was posted online," I said. The theme of the contest was "A Book That Shaped Me," and Katherine wrote about one that took place in Afghanistan, before the Taliban, and how the main character was once at school, and then a day later—once the Taliban was in—she was no longer able to go. Katherine did a nice job of juxtaposing this situation to America, where education is free and available to all.

"Thanks for checking it out," she said.

"What genre is your favorite?"

"Mostly historical fiction," she said.

"Anything depressing," Joe added, "war, poverty, the Holocaust."

Kate smirked at her father. "True, I like reading about kids in tough situations." She went on to tell me about a Newbery award winner she had just read, about a boy from Sudan who became a refugee after rebels ripped through his village, and another book—an MLK Literary Arts award winner—about a young girl torn from her village and forced onto a slave ship, where she was sold to a cruel master in Virginia. "I also loved another book about a girl who had cerebral palsy and couldn't communicate, but inside she was brilliant."

Katherine Santelli was thoughtful, articulate, and so far, not at all acting like a teenager. There was no eye rolling, no "whatevers" or "yeah rights." Talking to her was like talking with an adult, but then again, as I thought back, I was the same way. I had had an easier time relating to adults than teenagers, when I was Kate's age. When the waitress came, I said, "I don't know if you like clam chowder, but it's really good here."

Katherine loved clam chowder and ordered a bowl, as did Joe and I.

After a few bites, Katherine said, "Do you mind if I say this is the best clam chowder ever?"

"I don't mind at all," I said. "Because I'm in total agreement."

For dinner, Katherine ordered the grilled shrimp over wild rice, I chose the crab cakes, and Joe got the snapper. We passed on dessert. "There's a place right down the road," I said. "The chocolate soufflé is worth the wait."

While the soufflé cooked, Joe and I sipped coffee and Katherine enjoyed a hot cocoa with whipped cream. "My dad told me about the work you're doing in India," she said. "When I grow up, that's the kind of work I want to do. I want to help people. Somehow."

"I believe you," I said, "after listening to you talk about your reading. You certainly have the heart and the mind for it."

At the end of the night, we said our good-byes. "Thanks so much for meeting me," I said. "It was really nice talking with you."

Katherine took an awkward step forward and then stuck out her hand. I took it in mine and then decided to be brave. I pulled her in for a quick hug. "Good luck tomorrow!"

She looked at her dad, and then at me. Hesitantly she said, "Do you want to come?"

"Would you?" Joe said.

"I'd love to," I said.

That night, I lay in bed with my phone, texting Joe. She's amazing.

I worry so much about her, he wrote.

Me: She's perfect exactly how she is.

Joe: But she doesn't fit in.

Someday, I typed, but couldn't finish my thought. Wasn't my life an anthem to "someday"?

The next morning, I left my town house and walked to the King Street Metro station. The morning was brisk and cool yet sunny. By the time I hit the station, I had already shed my jacket and scarf. I rarely rode the Metro, and this morning, on such a quiet day with low ridership, I relished the thrum of the car zipping over the tracks. At the Smithsonian station, I disembarked. Once on the National Mall, I walked toward Fourteenth Street. Joe and Katherine were approaching our meeting spot, coming from the opposite direction. The book festival was setting up, giant white tents spanning ten blocks. We found the location where Katherine would be awarded her prize.

The ceremony was lovely. As a finalist, Katherine was called up onstage. She posed for a photo with the director of the contest, as well as the editor of the KidsPost for the *Washington Post*. Afterward, we spent some time in the tent, which was set up like a bookstore. While

Katherine browsed, Joe and I held hands, and the electricity between us—our want for one another, especially during this weekend, when we couldn't be alone—jolted shocks through my limbs. After checking that Katherine was absorbed in a book at one of the tables, I leaned into Joe, put my mouth on his neck. Risk-averse Missy Fletcher had the urge to make out with her boyfriend, right then and there.

"I'm going to need to see you again, soon," Joe whispered into my ear, kissing the top of it, sliding his fingers along my neck and into my hair. "You're killing me."

The following weekend, Joe returned to Virginia to see me. He knocked on my door, and when I opened it, we rushed to each other. We were frenzied, clawing at each other. Stripped of our clothing, disrobed of any pretense, we slipped into bed. I kissed his gorgeous neck, ran my fingers over the marine tattoo on the crest of his hip. He rose to sit on the edge of the bed and removed his prosthetic half leg. I turned away to give him privacy, but it didn't matter because Joe's missing limb meant nothing to me in terms of my love for him. I ached for his loss, but not for mine.

Then I felt Joe's body next to mine, his chest against my back, his arms around me. I turned so that we were face-to-face. I closed my eyes and I was there again, at the beachside hotel, the first time Joe and I made love. Then I opened my eyes, and I was here and so was he. I no longer needed to fantasize. Joe was in my bed, loving me.

Later, we slept, wrapped in arms of animal warmth. When we awoke, it was three in the morning. A thin stream of light slanted through from the bathroom night-light.

"What are you doing to me?" I asked, tracing my finger along the ridge of his cheekbone.

"Loving you," he said.

"For how long?"

"I've always loved you," he said.

"But will you love me forever?"

"I'm no longer a guy who makes promises," he said. "Life has shown me that even the most heartfelt promises can break."

"If you don't promise me forever," I said, kissing his mouth, "what will I believe in?"

"In yourself," he said, kissing me back. "Believe in yourself, Missy Fletcher."

Later, with Joe's head on my lap, I drew maps on his back, an elegy to our past, a sonnet to this moment in our present, a ballad of love never forgotten. We knew enough to respect time and space in this moment, were aware that the air and light around us would forever be the touchstones we'd rely upon to remember it. We were optimistic, yes, but we were wary, too, enough to know that a moment like this might never come again. As archivists of our love, it was our job to carve etchings of it on our souls.

PART THREE
DAUGHTER

CHAPTER FIFTY-THREE

The next week, sitting at my desk at Fletcher Financial, I slipped into the cozy sweater of nostalgia, remembering Dad and five-year-old me and our Saturday morning routine. How the two of us climbed the steps up to the office, me holding my McDonald's breakfast in one hand and the Holly Hobbie doll that Mom had given me in the other. There, Dad would take my doll from me and hand me the big copper key, and his titanic hand would guide my miniature one as I inserted it and strained to turn it. Then the sense of delight when the lock clicked and the door swung wide—an *Alice in Wonderland* entry into the enchanted space— draping me with the familiar scents of worn leather, musty files, and mahogany. Dad's office, his space—the coveted, comfortable, cavernous clubhouse he loved so much. A space I learned to love because I knew it was the portal to bring me close to Dad.

The phone rang, knocking me from my daydream.

"Ms. Fletcher, please," the formal voice said.

"Speaking."

"Ms. Fletcher, this is Marcus Arnold, Director of Giving at the One by One Foundation."

My heart thundered. Mrs. Longworth's charity. I flipped open my binder to the tab marked "One by One." By now I knew much about this sizable philanthropic organization that issued so many grants to NGOs and individuals. They had been operational since the early '70s with the mission of helping the socioeconomically marginalized children of the world become self-reliant.

"Yes?"

"We are in receipt of your grant application and are interested in learning more about your project in India."

"Wonderful," I said.

"We know this is short notice, but the board would like you and your partner, Reina Shephard, to present next Tuesday, at our monthly appropriations meeting. Would you be willing to come to Chicago to meet with us?"

Next Tuesday. Suddenly, I was tasting metal. I wasn't exactly sure of Reina's whereabouts and hated to schedule her without first connecting, but I had to say yes. Reina would make it work, I reasoned. She'd get here.

"Yes, definitely!"

Mr. Arnold spent the next five minutes apprising me of the protocol. How we would be called in when it was our turn to present, how there would be a projector for our use, should we need to plug in a laptop. He explained that the board would expect a bound copy of our proposal with all of the financials clearly delineated. I jotted down all of this information.

I sucked in a few deep breaths, looked at my notes. *I could do this.* I had six days to prepare for this meeting. Already I could picture my PowerPoint presentation, my neat graphs and charts, the net worth statements with pie charts. This was right up my alley. Preparation was my forte. And stunningly magnetic Reina would do the speaking. We could pull this off.

"Thank you," I said. "Thank you so much."

"I'll e-mail you the specifics," he said. "See you in a week."

When I hung up, I walked to the mirror on my wall and looked into my eyes. "You can do this!" I would do this. I might die in the process, but there was no doubt I had started something that needed to be finished.

I called Reina and hit FaceTime, something I never did. When she answered and her cheerful face greeted me, I said, "Guess what? Guess who wants to meet with us?"

Reina screamed, hooted, and hollered for the next five minutes. "You have got to be kidding me!" she kept saying. "Oh, this is good; this is *so* good."

When I told Reina that the presentation was scheduled for next Tuesday, that she would need to meet me in Chicago, her face fell. "Miss, hate to tell you, but I'll be in Spain."

A marble lodged in my throat. "Are you serious?"

"I can't get out of it at this late notice," she said. "UNICEF conference, and I'm leading a session."

"I'll reschedule," I scrambled. "Let me call him back, and see when the next appropriations meeting is— "

"Missy, no. You'll do it yourself, and you'll be fabulous," Reina said. "This is your thing—the numbers, the details. You'll nail this baby."

"Reina, I can't," I said. "I can't make the presentation."

"You can, and you will." Not a centimeter of wiggle room.

"You sound like my father."

"Missy, I know how much you loved your father—but enough with it! You're not him, and he's not here, and you're entirely perfect just as you are. You will present how *you* present, not how he presented. You will do this, and you'll be great."

"Yeah, okay," I said, knocking my head against the wall.

When I hung up with Reina, I called Joe and, in his usual optimism, he said, "I knew you'd do it. I knew you'd take the world by storm. How can I help?"

"Will you go with me?"

The next five days I kept my head down and plodded through the numbers. Reina did her part, e-mailing me ten times a day. She knew the region so well, the conditions of the children from her work with UNICEF. In our opening paragraphs, she wrote of the quarter of a million children in New Delhi who live in slums or on the streets. These children did not go to school. The literacy rate was only 33 percent. For our objective, Reina wrote: "To identify known orphans, to educate them while tending to their basic needs of food, shelter, and protection from victimization."

Under the section headed "How we will proceed," she explained how we would partner with an existing NGO whose mandate was to work on issues affecting the urban and rural poor, with a specialized focus on children. Reina went on to include non-orphan girls, as well.

Reina spoke of the fathers: how it was they who were called upon to care for their daughters, to ensure their fair treatment, their rights; how their own poverty had most likely led them to keep the daughters at home, rather than send them to school. Part of our outreach would be to the fathers, to educate them about their future as well as their daughters', should the girls remain unschooled.

For my part, I created a financial report detailing the costs of the school. Tuition, books, uniforms, extracurricular activities. Reports, audits, office needs. Electricity, construction, janitorial. Vehicle use, faculty salaries.

For our scope, I wrote that our school would open to forty girls, the twenty-two orphans currently living in Rohtak, plus eighteen others. Class sizes would be segregated by age: the youngest girls to age seven, the girls aged eight to twelve, and the girls beyond the age of twelve. We would hire three teachers, each responsible for her educational curriculum as well as a hefty program of singing, dancing, and making art. So many of these girls had been robbed of a joyful childhood. We were determined to restore a portion of this. They would learn while they played.

The days passed and the adrenaline pulsing through me kept me focused until finally only two days remained before I would meet with the One by One Foundation and convince them to give us a grant.

Joe called. "You're ready! You'll be great!"

Jenny called. "I was cleaning out one of your dad's drawers," she said. "I came across a handwritten quote. 'In the end, we only regret the chances we didn't take.' Pretty appropriate, huh?"

Then Monday came and kicked through my door with its jackboot. No amount of Dad's affirmations could free me from my doom.

Joe was scheduled to drive down from Jersey tomorrow, but I needed him tonight. I stared in the mirror and attempted to steady myself against the dotted mirages that flashed before me. *Who the hell did I think I was?* Missy Fletcher, who had one skill—managing money—was going to miraculously morph into an oratorical genius? I was going to stride forth in my power suit with my PowerPoint and PowerBar and deliver to this committee a presentation that would leave them shaking their heads, wiping their eyes, and looking for their checkbook? *That was your father, you idiot.*

I was in mid-heave when the phone rang.

I sobered up immediately. I couldn't say why. In a matter of seconds, my sticky skin dried, my heaves subsided, and my mind arranged itself back to normalcy.

Something was wrong.

CHAPTER FIFTY-FOUR

I had heard people speak of premonitions, of a twin feeling a twinge when her sibling was hurt, a mother stopping dead in her tracks when she sensed her little one was in danger. The ring of the phone was like that. Spooky. Eerie. It was Joe.

"Is everything okay?" I asked.

"We're just getting home from the ER."

"What?" I shrieked. "The ER?"

Joe sighed, let out a moan of frustration.

My heart punched at the walls of my chest. I needed to know, but didn't want to know. If I knew, it would be real. I forced my mind to think of something common: Jake sprained his wrist. Olivia had a raging ear infection. But in my heart of hearts, I knew it was Katherine. At-risk Katherine. The girl who wanted to be invisible.

"What happened?" I asked, and then held my breath and waited for the earth to shatter.

"Kate," he said, and this one word alone produced bile in my throat because Katherine hurting herself had been on my mind for some time now. "She was in the bathroom tonight. After a few minutes, I knocked on the door to check on her. She wouldn't open up."

"Why?"

"'Open up!' I yelled through the door, pounding on it with my fist."

"Joe," I begged. "Please tell me she's okay."

"She wouldn't open it, so I busted it down. She was in the corner like a cat rolled into a ball, crying quietly. When I peeled her off the floor, she shielded her arm. I pried it into the light. There were burn marks inside her arm."

"Joe," I cried.

"She had lit matches—many matches—and pressed them into her arm."

"Joe," I wept, pressing my forearm into my stomach. "What did she say about it?"

"She said the pain, the physical pain, hurt less than how she was hurting inside. She just wanted a distraction." Joe's voice broke, and he started to cry. I had heard him cry only once. When his grandfather passed away, a good seventeen years ago.

"She's asleep now," he said, a gauzy calm lacing his midnight voice, the sound of a guy who had spent the last three hours in a hospital room.

"Joe," I said. "I'm so sorry."

"My kid's in pain, Missy," Joe said, and then lost it—waterfall lost it. He sobbed, and all I could do was cry on my end of the line.

After a while, he pulled it together like guys do, kind of yelled and punched at the bed, I imagined. "Enough!" he said to himself. "Listen, Miss, I can't tell you how horrible I feel about leaving you in the lurch, but I don't think there's any way I can go with you tomorrow."

"Oh, please!" I said. "That's so unimportant! The only thing that matters is Katherine. The *only* thing that matters. I'll just cancel the meeting, try to reschedule it. Can I come up to Jersey and see you guys?"

"Missy," Joe said. "Kate's not the only girl that matters, and you know it. You're fighting for an entire school of them. Don't blow off your meeting. Go to Chicago. Make your presentation. And then come see us, okay? Promise?"

When I hung up, I could barely breathe. My heart raced, and I pounded my hands on the kitchen table. I wiped my eyes. "Help her!" I pleaded, because Katherine Santelli was the good in this world, and yet, this world was going to kill her. There had to be something I could do!

And as for my sorry state of affairs—no Reina, no Joe, no Dad. Just me.

CHAPTER FIFTY-FIVE

The next morning I flew to Chicago and took a cab to the towering glass headquarters of the One by One Foundation, right on the Magnificent Mile. Before I knew it, I was waiting outside the conference room for my name to be called. Before I knew it, I was asked inside. Before I knew it, I was standing at the head of a giant conference table, surrounded by twenty board members. Before I knew it, I was talking about the financials of the school as easily as I had once talked to Dad or Paul about the technical aspects of a client's account. I knew my stuff, was able to answer any questions, and though the sense was otherworldly—surreal—I was as calm as could be.

And when I was finished, I texted Joe to check in on Katherine. She was at home, in bed. Joe's mother was by her side. A marathon game of Scrabble was under way. Enough homemade cookies to last a few weeks.

Can I come to Newark? I asked carefully. I have some thoughts on Katherine, and I was hoping to meet with you and Lucy.

Both of us? he texted back.

Yeah, I typed, holding my breath. Can you arrange it? Text me the details?

A seed—from where, who knows?—had been planted, and all of a sudden I had a plan, a crazy, outside-of-the-box plan. A Frank Fletcher plan. A Reina Shephard plan. A visionary plan. I would need both Joe and Lucy on board.

Trust me? I texted. And I love you. And say hi to Katherine.

Once in Newark, I took a cab to the Rise N Shine coffee shop. Joe had texted me that he and Lucy would meet me there. From the window I could see them sitting at a table. Joe was rubbing at his face, overwrought, mired in pain. Joe, my indomitable hero, my unstoppable champion, wore gray stubble on his face and a crushing sadness in his eyes. When he saw me, he brightened and waved. Lucy smiled tightly. I approached their table and said hello. I removed my jacket and went to the counter for a cup of coffee. Back at the table, we volleyed perfunctory pleasantries about my flight, the weather, the aroma of the French roast.

The strange thing was, I wasn't scared. I was confident. I was calm. I finally got it, finally understood: So long as I was pursuing my passion, I would always find courage. I would be restored. My history of silence didn't have to be my future.

When we settled in, Joe provided the preamble to our conversation. He looked at Lucy, then at me. "I think Missy wanted you to join us, Lucy, because she had some similar experiences when she was in middle school that Kate is having." Joe looked toward me. "Is that right, Missy?"

I nodded at Joe, because he was right in a thousand ways. "That's true," I said. "But that's not why I wanted to meet."

This surprised Joe. "Oh," he said.

I looked up at Lucy, at Joe. "I have an idea for Katherine, and before I say it, I want you *both* to know that it is not at all hinged on the relationship that Joe and I have started up." I met Lucy's eyes and held them. "I like Katherine a lot," I said. "I think she is a gem of a human being with a heart of gold. She's smart and lovely and a true joy to be around." My throat filled with tears, and it took all of my power to not let them flood the gates. "Anyway, I want to be clear," I went on. "I'm here because I care about Katherine, and for no other reason."

Lucy clearly had no idea what I was talking about. Why should she? I was a stranger to her, and all but a stranger to her daughter. Who knew what I was about to come out with? But to her credit, she seemed sincere when she said, "I appreciate that, Missy. And I agree with all of it. Katherine's a wonderful girl"—she glanced at Joe, then turned back to me—"and we're worried sick about her."

I pressed on. "None of us knows what tomorrow will bring. I don't for a second believe that your marriage wasn't wonderful for a lot of years." They were a beautiful couple, I saw that, even now. "And Joe, what you saw at war . . ." I stopped, took a sip of water. They were staring at me, and why wouldn't they be? What I came to say was sounding like nonsense.

I braced my hands on my legs. "I'm not making sense," I said.

I took another gulp of water. "Here goes," I said. "I'd like to bring Katherine with me to India."

"What?" Lucy gasped.

"Missy." Joe echoed his wife's shocked reaction.

I went on. "Hear me out. Katherine has already tested two years beyond her grade," I said. "Joe, you told me that. And here we are, already in December. Would it really hurt to pull her from school for the rest of the year? And in January, when I go to India to get the school ready to open, Katherine could come with me. I could homeschool her while we're there. "

"She's only fourteen," Lucy objected. "She's my daughter. What you're suggesting—"

"I know it sounds crazy," I said. "But Katherine is mature beyond her years, and it's obvious she honestly desires to help others with this kind of work."

Lucy twisted at her napkin. "How long will you be gone?"

"About a month and a half—six weeks, give or take." I looked at Lucy expectantly. *Was she really considering this?*

"She *is* only fourteen," Joe said.

"I'll care for her. I promise you both," I said. "She will be well taken care of. I adore her, and I would love the chance to spend some time with her. And don't get me wrong: she'll be working. There is so much she could help us with: hiring teachers, working on their English, setting up the classrooms, choosing books and materials, and just being a positive role model for the girls who'll come to the school."

Lucy covered her face.

"She would feel worthy," Joe said, as if to himself. "She would have a purpose."

"That's exactly why I think it would be good for her," I said. "Working there will be a great healing experience for her. I really believe it. Gandhi said it: 'The best way to find yourself is to lose yourself in the service of others.'"

Lucy looked up and wiped her eyes. "I don't even know you, Missy."

"We could get to know each other," I said.

She trained her eyes on Joe. "What do you think?"

"I think it's a radical idea—pulling her out of school, sending her to India," Joe said, then fell back against his chair and shook his head, smiling. "But I think it might be the perfect plan. I can see it feeding her in a way nothing else could."

"Are we really considering this?" Lucy asked, then laughed. "Is this for real?"

They were on board; I knew it. They wanted to pull Katherine from her school as badly as I did. "The next step would be to talk to Katherine, to see if she has any interest in this."

There was no turning back from my adulthood now. I only hoped the yoke on my shoulders didn't snap.

CHAPTER FIFTY-SIX

On the seventh day of January, Katherine and I boarded a jumbo jet to New Delhi, India. I had flown to Newark to "pick her up." At the airport to see us off were Joe and Lucy, Olivia and Jake. There were concentric circles of hugs: Joe hugging Katherine, then me. Olivia following suit. Then Jake. I pivoted and held open my arms, without awareness that in front of me was Lucy. Her hug was tight but not warm: perhaps a warning; perhaps she was scared. It didn't matter. What I'd worried about in the beginning—me, trying to graft myself onto a family that was already rooted—was no longer a fear. There were no promises in life. A four-year-old's mother could be clobbered by an HVAC truck. A woman could spend two decades of her life without a love affair. Fathers died. Men went to war and were killed every day. Some came home changed. Marriages dissolved over much less. And girls around the world were disenfranchised in a variety of ways—lovely Katherine, so overlooked; the society of girls in India, so undervalued.

On the plane, Katherine and I buckled up. I made sure she had everything she needed: a blanket, a pillow, a bottle of water. On her lap was her Kindle, her iPod, her stuffed walrus.

Katherine looked at me expectantly. "Can I ask you a favor?"

"Anything," I said.

"Would you call me Kate instead of Katherine? I'd kind of like to leave Katherine behind."

"Of course," I said, curious, but not wanting to pry.

She offered anyway. "My mom's kind of famous for calling me Katherine. You know, three syllables Katherine: *Kath-er-ine!* Usually when she's disappointed in me."

I hadn't expected Kate to be so forthcoming, and all of a sudden I wondered if I was equipped to be her adult chaperone. "Why on earth would your mother be disappointed in you?" I asked.

She shrugged. "My mom was hoping I'd be the 'it' girl." Kate held back for a second. It seemed she was gauging my reaction. I nodded. "You know the one?" she went on. "The girl with the perfect 2400 on her SATs, homecoming queen, athlete of the year, all while volunteering at the homeless shelter every weekend?"

"Yeah," I said. "We had one of those girls. It wasn't me, clearly!"

Kate smiled. I wondered if she felt a kindred spirit in me.

"Your mom loves you to death, though," I said. "I can see that."

"Sometimes I feel bad for her," Kate said. "She likes things 'just so.' She used to pose us for Christmas photos, and I have to admit, when Dad was in his dress uniform and the three of us kids were little, we looked pretty good. Then Dad lost a leg and I started to freak out over everything. All of a sudden, none of us were 'just so.' I think that's why she took a job. To get away from us."

I looked straight at her and willed my face to appear normal, even though I wanted to crumble. "No one would run away from you, Kate," I said. "Your mom might have some of her own stuff she's dealing with, you know?"

The flight attendant made her announcements, and soon we were in the air.

"Is this the time where we say good night?" Kate asked. Prior to the trip, we had talked on the phone and I had gone over with her my airplane routine, my fear of flying, the precision with which I had to follow my steps: Xanax, relaxation tape, breathing, counting.

"I feel like I'm okay," I said. "Maybe I'll skip the Xanax this time."

"Don't worry about me," she said. "I'm not going anywhere."

I looked at her and grinned. Just being next to her, knowing in some sense she was mine—at least for this trip—filled me with pride. I knew I was only borrowing her. Joe and I might not work out; I knew that, too. But for the next six weeks, I had the opportunity to be someone to Kate. Plenty of people had been someone to me through-out my life—my father, of course. Jenny, Paul, now Reina. But could I honestly claim that I have ever been *someone* to someone else? I took the responsibility seriously. Kate was in my hands, and I wasn't going to let her down.

I skipped the Xanax but went through my other steps. Before I knew it, we were soaring through the sky. Over the next five hours, Kate and I played cards, we raced each other on the Sudoku puzzle in the airplane magazine, I read a book off her Kindle—*A Long Walk to Water*, a book she had chosen because of its topical relevance—and she read the grant proposal that had secured us money through the One by One Foundation. We brainstormed names for the school, imagined what the uniforms would look like, talked about the curriculum. We ate dinner, we ate candy bars, we listened to music from her iPod, and then we discussed the schoolwork she was required to complete dur-ing her absence. Science and math were fairly self-explanatory: a few pages of math problems each day, a ton of worksheets to complete for science. History was basically reading, as was classics. The big project was for English.

"I need to write my own 'hero's journey,'" Kate said. "Ever heard of it?"

"Joseph Campbell," I said. "The heroic monomyth." I'd studied the hero's journey in middle school, reading *The Hobbit* and *The Lion, the Witch and the Wardrobe.*

"Exactly!" she said. "Though it shouldn't be too hard. Surviving middle school is kind of like going on a hero's journey."

"True," I said. "And so is this trip. We're definitely crossing the threshold into the unknown."

Kate dug into her backpack and produced a visual representation of the monomyth. We looked at it together, traced the challenges and temptations that followed stepping from the mundane known into the unknown. How death and rebirth were the result of falling into the abyss. How transformation and atonement led the hero back home.

"Is it okay if I say I hope our adventure isn't quite *that* eventful?" Kate said.

"If it is, your parents will murder me."

With hope for an adventure, we fell fast asleep.

The next morning we landed in New Delhi, one of the largest cities in the world, with over twenty million residents. Our plan was to settle in, to adjust to the time difference, to let the jet lag slough from us gradually. After a night of rest, we'd take the train to the Taj Mahal before heading in the direction of the orphanage. Kate had been a real trouper on this long flight, but now she was showing signs of wear. I couldn't forget that she was still a young girl in need of a good night's rest. And most likely, she missed her parents.

Once we checked into the Marriott, Kate called her mother first, and then her father. When she finished with Joe, she handed me the phone. I watched her wipe her eyes and walk into the bathroom. She was jet-lagged, tired. She was homesick. This might be harder than I thought.

"She's amazing," I said.

"I can't believe she's there, with you," Joe said. "This is a bit surreal."

"We're fine," I assured him. "She's tired, but all's well."

When Kate emerged from the bathroom, I asked her if she wanted to get into jammies and order room service. She brightened at this idea. "I don't know why I'm sad," she said. "I'm having so much fun."

"Oh, honey," I said. "It's okay to be sad. You're away from home. Please don't feel that you need to be cheery for me." I handed her a tissue. "Besides," I said, "this is good material for your monomyth. 'The road of trials'—the challenges you must undergo."

Kate blew her nose, then nodded. "Good point! All heroes must fail some of the tests they're given."

"Not that you've ever failed a test for real."

"I'm doubting you ever have, either."

"Not an actual test," I conceded. "But then again, I've never been on a hero's journey before."

"Same," she said.

And then we crawled into bed and ordered room service—cheeseburgers and fries and Coke—as we flipped through the channels on the television. When we came across *The Wizard of Oz* in Hindi, we knew we had found the perfect hero's journey to lull us to sleep. So long as we got there before the part with the flying monkeys.

CHAPTER FIFTY-SEVEN

The next morning, Kate and I peeled our way through the breakfast buffet in the dining room of the hotel restaurant. Kate peeled an orange and banana. I peeled us two hard-boiled eggs. Peeling was our mantra. To peel away any contaminant. Just to be safe. While we were at it, we peeled at our own pollutants, picking at the parts that were tainted by suffering and struggle.

"My dad said you were supersmart in high school," Kate said.

"Like you," I said, skimming my knife under the skin of a mango.

"It's just that"—she halted, then picked it up again—"schoolwork is easier than the other stuff." Kate picked at the poison that covered her skin. The arsenic of bullies.

I nodded, slid a few pieces of mango onto Kate's plate. "That's how I felt, too," I admitted. "Schoolwork I understood, but the social scene . . . well, that was like . . ."

We looked at each other, shrugged.

"Translating Greek!" Kate said, and then we both laughed and said "Nah" because translating Greek really wasn't that hard.

"More like starring in the lead role of the school musical," I said.

"Exactly," Kate agreed. "That would be torture."

"But then I met your dad," I said, "and he was like my good luck charm. He thought it was cool to get good grades *and* star in the school musical *and* play sports."

"I heard," Kate said. "He was the 'all-around guy.'"

"There wasn't much he couldn't do," I admitted.

"My mom was hoping I'd be the 'all-around girl,' but alas . . . no." Kate's eyes drooped, as if she had swallowed a vial of shame. A toxin of a different source. From inside her own house. As confusing as a seemingly fresh glass of water infected with an invisible disease. How was Kate to process the notion that her mother wished her to be someone different?

"You have a giant heart, Kate," I said. "I wouldn't trade an ounce of it to be more 'something.' You have an amazing amount to offer. It's still a little buried. Same as me. We just need to peel back our layers." I lifted an orange peel for illustration.

She rolled her eyes at the heavy-handedness of the metaphor, but I could see she was with me.

"That's what's so cool about your dad," I said. "He sees under everyone's peel. He once gave me this Neruda poem that talked about 'the light of hidden flowers.' It's easy to believe in people when they have it all together on the outside. It's way cooler to believe in them when what they have is still a little buried."

"Speaking of good luck charms," Kate said. "We kind of need a talisman. If our hero's journey is going to be complete. To aid us in our quest."

"Fair enough," I said. "Let's keep our eyes out."

After breakfast, we returned to our hotel room and went through our checklist, made sure our backpacks were securely zipped and locked, that our money and passports were safely strapped inside the waists of our shirts.

"We have to be on the defensive," I said. "Some of the street people are very persistent."

Once we were dressed in clothes that covered us from head to toe and rendered us as inconspicuous as possible, I checked the zippers on Kate's backpack. I dug into the small zipper of my own backpack to make sure I had ready money so that I wouldn't have to open my money belt in public. As I jammed my fingers into the small space, I felt something hard. I made tweezers with my fingers and pulled it out. It was the charm of St. Brigid! The patron saint of travelers! The charm Dad had given me that I was so sure I had lost. "Kate, you're never going to believe this," I said.

"What?"

"We found our talisman!" I held it out for her to see and told her about it, how my father had given the charm to me on my birthday with the hopes that I would take a trip, how I'd thought it was lost for good.

"It's our talisman!" she said.

I reached around her neck and secured the clasp.

"You're letting me wear it?" she asked, reaching up to feel it.

"I'm letting you *have* it," I said. "If you want it. I'd love for you to have it."

Kate lunged into my arms.

We were ready for our next step.

We bought train tickets to Agra and after a 220-kilometer ride, we exited the rails and headed toward the Taj Mahal. Immediately we were accosted by souvenir vendors, unofficial guides offering us private tours, and children selling trinkets. I took Kate by the arm and pushed through them. Protecting Kate was my priority. I had assured Joe and

Lucy of my ability to do so, but now that we were here, I questioned whether I would have the skill to get us through these aggressive crowds. "No, thank you! We're all set!" I pushed us forward.

We made it to the guards with the guns, who frisked us and checked our bags. After the guards passed us along, I reclaimed my grip on Kate's wrist, a hold she tried to twist from every so often, trying to point at something, but that was *not* going to happen. Not on my watch. With my sunglasses perched atop my head and my money belt strapped tightly around my waist, I squeezed Kate's wrist with one hand and the brochure in the other and read: "The Taj Mahal is the finest example of Mughal architecture, combining the style of the Persians, the Indians, the Islamic, and the Turkish."

"Missy!" Kate said.

"Hold on," I told her. "Listen to this. Construction began in 1632, and over the course of its building, over twenty thousand laborers worked on it."

Kate tugged at my sleeve. "Missy! You're missing it."

I looked up and saw that we had passed through the archway, and what stood in front of us—our first peek at the Taj's dome—was otherworldly. White marble so pristine its purity seemed ethereal. The sun beamed gloriously on the unspoiled palace. Just then, a clump of clouds shrouded the brightness, and in its shade, the Taj mellowed to a dreamy pink.

Kate and I stared at each other in wonder.

"It says here that the white marble often looks as though it's changing colors, depending on how the sunlight and moonlight hit it," I said.

"Kind of like getting away from school," Kate said. "Everything looks different in a new light."

I gawked at her. "You *are* just fourteen, right?" I joked, nudging her, this little mystic who seemed to have it all figured out. The fact that she almost let a group of middle school girls derail her cut me in half.

"I'm totally serious," she said. "Just getting some distance—being here—I already feel totally more equipped to go back, you know?"

I knew we were only a few days into this trip and that it would take time for Kate to find the strength and confidence to weather the storms of her teenage life, but this—getting some distance, gaining perspective—was as good a first step as I could hope for.

The next day we boarded the train back to New Delhi. The minute we stepped from the train there, we were crowded by beggars. I pulled Kate through the train station and when I saw her eyes focused on a group of children—a few of whom were deformed or missing limbs—I pulled her close to me and told her she needed to be prepared, that she was about to see more sadness than she had in her lifetime. I had already told her about the multitude of orphan children, many of whom had been abducted by crime rings and mutilated so that they would appear needier when sent out to beg. An entire society of orphan children spent their lifetimes—barely out of infancy—working for others, every day, long hours, for very little food and wage. Though I had already told Kate about the horrors of India, I watched her face grow pale. She could not look away from the band of children.

I took Kate's arm and led her inside the train station and sat her on a bench. I pulled out our bottle of water and gave her a swig.

"These kids," she said, grasping for words, her solemn eyes glued to mine. "Their problems . . ." She covered her face and began to cry. "I feel so stupid. So selfish, complaining about . . ."

I hugged her. "Kate, no," I said. "You cannot make comparisons. Each person has her own struggles. Your struggles were . . . *are* . . . real. Don't minimize your feelings just because we're staring at kids worse off."

"Still. There has never been a day of my life when I haven't had my basic needs met: food, clothing, shelter, love. I've never been too hot or too cold. I've never been forced to do anything against my will." Her shoulders bobbed and she cried some more.

I planted a kiss on her forehead. "Oh, honey, thank God that's true. And yes, it is true. We're First World girls with First World problems. But we're here now to help these Third World children with their Third World problems. We're going to make a difference, Kate."

"I want to help them," Kate pleaded. "We have to help them."

"We will," I said. "And meanwhile, we can definitely say we've 'crossed the threshold' on our hero's journey, right?"

"Good point!" Kate said, wiping her eyes. "We have definitely left the known limits of our world and are venturing in a realm where rules and limits are not known." She pulled out her journal and poured her heart into three pages of notes.

A half hour later, I was greeted by a vision far more beautiful than the Taj Mahal. In front of me was Reina—golden-ray-of-sunshine Reina in cheerfully red capris and a skintight T-shirt, not the least bit concerned with looking conspicuous. And the fact was, Reina blended in any-where; she belonged everywhere. She didn't need to cover up to meld with the local culture; her attitude did it for her.

"That's Reina," I whispered to Kate.

"Wow," said Kate.

We stood and I wrapped Reina in a giant hug, then stepped aside. "And this," I announced with ceremony, "is Kate Santelli."

"There ought'a be a law," Reina said, hugging Kate, "against being this gorgeous."

Kate beamed.

There were gleeful moments of hugging and touching and appreciating each other, incandescent smiles filled with joy, admiration for haircuts and clothing choices, backpacks and jewelry. Just as Reina was complimenting the matching friendship bracelets Kate and I had made on the flight over, Kate pulled out a third one and handed it to her.

"We made one for you, too."

Reina lit up, rolling it over her wrist, and then walked to a street vendor and purchased three colas.

We returned to the bench, and after Kate distributed candy bars from her backpack, Reina briefed us on our next leg. She had once again hired her pal Salim to be our driver and translator. He would be here shortly to drive us to the orphanage. While Kate kicked back for a minute, Reina filled me in on the latest legal machinations. Her buddy from HBS was able to secure us our license to operate, and his family had been happy to purchase the parcel of land that stood adjacent to the existing structure. Demolition would soon begin and our new building would be erected.

"Bribes—large and small—greased the wheels," Reina said. "But this is India. Bribing is SOP."

According to Reina, the community was already buzzing, and if early interest was any indication, outreach to area fathers wouldn't present the challenge we feared it might: they had already taken to waiting with their daughters outside the existing building, hoping to enroll. Though Mrs. Pundari took their names and assured them she'd be in touch when registration began, they still returned, day after day.

When Salim arrived, we greeted him like an old friend. I hadn't noticed the first time around, but he was probably only eighteen years old himself, a good-looking guy with low-slung slacks and seriously styled hair. It was the way he looked at Kate that clued me into his youth.

"Kate's fourteen years old," I said to Salim. "Fourteen."

In Salim's car, we drove first through the congested city streets and then into the countryside, where the crowding and shocking poverty scarcely lessened. Kate was shell-shocked, and because I felt my words were weightless against the demands of her grief, I simply draped my arm around her and offered her my shoulder. To see the barefoot children wading through the mountains of garbage, the preteens asleep on the edges of the street, and the girls soliciting themselves in alleyways was belladonna to the brain.

Thunder rumbled; rain dumped from above, roads filled with ankle-deep water. With Kate still glued to my shoulder, I wondered about the shoddy rooftops and dirt floors and children on the streets we were passing. What did a deluge like this mean to them? How many times could one family rebuild before they lost the will to survive?

The rain had stopped by the time we pulled up to the orphanage.

"Home for the Orphaned and Malnourished Girls. Home for the Destitute," Kate read quietly.

"Don't worry," I said, squeezing her hand. "It's actually quite happy inside. Wait'll you see the girls."

Reina and I gathered backpacks and bags from the trunk of Salim's car and led Kate to the building. We entered through the back and wended our way until the chorus of chatter and girls filled our ears. When the girls saw us, they greeted us with smiles wide enough to bridge the garbage-laden country.

Mrs. Pundari had prepared lunch for us: flatbread grilled on her griddle and topped with vegetables. While Reina ate according to Indian culture, using her hand as a utensil to tear up her bread, mixing in the vegetables and sauce, and scooping the contents into her mouth, Kate and I opted to keep our bread whole, and instead wrapped our veggies inside, like a burrito. The girls sipped from their small steel cups, ate, and never stopped giggling.

Hours later, as the afternoon sky darkened, Salim drove us three miles down the road to town and the motel we would call home for the next six weeks. It was a provincial little motel, far from the Marriott in the city, but it was nice and clean and would provide a safe refuge for us each night.

The next day, we got to work.

CHAPTER FIFTY-EIGHT

It was only our second day at the orphanage. Kate and I were working outside, curriculum materials spread out on a flat piece of scrap wood set atop two old sawhorses, when a teenage girl hobbled up. She was an amputee—one leg, the other stopping below her knee, just like Joe's, but no prosthetic. She was pretty, with a long, glossy braid and bright eyes. She told us her name was Aneeta. "It means Grace," she said.

"My middle name is Grace," Kate said.

Aneeta told us she lost her leg when she was trapped in a house fire when she was little. Kate told her about her father. And like that, they became BFFs.

Aneeta wasn't typical of the kids in the area. She actually had two parents and both of them supported education. Though her mother hadn't been educated formally, her father had, and taught Aneeta to read when she was little. Kate told Aneeta about some of her favorite books. They went off to look at them, and from that moment on, they were nearly inseparable. Kate Santelli, a kid who couldn't make a friend all year in middle school, even if her GPA depended on it.

Aneeta helped us out, as well. She was able to tell us what most Indian kids in this region knew and didn't know. Many of them were wise in math because of the bartering and selling of goods they were forced to do. While most of them had at least a basic understanding of English, their reading skills were poor. And as for history, what was going on in the rest of the world, most had very little idea.

"With a population as large as ours," Aneeta said, "you would think that there would be more to our lives, but they're actually quite simple, quite small."

Every minute of every day, we worked. In the morning, crews of laborers would show up, or they wouldn't. Some days we were hopeful, watching the men demolish walls, knowing that soon new ones would be rebuilt. But then days would pass and the workers wouldn't arrive on the site, and we were left trying to maneuver around yet another pile of rubble.

One week, the construction crew rolled up, ready to install the toilets, a luxury the orphanage heretofore hadn't enjoyed; only, the workers couldn't begin because the water taps and plumbing had yet to be fully connected. In order for the water work to be finished, we needed new paperwork to be signed and stamped, even though we had already completed sheaves of forms the month earlier. The ironic thing was that it wasn't about the big money; it was about the small money. Between my start-up capital, the grants we'd received from One by One, and a number of alliances we had forged—chief among them one with water. org to provide for safe water and sanitary conditions—we had the operational budget. The problems we encountered were largely bureaucratic, structural, political—all of which required incentive money.

Aside from the construction issues, we continued to be swarmed with interested girls and their fathers. Notices had been posted in the village alerting the families of the school's opening. Each day, girls and their fathers, sometimes their entire families, would walk to the construction site, drop off their applications, and ask to be accepted. So far we had more than one hundred applications for only a handful of available spots.

Every night Reina and I read applications and made piles, aware that our decisions meant choosing to give opportunity to one girl while denying it to another.

Each morning, Kate worked alongside Reina and me. In the afternoon, she gave reading lessons to the orphanage kids and any other curious kids who'd come to check out the school. With Aneeta's help, they split the youngest from the oldest kids into groups and worked on their English.

I had only known Kate for a short time, but I knew her well enough to savor the glow that now emanated from her. There was no hint of the anxiety that had once muffled it. Her face was now wide-open and joyful, eager and expectant. She had traveled overseas and seen a much bigger world. She had lived in a village hemmed in by tradition and environment and seen a much smaller world. Somewhere in there, she had found her place. Much of the same could be said for me.

Because the daily operation of the orphanage had no choice but to continue on in the midst of the construction, it did, shuffling living quarters and kitchen supplies to one side of the building, and then again to the other. Meanwhile, the construction crew did its part to accommodate the residents, building new walls and structures on the outside, before knocking down the old facades on the inside. For many weeks, the image was one of a building wrapped around a building, a graft and a host, scaffolding encasing an ailing edifice.

We had been working for exactly a month when the Dynamic Duo—Kate and Aneeta—approached me with mischievous smiles.

"Cat? Canary? What are you two up to?"

They looked at each other, holding hands, and grinned conspiratorially at me. "We have the most awesome idea!" Kate said.

"And by *awesome* you mean you have a way to get the construction workers to work more than four hours a day?"

"More like awesome for *us*," Aneeta said.

Kate looked at me with puppy-dog eyes, an expression that struck me as extraordinarily childlike—a state I didn't think Kate was altogether familiar with, worrying for her father at war, assuming her position as the eldest child, maintaining her straight-A averages. "We want to have a sleepover."

"Here?" I asked, already thinking that there was no problem with that. There were plenty of new beds in the dormitory.

"At Aneeta's," Kate said. "Her parents said it would be okay and they would be home the entire time and they would walk us both ways."

I looked at Aneeta, not wanting her to think I didn't trust her parents. "Aneeta, you know I adore you and your parents, but I kind of vowed—like promised on my life—that I wouldn't let Kate out of my sight."

"It is only a mile away," Aneeta assured me, in her mature British-English voice. "And our house is substantial, with a real door and lock."

I knew this to be true. Kate and I had walked Aneeta home on a few occasions. Her family lived in a relatively nice neighborhood.

"It's a mile from here," I said, "but it's at least four miles from the motel where we stay every night."

Now the two of them were giving me puppy-dog eyes, their hands clasped together in begging position.

"I need to mull it over," I said, thinking I would find Reina and run it by her. "When do you want to do this?"

"Tonight," Kate said.

"Tonight!" I gasped. "Why tonight?"

"Because there is a lunar eclipse," Aneeta explained, "and my father has a telescope and said we could watch it."

Kate leaned in close to me and whispered, "I've never slept over at a friend's house."

"Never," I said. A statement, not a question. I had gone my childhood, tween, and teen years without a sleepover, too. I'd overheard girls talking about them—pricking their fingers to become blood sisters, painting each other's nails, confessing truths that made sense of adolescent confusion.

"Once a girl slept over at our house," Kate said. "But I've never slept over at a friend's house. Please?"

I looked at the two of them, then shooed them away. "Go, you little beggars. Let me think about it."

I found Reina hunched over a giant blueprint, discussing with our foreman the plans for the water lines. I listened in for a while, and then walked away with the thought that I would catch her later. I could text Joe or Lucy, and gauge their reaction. But how would that sound—me, the supposed adult in charge, looking to them for advice as to whether Kate could have a sleepover with Aneeta? They didn't know Aneeta, or her parents, or the town, or the risks attendant to her leaving my side. It would only make them worry.

I got back to work, screening candidates for the headmistress position. She would work alongside Mrs. Pundari, though Mrs. Pundari would continue management of the food and housing, whereas the new hire would be in charge of the school and the teachers. There was one woman in particular in whom I was particularly interested. Her name was Ms. Chopra, and she was educated in Mumbai at the university, though had returned home to Rohtak to care for her parents. Although she hadn't had the opportunity to graduate, she had taken numerous classes in education, special ed, and curriculum development.

When Reina was free, she sauntered over, glimmering from the diamonds on her sunglasses and the diamonds in her eyes and the diamonds she kicked up in the dust. "Need me?" she asked.

I outlined for Reina my dilemma about letting Kate go home with Aneeta. "What if something happens while she's out of my reach?"

Reina looked at me with disapproval. "Let the girl go," she said. "It's Aneeta! Her family is lovely and educated. Nothing will happen to her."

"You're right," I said. "Of course, you're right."

When I delivered the news to the girls, they yelped and jumped in the air and hugged me until I couldn't breathe. Hours later, after we had put in a good ten hours, Aneeta's parents arrived at the orphanage. The girls ran to greet them, and when Shri and Aadesh nodded their heads and smiled, I knew the news of the sleepover had been delivered.

"Thank you for having her," I began, when they joined me on the steps.

"This will be such a treat for Aneeta," Shri said. "She and Kate have become . . . how do you say?"

"Two peas in a pod," I said. "Yes, indeed they have."

"The walk is not far," Aadesh said.

"This sounds crazy on my part, I know," I admitted, "because you walk this walk every day to get Aneeta. And I know she walks it herself much of the time. But . . ." I stalled, worried about insulting them. "Would you mind if Salim drove you all home?"

Shri laughed. "Of course, that would be fine."

"Let me just make sure Kate has everything she needs."

I went inside and held Kate by the shoulders. "Kate, you know that your life is in my hands, right? If something happens to you, I would *die*—like, hero's-journey, throw-myself-into-a-fiery-pit *die*. I need you to tell me that you will be safe. That you will make only safe decisions. Okay?"

"I get it," she said. "I promise we'll stay inside Aneeta's house, except to look out the telescope."

"You have your phone?"

"Got it."

"Text me the second you get there."

"Got it."

I reached for her and squeezed her into a bear hug. "Promise me you'll be safe and smart."

As Kate drove away with Aneeta's family, my heart seized into a fist. I had just let a fourteen-year-old girl in my charge out of my sight in India. I flashed to a time I'd gotten lost in the supermarket when I was little. "Where's your mother?" I remember a woman asking me. I stood there shaking my head *no* because I didn't have a mother and this lady asking me about her whereabouts made that reality ache in my heart. When my father found me, the lady gave him a disapproving nod, and then she looked at me and dumped the responsibility into my lap: "Stick close to your father, in case he loses you again."

A few minutes later, Kate texted that they were at Aneeta's and that she and her friend were inside and were planning to read books for a while.

I calmed down. Just a bit.

Around seven, Reina announced that she was ready to call it a night. I agreed that I was finished working, too . . . but the idea of returning to our motel a good three miles in the opposite direction made me nervous. Here at the orphanage I was only a mile from Kate, should she need me. On the other hand, if I let Salim and his car go for the night, I would be at the orphanage without transportation, so what good would my proximity do? At least at the motel I could hail a taxi if a situation came up.

"You're kind of green," Reina said. "You look like you're going to puke."

"I might just do that," I admitted. "I'm worried about Kate. What if something happens to her?"

"She's fine. It won't."

"Gang of thugs? Earthquake?"

Reina shook her head.

"Fire?"

"Unlikely."

"Don't tell Aneeta that," I said. "She got stuck in a fire, remember?"

"I'll tell you what," Reina said. "Why don't you and I stay the night here at the orphanage? I'll have Salim run me into town for some takeout for us. I'll ask him to stay 'on call.' The proximity will make you feel better."

Near midnight, after Reina and I and all the girls in the dorm had eaten a feast from a restaurant in town, played hours of cards, we retired to our bedroom, a newly constructed room where the live-in headmistress and a few teachers would sleep. The room smelled of fresh-cut pine. Reina and I flopped onto the new bunk beds, exhausted from the day. After a few big breaths, Reina pulled herself up, walked to the desk under the window. Kate had been working at that desk, doing her homework and other projects for the orphanage and school.

Reina rubbed her finger along the touch pad on Kate's laptop, stared at it for a minute.

"Snooping around?" I said, yawning, a little surprised that Reina would be looking at Kate's laptop.

"I was actually just checking to see if our new electricity was working," she said.

"Is it?"

"Yeah . . ." Reina said, distracted, clearly reading something on the awakened computer's monitor.

"What are you reading?" I asked.

"I didn't *mean* to read anything," she said. "But I just happened to see Kate's writing."

I stood and joined Reina at the laptop. I recognized the document on the screen as Kate's monomyth—the hero's journey she was writing for English. She had it dissected into steps: the call to adventure, refusing the call, answering the call, supernatural aid, crossing the threshold, entering the belly of the whale. She was currently writing about one of the trials her hero encounters: temptation. Her protagonist, Prosperina, had left the village and gone into town with a girlfriend. The girlfriend tempts Prosperina with an ancient herb. She tells her it's harmless, but wonderful, like standing in the middle of a diamond shattered into a million pieces. Prosperina hesitates, but the girlfriend persists, until finally she submits and smokes the magic herb.

My heart gonging feverishly, I looked at Reina and found her biting her lip. In the margin of the story in a comment box was Kate's note to herself. "Aneeta's house, record feelings, details."

"They're going to do drugs!" I shouted.

"Well, now . . ." Reina said, with maddening calm.

"Reina! We've got to get to her. What if she's already done it? What if they were 'bad' drugs? What if she's sick . . . or worse? Oh my God, Reina. We've got to get there."

"Okay, okay, let's think. Let's calm down and think. On one hand, this is just a story—"

"Reina!"

She jumped. "All right! You're right—it does seem to be pretty fact-based. I'll call Salim and see if he can come get us." She pulled out her phone.

At the same time, I texted Kate. No response.

"Salim's not answering. It's going straight to voice mail," Reina said.

I shoved my feet into sneakers and found a flashlight in the store-room. "Forget it, I'm walking," I said. "More like running."

Reina pulled on her sneakers, too.

When we got outside, we were met with a darkness I could never have imagined. As if blackout curtains covered the sky, as if a black

Sharpie underscoring my grievous error in judgment had been swiped across the heavens. I should have never let Kate go. I had lost her. I had failed. I wished the night sky would swallow me whole.

We were out in the middle of nowhere with not a house light or streetlamp or car passing by. Just inches outside our flashlight's anemic beam, we literally could not see our hands in front of our faces.

When at last our eyes had adjusted slightly, we could just make out the road. After Reina walked directly into a fence, I stepped clumsily into a hole and twisted my ankle.

"How are we going to walk a mile like this?" Reina asked.

"We're not," I said, reaching for her hand.

"We can't see a damn thing."

"Kate!" I hollered, though she was nowhere around. "Kate!"

Then I fell to my knees and heaved a tidal wave cry because there was a chance I had made a mistake that couldn't be fixed. There was a chance that I had ruined a life—more, lives. "Kate," I cried. "I'm sorry, please. Give me another chance."

Just then my phone issued a beep, alerting me of a text message. Maybe it was Kate. Please, let it be Kate.

It was Lucy.

Hi Missy, Just checking in. Haven't heard from you or Kate yet tonight. Have her text, okay?

I covered my face and cried. In my stupidity, in my childish, lethal naïveté, I had assumed that I would always be saved from whatever trouble I happened to fall into—by Dad, by a safety net, by my risk-averse behavior. But what I'd fallen into now, I couldn't see to the bottom of.

CHAPTER FIFTY-NINE
JOE

Tuesday again. Up on the fourth floor of the veterans' hospital, I found my group of guys. Five minutes in, I could already tell that Tony was in a mood.

"F— this, f— that. Food sucks, pain never ceases, f—ing headaches getting worse."

I let him bitch for about five minutes without correcting any of his language, without pointing out the bright side to still having one leg and two arms and a more-than-well-functioning mouth.

Andy, though, was in a good mood. He told the group that he had been reading a lot of books about "crossing over" and how thin the line was between life and death. "I think I have a better sense of life because I was so close to death," he explained, his eyes dreamy.

"That's one of the freebies of war," I said. "How close you come to death gives you a hell of a perspective on life."

"That's it," Andy said.

"It's not just war," I said. "I once was on an airplane, sitting next to this brilliant pediatric oncologist. Kids died around him every day, yet he had this look to him—this understanding that put him at peace. 'How do you do it?' I asked him. You know what he said? He said that spending time with someone who is so close to leaving this world almost makes you feel the next world."

"Bunch of shit," Tony grunted. "Dead's dead. Worms in your head, dead."

"What do you say, Carlos?" I asked.

Carlos hung his head low. "I'd deny this if any of you jerks repeated it," he said. "But when I was lying there—blown to bits—all I felt was anger. I was angry I was being cheated out of the rest of my life. I'd never get married, hold a kid, drink another beer. It was this anger that saved me, though. I channeled it into my will to live, to see another sunrise. I was angry but calm, like I knew if I stayed mad enough, I'd survive."

"Same for me," Andy said. "I felt the same way." He looked right at Tony, raised an eyebrow. "Bro, you can't tell me that after what we've been through, you don't feel that there is more than meets the eye. Life as we know it—this mortal, amputee-learning-to-walk-and-live-again life—is just part of it. I feel it, I really do."

Tony opened his mouth to spew some more garbage but stopped, hung his head. "Whatever," he said. "I guess."

I looked at the guys—one at a time. "I'm not saying that any of this was set in the stars, anything preordained or such. I'm just saying that we set out on a path, made choices based on what we were good at, what our interests were—for us, we became soldiers, sailors, airmen, or marines. But at some point that path ends and another path is placed before us. It could seem random, but to me, if you give it enough thought, doesn't it seem like all the paths know each other, like they knew all along they'd intersect?"

"That's it," Andy said. "That's how I look at it, that everything that has happened did so for a reason, and as screwy as it sounds, I wouldn't change a thing."

I left the meeting feeling incredibly hopeful, as if my group had made some sort of emotional progress. I drove to Holy Angels to pick up Olivia and Jake. Olivia started chatting before she was even buckled up. "Daddy, Daddy, guess what? There's going to be a talent show . . . and I can sing in it, or say a poem, or even do comedy . . . wouldn't that be hilarious?"

I just stared out the windshield and grinned because things were looking up. My two youngest kids were happy as could be, Kate was in India with Missy opening a school for girls and feeling good about the work she was doing, my group of wounded warriors was talking philosophy and theology and finding meaning in their situations. It had been a long time since I felt so optimistic about everything. Just like when I was eighteen. I loved that feeling.

When we got home, I found Lucy's car in the driveway. She wasn't scheduled to pick up the kids until Thursday night, so I wasn't sure why she was at the house unless she needed to pick up or drop something off. She had already moved everything she wanted from the house to her new condo, so I couldn't imagine what she would need. When we opened the front door, a delicious aroma wafted toward us.

Lucy stepped out from the kitchen and held her arms open for the kids, who ran to her.

"What's going on?" I asked.

An apron covered her T-shirt and jeans. "Oh, nothing! Just thought I'd cook you dinner so you'd have it for later," she said, stepping back into the kitchen and scooping up a pile of cut carrots to add to the salad bowl. "Chicken cutlets with mushrooms in a white wine reduction."

If the kids were in a good mood before, they were over the moon now. Mom's home! They chattered excitedly all the way up to their rooms.

"You're fixing us dinner?" I clarified, going to the stove to take in the chicken and mushrooms simmering in a creamy sauce. Lucy could cook, but Lucy didn't *like* to cook. Tacos from a kit or pasta with jarred sauce was much more her speed.

"You object?"

"Not really," I said, stabbing a mushroom, placing it into my mouth. "I'm just a little surprised."

"Once it cools, I'll put it in the fridge," she said. "You can heat it up later."

"If it makes it to the fridge," I said, spearing a piece of chicken.

"I haven't heard from Katherine today, have you?"

"No, but that's not unusual, right? We don't hear from her every day."

"Most days," Lucy said. "You think she's all right?"

"Of course I think she's all right," I said, still examining Lucy closely; the dissonance of her wearing an apron and cooking a dinner that required wine and deglazing was like trying to make sense of a kangaroo in our yard.

"You trust Melissa," she said. "I know that. And so do I." Lucy bit into a baby carrot. "She's great, Melissa. Right, she's great?"

"Agreed," I said. "She's pretty great."

I looked at Lucy and she looked at me. Our eyes locked. What the hell was she up to?

I changed the subject. "How's work?" I sat on the sofa and removed my prosthetic, leaned it against the wall, hung the silicone sleeve that protected my skin over it.

Lucy shrugged her shoulders. "It's good, busy." She went to the refrigerator and cracked open an ice-cold beer for me. "I'm a little tired of all the travel." She poured herself a glass of white wine.

Lucy came and sat down next to me. Close to me. Too close. For some reason, I was self-conscious about my stump. It had been a long time since Lucy and I had sat on the sofa together. A long time since she had seen my half leg. "What's going on, Lucy?"

"I don't know," she said, sliding in even closer, curling her legs under herself like a cat. "I guess I just miss being here. With you, with the kids."

"Uh-huh," I said, attempting to scoot closer to the edge, to make at least an inch of space between us.

"Seeing you and Missy—how she looks at you, how you look at her. Kind of makes me *jealous*. Kind of makes me wish things were different."

I stood up, hopped a foot over, fell into the chair. "I thought *all this* is what you were sick of."

"I think I made a mistake," she said, standing, coming to the arm of my chair, leaning into me.

"Lucy," I said, getting up, hopping toward the table, holding on to the wall, wishing I hadn't removed my prosthetic. "You left us. We've been legally separated for over a year. We signed divorce papers."

"We could reverse it," she said, walking toward me. I was pretty much helpless, leaning there. With her hands against the wall on both sides of my face, she leaned in and kissed me. I felt her lips before I turned, ducked under her arm, sprung to the chair. Reached for the silicone sleeve, my damn prosthetic, snapped it into place. "Goddamn, Lucy, what's gotten into you?"

"I want you," she said. "That's all. I just want to be with you."

"Are you sure?" I asked. "Or am I just looking good from a distance? Because nothing's changed, Lucy. I'm still wounded, still have PTSD. I'm still a marine, still the guy who deployed when you wanted me to stay. What's changed?"

"Nothing's changed," she admitted. "It's just hard seeing you with someone else, okay?"

"That 'someone else' is taking care of our daughter at the moment. Don't you think this is a bit inappropriate, given that?"

Lucy's face turned to stone. "Perhaps," she said. "But let's be real, it's Game Over for me. You know Missy and Kate are bonding. You know Missy is a better mother than me."

With that, Lucy grabbed her purse and walked toward the door.

"Are you going to say goodbye to Olivia and Jake?" I asked, pointing upstairs.

"Tell them I got called back to work," she said. "They'll understand that. Work comes first. You taught them that, right Joe?"

CHAPTER SIXTY

The good thing about hitting rock bottom is that there's only one way up. My father's words whispered through my brain. I sat up, wiped my eyes with the bottom of my shirt. I had an idea.

With my pathetic flashlight, with squinted, straining eyes, I pulled Reina back up the rutted road toward the school.

"Where are we going?" she asked.

"You'll see."

I led her around to the work shed. Once inside, I lit the kerosene lantern I had seen Mrs. Pundari light a few days before when she and I had come to the shed for extra mattresses.

Looking up at the corrugated metal roof, Reina asked, "What's in here?"

"A motorcycle, I believe."

In the back corner, obscured by cobwebs, was a little Suzuki 125.

"Whoa, wait!" Reina said, digging her nails into my wrist.

I looked at her. "Help me," I begged.

Reina and I pushed and pulled furniture and boxes out of the way, unearthing the bike. I had ridden a motorcycle exactly one time in my life, when I had gone on a camping trip with my schmuck of an ex-boyfriend, Jason. He had given me a perfunctory lesson on how to start and shift, and then had taken off without me. When my bike stalled and I was all alone, I had no choice but to persist in executing the steps he had taught me until the bike roared to life.

Now, I placed my hands on the handlebars, swept up the kickstand, and lunged forward with the bike. We brought it toward the kerosene lamp and inspected it. It had a key in it, which was good. The gas tank was empty. That was bad—but only a temporary setback: in a red container we found some fuel, and emptied it into the chamber.

I sat on the bike, squeezed the clutch with my left hand, and clicked it into neutral. I flicked on the headlights, and then found the button I believed to be the ignition. I turned the key, held on to the left brake, and then pushed the button. It sputtered and then died. I looked at Reina. I primed the pump and then tried again, and this time it revved to life, momentarily, before it died. I gave it some throttle and it roared, but then gave out again.

"Come on!" I hollered at it, trying again, wiping at my stinging tears. This time it bucked under me, and kept running. I looked at Reina and smiled. "Hop on."

The two of us burst into tears, laughing at the same time.

She climbed on behind me and clung to my waist. I gunned the engine, put it in first gear, and released the clutch gently. We began to move forward. The bike's headlights were hardly an improvement to my sad flashlight. Even so, we found the road and cruised along in only second gear, as we strained to see the few feet in front of us.

"Look out!" Reina shouted, pinching my sides.

Too late to brake, I saw what she saw: a scrawny cow sauntering across the road. I swerved and missed him by a few inches. After that, I took to honking my horn every minute or so.

After a time, the blackness that circumscribed us, the drone of the bike, the cool and crisp air, the confetti of stars in the sky all enveloped me like a hug. The terror I had suffered at first was gone. The adrenaline that had fueled us to this point receded. Now, even though I had yet to reach Kate, I felt as though I were being transported toward her, as though I were floating her way, somehow both leaving and entering at the same time. I would save her. I knew who I was and I knew where I was—exactly on the line that separated safety from risk. I had a toe on each side. If Kate was in danger, I would save her. I would risk life and limb to rescue her.

"I can see civilization," Reina said, digging her chin into my shoulder.

Once the outskirts of town emerged from darkness, we were able to see streets populated with a scattering of homes. We veered right at the stop sign and then left at the next one. Aneeta's house was the fourth on the left, down a narrow dirt road. I stopped the bike, killed the engine, and we climbed off.

"Now what?" I said. "It's after midnight. Do I just go up to the door and ask if Kate and Aneeta are smoking ancient herbs?"

"Yeah, you do that." Reina rolled her eyes.

"There's no way to do this without looking like I'm checking in."

"You *are* checking in, and Aneeta's parents won't think a thing about it. They're parents, too."

I opened my eyes wide, reminding her that I wasn't a parent.

"Well," she said. "You're *acting* like a parent."

"Fair enough."

I worked through my options as we walked up to Aneeta's family's house. *Hello, Shri and Aadesh! We were just out for a drive. Thought we'd check in. Thought I'd talk briefly with Kate about the Just Say No campaign we were subjected to as kids.* Or maybe I'd speak with Shri and Aadesh alone, tell them about Kate's issues at school this year, how peer pressure to fit in had led her to some at-risk behavior.

I'd come to no decision before we found ourselves standing at the door. Reina knocked. Shri opened the door, wrapped in a blanket, seemingly half asleep.

An awkward silence.

"Forgive me," I said. "I just wanted to check in. Do you mind if I go see Kate?"

"Of course," Shri said. "But she's not in Aneeta's room."

I swallowed hard. Here it was, the news that Kate and Aneeta were unsupervised, smoking dope, or worse, with boys, in a club . . .

"Where are they?" I asked.

"On the roof," Shri said. "With Aneeta's father. They're waiting for the eclipse."

"Oh yeah, the eclipse," I said, having totally forgotten about that detail.

Shri led us through the house, a modest two-room structure. I noted the efficient use of space, how every table or countertop was fitted with shelves underneath. We passed through the kitchen—a space the size of a walk-in closet, with pots stacked carefully atop the one-burner stove—and exited through the back door. Shri pointed to a ladder, secured against the side of the house.

"You check it out," Reina whispered.

Quietly, I climbed the ladder. When I reached the top rung, I stopped. Above me I saw a wonderland of purple-black sky dotted with an explosion of pink stars, and on the tin rooftop before me, I saw Kate and Aneeta sprawled on their bellies on a picnic blanket, absorbed in a game of Scrabble under a flashlight's beam. Kate's smile bloomed in the darkness—so natural, so at ease, so the opposite of the anxiety-ridden girl who'd almost made a bad decision in middle school. Aadesh was absorbed, too—kneeling on a pad, his eye pressed against the telescope. I beheld a palette of beauty—the visual, the sensual, the ephemeral. A girl, her friend, her friend's father. The limitless sky in all its splendor. Peace and joy on a tin rooftop.

This was it: the ultimate boon. The step in the hero's journey that represented the goal of the quest, the reason the hero took the journey to begin with. Kate's heart had found a soft landing. She had experienced her revelation. She had felt friendship at its sweetest.

I edged my way down the ladder before any of them had had a chance to detect me.

"Everything okay?" Reina asked.

"Everything is great," I said, and then I turned to Shri. "I'm not Kate's mom, you know. But on this trip, she's like my daughter. She's my responsibility. And the simple fact is, I just had a panic attack and felt like I needed to see her. I hope you understand."

"I do," she said. Her voice was soft.

"Don't tell her I was here?"

"Mom is the word."

"Mum," Reina corrected. "Mum's the word."

"Mum and Mom," I said.

"They go hand in hand," Shri assured me.

"Let's vamoose!" Reina said, hopping on the back of the bike. We absconded into the blackness, with Reina's arms wrapped tightly around my waist, her head resting on my shoulder. A safe distance from Aneeta's family's house, I laughed out loud, let loose a giant whoop.

I had found my ultimate boon, too.

Reina and I drove home beneath the light from the penumbral moon. Though a shadow obscured us, I never felt so entirely bathed in light.

After we returned the bike to the shed, I told Reina I needed to send a quick text. By the glow of the kerosene lamp, I texted Lucy:

Kate is perfect. Still awake in middle
of the night with Aneeta and her family, watching the lunar eclipse. She'll
fill you in tomorrow. You have an amazing daughter. Thank you for sharing her
with me.

CHAPTER SIXTY-ONE

By the fifth week, a metamorphosis had undeniably begun. The old walls had been demolished and hauled away; the frameworks that encased the building were removed. The chrysalis had begun to disintegrate; a beautiful butterfly had begun to emerge. Roof tiles were laid. Painters rolled on coats of fresh white paint. Shutters were hung. The earth was smoothed, new dirt poured around the foundation, plants welcomed into rich soil. Inside, rows and rows of bunk beds were built, crisp linens delivered. A modern kitchen came into being, bearing no remnants of the old: stoves with ovens, refrigerators. Deep drawers; high, secure cupboards.

Reina and Kate and I would leave in four days. Direction and control would be conveyed to Ms. Chopra, the woman hired to manage the school and the orphanage. A board of directors was already in place. Teachers had been hired. Caregivers, too, to help out Mrs. Pundari. Ms. Chopra would report to One by One, whose local NGO had partnered with us to provide local administration of our operation. Accountings would be filed monthly. The start-up money I'd donated to the project was spent, plus some. It was the greatest purchase of my life. The One by One Foundation grant would supply enough funds for the next year, and was willing to provide more, contingent on our success. Mrs. Longworth stood behind the scenes of this windfall.

On one of our last nights, I sat on the edge of Kate's bed. She handed me a thick packet of paper. "I want you to read my hero's journey," she said.

"I can't wait to read it," I said. "Should I save it for the plane trip, or read it now?"

"The plane trip, definitely."

I studied the sheet atop the story. It was a map of the seventeen stages of the monomyth. Next to each stage, Kate had written chicken-scratch notes, indicating with a large check mark that she had covered that step. I'd been with her through them all, from entering the belly of the whale, down the road of trials, amid the fear of temptation, and now her desire torn between not wanting to leave and the wrenching pull to go home.

But there was one step—Meeting with the Goddess—I asked her about. "We didn't really meet with any goddesses," I said. "Did you just make her up?"

"Well," Kate said, turning a little pink, "it didn't have to be an actual supernatural goddess. The step actually involves experiencing all-powerful, all-encompassing unconditional love."

"Oh, cool," I said. "So did you use Aneeta as your goddess?"

"The type of love an infant experiences from her mother," she clarified.

"So probably not Aneeta."

Kate scooted near me. "Silly, I chose you."

Of course I knew about maternal love. I'd heard and read about a mother's aching devotion to her children all my life. But nothing had prepared me for the reverberations that rolled through me in this moment. I pulled Kate in for a hug to ground myself against the trembling.

"I love you, Missy," Kate said.

I didn't give those words easily. To Dad, to Joe. To my mother, once upon a time. But never had I felt more certain of who I was and how I felt: "I love you, too."

CHAPTER SIXTY-TWO
JOE

Some might say each of us was born whole and perfect. They might contend that life chipped away at us day by day: the first time we were scolded for spilling milk, that deflating moment when we were called out at first base, the lingering betrayal when our best friend aligned with someone else.

Chip, chip.

Parts and pieces crumbled away when we gathered the courage to approach the prettiest girl in school, and she looked at us as though we were joking. We patched ourselves up, but fractures would always hold weak spots, so years later, when our wives blamed our children's failings on us, when she looked at us as if she could have chosen better—a doctor, a lawyer, anyone but a marine—the fused bone cracked again.

Chip, chip.

These people might argue that the older we got, the bigger the falling chunks got. When we were ambushed by mortars, when our buddies died in our arms because our fingers couldn't catch enough of their blood, when we sat with their widows and told them how their husbands never stopped fighting. When we came home to a wife who used to adore us but now looked at us like our time in Afghanistan was only a selfish sojourn of "me time," like a guys' weekend at the Bellagio, while she had been taking care of the real life of kids and the house and the bills.

Much of this was true. Anyone who had been to war—real war, or metaphorical war—knew that it required every piece of who we were. We were all in. We gave selflessly. We gave greedily, with no thought of what our giving did to the people left back home.

But just because we gave it our all, didn't mean we were incapable of regeneration.

If we didn't regenerate, if war robbed us blind, if life chipped away at our whole and perfect selves, then none of us would be standing now.

I'd come to look at it all differently. I now thought we were born, and our infancy was exactly that—a beginning, our first stage of existence. My genius daughter would tell me the prefix "in" meant just that: *without, not*. We were born *without* knowledge, without experience, without protection. As infants, we were *not* suited, not equipped, not prepared.

We were not born whole; we were born *new*, and each life experience coated us with another layer. These layers protected us like armor, but they also covered us to the point where we no longer could feel. That was the balance: to open up to the experiences, to strategically place the layers, but to leave the heart open. The heart had to be sent into the front lines every day, naked, unarmed, willing to take fire. That was the only way to live. With risk. On the cusp of dying.

I'd also come to believe that many lives made up a life. Just like chapters make up a book, or seasons make up a year, or battles make up a war. I thought about my life with Lucy, and for all but the last of our years together, it was right and good. I wouldn't go back in time and change a thing. She was the perfect wife for a guy who wanted nothing more than to defend his country and make his family proud. We shared that.

And the kids. They're the reason for it all.

But now. A flip of the chapter, a change of seasons, a new battle. My oldest daughter at war with her self-esteem, and my high school sweetheart was the one navigating her through the land mines. I couldn't have predicted that. I loved that I couldn't have predicted that. I loved everything about it, especially Missy. I loved Missy. I *love* Missy Fletcher. I always had, in some sense—first in the sentimental "first love" sense and now, in the thirty-six-year-old man's sense. Like I wanted to be with her more than I wanted to breathe.

She and Kate were scheduled to leave India tomorrow with a stopover in Paris. Missy wanted Kate to see the Louvre. If I hopped on a plane tonight, I could meet them there. Surprise them. Show them how much I love each of them. We could eat dinner in a little café, walk along the Seine, peer down the Champs-Élysées from atop the Arc de Triomphe.

I opened my laptop and searched for flights. A nonstop to de Gaulle leaving tonight at ten. I picked up my phone and called Ma.

"Of course I'll watch Olivia and Jake," she said. "That way I'll be there when Kate gets home, anyway."

I packed my suitcase and then headed to the school to pick up the kids. When we pulled into Friendly's, the kids squealed. "Ice cream?"

"Yep," I said. "Order whatever you want."

And while we stuffed our faces with the sugary goodness of mounds of ice cream covered in hot fudge and caramel, I told the kids the plan. How I was going to fly to Paris to surprise Kate and Missy. How by this time two days from now, we'd all be together. How it was important to tell the ones we love how much we love them.

CHAPTER SIXTY-THREE

On our last night, Reina, Kate, Aneeta and her family, and I sat outside on lawn chairs admiring the beautiful building in front of us. Mrs. Pundari and the children played on the grassy lawn. The sun had descended just enough to shade the sky a magnificent purple, casting mystic shadows on this special home and school for girls.

"The white paint no longer looks white," Aneeta said.

"Just like the Taj Mahal," Kate said. "In new light, everything can seem different."

"This school is a thousand times more beautiful than the Taj," I said.

Reina smiled.

"I'm serious," I said. "Because its beauty isn't just external, it's internal. It's in the walls, in the bunks, in the girls who sleep in them. The ovens that cook the food, the tables and desks for the students. Ms. Chopra and Mrs. Pundari. The books and the playground and the music room. Every inch of this place is beautiful."

"You're right," Reina said. "The Taj is just a show-off. Like a popular girl prancing around in her Prada in a poor part of town."

This made me laugh. "You think the Taj ever looks down on all those people and wonders what it would be like to be part of it all?"

"To have real friends, not just admirers?" Kate said.

Kate and I both knew what this meant. Neither of us had ever been the popular girl, but we had certainly been the outsider. Now we were part of something. I had taken on adulthood, and because of it, I now had meaningful relationships with the people in my life. I was no longer anyone's dependent. I was proud to be the mom, the dad, the boss, the friend, the benefactor. I wouldn't get straight As in all my roles; I knew that. But life wasn't lived on a report card.

And Kate. She had slain the dragon and won the prize. She would go home with a bag full of confidence and the knowledge that she could be someone's treasured friend. I didn't believe she would get mired in the middle school pettiness again. Her view now extended to a much farther horizon.

The color of the sky changed again, now a glowing rose. The adults drank from plastic cups filled with wine. Kate, Reina, and I would leave, but part of us wanted to stay. Of course we wanted to stay with our new friends and family. I was happy, so happy. I loved Kate and Reina and Aneeta and her family and this orphanage. I loved Joe. I would always love Joe. I couldn't wait to see him, and I hoped with all I had that he couldn't wait to see me. I no longer thought in terms of "ending up" with Joe, as though there were an objective to our relationship beyond simply being with each other. I just wanted to spend time with him. I just didn't want another year to go by without knowing him. I just wanted his lips on mine.

I rested my eyes on the school, the fruit of our labor, funded in part by my father's money. He would be proud, because building a school in India was a Frank Fletcher plan.

My father was extraordinary in a million ways, but he wasn't perfect. I saw that now. He held me to the only standard he knew—his own gregarious, bold, outgoing standard—and in doing so, he cast a shadow that would always chill me with the breeze of inadequacy. Only now—so many years later, as I loved Kate with motherly affection—did I realize how robbed I was of my own mother's love. Her death had disassembled me in ways that were never addressed by my exuberant, cliché-loving, glass-half-full father. I loved my father, but I had never much loved myself because I always judged myself through his eyes— and those optimistic, can-do eyes could only find me lacking.

If I wanted to, I could harbor an animosity for my father for the rest of my life. I could hold a grudge, and let it fester. After all, it was pretty insulting of him to leave me a *You could do better!* letter at his death. It was hurtful in a thousand different ways. It was low because my father should have loved me for exactly who I was. He should have championed my introversion, appreciated my quiet, contemplative ways as a viable alternative approach to life. His letter was degrading in a thousand different ways. Except for the one way that mattered: he was right.

I *did* need a push. I did need to be called out on my cowardice. I needed a microscope turned upon my parochial, hemmed-in life. And I needed it from Dad, the man whose opinion I valued the most. That's why it hurt the most. Because the truth hurts.

I get it, Dad! Here I was, nearly as far from home as was possible without leaving the planet, with less certainty and safety than I had ever known, and I saw myself and my world with the clarity of a crystal.

I looked again at the orphanage and school. Now that the sun had plunged even deeper and nightfall had yawned across the giant sky, the structure shone gold. A week from now, a month, a year, how would I remember this moment? I knew. It wouldn't be a memory drawn from my beautiful mind. It would be a feeling—a tender, warm, resounding pulse—pulled from my teeming heart.

ACKNOWLEDGMENTS

Before I had my "pitch" ready, people would ask, "What's your new book about?" and I would juggle a bunch of words in the air: father, daughter, Afghanistan, India, introversion, bravery, and they'd look at me like maybe I didn't know myself. In fact, I hadn't randomly drawn a bunch of words from a hat. The seeds for *The Light of Hidden Flowers* were planted much more naturally.

Years ago, I happened to be sitting in the audience of a business conference listening to a speaker. This guy was one of those larger-than-life, charismatic born storytellers. Then, a few years later, I read a book about introversion, kind of the exact opposite of this guy. Somewhere along the way, I got an idea for a novel. My protagonist would be introverted—brilliant, but quiet. She would work with her father, the charismatic superman of her life. But the father would leave her. He would get sick and die, and she would need to stand on her own two feet.

From there, the flowers grew. The story of lost love, the travel to India, the responsibility of adulthood for my once-diffident protagonist. At some point I realized my character was on a modern-day hero's journey. My kids had taught me about the monomyth, so that made the writing of this especially meaningful. A little bit of them woven into the words.

I am grateful to Lake Union Publishing for their continued support, for Jodi Warshaw's steady leadership and David Downing's superior editing, and for the efforts of the entire marketing and publicity team.

I am humbled by the help I received from Colonel Matt Day of the USMC. Matt is a friend of our family, and while I'm typically a bit shy about asking for help (a little like Missy!), I asked Matt to review the sections that pertained to being a marine and the USMC, in general. He corrected some of my word choices, phrases, descriptions, but what Matt's commentary mostly did for me, was "make it real." Reading his firsthand stories of IEDs, night terrors, and the lifelong haul (physically and emotionally) that our service people carry, hit me straight in the heart. To know that this is for real, that our men and women are out there, fighting this fight, every day. My gratitude for their sacrifice is great.

I am thankful to my husband, Kevin, for his constant love and praise. He is my beloved, and I am grateful for his unwavering encouragement.

I am fortunate to have the most supportive group of friends, who cheer my every accomplishment and celebrate me as though I really were hot stuff. More than a year later, we're still using the leftover "Cheers to Jen!" cups and napkins from the last book party.

A Q&A WITH JENNIFER HANDFORD

Q. Missy has taken longer than most to "become an adult." Has loving her father too much—and thus, staying by his side—proved to be her downfall?

A. Missy is a high achiever who relies on her book smarts, but in many aspects of her life, she has "failed to thrive" because she has chosen to stay near her father rather than branching out on her own. We can trace this behavior back to the childhood trauma of losing her mother. Whether consciously or not, Missy internalized this loss and compensated for it by staying close to home. In her naïveté, she neglected to consider her father would someday grow old, or in his case, get ill. Missy's role as child is quickly exchanged for the role of parent as she assumes the care of her father. Because it happens quickly, her adulthood accelerates from zero to sixty. Before she knows it, in her lap she has the burden of her father's illness, the firm's future, an eager boyfriend, a love from the past, a school in India, and the tender soul of a teenage girl.

Q. You have described this story as a "hero's journey," referring to mythologist Joseph Campbell's famed monomyth. Did you set out to write a hero's journey?

A. I set out to write a story about a shy daughter and her gregarious father. I knew the father would die and the daughter would be left on her own for the first time in her life. Courage, strength, fortitude would be needed for her to carry on. As I came to inhabit this space, it occurred to me that Missy would embark on an adventure—riddled with trials and challenges—and much would be required of her. I suspected Missy had it in her to overcome these obstacles, and in the end, she would emerge with not only the prize but also a boatload of self-esteem.

Q. For Missy, what was the prize? What was her payoff for taking the risks?

A. Missy returned with many prizes: (1) the self-confidence in knowing she could lead rather than follow, (2) the courage to stand up and fight for what she believed in, (3) the permission to stand on the edges of the bell curve and experience the risky side of life, and (4) the insight that she and Joe may not be forever, but they are for now, and now is the only place to live. But her biggest prize was Katherine. Missy had never been an influence to anyone. It was always the other way around—people were an influence to her. With Katherine, she got to be that special person. Missy got the chance to be the mother she never had to an insecure middle school girl.

Q. Missy held her father in the highest esteem, believing him to be the ideal man, and in doing so, turned a blind eye to his flaws. As she grows into a stronger person, she begins to see him through a clearer lens, don't you think?

A. Frank Fletcher loved his daughter, and he admired her intellect, but he wasn't shy about pointing out her shortcomings. He wasn't outwardly critical of her, but in their daily conversation he would insinuate that her life was lacking. "Why don't you go shopping with some girlfriends? Why don't you play tennis at the country club?" He meant well, but Missy wasn't a shopping-and-country-club type of girl. Frank Fletcher believed she'd be happier, better, more successful if she were. Herein lies the dissonance between who Missy was and who her father wanted her to be.

Q. How does the brain play a thematic role in this story?

A. We are each given certain talents on which to hang our hat. I made my protagonist exceptionally smart, but she's a bit of an introvert and shies from too much sociability. Frank, in contrast, may not have a genius IQ, but he's outgoing and friendly and could talk his way through any situation. Thus, each relies on her/his brain in a specialized way.

Q. Frank gets Alzheimer's. Was there any question as to which disease you would assign him?

A. Frank had to get Alzheimer's because what could be more devastating to a storyteller? For a man who lived to retell stories from the war, from his lifelong career, of his beloved wife—what could be a worse fate than losing his memories, his words?

Q. You inhabit the space of an Afghanistan war veteran—an amputee, no less—as well as a Vietnam War veteran. Was it important for Joe to be a marine and for Frank to be an army vet?

A. I am hugely patriotic and have great appreciation for the men and women who serve and have served in the armed forces. As an eighteen-year-old headed off to college, Joe was nearly perfect—at least in Missy's eyes. He was strong, optimistic, determined. He was a guy on a mission. And I knew he would end up a marine. So when I considered him fifteen years later, and the challenges he might have faced, in addition to a fed-up-with-the-Marines wife, I thought of an amputation. It was the type of issue that would give Joe pause, but I knew Missy wouldn't flinch. And Frank—outgoing, gregarious Frank—wasn't without his share of pain. He'd been to war and buried his wife. These facts make his rosy outlook on life even more spectacular.

Q. There are similarities between Frank (Missy's father) and Lucy (Kate's mother) in that they both push their children to be different from their true nature.

A. A child loves her parent no matter what, and we see in Missy how forgiving she is of Frank's implied criticism of her. She lives with it because she loves him so much and believes that his drive for her to be more outgoing is the only way he knows to root her on. Frank was a great man, and maybe he did all he knew in terms of being a father, but he wasn't flawless. Missy finally sees that.

And Katherine, once she's in India with Missy, sees that love comes from unlikely sources and "family" can be made of people we just met.

Q. You set the scene in a financial planning office and give Missy the profession of a financial planner. Yet we come to see that Missy's passion resides more in policy and philanthropy. Do you think most people have dual interests when it comes to their careers?

A. Speaking from my own experience, I've wanted to be many things. When I moved to Washington, DC, in my early twenties, it was because I was single-sighted on working for the CIA. I very much wanted to travel overseas and live in DC and research foreign lands. But around the same time, I got involved with stock picking and investing. Investment clubs had popped up everywhere, and I became interested in the financial world. I eventually chose it as my career and went on to work as a financial planner for nearly fifteen years before I tried my hand at writing. That's when I entered a novel-writing contest. My "next" career was launched from there.

DISCUSSION QUESTIONS

1. When we first meet Missy, we get the sense that she is a "behind the scenes" type of gal. When Frank falters at the seminar and forgets what he's talking about, Missy knows what she should do. She knows she should shout from the back of the room to help her father, but the words won't come out. Her shyness has debilitated her. Are some people too nervous to act, even in a situation such as this?

2. Missy lurks on Facebook as her way of living vicariously through others. In a sense, watching others is her "call to adventure." Some contend that Facebook and other forms of social media have created more loneliness, rather than less, because the sense of inclusion is merely implied, rather than real. What do you think?

3. Joe, in his youth, was the type of guy who wanted to save the world. Now that he's older, he sees that there are a lot of things he can't control. He volunteers at the veterans' hospital, but he can't cure the guys. He's there for Kate, but he can't go to middle school for her. Are guys—in general—fixers? Is it hard for them (and women, too) to accept that there are some things that can't be fixed?

4. Missy admits that her father has aged and she hasn't seen it. How reliable is our memory? Do we hold on to our best images? Do our minds see through "rose-colored"

glasses? Is there anything wrong with remembering the past more fondly than perhaps reality demands?

5. Missy has a real identity crisis, and we often find her asking, "Who the hell are you, Missy Fletcher?" Does life have a way of passing faster than we had planned, until the point when we wake up one day and we're older than we realized, looking at ourselves in the mirror and wondering the same thing: "Who the hell are you?"

6. Missy is irritated by Lucas because they are so much alike, but she's smart enough to do the math. If his characteristics annoy her, then perhaps she annoys herself. Is it hard to see ourselves in others, in our children? Do we tend to like people who are like ourselves, or are we too critical for that?

7. Missy has a fear of flying, but in a sense, it's another excuse for her to stay put. She'd *love* to travel, if only she could board a plane. And we find her goading Lucas into taking trips that she herself has shown no ability to take. Why has it taken her thirty-six years to overcome this fear?

ABOUT THE AUTHOR

Photo © 2012 Marty Shoup

A native of Phoenix, Arizona, Jennifer Handford now lives in the Washington, DC, area with her husband and three children. One of three first-place finalists in the Amazon Breakthrough Novel Award contest in 2010, she published her first novel, *Daughters for a Time*, in 2012. *People* magazine hailed it as "a wrenching, resonant debut about infertility, cancer and adoption. Grab your hankies." In 2014, *Acts of Contrition* was published. *The Light of Hidden Flowers* is Jennifer's third novel.

Please visit Jennifer at www.jenniferhandford.com.